Riverbay Road
MEN'S DORMITORY

NOVEL 2

Riverbay Road
MEN'S DORMITORY

NOVEL
2

WRITTEN BY
Fei Tian Ye Xiang
(ARISE ZHANG)

TRANSLATION BY
Xia

ILLUSTRATIONS BY
Tamtam

Seven Seas Entertainment

RIVERBAY ROAD MEN'S DORMITORY VOL. 2

Published originally under the title of 《江湾路7号男子宿舍》 by 非天夜翔 Fei Tian Ye Xiang
Author© 2017 非天夜翔 (Fei Tian Ye Xiang)
This edition arranged with JS Agency
English Translation copyright ©2025 by Seven Seas Entertainment Inc.
All rights reserved.

No portion of this book may be reproduced or transmitted in any form without written
permission from the copyright holders. This is a work of fiction. Names, characters, places,
and incidents are the products of the author's imagination or are used fictitiously.
Any resemblance to actual events, locales, or persons, living or dead, is entirely coincidental.
Any information or opinions expressed by the creators of this book belong to those individual
creators and do not necessarily reflect the views of Seven Seas Entertainment or its employees.

Seven Seas press and purchase enquiries can be sent to
Marketing Manager Lauren Hill at press@gomanga.com.
Information regarding the distribution and purchase of
digital editions is available from Digital Operations Manager CK Russell
at digital@gomanga.com.

Seven Seas and the Seven Seas logo are trademarks of
Seven Seas Entertainment. All rights reserved.

Follow Seven Seas Entertainment online at
sevenseasentertainment.com.

TRANSLATION: XiA
ADAPTATION: Max Machiavelli
COVER DESIGN: M. A. Lewife
INTERIOR DESIGN: Clay Gardner
INTERIOR LAYOUT: Tanya Sokolovskaya
COPY EDITOR: Ethan Demedeiros
PROOFREADER: Amanda Eyer, Pengie
EDITOR: Harry Catlin
PREPRESS TECHNICIAN: Salvador Chan Jr., April Malig, Jules Valera
MANAGING EDITOR: Alyssa Scavetta
EDITOR-IN-CHIEF: Julie Davis
PUBLISHER: Lianne Sentar
VICE PRESIDENT: Adam Arnold
PRESIDENT: Jason DeAngelis

ISBN: 979-8-89160-997-6
Printed in Canada
First Printing: July 2025
10 9 8 7 6 5 4 3 2 1

CONTENTS

Chapter 27	7
Chapter 28	21
Chapter 29	31
Chapter 30	51
Chapter 31	65
Chapter 32	75
Chapter 33	91
Chapter 34	103
Chapter 35	123
Chapter 36	133
Chapter 37	151
Chapter 38	169
Chapter 39	177
Chapter 40	199
Chapter 41	219
Chapter 42	233
Chapter 43	249
Chapter 44	261
Chapter 45	271
Chapter 46	285
Chapter 47	307
Chapter 48	329
Chapter 49	347
Chapter 50	369
Character & Name Guide	391

CHAPTER
27

THAT NIGHT HUO SICHEN sat on the futon and applied himself seriously to the task of replying to his text messages. The way his fingers flew across the keyboard belied his anger. His phone had been ringing all night, and now, at last, he had the time to settle all these headaches.

Zhang Yuwen watched him without disturbing him. At times, Huo Sichen just frowned; at others, his face went dark with suppressed fury. After almost an hour, he finally threw his phone aside and let out a long sigh.

Zhang Yuwen raised a questioning eyebrow at him. The guy looked utterly exhausted. Zhang Yuwen picked up Huo Sichen's phone in a silent gesture, asking if he could look through it—an act that crossed the boundaries of a typical relationship. Not even married couples normally checked each other's phones. Even so, Zhang Yuwen knew that Huo Sichen would agree. His views on love were conservative and traditional, just like his understanding of their relationship.

As he expected, Huo Sichen nodded. Zhang Yuwen scrolled through Huo Sichen's chat history with the other guy, Peifeng. There wasn't much useful information in the chat—most of it was the two of them rehashing old scores and talking tough. Peifeng was clearly furious, too, and they were acting like two petulant children in a fight. Zhang Yuwen scrolled for a long time but never quite identified the reason for their argument.

"So what were you arguing about?"

"He told my subordinate in the group chat to find a shipping order. I told him privately that everyone's on vacation right now, and it's not like it's urgent. Then, he blew up at me."

"Maybe he's anxious too. That's just how bosses are."

"The company hasn't paid out the year-end bonuses yet, and it's looking like they won't give them out before the Spring Festival," Huo Sichen said wearily. "We might all be out of jobs next year, the performance bonuses are all being delayed, and he's still asking people to work during their vacations."

With a smile quirking at the corner of his mouth, Zhang Yuwen read more of the chat. After a while, Huo Sichen asked, "What do you think?"

Zhang Yuwen smiled at him. "Do you want the truth, or just words of comfort?"

"The truth, of course."

"He's got a chip on his shoulder because he thinks you're getting paid too much." Zhang Yuwen lay down. Huo Sichen followed suit and hugged him, allowing the tender moment to cast his stress and irritation to the back of his mind.

Zhang Yuwen was dying of curiosity. He wanted to ask about Huo Sichen's erectile dysfunction, but ultimately, he didn't. Instead, he stroked Huo Sichen's face. The longer he looked at him, the more handsome he found him. Huo Sichen wasn't as dashing as Chang Jinxing, but he was still an attractive guy, with thick brows, big eyes, and an air about him that was slightly aggressive, yet still reserved.

At first glance, he seemed like a seven out of ten, but the more Zhang Yuwen looked, the more pleasing and manly Huo Sichen seemed.

Zhang Yuwen felt Huo Sichen's reaction to their closeness. "What happened to that erectile dysfunction, huh?"

"It got better after I met you," Huo Sichen whispered.

"That's some high praise."

"I'm serious."

Zhang Yuwen tried to push Huo Sichen away a little, but Huo Sichen hugged him tighter, burying his face in Zhang Yuwen's shoulder. They were so close together they could almost hear each other's heartbeats. It was in that moment that Zhang Yuwen finally realized: He liked Huo Sichen.

That night, they did nothing but sleep, hugging each other close.

If someone were to set their love for one another on a seesaw, Zhang Yuwen had no doubt that Huo Sichen's love would be as heavy as a mountain and his own as light as a feather. But it was this gravitational force that pulled Zhang Yuwen inexorably toward Huo Sichen.

Tonight, Zheng Weize was caught up in an emotional whirlwind. He was certain that he didn't stand a chance with Chang Jinxing, but that kiss had ignited a love inside him that he couldn't control. He'd always wanted to find an assertive top who could dominate him, but learning about Chang Jinxing's sexual preferences during the heartfelt truth-sharing only made Zheng Weize like him more. His love for Chang Jinxing was a tangled mess of wanting to be fucked by him and wanting to dote on him, and for Zheng Weize, this was uncharted territory.

That night, while Chang Jinxing was charging his camera and looking through the photos on it, Zheng Weize sat in the corner, hugging his knees and texting on his phone.

"Look at these," Chang Jinxing said. He showed Zheng Weize the photos he had captured of everyone when the fireworks went off; each guy's expression told its own unique story.

Zheng Weize looked at the photos and smiled. The look on Chang Jinxing's face whenever he was engrossed in photography was mesmerizing. This was a man who adored photography, and with his dedication to and passion for his craft, he had Zheng Weize completely in his thrall.

"Bedtime?" Chang Jinxing asked.

"Yeah." Zheng Weize arranged their futons and set them side by side. He lay down, still texting, and Chang Jinxing settled down with his back to Zheng Weize, messing around on his own phone.

Zheng Weize did not hug Chang Jinxing that day.

Under the dark cover of the night, he lay awake, feeling sad and torn. Something had happened between the two of them and not even very long ago, but at this point, Zheng Weize almost felt like he had imagined it. It was hard to know where to draw the line. Not long after Chang Jinxing returned from his business trip, Zheng Weize, who'd missed him a lot, bought him some gifts. While he was on the cruise, Zheng Weize even aired out Chang Jingxing's quilt and tidied up his bedroom like a good girlfriend.

Even before that, their relationship had always seemed ambiguous. Chang Jinxing took care of him and pampered him. Short of spending money, he seemed willing to do anything for Zheng Weize, from hugging him to carrying his bag and buying him water. He let Zheng Weize lean on him and engage in all sorts of physical affection. Even when Zheng Weize kissed him, Chang Jinxing didn't refuse, though he never took the initiative to kiss Zheng Weize himself, and he never let Zheng Weize kiss him on the lips.

What gave Zheng Weize hope was that, while Chang Jinxing rarely spent money on him, he also never spent Zheng Weize's money. He wasn't like that straight guy, who had accepted everything Zheng Weize bought for him. And Chang Jinxing did occasionally spend a little on Zheng Weize—buying him a cup of milk tea, paying for his bus or subway ticket, or helping him make small purchases from online stores.

He's just a little tight on money lately, Zheng Weize thought. *He does like me.*

When Chang Jinxing returned, Zheng Weize was thrilled to see him again, and he kept pestering and talking to him. Chang Jinxing showed him the photos from the cruise, and when the night grew late, Zheng Weize didn't want to go back to his room. He decided to sleep over, and Chang Jinxing didn't refuse.

That night, as Chang Jinxing lay in bed in a T-shirt and underwear and chatted with Zheng Weize, Zheng Weize hugged him. Chang Jinxing still didn't turn him away. Taking this as tacit consent, Zheng Weize tried touching his body, keeping his movements light and slow. At first, Chang Jinxing acted as if he was a little uncomfortable, but he didn't push Zheng Weize's hand away. It was only when Zheng Weize touched Chang Jinxing's nipple that Chang Jinxing indicated for him to stop.

Zheng Weize was as enamored with Chang Jinxing's body as he was with his face; he loved those pecs, those abs, those long legs. This guy had everything in the right place, and he wasn't too bulky like Chen Hong was. Sometimes, Zheng Weize even fantasized about Chang Jinxing being overcome by his lust for Zheng Weize and having his way with him. He wanted to tempt Chang Jinxing into fucking him, and he figured that once they had slept together, he could emotionally blackmail Chang Jinxing, pressure him to take responsibility. Maybe Chang Jinxing would agree, even if he only went along with it half-heartedly.

Besides, even if the blackmail plan failed, Zheng Weize had nothing to lose by sleeping with a handsome guy.

He stroked his hand over Chang Jinxing's chest and down to his abs. "Your dick's so big."

In the darkness, Chang Jinxing laughed and fended off Zheng Weize's hand. He was still busy replying to messages on his phone.

When Zheng Weize touched Chang Jinxing's clearly defined cock through his underwear, he found it was already hard. But before he could push the limits further and reach inside his underwear, Chang Jinxing finally pulled his hand away.

"Don't," Chang Jinxing said with a warning smile.

Zheng Weize clung to him, pressing their bodies together, and Chang Jinxing allowed it. But when Zheng Weize attempted to cross the line a second time, Chang Jinxing issued a severe warning.

"No groping!" he snapped, sounding a little angry.

Zheng Weize released him, providing what he thought was an obvious window of opportunity for Chang Jinxing, but there was no reaction.

Chang Jinxing got up, put on his pajama pants, and lay back down. He glanced at Zheng Weize and petted him on the head— perhaps he'd been a little too harsh.

"Who are you messaging?" Zheng Weize asked.

After a moment's thought, he replied, "A girl."

"Girlfriend?" Zheng Weize knew that Chang Jinxing was bisexual.

"Not yet."

"Which means she will be. Lemme see?"

Chang Jinxing generously showed Zheng Weize his phone.

Zheng Weize was taken aback. "She's calling you hubby, and you say she's not your girlfriend yet?" he said in disbelief. He'd never been with a fuckboy like this before; he had no natural defenses against this kind of behavior.

"She's just joking around," Chang Jinxing said with a smile. He ran a finger across Zheng Weize's cheek. "She's just a friend. Are you jealous?"

Zheng Weize was at a loss for words. He lay down with his back to Chang Jinxing, wanting to cry, and Chang Jinxing made no move toward him. He didn't finish chatting with his "girl" until nearly two in the morning, at which point he turned around, wrapped his arms around Zheng Weize from behind, and fell asleep.

Zheng Weize felt the urge to sit up in the middle of the night and ask what exactly he was to Chang Jinxing, but he didn't have the courage. Besides, Chang Jinxing was sound asleep. This was the skill of a fuckboy, and Zheng Weize was finally experiencing it firsthand. Guys like that wouldn't profess their feelings or define the relationship, but they wouldn't reject you either; when you demanded an explanation, you were left feeling like you were making baseless accusations, swinging your fist at empty air. Then, the jerk would adopt an innocent, wounded look, like he was the real victim.

And the only thing worse than a fuckboy was a bisexual fuckboy. Zheng Weize didn't understand why the Almighty would test him so cruelly as to put such a species in his path. But who else could he love if not Chang Jinxing?

In fact, Zheng Weize did have another candidate, but he was an even riskier option than Chang Jinxing, because he was straight.

For now, Zheng Weize would call him "Whiskey." And yes, he was yet another straight guy; somehow, Zheng Weize always seemed to get involved with straight guys.

Recently, Zheng Weize's feelings had been oscillating between Chang Jinxing and Whiskey, making him feel conflicted and distraught. He couldn't get a proper response from Chang Jinxing, and he didn't dare to reveal too much to Whiskey; especially not while Whiskey was the top fan on his female live stream account.

After he returned home on Christmas Eve, Zheng Weize had put on his wig and turned on his voice changer in preparation for a few hours of streaming, trying to recoup the money he'd spent on gifts for his roommates. Then, a man named Whiskey entered his channel.

"Thank you, Whiskey, for the roses," Zheng Weize said with a smile. "Is everyone safe and at peace this Christmas Eve? Or are you spending it alone like me...?"

Whiskey sent him more roses, never once leaving the channel. It was Christmas Eve, so there were few viewers, and Zheng Weize was too full from dinner to turn up the charm, so he started talking about his childhood. As midnight approached and the countdown was about to begin, Whiskey was still there.

"It's time for the countdown!" Zheng Weize grinned. "Let's count down together. Three, two, one...YAY!"

The viewer count was dismal; it was only Zheng Weize and this stranger named Whiskey. After the countdown was over, Whiskey silently left, and Zheng Weize ended the stream to count his meager Christmas Eve earnings.

But the next day, Whiskey came again, and for three consecutive days, he sent Zheng Weize gifts worth several thousand yuan. He made his way to the top of Zheng Weize's fan contributor leaderboard in no time. Zheng Weize tried harder to please him and engage him in conversation: "Do you like drinking whiskey?"

Finally, one day, after he was done sending gifts, Whiskey responded. "Yeah. Do you drink?"

"I can, but I don't do it often."

So, they started chatting, and perhaps because he was online and talking to a streamer who was a total stranger to him, Whiskey seemed to feel free to reflect on his life. He shared quite a lot about himself. Zheng Weize learned he was a thirty-three-year-old man who had once gone to Africa for work and returned to divorce papers from his wife. His wife took the child and money and remarried, and now, Whiskey lived alone. During the quiet hours of the night, he drank alone and watched streamers online, often opening several channels simultaneously. Lately, though, he rarely watched the other streamers... In his own words, Zheng Weize was "different from the others," though Whiskey himself couldn't quite articulate why.

Deep down in his heart, Zheng Weize knew the answer: *Because I'm a guy.* It was only natural that a man could do a better job of understanding what other men were thinking and relating to them— for example, when it came to the loneliness of drifting in a foreign country, or their uncertainty and wistfulness about their career and life plans. They chatted enthusiastically, and Whiskey wasn't like the other straight guys, who asked to see Zheng Weize's boobs and thighs once they were on more familiar terms—even though Zheng Weize had fake bras prepared in advance.

All along, Whiskey believed that Zheng Weize was a girl. He said "she" was pure, enthusiastic, and generous.

But a few days later, their conversation took a turn for the inappropriate. Whiskey began talking about his loneliness and his girlfriend in Africa; about how he'd cheated on his wife in Africa while his wife was cheating on him back home. This affirmed Zheng Weize's belief that straight guys were all equally rotten, but even so, he accepted Whiskey's gifts and hoped for more. He'd been a streamer for a while now, and he was beginning to grasp the trick of making others offer him gifts willingly.

Whiskey kept showering Zheng Weize with gifts as they chatted about all sorts of things. Zheng Weize disdained Whiskey as a crude straight guy, but he was also drawn to his experience. He shared his own story of life in Jiangdong City after he'd moved there, including his struggles being bullied at his job at the sales counter and moving from house to house...

Finally, there was someone who would listen to his story. By switching his gender in these stories as he told them, Zheng Weize was able to seamlessly make himself out to be a beautiful, delicate, yet strong-willed girl struggling in the big city. This stirred Whiskey's protective instincts, and the gifts kept coming.

In just one week, Zheng Weize had made over ten thousand from Whiskey. He was genuinely grateful to his patron, but he also felt uneasy knowing that, in truth, he was a guy dressed up as a girl—to put it bluntly, he was running a scam. But when Whiskey gifted Zheng Weize four virtual villas and two virtual sports cars, Zheng Weize finally succumbed to the allure of money.

He was deeply moved—this straight guy must have fallen in love with him. Why else would he spend so much money on a live streamer otherwise?

They exchanged contact information, moving their conversations from the live stream channel to their mobile phones. The content of their chat also became more personal. Zheng Weize shared part of his life with Whiskey, and he learned that Whiskey liked smoking and drinking. The only thing stopping him from getting closer to Whiskey was Zheng Weize's fear that he might be a balding, middle-aged man with a pot belly.

Besides, he still liked Chang Jinxing. Whiskey's presence in his life often made him feel as if he had a main partner and a backup. Sometimes, when he was with Chang Jinxing, he sneakily replied to Whiskey's messages; it gave him a kick to feel like he was "two-timing" them.

Zheng Weize was disappointed by Chang Jinxing's subtle rejection, but in his disappointment, he thought, *Luckily, I still have Whiskey.* On the first night of the new year, with his back to Chang Jinxing, Zheng Weize sent Whiskey a message. He had told Whiskey before he left that he was going to spend the new year with his "girlfriends."

Whiskey wanted to see Zheng Weize's girlfriends, but Zheng Weize saw through his ploy. *Nah, not showing u.*

U wanna see me? Whiskey asked him. *Aren't u curious about my looks?*

Zheng Weize wanted to, but he was afraid. He wasn't mentally prepared. *U look like u, what else could u look like?*

Whiskey sent a smirk emoji followed by a photo of himself. Zheng Weize blinked hard.

The photo showed two guys sitting and drinking under some lights by the riverside at night. The one at the forefront was taking a selfie and the guy behind him was smiling for the camera.

Which one is you? Zheng Weize asked, sacrificing his composure. The guy in front appeared slightly more mature, perhaps because of the dim light, while the one at the back was a typical pretty boy. He wasn't on the same level as Chang Jinxing or Zhang Yuwen, but he was handsome nevertheless.

wat do u think? Whiskey replied. *the one in the back is my nephew.*

Zheng Weize studied Whiskey's face, a little disappointed. *Hm, not bad,* he thought. At least he had his hair and no receding hairline. He wasn't handsome, but he was a clean-cut, mature guy who rated a solid five—no, five and a half out of ten. All in all, better than Zheng Weize had imagined.

Next, Whiskey sent him a few older full-body photos of himself. There was even one from his younger days as a student; he'd looked much more handsome back then. Zheng Weize carefully studied each photo and snuck a glance over his shoulder at Chang Jinxing, who was sleeping with his back to him. Zheng Weize sighed, but as he looked at the photos, he found some attractiveness in Whiskey's looks. He wasn't five foot eleven, but his proportions were passable. It wasn't like Zheng Weize was all that tall or good-looking himself. He couldn't afford to be too picky.

Whiskey pestered him for his photos again. Zheng Weize was prepared for this and sent him a few, and Whiskey said, *I'm on vacay for the next few days. was thinking of going to Jiangdong. wanna meet me for a meal?*

Of course, Zheng Weize made an excuse to turn him down. Whiskey asked him for his mailing address, and, after a moment's thought, Zheng Weize gave him the address of a parcel pickup point at the department store where he used to work.

Whiskey bought him a mystery gift for the new year and asked Zheng Weize to call him "hubby." Touched and emotional, Zheng Weize turned on the voice changer on his phone and fulfilled Whiskey's wish. Then, he turned to look at Chang Jinxing, wondering if he was asleep.

Whiskey sent him a voice message too, and Zheng Weize put the phone to his ear. "I love you, my darling, and I've loved you for a very long time," the mature voice said. "Go to bed early. Staying up late is bad for your skin. I'll head home as soon as I've finished my drink."

Tears began to flow freely from Zheng Weize's eyes. He knew that this romance would never be, but he was deeply moved all the same.

Riverbay Road
MEN'S DORMITORY

CHAPTER
28

THE NEW YEAR'S OUTING came to its end, and everyone returned to their exhausting, stressful lives.

All of Zhang Yuwen's roommates thought, *Man, if only I were rich and didn't have to work.*

Meanwhile, Zhang Yuwen was thinking, *When the hell will I finally get my manuscript approved?*

Zheng Weize had scammed his first pot of gold from Whiskey; a gift worth more than thirty thousand yuan. Despite the sudden windfall, he was anxious. What if Whiskey discovered his real identity and reported him to the police? Every time he saw a message from Whiskey, he felt like a thief; apprehensive and guilty.

Chen Hong's gym members were mostly gone. He needed to scout for a new location and open a modest gym this year, but this time around, he planned to start small and go with a private club format. Despite everything, he still had ¥120,000 left in his savings, enough to take another gamble and see if he could turn his fortune around.

He was thirty years old, and this was his last shot. If he failed again, he decided, he'd resign himself to his fate, return to his hometown, and open a shop to make a living there.

Yan Jun's job was the same as ever. He kept on going to work every day and strived to hit performance targets. His living conditions had improved significantly now that the others were helping with Xiao-Qi; now that he no longer had to rush between work, the childcare center, and home, his spirits had improved. Every morning, he drank coffee that was lovingly made by Chang Jinxing, and he could even swipe Chen Hong's fitness meal from the refrigerator for breakfast. His commute decreased significantly. Meanwhile, as Xiao-Qi grew older, she required fewer nighttime feedings, and she woke less frequently in the night. On occasions when he had to work overtime, his roommates were able to pick Xiao-Qi up on his behalf and feed her her baby food.

In short, Yan Jun was getting enough rest, he was in a better place mentally, and his future seemed bright. On his first day back at work, his boss told him that he was being promoted. Just like that, Yan Jun became a mid-level manager of a team of seven—and, most importantly, his salary saw a 70 percent boost.

That evening, following the standard protocol, Yan Jun treated his subordinates to some drinks. It was ten at night when he finally returned to No. 7 Riverbay Road.

Zhang Yuwen was still at his computer, tackling his own pile of trash. He had picked up Xiao-Qi for Yan Jun and fed her with Chang Jinxing, and then Zheng Weize had lulled her to sleep. Now, Yan Jun finally returned home, slightly unsteady on his feet.

"Go out drinking again?" Zhang Yuwen asked.

Yan Jun merely smiled, pink-cheeked, and said nothing.

Everyone else was asleep. Zhang Yuwen went to the kitchen to make some tea to sober Yan Jun up. Although he'd had a lot to drink,

Yan Jun was still sober enough to ask about his daughter. "Where's Xiao-Qi?"

"She's asleep," Zhang Yuwen replied as he opened a tea bag.

Yan Jun followed him into the kitchen and wrapped his arms around Zhang Yuwen from behind.

"Hey!" Zhang Yuwen said, surprised. This was out of character for Yan Jun. He tried to push him away, but he couldn't break Yan Jun's strong grip.

"I know it's you. Just let me hold you for a while. Just a little while." Yan Jun closed his eyes and savored this fleeting tenderness—the illusion that, on this night, someone had been waiting for him to drag his weary body home, leaving a light on for him in the dining room while his daughter was already fast asleep... This was probably Yan Jun's greatest dream in life, and he knew that once he let go, it would all vanish into thin air.

Zhang Yuwen realized that Yan Jun was feeling wistful, and his irritation faded. Yan Jun must have been exhausted, he supposed, and their home on Riverbay Road brought him momentary peace and comfort.

After a moment, Yan Jun let go and went to his room to check on Xiao-Qi. Then, he came back out to sit at the dining table and accepted the tea Zhang Yuwen offered him. The night was quiet, the only audible sound being Zhang Yuwen typing away on his keyboard.

"I got a promotion," Yan Jun said finally.

"What?" Zhang Yuwen glanced at Yan Jun and processed what he'd said. "Congrats! Wow!"

Yan Jun's answering smile was a little shy.

"What about the salary?"

"I got a raise too. I'll treat you all to a meal next week."

"This is great news!" Zhang Yuwen went over and hugged Yan Jun, who heaved a long sigh, touched by the gesture. "It's always good to have extra money on hand."

"I'll be able to send more money home now."

"Make sure you eat better too. You're too thin."

Zhang Yuwen knew that while Yan Jun was frugal in his day-to-day life, he was still better off than their roommates. He only scrimped on himself, never on Xiao-Qi, and he wouldn't spend a cent on anything he didn't need. He hadn't touched the pensions and insurance payouts from his deceased brother and sister-in-law—those were being saved for Xiao-Qi's future dowry—and his mother, in the countryside, relied on him completely for her living and medical expenses; she had cataracts and diabetes and needed regular medication and checkups. Yan Jun alone had to support his mother and raise his daughter in the big city—a monumental task for one man.

Yan Jun looked at Zhang Yuwen as if he wanted to say something, but in the end, he simply said, "It's twenty thousand now."

"Wow!" Zhang Yuwen exclaimed. A salary of twenty thousand was impressive. It wasn't in the same league as Huo Sichen's, but it was a solid middle-class wage. "That's so much!"

"Are you going to raise my rent?" Yan Jun joked.

Zhang Yuwen laughed, closed his computer, and studied Yan Jun. For a moment, he wanted to tease him and ask him to pay for the roommates' babysitting services, given how often they looked after Xiao-Qi, but he reconsidered it. "You need to make sure that you spend time with Xiao-Qi. I know it's hard, but you've got to learn to balance family and career."

"I know," Yan Jun reassured him. "It'll only be for a few more days. I promise there will be no overtime, just like before."

Zhang Yuwen nodded.

Yan Jun fell silent for a moment, thinking. Then, he said, "I want to buy a house in Jiangdong."

"Oh. That'd be quite the substantial down payment, wouldn't it?" Zhang Yuwen wondered if he could lend Yan Jun some money.

But Yan Jun had a different idea. "I'll put it in Xiao-Qi's name and use my brother and sister-in-law's insurance payout for the down payment."

In truth, Yan Jun was starting to nurse the notion of pursuing Zhang Yuwen romantically. At first, he'd thought he didn't stand a chance; Huo Sichen was the perfect match for Zhang Yuwen. But his promotion and raise provided a bit of much-needed encouragement and confidence. Love still seemed distant to him, but these new circumstances had at least given him a push forward.

He still had vivid memories of doing high jumps in his student days. The bar seemed insurmountable, but he'd always charged ahead, flipped over the bar, and landed. He kept challenging it, and the bar kept rising until it reached the point where he hesitated. Looking at the bar from afar, it seemed difficult...but if he just gave it his all and forged ahead, he might just manage to reach it.

In his vision of a perfect life, he would buy a house in Jiangdong and settle down in this unfamiliar environment. He would woo Zhang Yuwen, give him all the money he made, and let him manage Yan Jun's life—not just his body, but also his soul and everything else he had to give. His entire existence.

"I can help you ask around," Zhang Yuwen said. "I have a friend who knows someone in real estate, but I wouldn't recommend buying a house now. The price might drop if you hold out for a while."

"Hm." Yan Jun considered Zhang Yuwen's suggestion. "So you think it's better not to buy now?"

"Yeah. It'd be a heavy burden. Maybe you can wait until Xiao-Qi starts kindergarten or elementary school before deciding? It'd help with choosing a good location near the school."

Yan Jun nodded in understanding. "How's it going with you and Huo Sichen?" he asked.

"As well as can be expected." Zhang Yuwen laughed. "What exactly do you want to hear about?"

Yan Jun's intuition told him that Zhang Yuwen and Huo Sichen weren't official yet; if they were, circumstances would be a little different. Since they'd left the hot spring resort, Huo Sichen had been busy with his company, and Zhang Yuwen hadn't asked him about his decision to switch jobs. After all, some people hated their jobs but still had to get a handle on their feelings and continue working. They still met for dinner twice a week, but this week's date had been canceled because Huo Sichen was busy. They did still chat frequently online, though.

"Are you guys official now?" Yan Jun asked.

"I guess so?" Zhang Yuwen thought about it. "Hm. Yeah, we are. I don't know where it'll lead, but we both think it's worth a try."

"So, you're both just trying things out now?"

Zhang Yuwen smiled and avoided Yan Jun's gaze. He hadn't demanded to meet Huo Sichen because he understood what it was like to have work commitments. Several years ago, when his career was on the up, Zhang Yuwen had been in Huo Sichen's shoes and unable to do a thing about it. Men and women alike had to make sacrifices for their partner's career.

And after Zhang Yuwen and his ex broke up, he found the separation wasn't all that bad, or rather...

"You don't really like him that much," Yan Jun said plainly.

Zhang Yuwen didn't speak for a long moment. Then, he said, "I actually do," understanding in the same moment what Yan Jun had left unspoken: *He doesn't like you that much either.*

"When you like someone, you want to see them all the time," Yan Jun said. "You can't help yourself at all."

"That's teenage love. You're twenty-seven. You'd still act that way?"

"Of course." Yan Jun smiled at Zhang Yuwen.

"Yuwen... Yuwen!" Their conversation was interrupted by Chang Jinxing hurrying down the stairs. He looked conflicted when he saw Zhang Yuwen and Yan Jun chatting, but Yan Jun gestured for him to sit, standing to return to his room for a shower and to keep Xiao-Qi company.

It was okay with him if Zhang Yuwen wanted to "try things out" with Huo Sichen. Intuition told him that Zhang Yuwen and Huo Sichen weren't meant to be. For one, their financial statuses were so disparate; they didn't come from the same world. He also felt confident that Zhang Yuwen was just lonely and that Huo Sichen wasn't sincere—or at least, not *that* sincere—so it wouldn't be long before they parted ways.

He was a little jealous of Huo Sichen, but he wasn't about to resort to anything devious. His thoughts were complicated, and in a sense, he'd projected another side of himself—a successful Yan Jun—onto Huo Sichen. Zhang Yuwen had accepted Huo Sichen's overtures, so if Yan Jun were to sincerely pursue him as someone of the same caliber as Huo Sichen, he'd certainly accept him too...

"Did you recommend me for a job?" Chang Jinxing asked in bewilderment.

"Did I?" Zhang Yuwen was just as puzzled. "You did ask me to... Oh, right! I asked a friend."

"Someone called just now and asked me to report to the film production crew tomorrow. I thought it was a scam!"

Zhang Yuwen remembered now. Before the new year, he asked a director friend who was his junior to find a job for Chang Jinxing, but he'd completely forgotten about it after a few days.

"Didn't you ask me to help you ask around?" Zhang Yuwen said. "I doubt it's a scam. Did he say who he was?"

Chang Jinxing sat in Yan Jun's seat, looking anxious. "He said they were filming a short, twelve-episode drama. No mention of the pay. He just said to join the crew tomorrow as a camera assistant and gave me the address and the number for a contact."

Zhang Yuwen glanced at the note Chang Jinxing had written. "Oh, I see. In that case, you should go."

"Your friend's in the film industry?" Chang Jinxing couldn't believe it. In most people's eyes, filming drama series or movies was a high-end, unattainable job.

Zhang Yuwen couldn't reveal his identity, of course. He didn't want to risk waking everyone up by making Chang Jinxing yell. "They're an HR agent who recruits employees for various production crews," he said. "All I said is that you have a background in photography."

And this was where Chang Jinxing completely exposed himself.

"But I know nothing about set photography and cinematography." He was so nervous he didn't know what to do. "What're they gonna have me do?"

"Aren't you a photography major?"

Silence hung in the air between them. "I've forgotten everything I learned," Chang Jinxing said, hastily correcting himself.

"It's okay. A camera assistant mostly, you know, assists. Someone will guide you."

But Chang Jinxing was still panicking. "What should I take note of the first time I join the crew?"

"Don't worry about it," Zhang Yuwen reassured him. "Don't panic. Just watch and learn. Ask questions if you must, and follow the camera people. Address them politely, be proactive in passing them the equipment, and run errands for them—that's all. Besides, you're so handsome, they'll definitely like you. Who knows, they might even ask you to try out for a role."

"How do you know all this?" Chang Jinxing asked. Zhang Yuwen was dangerously close to giving himself away too.

"Isn't that how it usually is? It's just common knowledge," Zhang Yuwen said hastily. Chang Jinxing sighed. "Do you want to give it a try? You could just turn it down. I remember..."

Chang Jinxing glanced at Zhang Yuwen and saw encouragement in his eyes. "It's a job I want to try," he said. "That's right. Thank you, Yuwen. I've always wanted to be a real photographer."

Zhang Yuwen nodded in understanding. "You're just worried that you aren't up to the task, now that the opportunity has come knocking."

"Yeah, exactly!" Chang Jinxing was very worked up. "You took the words right out of my mouth. Makes sense, I guess, since you're a writer. I'm just worried that I won't know what to do when I'm there, and I'll end up ruining my shot..."

"Nah, that won't happen," Zhang Yuwen said. "You can do it. Your photos are some of the best I've ever seen. Your shots are very emotive."

This encouragement didn't help a great deal, but it was better than nothing. Eventually, Chang Jinxing made up his mind and nodded. "Can I borrow some of your clothes to wear?" he asked. "Mine are still wet from the wash."

Just go as you are; no one cares what a camera assistant wears, and with that gorgeous face your parents gave you, you'd look great in anything. Zhang Yuwen wanted to voice these thoughts aloud but, to give Chang Jinxing some confidence, he went up to his room and picked out a handsome jacket for him. "My ex scrimped and saved to buy this for me. It's from a Parisian designer. I've only worn it twice."

Chang Jinxing always seemed to wind up associated with other people's exes. First, he'd worn Chen Hong's ex's clothes at Chen Hong's house, and now he was wearing a jacket Zhang Yuwen got from his ex.

"Great! You look very spirited!" Zhang Yuwen patted him on the shoulder. "You're good to go."

Chang Jinxing tidied his hair and nodded apprehensively, looking as if he'd received a protective amulet instead of a jacket. From the bottom of his heart, he said, "Thanks. I love you, Yuwen."

Laughing, Zhang Yuwen shoved him out of the room and told him to get the hell back to sleep.

CHAPTER

29

CHANG JINXING TOSSED and turned in bed that night, his mind swimming with weird thoughts. It was almost dawn when he finally fell asleep, but he still woke up early to begin his day. He sat at the dining table, drinking coffee with trembling hands and checking the time over and over.

"You just got back?" Zheng Weize asked in a disbelieving tone.

"Nope. I have a thing today," Chang Jinxing told him. "I'm going out later."

After a while, Chen Hong came home. "Did you stay up all night again?"

"Nah," Chang Jinxing said. "I'm getting ready to go to work."

Yan Jun got up, too, to take Xiao-Qi to the childcare center. "Did you sleep at all last night?"

"Did you?" Chang Jinxing countered.

Yan Jun rubbed his eyes. "I did eventually. I always have trouble sleeping in the spring."

Zhang Yuwen was the last to get up. He glanced at Chang Jinxing. He could tell he was still nervous. "Shall I drive you?" he asked.

"I'm taking the subway," Chang Jinxing replied quickly.

Chen Hong put on his helmet. "Where are you going?" he asked.

And so, riding his motorcycle through the chilly spring wind, Chen Hong drove Chang Jinxing to his first formal job. He could tell that Chang Jinxing was heading to an important job interview, so he made conversation on the way to ease his anxiety. When they reached the meeting point, he blew Chang Jinxing a kiss. "Break a leg! Love ya!"

Chang Jinxing blew him a kiss back, and off went Chen Hong to scout for his venue.

Seeing a big group of people gathered in front of a large bus, Chang Jinxing dialed the number his contact had given him. A woman answered, and she looked around and waved him over.

"Hello, I'm—"

"Where's your manager?" the woman asked impatiently. She looked to be in her thirties and had a pass pinned to her chest that said *Coordinator*. "Why are you alone?"

"I don't have one." Her question made Chang Jinxing nervous. He got even more nervous when he saw a few girls staring at him and whispering to each other, and then smiling at him.

"Huh?" The coordinator looked stunned, and Chang Jinxing's heart skipped a beat. They couldn't have gotten the wrong person, could they? But then it finally dawned on the coordinator. "Oh! You're the camera assistant Director Zhu referred to us! I thought you were an actor."

"Whoa!" the onlookers exclaimed in surprise.

Chang Jinxing blinked. "Huh?"

The coordinator laughed, adopting a dazzling smile. "You're so handsome!"

A bit embarrassed, Chang Jinxing nodded.

The coordinator found an ID badge for him. "You can affix your photo to it later. We'll meet here every morning at eight. All right, everyone, on the bus."

"Add me on WeChat," said a young woman, approaching him. "I'm the production assistant."

"I'm from the production crew," someone else said.

The coordinator held up a hand to stop them. "I'll add him to our group chat! Everyone get on the bus already! Now!"

Chang Jinxing glanced at his ID badge, which told everyone that he was a camera assistant. He got on the bus in a daze. Everyone else on the bus seemed to know each other; they talked among themselves, shooting him curious looks.

Gradually, Chang Jinxing's nerves subsided. Not knowing what to do in this unfamiliar environment, he took out his phone. He had a message from Zhang Yuwen: *Hows it going?*

Chang Jinxing replied that he was on the bus, but he didn't know what to do, and he wondered if they would ask him to act. He also took a photo of his ID badge for Zhang Yuwen.

Dont just mess around, Zhang Yuwen told him. *Find ur team leader. Look for the ppl from the camera crew and sit with them.*

Oh, right! *But I can't see their IDs,* Chang Jinxing replied.

Ask around. Ask anyone. They'll tell you.

So, Chang Jinxing tucked away his phone and asked around. Someone pointed the camera crew out to him, and he hurried to the back of the bus and greeted them.

"Oh! So you're Jinxing!" said a middle-aged man. He was in his forties with a weathered face and graying hair, which poked out from under his hat. "Wow, you're a handsome one, aren't you?"

The four members of the camera crew broke into laughter.

"I'm Wang Botao," the middle-aged man added. "Just call me Botao. I'm the first camera operator. This is Liu Peng, the second camera operator."

Chang Jinxing greeted them politely. Each cameraperson had an apprentice who seemed to have even more social anxiety than Chang Jinxing. They bowed and greeted each other humbly, and the apprentices added Chang Jinxing's WeChat contact. Wang Botao motioned for Chang Jinxing to sit beside him, so he did.

The bus was almost full, and the last person to board was another middle-aged man. The others greeted him, and Wang Botao told Chang Jinxing, "That's the director."

The director walked to the back of the bus and stopped in front of the camera crew. Chang Jinxing hastily stood up and bowed.

"You must be Jinxing!" the director said. "My word, what a handsome lad!"

The director even shook his hand, earning Chang Jinxing a lot of questioning looks from other parts of the bus. The whole thing made him uneasy and anxious; he felt like he was getting special treatment.

The director turned around. "Well, if everyone's here, let's go!"

With that, the bus departed, leaving the city and heading to the filming location. Chang Jinxing's phone had been buzzing nonstop since he boarded the bus, and when he took it out, he found that he'd been added to several *Under The Spring Breeze* group chats for the film, coordination, camera, and production crews.

The deluge of messages overwhelmed Chang Jinxing, but a new text from Zhang Yuwen stood out: *When ur with ur mentor, dont look at ur phone unless necessary.* Chang Jinxing immediately set his phone to silent mode and put it away.

Wang Botao leaned over and asked, "Xiao-Chang? Is this your first time on a production crew?"

"Yes. What should I do when we get there?"

"Just follow me," said Wang Botao. He'd clearly been briefed about Chang Jinxing.

Chang Jinxing nodded obediently. "Okay."

The bus drove for almost an hour. It left Jiangdong and ultimately stopped at a corner of a suburban park on the west side of the city. There was a villa in the park, with a stream and a forest, that the film production crew had rented to film a twelve-episode youth idol drama. The content of the drama was contrived and unremarkable, but the producer clearly didn't care about viewership and was only out to make some money. There wasn't much investor interest, and all that really mattered was that the company had some projects to keep them going.

The film production crew set up an altar and hung banners outside the villa. Everyone scrambled to get ready, and the male and female leads arrived in their respective vans. Together, they prayed to celebrate the commencement of filming, and the camera crew took promotional photos that would be handed over to the producer to use for publicity back at the company.

As this was Chang Jinxing's first drama shoot, he was curious about anything and everything, and he noticed that all the actors had very typical features: skinny, with small faces. He didn't find the male lead particularly handsome, but the female lead was quite attractive.

The morning shoot officially began, and the first scene featured the leads arguing inside the villa. That was when Chang Jinxing learned that filming wasn't done in chronological order. He received the scene schedule breakdown and followed the lead camera operator around, assisting him by handing him the equipment and coordinating with the lighting crew and the others. They filmed the same scene two or three times. The leads' acting skills weren't just poor; they couldn't even remember their lines. The director rubbed his forehead and, with a look of resignation, approved the take.

At first, Chang Jinxing was engrossed in watching them, but fortunately, before long, he remembered why he was there. His job as the camera assistant was fairly simple, and Wang Botao, with an unlit cigarette in his mouth as he filmed, often told Chang Jinxing to watch while he explained concepts such as focal distance, aperture, and the difference between front and back lighting. Although Chang Jinxing was familiar with photography, he only had a rudimentary understanding of the theory behind it, and the lack of formal knowledge made it challenging for him to learn. He couldn't even take out his notebook to jot down some notes. The gears in his brain were working so hard they were practically smoking.

They took a break for lunch after filming two scenes, and Chang Jinxing took the opportunity to check his phone. Acting on the tip from Zhang Yuwen, he quickly collected lunch for the entire crew and went to the nearby supermarket to buy drinks.

"Excuse me," someone said, but the question they wanted to ask Chang Jinxing died on their lips when he turned around. "Whoa. Are you an actor?"

Chang Jinxing waved this question away and showed the person his ID badge. "No. I'm a camera assistant."

"Where's the restroom?"

Chang Jinxing pointed, and the person left.

Everyone who saw him wore the same look on their face: "Whoa, what a hottie." He was used to this, but the members of the film production crew were very direct about it, as if "handsome" was a product attribute that people remarked on with the same frankness with which they might pronounce a bag expensive. It made him a little uncomfortable. On the other hand, the lead and second camera operators were kind to him, and the director even made a point of coming over to check on him during the lunch break.

After lunch, Wang Botao smoked his cigarette and took a nap, as was apparently his habit. Chang Jinxing, feeling sleepy himself, dozed off for a while too. The lead cameraman's apprentice came to wake him up in the afternoon, at which point he went back to work, helping to push the camera. The job was hard, but Chang Jinxing didn't mind it. Here, with the film production crew, he felt like a person, not an object.

That afternoon, the second male lead arrived for his scene, which took place in the garden during early spring. He was with the supporting actor who played his childhood friend, sharing his impressions of the female lead as he waited for her favor.

"Push the camera to him later," Wang Botao said to Chang Jinxing. "Pay attention to the focus."

And just like that, Wang Botao let Chang Jinxing take over. Completely oblivious to what this meant, Chang Jinxing took over the camera and aimed it at the scene. The apprentices stared, shocked. What kind of connections must this guy have to get to touch the camera on his very first day?

The clapperboard clacked, and now, it was Chang Jinxing's turn to be shocked. A familiar face appeared in the frame—Kong Yu! The second male lead was Kong Yu, the small-time actor he'd met on the cruise ship!

Chang Jinxing had always had a good memory, and he rarely forgot a face or name. It was one of his survival skills. He stared nervously at the viewfinder, adjusting the focus as Wang Botao had taught him and observing the scene.

Kong Yu looked completely different here. In Chang Jinxing's memory, he was one of the underdogs on the cruise: timid and restrained, no better off than Chang Jinxing. But the moment he was on camera, he became a different person. Exuding the charisma of an actor—getting into character with the flip of a switch—he owned the role of a lovestruck second lead right down to his gaze and expression, radiating deep emotion from every pore. Chang Jinxing, who'd met him recently, focused harder on Kong Yu.

"This guy isn't cutting it," the director said suddenly from behind Chang Jinxing. Chang Jinxing, startled, thought for a moment that he was talking about Kong Yu, but he listened closely and realized the director meant another person—the childhood friend who was sitting beside the second male lead. "He can't act for shit."

"The childhood friend is an internet celebrity," came a woman's voice, also behind Chang Jinxing. "His company pushed him on us."

Wang Botao tactfully walked away from the conversation, but Chang Jinxing, who was standing right next to them, couldn't leave; he had to keep an eye on the camera.

"Talk to the company," the director said. "Let's just wrap up this scene for now. Cut!"

The director and the woman he was talking to left, and Wang Botao came back. Done with the scene, Kong Yu walked over to the camera crew, all smiles, to greet and speak to the director. Chang Jinxing glanced at him occasionally as he prepared the equipment for the next scene. It was interesting to see this other side of him. Noticing his gaze, Kong Yu met Chang Jinxing's eyes, and they traded knowing looks. Chang Jinxing smiled.

The woman who had been speaking with the director returned then. "Let me see the scene from just now," she said to Chang Jinxing, then added, "Wow."

Chang Jinxing assumed she was leaving a "you're so handsome" unsaid. He quickly nodded and played back the previous scene for her.

Wang Botao returned, sipping tea from his thermos cup. "This is the producer," he said to Chang Jinxing.

Chang Jinxing hastened to greet her. "Hello."

"Oh! So you're Jinxing," the producer exclaimed. "So sorry, I should have called you myself, but I was swamped last night. There's always so much to do before filming starts."

"No worries," he said with a smile.

The producer responded with a warm smile of her own. "Let me treat you to a meal after we wrap up the filming."

Chang Jinxing wondered who exactly Zhang Yuwen had contacted to get him this job. The way the film production crew treated him was like night and day compared to how they treated the rest of the camera crew. Did Zhang Yuwen know some kind of industry big shot?

"Yeah, this won't do," the producer muttered. "They're a company that grooms internet celebrities... Wang Shuo! Where's the assistant director?"

She left again, and the director continued filming like nothing had happened. Unbeknownst to Chang Jinxing, those few words had decided the future of an internet celebrity who wanted to get into acting.

The entire afternoon was scheduled entirely around the filming of the second male lead's scenes, and the main male lead had already left without even meeting him. Next up were several scenes between the second male lead and the female lead. At four p.m., the company sent over afternoon tea as a treat for the first day of filming. A twenty-minute tea break was called, and everyone snatched up coffee and cakes.

With a cup of coffee in hand, Kong Yu walked over to Chang Jinxing, who was sitting off to the side, using this precious break to check his phone and reply to messages. Seeing Kong Yu standing in front of him, he looked up.

Kong Yu smiled. "So, we meet again."

Chang Jinxing put his phone away, made a shushing gesture, and shook his hand with a smile. Kong Yu seemed to have an aura about him when he was on set—the air of a professional. It made him seem like a completely different person from the Z-list actor Chang Jinxing met on the cruise ship.

"Have you always worked as a cameraman for film production crews?" Kong Yu asked.

"No, I was referred to this job by a friend," Chang Jinxing replied. He really had to demand answers from Zhang Yuwen when he got home. This was no job referral from a random HR agency. Chang Jinxing might never have had a proper job before, but he wasn't stupid, and he could tell from the way everyone was acting around him that the person who referred him must have been a big deal.

Kong Yu hesitated, seeming to want to ask something, but then filming for the next scene began.

Chang Jinxing grinned at him. "I'll get a good shot of you," he said, laughing, and they went their separate ways.

Evening scenes were challenging to film, so Wang Botao took over again while Chang Jinxing watched intently from the side. Wang Botao had him adjust the props, and Chang Jinxing ran onto the set to do so, meticulously tweaking things to cover up any slips.

A couple of scenes later, the director announced a wrap on filming for the day. It was nearly eight p.m., and Chang Jinxing was famished as he packed the equipment. The film production crew wouldn't provide dinner unless there were night scenes to film.

Chang Jinxing was kept busy all day, and he was at his physical and mental limits. He had to push equipment, run errands, and scurry back and forth between the shooting site and camera to

relay messages, and now, he was hungry, cold, thirsty, and tired. He shivered in the chilly wind, his mind a foggy haze.

A man came over and, with both hands, offered Chang Jinxing a bottled drink and a sandwich. "Hello. Kong Yu got these for you."

"Thank you," Chang Jinxing said. From the solemn way the man held the items out to him, he wondered if this was some kind of token of love.

Finally, it was over. At half past eight, he took the bus back to the city and fell asleep. When he woke, he found that he had a friend request on his message app; to his surprise, the request showed Kong Yu's profile picture. He accepted it. He also learned he would have to wake up even earlier the next morning because they had to set off at seven o'clock. With his camera in hand, he took the subway home.

He was utterly exhausted when he got home. Was this how Yan Jun felt every day when he opened the front door? If there were a mug of steaming hot milk and a plate of piping hot dinner waiting for him on the dining table, he would marry the person responsible without hesitation and hold their hand until the end of the universe...

Chang Jinxing's reverie was interrupted by what he found when he walked into the dining room. Zhang Yuwen stared at him in silence, and Chang Jinxing stared back. There, on the dining table, was a mug of hot cocoa and a bowl of curry rice.

"Is that for me?" Chang Jinxing couldn't believe his eyes.

"Yeah," Zhang Yuwen said. "I figured you probably hadn't eaten yet." Chang Jinxing pounced on Zhang Yuwen and made to kiss him, but Zhang Yuwen pushed his face away, exasperated. "Oh, save it!"

Chan Jingxing didn't even remove his coat before he sat down, downed half a mug of hot cocoa, and started gobbling up his food. He finally felt alive again.

"Who exactly did you ask to refer me for this job?" he asked at last.

"Why? What did they say?"

"Don't try to fool me. There's no way this job came from an HR agency. Tell me the truth; did you work in the film industry? You couldn't be..." Chang Jinxing glanced around the house, wondering if Zhang Yuwen had been living a double life this whole time.

Before Chang Jinxing could see through his pretense, Zhang Yuwen jumped in with a clever cover-up. "Our publishing house published the autobiography of a renowned director in the industry, and I was the editor in charge of the project. I got along well with him, and even helped him write some of the content."

"Oh." Chang Jinxing remembered a name he'd heard. "Director Zhu?"

"That's him, but don't tell anyone—I wasn't sure at first what kind of job he would recommend. How did it go?"

Chang Jinxing shared some anecdotes, and Zhang Yuwen seemed to understand everything he described. "You really know a lot," Chang Jinxing said. His mental image of Zhang Yuwen was undergoing a strange transformation; he looked the same, but somehow, Chang Jinxing saw him differently.

"I learned all of it while I was working on the autobiography," Zhang Yuwen explained. "Your drama is a small one that will take twenty days to complete filming, so it's not all that tough, and you won't have to stay up late working." Chang Jinxing was completely worn out, but most of his exhaustion stemmed from the lack of sleep he'd had the night before. "How much are they paying you per project?"

"Uh, I don't know," Chang Jinxing replied blankly.

"You didn't ask?"

"Am I allowed to ask? It...felt kind of embarrassing to bring up."

Zhang Yuwen didn't know whether to laugh or cry.

"But I'd keep going there even if I wasn't getting paid. I really learned a lot today. This is exactly the kind of work I want to do. Thank you, Yuwen!" Chang Jinxing said, sincerely grateful.

Zhang Yuwen gestured for him to go to bed soon, since he had to wake up early in the morning. He didn't tell Chang Jinxing that the referrer was the reason the film production crew was so courteous toward him. Some jobs looked glamorous on the surface but were full of parasites underneath, and in this regard, the film and television industry was no better than any other. In some respects, it was actually worse. But Chang Jinxing had the same hopes and aspirations as every other newcomer who entered this line of work, and Zhang Yuwen didn't want to rain on his parade.

Chang Jinxing dragged his battered body upstairs to sleep, but Zhang Yuwen remained in the dining room, working on his novel. He had fallen into the habit of sitting in the dining room for a while during the evening, sometimes waiting for Huo Sichen to reply to his messages, sometimes reading a book. Today, he was writing. After eight, his roommates always returned home, one after the other, and each would sit beside Zhang Yuwen and say a few words to him.

Chen Hong, for example, set his motorcycle helmet on the table, opened the refrigerator, and found a sandwich. "Can I eat this?"

"That belongs to Jinxing," Zhang Yuwen said. "It might be his breakfast tomorrow. I'll heat some milk for you."

"I'll just buy him another one tomorrow." Sitting opposite Zhang Yuwen, Chen Hong drank his milk and made quick work of the token of love that Kong Yu had given to Chang Jinxing. "Where's Yan Jun?"

"Asleep," Zhang Yuwen answered. "Where did you go?" With the new year in full swing, everyone seemed tired, always busy, busy, busy.

Chen Hong took out his phone. "Help me out. I'm looking at these three locations." He showed Zhang Yuwen several potential sites for his gym and asked for his advice. "I have a hundred and twenty thousand in funds now. Was thinking of renting a cheaper one."

Zhang Yuwen examined the square footage and layout of each of the three locations. "That depends on how you want to market your gym. The locations are fine. They're just in different areas."

"Yeah." Chen Hong sighed. "Last time, I wanted to go high-end, but it didn't work out. I'm not keen on adopting a high-volume, low-margin model, either. It's too tiring and too little money for too much work."

Money, money, money. Chen Hong's life seemed to revolve around money. This was his last gamble; it would determine whether he'd stay in Jiangdong or return to his hometown. He had to act with prudence. He couldn't find investors at this point, so his only option was to use his own savings.

"Which are you better at?" Zhang Yuwen asked. "Running a high-end studio in an upscale neighborhood, or catering to the general public with affordable prices?"

"I don't know," Chen Hong said, feeling lost. "I've lost a lot of my confidence after all those setbacks."

"Sichen said you're an excellent professional in your field."

"Yeah, but that doesn't always translate to profit."

Zhang Yuwen pointed at one of the locations. "This one isn't bad, I think. But remember, it's just my opinion."

Running a business seemed complex to Zhang Yuwen, used as he was to trading his skills for money. Operating a company or shop came with so many uncontrollable variables, and there was always the risk of being forced to close down in an economic downturn.

"Hm..." Chen Hong took his phone back from Zhang Yuwen. Just then, a message notification sounded from his gay dating app.

Zhang Yuwen glanced at it. "Are you still using that app?"

"Yeah. I'd like to look for a potential partner too, I think. Why? You have an opinion on it?"

Zhang Yuwen laughed. He'd downloaded the same app before, but had deleted it before long.

Chen Hong said it for him: "It's just that the users there are only looking for hookups."

"Yeah. Especially when they see someone with a great physique like you. They get carried away by lust."

Chen Hong sighed and scrolled for a while. "What do you think of this one?"

Zhang Yuwen looked at the profile. It belonged to an elite business professional who matched Chen Hong's type. "Not bad, I guess, but don't bring him home. If you want a hookup, go get a hotel room."

"Nah," Chen Hong said. While he had sexual needs—and the sexual needs of a fitness trainer were even more potent than those of the average person—he mostly preferred to take care of them himself. "When you're single, do you ever hook up with strangers?"

"Not really," Zhang Yuwen equivocated, not wanting to hurt Chen Hong's feelings.

"How about acquaintances?"

"That's even weirder. The way I see it, sleeping with someone establishes some sort of relationship with them. Honestly, though, you don't need to worry about what I think."

"I'm not worried about what you think, really."

"Some heterosexuals also like to hook up," Zhang Yuwen added. "It's just a preference. Not hooking up doesn't give someone the moral high ground."

"I know."

Spring had arrived, and Zhang Yuwen knew his roommates were all a bit horny. Of course, he had desires too. Chen Hong had to wake up early the next day, so he went to bed after their conversation.

The next morning, Chang Jinxing woke up even earlier, and he and Chen Hong agreed that Chen Hong would drive him to the meeting point again.

"Where's my sandwich?" Chang Jinxing howled.

"I ate it," Chen Hong confessed, "but I got you this."

"Someone gave that to me!"

"Oh?" Chen Hong had learned Zhang Yuwen's art of asking "oh?". It said more than a thousand words of teasing. In fact, everyone from No. 7 Riverbay Road had picked up this habit.

Chang Jinxing remained silent. Chen Hong drove him to his destination and dropped him off.

"I'm leaving!" Chen Hong said. "Work hard! Do your best!"

Chang Jinxing hummed in response and handed Chen Hong a small envelope.

"What's this?" Chen Hong asked. "A love letter?"

"Cake voucher! You can exchange it for a cake and a cup of coffee." It was a gift from a fan of the lead actor who'd visited the set the previous evening. Everyone had one.

"Mwah!" Chen Hong blew Chang Jinxing a kiss.

"Mwah!" Chang Jinxing returned it. Chen Hong started his electric motorcycle and drove away.

Sometimes, Chen Hong wanted to kiss Chang Jinxing on the lips. If Chang Jinxing wasn't his roommate and was instead just some stranger he'd met on that dating app, Chen Hong would absolutely have had sex with him. Even better, with Chang Jinxing being such a player, Chen Hong wouldn't even need to take responsibility afterward...

But after that night when he and Chang Jinxing jerked off together, things had been a little weird between them. They were like "good bros"—closer than ordinary friends, but without the emotional bond that real buddies forged over years or decades. The only thing was that they had seen each other's naked bodies, touched each other's dicks, beat each other off...

After some thought, though, Chen Hong had curbed the idea of going any further with Chang Jinxing. He hoped they could be good friends; good friends weren't easy to come by in life. Come to think of it, after they left school, people who used to be friends often took different paths in life and gradually lost touch. Everyone in society wore a mask, only ever thinking about their own self-interest. The only people he could really call his friends were the ones he'd met at Riverbay Road—Chang Jinxing, Zheng Weize, Zhang Yuwen, and Yan Jun.

Chen Hong truly cherished these friends, but for the last little while, he had been feeling out of sorts. He kept dwelling on his failures, ramping up the pressure he put on himself until it became a kind of self-hypnosis and almost sent him spiraling into depression. Then, spring came, and seeing Zhang Yuwen dating Huo Sichen made him want to fall in love too.

He desperately needed to build up his confidence as a man. The last time he felt so confident was when...well, it was during sex with his ex. He was able to satisfy practically all of his sexual fantasies and try out all sorts of positions. The sex lasted a long time, and it was good; both facts led to satisfaction like Chen Hong had never experienced before. Chen Hong indulged his desire to conquer, and his ex achieved physical pleasure.

He desperately needed to have sex. It didn't matter who the other guy was. He needed to conquer him and recover the confidence he'd lost when life beat him down.

In short, Chen Hong decided to leave everything else on the back burner and find himself a hookup from the app.

Riverbay Road

MEN'S DORMITORY

CHAPTER

30

CHEN HONG TRADED his voucher for coffee and cake, then took his seat and opened his dating app.

He had uploaded a few of his workout photos to his profile a while back, wondering if he could find some clients through the app. Many had taken the initiative to reach out to him, but he'd never made the move to meet them in person because, deep in his heart, he still thought of himself as mostly straight. Maybe a 70-30 split? 70 percent straight, 30 percent gay. Perhaps he would one day go on to get married, have kids, and start a heterosexual family. But if he started dating a bunch of different guys, there'd be no turning back.

Armed with this odd mindset, he downloaded the app to see just how much attention he could garner with the abs and pecs he had so painstakingly developed over years of grueling workouts. Everything else was inconsequential.

Yan Jun used the same app. Chen Hong had once asked him about it, and Yan Jun's response was that he was just looking at guys on there and imagining dating them, nothing more. Chen Hong could easily believe that Yan Jun was too busy to have the time or energy for casual hookups.

Zheng Weize used it, too, but he didn't hook up with people from the apps. He had to live stream in the evenings; hookups would have held him back from making money. He was also wary of strangers, fearing he'd be bullied and scammed.

The only two who weren't on the app were Chang Jinxing and Zhang Yuwen. Chang Jinxing himself was a walking dating app—man or woman, everyone wanted to sleep with him. If he wanted to make friends, he could just sit in a bar for a few minutes, and someone would offer him drinks or book a hotel room. He wouldn't have to spend a dime. And Zhang Yuwen, for his part, was a bit of an ascetic. Maybe it was his lifestyle habits, or maybe he just didn't like hooking up...

Thinking over his roommates' love lives, Chen Hong updated his profile with a photo that Zheng Weize had touched up for him, one that revealed his face. Within twenty minutes, he received more than forty messages. Of course, these people only wanted a taste of his body; none of them wanted a relationship. Perhaps, in their eyes, someone like Chen Hong was just on the app to have a good time.

Wanna hook up?

Hook up?

Hook up, hook up, hook up...

Like an emperor choosing among his consorts, Chen Hong found one that best met his aesthetic standards: under 18 percent body fat, broad shoulders, long legs, and an austere vibe.

Now? Chen Hong replied.

I'm at work, the other guy responded.

I can go to ur office, Chen Hong suggested, inspired by Zhang Yuwen's kink. *How abt the restroom?*

Apparently, that startled the other guy. *Ain't that a bit risky?*

Where r u? Chen Hong asked. The guy sent a location—an industrial park a little over a mile away. Chen Hong sent him his own location from the cake shop. *I'll get a room.*

He found a nearby hotel with inexpensive rooms that charged by the hour. It would only become costly if they stayed overnight.

The other guy didn't reply for a while. Meanwhile, Chen Hong got up and started moving. Feeling proactive, he bought lube and condoms from the convenience store next door, then rode to the hotel. He received the other guy's message on the way: *Fine, I'll come earlier. Give me the room number once you've booked one.*

Chen Hong got a room that charged over two hundred yuan an hour. He knew that few could resist his allure. As he took his next step, his confidence washed over him like a tide—no, like a tsunami.

He waited in the hotel room for ten or so minutes before someone rang the doorbell. He opened the door without looking through the peephole. It was a man in his twenties, about the same height as Chen Hong. He wore black-rimmed glasses and was dressed in a suit, shirt, and tie, plus a trench coat to complete the look. A fair-skinned man, he looked gentle and refined.

When he saw Chen Hong, he hesitated for the briefest of moments, because Chen Hong's photo had clearly been retouched to make him look better. The difference wasn't drastic enough for him to change his mind about hooking up, though. Chen Hong pulled him in, wrapped his arms around his waist, and began kissing him. After a brief internal struggle, he accepted Chen Hong and deepened the kiss. Chen Hong closed his eyes and imagined his ex as he pushed the man onto the bed.

Panting, the man stripped down to just his shirt. Chen Hong put on the condom, applied the lube, and prepared to enter.

"No, wait...it's too big!" The elite-looking man started to panic. "Too big! Dude! Wait!"

Chen Hong bent over and kissed him. Then, pinning down his wrists, he thrust in.

The guy was very tight. He probably rarely got fucked from behind. Recalling his past sexual experiences with his ex, Chen Hong moved slowly and gently. After a few cries, the man gradually conceded. Chen Hong wrapped his arms around him and buried his face in his shoulder. He was inside this guy, but his heart was elsewhere, thinking of another man—like dreaming of a sumptuous meal he'd once enjoyed while he was eating a boxed lunch.

"Shit, it's really big... You..." Mr. Elite's voice even changed. "Slow down, ah!"

Given that Chen Hong often replayed his memories of fucking his ex during dark, lonely nights, the novelty of the sensation faded quickly, so instead, Chen Hong started to imagine Mr. Elite as Chang Jinxing. Now that was exciting. Next, he pictured Zhang Yuwen, and the sensation multiplied. Next up was Yan Jun, and as he fantasized about fucking Yan Jun, his stimulation hit its peak.

In Chen Hong's mind, Yan Jun was the least likely of his roommates to sleep with him. The others were unlikely, yes, but improbable wasn't the same as impossible. The thought of one athlete fucking another excited Chen Hong, and he came.

Post-nut clarity set in. The two of them looked at each other, speechless.

"Need a hand?" Chen Hong asked finally.

"I came too," Mr. Elite said expressionlessly. While Chen Hong fucked him, he'd been jacking himself off. They'd climaxed almost simultaneously, a rare occurrence in sexual encounters and a testament to their chemistry.

"Okay," Chen Hong said. "Then...that's goodbye, I guess?"

"I'm a top!" Mr. Elite fumed.

"Huh? Why didn't you say so earlier?"

"When did you give me the chance to?" Mr. Elite was on the verge of coming undone. Chen Hong's strength was too much for him to take, especially when he'd started out by taking his mouth and pinning his wrists.

"Why the heck did you contact me, then?"

"I thought you were a bottom." With a towel, Mr. Elite cleaned the semen off his abdomen and wiped himself in the back with a towel. Chen Hong tried to take the towel to help him, but Mr. Elite, red-faced, told him to get lost.

"Well...neither of us read the introductions on the app," Chen Hong said, "so we're both to blame."

Mr. Elite was finally starting to calm down. "I have bottomed before," he admitted.

I knew it, Chen Hong thought. *If you didn't want me to fuck you, why didn't you say no? You obviously enjoyed it too. Crafty bottoms like you just can't be trusted.*

"Are you going to take a shower?" Mr. Elite asked.

"This room is paid by the hour, and I only reserved it for two hours. It's... Oh, it's only been half an hour. Well, either way, I'll skip the shower until I get home."

"Let me extend the room for you."

"It's fine. I'm leaving soon."

After some thought, though, Chen Hong did go take a shower. A while later, Mr. Elite came in too. This was Chen Hong's first hookup with a stranger, and he wasn't really sure about the etiquette, but it seemed rude to just leave, so he waited for the other guy to finish showering.

"Are we splitting the cost of the room?" Mr. Elite asked him when he emerged, putting on his glasses.

"No," Chen Hong said. "Wait, is there a rule about that?"

Mr. Elite, who had been tidying his hair, burst out laughing. Chen Hong looked at him and realized that he was pretty handsome.

"Some people want to go Dutch," Mr. Elite explained, "but I never do when I get a room."

"Yeah, okay then. No need to split the bill."

"Let me treat you to lunch," Mr. Elite said as they left the room and went to the elevator. He didn't press the button, and Chen Hong waited for a while before pressing it himself. His experience with people told him that this guy was probably well-off.

"I've already eaten." Chen Hong wasn't too inclined to have lunch after dessert.

"Where are you going? I can give you a ride."

Chen Hong waved this offer away, and when they reached the hotel entrance, they said their goodbyes. Chen Hong watched as Mr. Elite walked to the parking lot, opened the door to a Porsche, and drove away. Feeling rather conflicted, he was no longer in the mood to go check out the potential gym locations. All he wanted to do was to go home.

What a mess. The more Chen Hong thought about the whole thing, the more he regretted it. He felt as if his vows of chastity had been compromised. What principles had he been upholding all these years? And why had he given them up today? He felt guilty, but then again, he was a free adult who could do anything he wanted as long as he didn't break the law...

I didn't betray anyone, so why do I feel guilty?

Fortunately, his mood improved when he got home and saw his friends. Huo Sichen and Zhang Yuwen were eating at home. It was obvious that Huo Sichen had taken some time off on his lunch break to visit Zhang Yuwen.

"Have you eaten yet?" Zhang Yuwen asked Chen Hong.

"I'll just have a black coffee." Chen Hong sat down at the dining table. "What do you have there, Sichen? Oh, you brought pizza? I'll have some of that, then."

Suddenly ravenous, he devoured half of it.

"What did you do today?" Zhang Yuwen asked him.

"Have you decided on the new gym?" Huo Sichen chimed in, knowing that Chen Hong was looking for locations.

"I went to meet a hookup," Chen Hong said, rendering Zhang Yuwen and Huo Sichen speechless. Belatedly, it occurred to him that the dining table might not have been the best place to bring that up. "Sorry."

"No, no, go on," Zhang Yuwen said. "What happened after?"

"That's it," Chen Hong said.

"You have a photo? Show us," said Zhang Yuwen.

"Why are you interested in his hookup?" Huo Sichen asked.

"Just curious. Why?"

Chen Hong took out his phone and pulled up the photo for him. "He used a filter."

"Oh, not bad." He looked a bit familiar to Zhang Yuwen, who elected not to mention that lest it lead to any wild speculation.

Huo Sichen glanced at the photo but did not comment on it. Feeling listless, Chen Hong went back to his room for a nap after his lunch.

"He's under a lot of pressure," Zhang Yuwen said.

Huo Sichen nodded. "I go fishing when I'm stressed."

"What kind of fishing?"

"The regular kind, but sometimes I catch something else."

"Such as?"

"You don't eat the pizza crust, do you?" Huo Sichen asked instead of answering him. "Rich kids sure are different."

"There are all kinds of rich kids. Don't change the subject. Go on, tell me. What else have you caught?"

"A fish that doesn't eat pizza crusts."

Zhang Yuwen paused, then realized that Huo Sichen meant the time they met at the laser tag arena last year. He burst out laughing.

"You..." Zhang Yuwen looked at Huo Sichen with doubt in his eyes. "Back then, you already..."

Huo Sichen thought about it. "I guess so. Yeah, I have to admit it. You're right. It's exactly what you're thinking."

Zhang Yuwen and Huo Sichen had a unique rapport. They didn't even have to finish their sentences to get their meaning across to each other. What Zhang Yuwen wanted to ask was "You already had feelings for me?" And Huo Sichen's answer was a resounding yes.

"You had ulterior motives," Zhang Yuwen said. "I won't let you leave today until you admit that."

Huo Sichen laughed and got up to make coffee. "I wanted to date a guy. I'd been thinking about it for a long time after I broke up with my ex. You remember I said that I have...erectile dysfunction, right?"

"Oh." Zhang Yuwen nodded.

"So, here's the thing. I don't feel a thing toward girls, or even guys for that matter. But somehow, I feel like if I change my lifestyle and find the right guy to live with, everything will feel a lot more natural. Or who knows—maybe I just want to escape responsibility."

"Mutual understanding comes a lot easier when it's a relationship between two guys, since they think similarly," Zhang Yuwen said. "My childhood friend is married, but apart from sex, I think he prefers hanging out with guys."

"Maybe that's how it is with marriage and families," said Huo Sichen.

"But there are also many families where both parties complement each other perfectly and achieve mutual understanding. All I can say is that it has nothing to do with personality. It all depends on whether you meet the right person."

"Yeah! Meeting the right person is very important. I won't go into my ex's flaws, but I began to doubt myself when I was with her. I felt like I wasn't a good boyfriend, and I lost faith in love because of it. And then there was the physical aspect of it..."

"Yeah." Zhang Yuwen wanted to laugh every time he thought about Huo Sichen's impressive endowment and erectile dysfunction.

"I don't even know why I went fishing that day, but I met you," Huo Sichen said. "At the time, I thought that if there was someone out there I'd want to spend the rest of my life with, it would be someone like you."

"But you didn't even know what kind of person I was."

"Someone who looks like you," Huo Sichen clarified.

Zhang Yuwen laughed. "So you're just shallow."

Huo Sichen took his phone out and showed Zhang Yuwen a photo. It was a candid shot Huo Sichen had secretly taken at the laser tag arena. They'd been by the lakeside, listening to the owner explain the rules, and Huo Sichen was standing a short distance away and snapped a photo of Zhang Yuwen's profile against the light.

Suddenly, Zhang Yuwen had less trouble believing that Huo Sichen fell in love with him at first sight.

"But you don't have ED, trust me," Zhang Yuwen said. "You just had some setbacks in your relationships on top of work stress. It was only temporary."

"Maybe? Later, I found that feeling again...when we went hiking."

"Oh? When specifically?"

"When I lifted your shirt to apply ointment for you," Huo Sichen said. "Your skin was very fair, with a certain sort of masculine appeal..."

Zhang Yuwen's first thought was, *Damn! Chang Jinxing's a real player—his observations are spot on.* Chang Jinxing, of course, had been the first to notice Huo Sichen's fleeting shift in expression.

"That night, we slept in the same bed," Huo Sichen went on, "and you hugged me in the middle of the night. My libido came back. You reawakened it."

Zhang Yuwen just smiled, but Huo Sichen was looking at him thoughtfully.

"I want to make love to you." Huo Sichen leaned in a little and looked into Zhang Yuwen's eyes. "Can I? I want to have sex with you. I want to love you properly. You can teach me. I'll do everything I can to satisfy you."

Zhang Yuwen looked at Huo Sichen and leaned in to kiss him. His request was too formal, too serious to refuse. "Okay. Now? I'll go lock everyone's doors right away."

Huo Sichen laughed. "I'll come find you in a few days," he said, seemingly thinking about the time. Zhang Yuwen hummed an acknowledgment. "Let me be the top. We agreed on it."

"I know, I know," said Zhang Yuwen. Huo Sichen glanced at his watch but didn't get up. "Going back to work?"

"I'm still hard," Huo Sichen said. "I almost came when you kissed me just now."

Huo Sichen had turned himself on with all the flirting, and when Zhang Yuwen kissed him, they both had a reaction. Zhang Yuwen was in his loungewear, but Huo Sichen was wearing a pair of suit pants, and his erection was straining against the fabric.

"We're the only ones here," Zhang Yuwen pointed out. "What are you shy about?"

Doing his best to calm himself, Huo Sichen put on his suit jacket and headed for the door. For a brief moment, he almost thought of No. 7 Riverbay Road as his own home.

"But if you make me feel too uncomfortable," Zhang Yuwen warned, half serious and half teasing, "there'll be no next time."

"I'll be sure to...prepare in advance," Huo Sichen said. "I'm leaving." Zhang Yuwen saw him to the door, and Huo Sichen gave him a peck before driving away.

Damn, Zhang Yuwen thought, *why do I feel like a wife sending his husband off to work?*

When Yan Jun came back that night, Chen Hong, feeling refreshed from his afternoon nap, went to his room to chat with him and play with Xiao-Qi.

"I had a hookup this afternoon," Chen Hong said.

"Oh?" said Yan Jun. Everyone was imitating Zhang Yuwen. Chen Hong sighed. "Did you top?"

"Yeah. He wasn't bad. Well-off, drove a Porsche."

"Uh-huh." Yan Jun sprinkled baby powder on Xiao-Qi like he was preparing a dish.

Zhang Yuwen knocked on the door. "Is Jinxing back yet?"

"No," Yan Jun replied. "Wanna come in and hang out, sir?"

Zhang Yuwen, it turned out, wanted to play with Xiao-Qi for a while too. "So cute!" he said. Xiao-Qi waved at him, calling out "Yuwen, Yuwen," so he got straight to the point, holding Xiao-Qi by her hands and doing some crib exercises with her.

Chen Hong sighed. A moment later, he asked, "Are you guys listening to me?"

"We're listening." Zhang Yuwen was helping to dress Xiao-Qi in a onesie after her exercises. She was such a soft, adorable baby.

"Keep going," Yan Jun said. "Who paid for the room?"

"That's not important," Chen Hong said. "But guys, what happens when a guy who's never hooked up with a stranger before finally does it?"

"He acts exactly like you: He goes around asking other people for their opinions," Yan Jun said.

"Exactly." Zhang Yuwen gave Yan Jun a nod of approval for saying what he had been thinking.

Chen Hong didn't know what to say to that. He didn't feel like he was "dirty," but he did decide not to go for any more casual hookups because, in the end, the experience hadn't changed his life in any way. At most, it just shifted his attention away from his career to his libido.

He intended to delete the app that night, but a last peek at it showed several messages from Mr. Elite. *How about exchanging contact info?* one of them read, providing his own contact information.

Chen Hong hesitated; maybe this rich guy could introduce him to some big clients. In the end, he steeled himself and added Mr. Elite, feeling like a sneaky thief. Then, he clicked on the red X in the upper right corner of the app.

Riverbay Road
MEN'S DORMITORY

CHAPTER
31

WHISKEY, ZHENG WEIZE'S number one fan, had already dropped almost thirty thousand on him. Zheng Weize's anxiety soared as he watched his savings grow, but at the same time, he found himself falling for Whiskey.

Yeah, yeah, I'm promiscuous. What about it?

Zheng Weize began to look deep inside himself. Aside from Chang Jinxing, he'd be able to accept any of his roommates if they were willing to be with him—Zhang Yuwen, Yan Jun, Chen Hong, and even their friend on the outside, Huo Sichen. Any time Zheng Weize laid eyes on one of them, he found them handsome, and then he'd glance at another and think, *Hey, he's not so bad either.*

But they weren't interested in him, and they were all out of his league. *Why? Because I'm ugly, of course, and a sissy to boot.*

Zheng Weize knew that they wanted to date guys, not men who looked like women. Maybe there were men out there who liked effeminate guys, but he was sure they preferred the pretty and delicate ones. He'd probably never have such good fortune. Even casual hookups turned their noses up at him.

Zheng Weize's life was a series of self-inflicted blows. In the past, he was too busy working to think about it, but now that he was staying alone in his room most of the time, he was becoming increasingly withdrawn. Sometimes he didn't even want to leave when he heard his housemates chatting in the living room. Everyone had seen him fail to woo Chang Jinxing, which was embarrassing beyond reason; he felt like a toad caught lusting after a swan that'd had its humiliation memorialized by a nature photographer.

He only felt like himself when he put on his wig, applied makeup, padded his chest, turned on the voice changer, and sat in front of the camera every night to wave to his viewers and live stream as a girl. Being a girl was the only time he felt authentically him.

But Zheng Weize didn't want to undergo gender reassignment surgery to become a girl. Maybe he just didn't want to give up the little bit of privilege he enjoyed in society as a man. He also felt like he wasn't entirely a girl—like his emotions weren't as delicate—and he didn't want to be a weakling who depended entirely on others. Of course, being a woman didn't equate to being dependent, but Zheng Weize didn't put a lot of thought into that.

Lately, Chang Jinxing had been leaving home early in the morning and returning later at night. Zheng Weize decided to avoid crossing paths with him. Every time he saw Chang Jinxing, it hurt; seeing him for a full week would be enough to break his heart. Their New Year's Eve kiss had been a beautiful moment, but it was ultimately just a consolation prize, a thank-you for participating—that couldn't be any more apparent to him now.

He began to open up to Whiskey. Whiskey, for his part, sensed something while Zheng Weize was nursing his heartbreak and seized his opportunity.

Zheng Weize poured his heart out, telling Whiskey about his "ex," a scumbag player who had hurt him. He embellished the story, drawing inspiration from both Chang Jinxing and the straight guy to fuse them into a character so intricate and conceiving a plot so novel that even Zhang Yuwen, a movie director, would have been impressed. Sometimes, he even burst into tears while they talked, at which point Whiskey would frantically send him money and soothe him with promises to meet, date, and marry him; to never abandon him.

Zheng Weize bought into it so fully, he almost forgot about his real identity. Weirdly enough, the only thing stopping them from meeting up turned out to be Whiskey's looks and height, which fell short of Zheng Weize's requirements for the perfect partner. After rejecting yet another of Whiskey's requests to meet, Zheng Weize ended his live stream and sighed.

Oh, right, I'm a guy, he remembered suddenly. *What a close shave; I almost agreed to meet him just now.*

He opened his phone and swiped through his chat history with Whiskey: The few photos he'd sent to Whiskey, and all the moments from Zheng Weize's life that he'd shared with him.

Whiskey was smart to have sent a few photos of himself from his student days, when he was fair, slim, and fresh-faced. While his facial features weren't exactly handsome, young men always had a vibrant air of vitality to them. Those photos further cemented the link in Zheng Weize's mind between the young Whiskey and his current, rugged, thirty-something self.

R u angry? Zheng Weize asked him. This was the third time Whiskey had asked to meet him.

After a significant delay, Whiskey sent him a long voice message: "No, baby, it's not that. Listen to me. You keep saying you aren't ready, and I get that you might really be afraid of men, but I'm not like that. I love you, baby. I love you. I didn't call you my wife just for fun. I know you're different from the other streamers. Look, I don't even go to other live stream channels anymore. As long as you come, I'll show up on time. I know you hide it well, but there's a sadness in your eyes. Gimme a chance, please? I'll cherish you. From the moment I saw you, I knew you were the one. You can't keep going on like this... The way you're living, always cooped up in your room. I dunno what your besties are like, but how can you just stay home all day and not come out to face society? It's not good for you to eat takeout every day either, and you still gotta pay rent... How is that little bit of income you have enough?"

It was so easy to lose yourself in a role when you had been playing it for a long time, no matter who you were. Hearing Whiskey's words, Zheng Weize buried himself in his blanket and cried.

Whiskey sent another voice message. "I want to meet you and talk about living together. As your hubby, I'll...support you. Gimme a chance. I wanna take care of you and protect you. Don't live stream anymore. Whether you have depression or some other illness, it's treatable. I believe you'll slowly get better."

Oh, right, I have depression too... Zheng Weize had completely forgotten that he'd been playing the sympathy card, using depression as a cover to deceive Whiskey. *I'm depressed...*

Zheng Weize cried himself a river. His tears soaked through his pillow. Everything Whiskey said was so touching, especially that "I'll support you"—it hit Zheng Weize right in the heart, where he was the most vulnerable.

Tearfully, Zheng Weize replied with a voice message of his own. "I'll think about it." Shortly after he hit send, though, it hit him: *Shit! I forgot about the voice changer!*

Panicking, he considered retracting the message, but if Whiskey had already heard it, then withdrawing and replacing a message in a guy's voice with one in a girl's voice would only make things worse. It would substantiate any suspicions Whiskey might have. But amazingly enough, Whiskey noticed nothing amiss. Maybe he thought "her" voice had gone all hoarse from crying, or perhaps that she'd turned on the text-to-speech function.

r u crying? sweetheart, baby, r u crying?

Zheng Weize quickly adjusted his wig and took a photo of himself on the bed, looking all sad and red-eyed. *Yeah!* he replied.

My heart's breaking, Whiskey responded.

Like every other day, he spent the night on an emotional rollercoaster. Zheng Weize was exhausted. He had lied, and now he had to lie even more to cover it up. But he'd fallen for this straight guy, touched by his sincerity and his money. Never in his life had anyone treated him this generously.

Whiskey pulled out his trump card. *I know ur afraid to have sex with men. we dont hv to do anything. we can just talk, and u can just lemme hold you while we sleep. thats all I ask for. I can wait til ur ready.*

Zheng Weize couldn't deny it: In that moment, his heart was a little swayed.

The next day, in all seriousness, Zheng Weize asked Chen Hong, "Do you think straight men can be turned gay?"

"You'll have to ask Zhang Yuwen," said Chen Hong. "He's the only one who's turned a straight guy gay recently."

"I'm not joking," Zheng Weize said. "Look me in the eye and answer me."

"I doubt it. Always seems like the ones who're turned weren't actually straight in the first place and already had a natural inclination toward guys. Why? You find yourself *another* straight guy to crush on?"

"Nah. Just curious."

A devilish thought was growing in Zheng Weize's mind. Meanwhile, Chen Hong was chewing on a pencil and looking over the floor plans of some potential locations for his gym. Zheng Weize hugged his arm and rested his head on his shoulder, seeking a moment of comfort; Chen Hong's physique made him feel secure and protected.

Chen Hong could tell that something had happened to Zheng Weize recently, something beyond his relationship with Chang Jinxing. He kept cooping himself up in his room. The other roommates were all worried about him and would have gone knocking on his door if he hadn't emerged from his room this week. Luckily, Yan Jun was hosting the next gathering, and he planned to bring everyone to the riverside for a barbeque, which would make an opportunity for them to socialize.

"What would a gay guy do," Zheng Weize asked, feigning detached curiosity, "if he wanted to convert a straight guy?"

"He'd go around asking questions, just like you are," Chen Hong replied without looking up. Zheng Weize was left speechless.

He wanted Chen Hong's opinion, but he was too shy to ask outright, and he also didn't want to show Chen Hong a photo of Whiskey. He was embarrassed that Whiskey wasn't up to scratch, especially compared to Chang Jinxing, his previous target.

"I had a client who was in the same situation," Chen Hong said.

"Oh? How so?"

"Maybe some straight guys might have a natural inclination to be gay, but they just haven't realized it."

Some straight guys weren't exactly straight by nature. If they never met a man who went out of his way to win them over, they would perhaps go on to get married, have kids, and live their entire lives as heterosexuals. But under the right conditions, brotherly affection could shift to something more, and they would be reluctantly converted. And once they got a taste of it, there would be no turning back. At first, Chen Hong was going to bring up Yan Jun as a classic example, but after some thought, he mentioned another friend instead. He had a client who enjoyed online games, and in one of those games, he met a girl and spent a lot of money on her.

Zheng Weize was shocked at the similarity to his own situation.

"Was the girl actually a boy in disguise?" Zheng Weize asked. "Did they end up together?"

"No idea." Chen Hong continued to contemplate his renovation plans.

Eventually, the girl couldn't keep up the lie anymore and revealed the truth when they finally met. At first, Chen Hong's client blew his top, but they had forged an emotional bond, and it was impossible for him to just let go. Instead, the guy started treating him like a buddy, and surprisingly, they went on to become good friends who often played basketball and went swimming together. As to whether they ended up as a couple, Chen Hong didn't know.

Chen Hong was also reminded of how his own lover deceived him.

"But be careful. Some straight guys will go crazy with rage and beat you up," Chen Hong added, dropping Zheng Weize a subtle reminder not to pin his hopes on this straight guy. The risk was too great.

"Really?" Zheng Weize asked worriedly.

"I guess?" Chen Hong wasn't sure. He hadn't really felt like beating the other guy up when he first met him. The idea of getting violent only crossed his mind when the guy threatened him with compromising videos—otherwise he might have ended up becoming friends with him.

He glanced at Zheng Weize. "It's not a given. It depends on the emotional bond between the two people. If the relationship has always been good, they could maybe stay friends. It also depends on the other person's personality. Are you dating a straight guy online?"

"No," Zheng Weize lied flatly. "A good friend of mine is asking for my opinion. He's gay too."

"Tell your friend not to meet him. He should keep his feelings to himself."

"But the straight guy has sent him a lot of money."

"Then he should give it back, or buy some gifts for him." Chen Hong had already seen through the asking-for-a-friend ruse, but he didn't want to expose Zheng Weize, so he tried his best to dissuade him.

But Zheng Weize only heard what he wanted to hear. "But he's already spent a lot of it," he said.

After returning to his room, he sat himself down to trawl the web for cases similar to his own and typed "turning a straight guy gay" into the search bar. Unfortunately, information on the internet suffered from survivorship bias—only those who'd succeeded stepped forward to share their experiences, while those who were beaten up tended to keep quiet—and what he found gave Zheng Weize a confidence boost.

The seed of a devilish thought that had been planted earlier in his mind sprouted and began to grow.

"What are you up to, dear?" Whiskey's voice message carried a hint of a smile. "It's a beautiful sunny day today."

That afternoon, Whiskey sent Zheng Weize a photo from a park. He lived in a city not far from Jiangdong, where he helped his older sister in her small business dealing with wholesale laminating film. Now, he was out walking his sister's dog.

Zheng Weize turned on the voice changer. "Taking a nap."

Whiskey switched to text message. *Not going out?*

Gonna have afternoon tea with my girlfriends later, Zheng Weize responded.

When do I get to have afternoon tea with u? 3rd time's the charm, I hope.

Zheng Weize smiled. Over the days, he'd been thinking about how to handle the situation with Whiskey, and he concluded that he couldn't keep going like this. Even if it all went to shit, they had to be honest with each other. But whether to meet Whiskey as a guy or a girl—that was the question that stumped him the most.

If he met Whiskey as a guy, he'd have to apologize to him and seek his forgiveness. Whiskey might be shocked and cut off contact with him for a time, but if he reached out to Whiskey first, he might be able to mend the relationship and slowly turn him gay, and then they'd eventually end up together as a couple.

But what if he met Whiskey as a girl? Continued deceiving him in real life? That would save him from having to deal Whiskey such a big blow all at once. Or he could dress in women's clothes and tell Whiskey that he was a cross-dressing bottom... Zheng Weize had seen something sparking between the straight photographers at comic conventions and the cross-dressing male cosplayers before.

After thinking it over, he decided that the second option would result in the least shock to Whiskey. He would meet Whiskey dressed as a girl and let Whiskey discover the truth on his own. That way, Whiskey would be less likely to suffer a mental breakdown. And Whiskey could also just see him as a girl, couldn't he?

He could disguise his appearance, but what about his voice? Tell Whiskey he had a cold? What about his Adam's apple? Zheng Weize looked in the mirror. His Adam's apple wasn't all that prominent; he could hide it with makeup and a scarf. The best time to meet would be at night, when the light wasn't too bright. That would reduce the risk of exposure.

Except...say he kept up with the lie. What if Whiskey started getting all touchy-feely? If he came to Jiangdong, would he stay in a hotel? And if Zheng Weize were to visit him there, would he want to have sex? He did say he didn't want to...but then again, maybe Whiskey wouldn't notice if they turned off the lights... This thought made Zheng Weize incredibly excited.

Having sorted out his plans, Zheng Weize suddenly felt hopeful. Whiskey was a gentle guy, and Zheng Weize had fallen for his tenderness. He was sure that even if Whiskey discovered his real gender, their emotional bond was strong enough that they would continue to be friends.

I love you too, Zheng Weize declared in his heart.

So when Whiskey asked to meet him for the fourth time, Zheng Weize agreed on the condition that he chose the time and venue—because he had depression and social anxiety, and he wanted to avoid crowded places.

Then, Zheng Weize prepared to face the greatest challenge of his life.

CHAPTER

32

CHANG JINXING GRADUALLY GREW accustomed to work on the set. Every day, Chen Hong gave him a ride on his motorbike to the meeting point; he greeted his colleagues, brought his mentor a thermos filled with coffee, and busied himself around the set. Thanks to his good looks and industry connections, everyone was friendly to him, and he used his skill at reading people, honed from all those years of playing the eunuch, to charm the first and second camera operators. In return, Wang Botao generously taught him a few things. Of course, Wang Botao, as a veteran cameraman, believed the old saying that "teaching the apprentice starves the master," but he had a hunch that Chang Jinxing was a young director being trained by some big shot and wasn't actually out to make a living in cinematography.

"Cinematography is tough work," Wang Botao lamented to Chang Jinxing.

"But it's also rewarding," Chang Jinxing replied.

Wang Botao smiled. All this for those tiny, fast-rolling credits after a drama episode or film? Did viewers even notice those names? In the end, it was all about making a living. He didn't want to put a damper on the young man's dreams, though, so he simply patted him on the shoulder.

"Do you know Kong Yu?" Wang Botao asked pensively.

These days, Kong Yu's manager often came looking for Chang Jinxing, and they occasionally chatted for a bit. The talent management agency was adept at sailing where the wind blew, and someone there must have discovered who Chang Jinxing's backer was. Such a deliberate attempt to get close to someone seemed a bit odd on the surface, but it was fairly normal for the industry.

"We've met once before." Chang Jinxing didn't want to elaborate too much in case he accidentally outed Kong Yu.

Wang Botao grinned. "It's been a while since he last got a role."

If Zhang Yuwen had been there, he could have explained the crew's secret lingo and doublespeak to Chang Jinxing. For example, if Wang Botao suddenly asked about an actor, it meant that he was hinting at something about that person. "Been a while since he last got a role" implied that the guy in question had no resources and was looking for people he could use as stepping stones to climb to the top. In essence, Wang Botao was telling Chang Jinxing to watch out.

But all of this flew right over Chang Jinxing's head. "Huh? He seems like a good actor to me."

Wang Botao nodded and said nothing else.

Filming began for the day. First up was another scene between the second male lead and his childhood friend. The director and producer rarely crossed paths on set, but this time they both walked over to the camera as if they'd agreed to do so beforehand.

The director was speechless. The childhood friend's acting was horrendous. Chang Jinxing, who was watching from the side, felt so embarrassed for him that he wished he could crawl into the ground on his behalf.

Finally, the producer couldn't stand it anymore. "Oh my god! Do you even know how to act?!"

Oh no, Chang Jinxing thought, *the mic is gonna pick up your voice!*

Kong Yu's expression shifted minutely, but no one had yelled cut, so he tried his best to keep going, trading lines with the internet celebrity playing his childhood friend. The actor who'd been publicly scolded pushed on too, not daring to look at the camera.

You guys have remarkable mental fortitude, Chang Jinxing thought.

"Cut! Cut! Cut!" the director hollered. "Step off the set and think about what your job title entails before you return!"

The producer sighed, and Wang Botao stopped the camera. The director and producer stepped aside and launched into a discussion. "Where's the assistant director?" the producer asked.

"Doing the casting for another drama," the director replied.

"This isn't working. We have to replace him. I'm about to die of secondhand embarrassment. Just look at this scene... Oh, was it already deleted? He looks like he's having a seizure when he gets all worked up! How does Kong Yu even manage to keep acting with him?!"

Thank God, Chang Jinxing thought, although he pretended he hadn't heard that. *I can't take it anymore.*

"We already spoke about replacing him last time," the director said.

"But we haven't found a suitable replacement, have we? Their agency said they'd give him a two-day crash course."

"Then what do we do now? We don't have a replacement, and his character is in a lot of scenes."

"Change it into a monodrama?" the producer suggested. "Or pair him up with the female supporting role?"

"We'll have to call the screenwriter and see how she can change it," said the director.

Oh, that's an option? Chang Jinxing thought.

The producer and director went over the script. Then, the director made a phone call to the screenwriter while Kong Yu and the supporting actor took a break off to the side. The actor playing the childhood friend still looked bewildered; he didn't know that his fate was already sealed and he was about to be booted out the door.

Kong Yu threw Chang Jinxing a questioning look, and Chang Jinxing gave him an imperceptible shake of his head, signaling that there was trouble. That brief moment of eye contact was all it took; Kong Yu got the idea.

The screenwriter's voice came from the phone. "We can't change it! He's a very popular character from the original work, and we'll need them for fan service and publicity later!"

"Oh, right!" the producer said. "I almost forgot about that!" Chang Jinxing was stunned. "Find someone else, then," the producer said decisively. "Someone handsome. Tell the assistant director he has until tomorrow morning to scrounge up a replacement. We'll shuffle things around, shoot the birthday party first..."

"The male lead isn't here yet," the director pointed out. "Get the coordinator to call him."

"Oh, for God's sake." The producer was beyond frustrated.

The director was just about to take another look and see if he could salvage the situation when he glimpsed Chang Jinxing out of the corner of his eye. Three seconds later, the director asked him, "Give it a shot, won't you?"

"Give what a shot?" Chang Jinxing opened the footage from the earlier scenes to show the director. "Which scene?"

But the director was calling out to the producer. "Lao-Wang! Come back! What do you think of him?"

The producer turned around. "Oh, he works! Give it a try!"

"Um, give what a try?" Chang Jinxing asked.

"The role!" the producer said. "Where's the makeup artist? Take him to get his makeup done."

"Wait, what?!" Chang Jinxing blurted. "What do you mean? You want me to act?"

"He has a great facial structure," Wang Botao commented, sipping the coffee Chang Jinxing had given him. "Very photogenic. He has a small face too."

The producer grinned. "You're right! How did I not notice before? Come on, Jinxing, help us out here..."

"But...but I've never acted before!"

"Kong Yu will lead you, and the director will walk you through the scene later. Just give it a try. If it doesn't work out, we'll find someone else. No harm in trying, right?"

"I'll get you an extra chicken drumstick for lunch!" the director added. "Where's the production assistant? Get the other guy out of here."

With that, the pitiful actor who played the childhood friend was sent packing. Whether Chang Jinxing suited the role or not, the producer had no plans to use that actor again.

"No, no, no." Chang Jinxing was panicking. "I really can't do it. Oh my god! Why are you even asking me to do this? I'm here as the camera assistant, not an actor!"

"Just try it," said the makeup artist, joining in. "Acting is fun."

Several girls from the crew entered next, laughing. "Yeaaah! We were just saying that you'd do a better job than that guy if you took over..."

Pressed into the chair, at first Chang Jinxing tried to wriggle his way free, but he didn't want to lose face in front of so many girls, so he tried his best to calm down. Panicking would only embarrass him further.

The makeup artist quickly applied foundation. The girls giggled, wanting to take photos of him, but then, suddenly, they fell silent. Kong Yu walked in, and the others scattered.

"Here's the script," Kong Yu said. "Take a look. I've changed the lines for you. You only have four lines in this scene."

Chang Jinxing's mind went blank as he looked down at the script. Kong Yu watched him in the mirror.

"I really don't know how to do this..."

"Zhou Rong doesn't either," Kong Yu said. "He's even more clueless than you. You can't be worse than him. Just relax and start by memorizing the lines."

"Oh my god," Chang Jinxing exclaimed. "What is even happening?!"

Kong Yu left the makeup room and chanced upon the director and producer in another deep discussion.

"But Director Zhu was the one who recommended him," the director was saying. "Should we check with him? What if he's a relative, and Director Zhu doesn't want him to get into acting?"

"Let me ask." The producer made the call. "Oh, hey. Hi, Director Zhu. Sorry to bother you again, but uh, we've got a situation right now... One of the supporting actors can't keep up with the role. Jinxing has the looks for it, and we're thinking of letting him try... What? Oh...okay."

Off to the side, Kong Yu kept eavesdropping.

"Director Zhu said he referred him as a favor to someone else." The producer shot the director a questioning look. "Who could it be?"

While the director and producer looked at each other, a subtle change came over Kong Yu's face.

The director asked, "What else did he say?"

"He said it's not up to him to decide. We have to ask Jinxing. It should be fine if he's okay with it— Hey, Jinxing!"

"Are you going to ask him?" said the director.

With his makeup already done, Chang Jinxing stepped out. He'd changed into a loose-fitting casual suit and looked like a completely different person. "Oh, man," he groaned. He was clutching the script in one sweaty hand.

"Are you willing to try?" asked the producer. "Director Zhu said it's your call."

"This isn't going to work!" Chang Jinxing cried. "I'm not prepared at all!"

"He says okay," the producer said. "That settles it, then. The director will guide you through the scene. Let's get ready to continue."

Chang Jinxing had no words.

The director pulled Chang Jinxing aside and patiently walked him through the scene. Kong Yu stayed by his side until it was time for the camera to roll. Chang Jinxing and Kong Yu sat at the bar in the villa, and the camera panned to them.

"Action!"

"The more I think about it, the worse I feel," Kong Yu began.

Chang Jinxing said nothing. In fact, he was nervously rehearsing his lines in silence. He met Kong Yu's eyes, and Kong Yu gave him an inquiring but encouraging look.

"When a person is lonely, they tend to make a lot of bad decisions," Chang Jinxing recited.

"Not too bad," said the producer. "Much better than the earlier guy."

"It's almost as bad, but at least Kong Yu can play off of him, and they won't talk past each other."

Kong Yu heaved a long sigh. Chang Jinxing was at a loss for what to do. It was awkward to simply sit around doing nothing, so he took the two glasses of whiskey from the bartender and set one in front of Kong Yu.

"He even knows to improvise," the producer observed.

"Cut!" yelled the director. He went over to whisper to Chang Jinxing. "The script says you have to look at Kong Yu when you're talking, but you actually have to look at the camera, because it's from his perspective now."

Chang Jinxing assumed the director was going to chase him off, throw a sack over his head, and beat him up, but no—so did that mean he did okay with his line? That gave him a confidence boost.

They redid the scene, and this time, Chang Jinxing looked into the camera and delivered his lines with a smile. Meanwhile, a dejected Kong Yu took the liquor Chang Jinxing handed him and downed it all. Then, he nudged the whiskey glass toward Chang Jinxing, indicating that he should drink too.

"Kong Yu's leading him," the producer said. "This is going to work."

Following Kong Yu's lead, Chang Jinxing drank it—and promptly grimaced. *Isn't this lemon tea?!* But his expression was spot-on, and the director didn't yell cut.

Kong Yu put his arm around Chang Jinxing's shoulder and slurred drunkenly, "Loneliness is the devil. You won't understand if you've never been haunted by the devil."

He's seriously handsome. Chang Jinxing gazed blankly into Kong Yu's eyes, forgetting for a moment that they were still filming. Then, he snapped back to his senses and shifted his gaze to the bar. "So, you've decided to make a deal with the devil?"

"Slightly better...but still not good enough," the director said.

"Looks good to me, actually," said the producer. "Didn't you see that? Their eye contact was interesting."

The director glared at the producer, who stopped talking. After the reminder from the screenwriter, her attention had completely shifted from acting to fan service, and now, all she could think about was generating hype and boosting traffic to hit their promotional targets.

Chang Jinxing's acting was awkward, but it was much better than the previous guy's—it fell within a tolerable awkwardness range, likely because of Kong Yu's cooperation. In the end, the director gave his approval.

"Phew..." Chang Jinxing's undershirt was drenched in sweat.

Wang Botao gave him a thumbs-up. "Nice work."

Chang Jinxing hurried over to watch his scene, and the producer said to the director, "Let's reshoot the childhood friend scene from the other day while everyone's here. That's all for now. I'm heading out."

The director had no choice but to go with it. Chang Jinxing was better than his predecessor, at least, so he dropped it for the time being.

During lunch break, Chang Jinxing received two lunch boxes and two drinks, since he was now a camera assistant *and* an actor. Kong Yu invited him to eat with him, but Chang Jinxing insisted on staying with the camera crew.

By afternoon, when they began reshooting the scene from the first day, everyone was exhausted and sleepy. With a bit of prior experience under his belt, Chang Jinxing's second scene went a lot better. He'd already memorized the lines from all those bad takes the previous actor had to redo, too, so he made it through the reshoot without a hitch.

Once the scene was done, Chang Jinxing quickly removed his makeup and returned to the set as a camera assistant. "How many scenes do I have in total?" Chang Jinxing asked.

"Not many," Kong Yu said, watching from the side. He rarely concerned himself with watching back his scenes, but Chang Jinxing was so nervous that he came over to provide some support. "About ten. Our scenes are pretty minor. The focus is on the leads."

Chang Jinxing nodded. A thought occurred to him then: Would he get more pay now that he'd taken on this role? That would be awesome. Since filming began, no one had said anything to him about his salary, and Chang Jinxing couldn't muster up the courage to ask.

Kong Yu leaned in a little. "You did good there."

"Why is my face so wide?" Chang Jinxing wondered aloud.

"The camera will do that," Kong Yu replied. "This is already good."

Chang Jinxing laughed. He thought he looked a little silly on screen, although he didn't feel that way at all while filming. He cast a sidelong glance at Kong Yu and realized that they were standing too close together, so he took a hasty step away.

"Where are you staying?" Kong Yu asked. "I could drop you off tonight."

"It's okay, I can go back myself," Chang Jinxing said hurriedly.

Chang Jinxing thought about calling Zhang Yuwen to fill him in on everything, but filming had wrapped for the day, so he decided to just talk to him and ask him for his opinion in person when he got home.

He thought Zhang Yuwen would find it amusing or be happy for him, but that night, he realized that he didn't know Zhang Yuwen as well as he thought.

"What?!" Zhang Yuwen blurted in disbelief. "They had you stepping in to act? What is this production crew thinking?!"

Chang Jinxing tensed, not knowing what to say. "I...I don't know. I wasn't sure what happened either. They put makeup on me and sent me in front of the camera..."

Zhang Yuwen went silent for three seconds and then started making calls, visibly suppressing his anger. Chang Jinxing found himself stupefied. This was the first time he had ever seen Zhang Yuwen angry, and he would never have expected anger to transform his good-natured friend into a different person altogether.

"What happened on set?" Zhang Yuwen demanded into the phone. Chang Jinxing didn't say a word. "Why would they send someone with no experience to stand in at the last minute?!"

The person on the other end seemed to be apologizing profusely, and Zhang Yuwen listened with a grim expression on his face. While this was happening, Yan Jun, Chen Hong, and Zheng Weize came out to see what was happening. Chang Jinxing gestured to them to go back to their rooms. Zhang Yuwen remained seated, and Chang Jinxing, at a loss for what to do, stood next to him.

After hearing the apologies, Zhang Yuwen hung up, looking resigned.

"What's your producer's phone number?" Zhang Yuwen asked Chang Jinxing.

"Don't! Please, Yuwen! I don't want to lose this job."

Knowing Chang Jinxing wouldn't dare to give him the number, Zhang Yuwen made another call. "Do you know the producer of *Spring Love*? Can you give me her number? Thanks."

Chang Jinxing was dumbfounded. It was only now dawning on him that Zhang Yuwen was probably some kind of big boss behind the scenes.

Zhang Yuwen next dialed the producer's number. "Hi, Wang-jie. This is Zhang Yuwen." He introduced himself right off the bat. The person on the other end was clearly just as stunned as Chang Jinxing was. "I was the one who asked Lincoln to introduce Jinxing to Director Zhu."

"Oh! So it was you!" The producer's voice was audible over the phone.

"I've heard from Jinxing that he was asked to stand in for another actor today?"

"Uh, about that..." Palpably nervous now, the producer's voice sounded a lot smaller. Watching on, Chang Jinxing couldn't even begin to describe how shocked he was. As Zhang Yuwen listened to her explanation, he sized Chang Jinxing up, determining the veracity of his words. *Good thing I didn't lie to him!*

"Uh-huh, okay, okay, I got it," Zhang Yuwen said. "In that case, I'll ask him first. Yeah, let him decide for himself. I might call you again later."

Zhang Yuwen hung up, looked at Chang Jinxing, and heaved a tired sigh.

"I'm sorry, Yuwen...ge," Chang Jinxing said. He may have been the same age as Zhang Yuwen, but the guy in front of him had such an imposing aura that Chang Jinxing concluded there was no way he was a proofreader at a publishing house.

"Do you want to act?" Zhang Yuwen asked. "Are you mentally prepared to debut?"

"Huh? No, I really wasn't thinking of it like that! They asked me to step in because the original actor was a disaster and his acting sucks." Zhang Yuwen looked into Chang Jinxing's eyes, and Chang Jinxing continued in all earnestness, "And then I kind of found it fun after filming those two scenes. I didn't really give it that much thought.

If you don't think it's a good idea, I won't go tomorrow. Maybe I'll just quit, even."

Zhang Yuwen shook his head.

"I'm really sorry if this puts you in a difficult position," Chang Jinxing added. "You gave me the opportunity, but I didn't appreciate it properly."

"No, that's not what I mean." For someone who prided himself on having seen and experienced a lot, Zhang Yuwen still fell for the classic playboy trap of taking a step back in order to move forward.

"I meant it," Chang Jinxing said. "I won't go tomorrow."

"That's not it." Zhang Yuwen wanted to explain, but instead, he asked, "Are you angry?"

"Nah, I'm not. But I know I must have caused you trouble earlier."

Zhang Yuwen looked at Chang Jinxing quietly for a while. Eventually, he said, "I should be apologizing to you. I didn't make things clear to you." He took a deep beath, looking as if he was contemplating his words. "Do you want to be an actor? Tell me the truth. Do you want to be a star? If so, I can help you."

Chang Jinxing looked at Zhang Yuwen, thunderstruck. "I..." He thought for a moment. "Yuwen, are you the boss of a film production company?"

"No, but that's not important. You have to think it over carefully. What exactly do you want? Let's assume that filming wraps up, and you shoot to stardom—"

"It's not that easy," Chang Jinxing said. He wanted to laugh, or maybe cry.

"No one can say for sure what the future will bring," Zhang Yuwen said. "Let's just assume that they'll tell you and Kong Yu to play up the bromance for fan service, right? That'll definitely generate hype once the drama airs. The production company needs traffic for their viewership ratings, and the platforms need the clicks. And Kong Yu's talent management agency needs the hype to boost their popularity.

"Once you stand in the public eye, more and more people will start paying attention to you. Your dark past will be dug up. Your family, your secrets, the people you love, and those you've slept with...it will all become fair game. People who've slept with you, men and women, will take any photo they have of you and post it online for attention. They will discuss your dick like they're talking about a dish."

The color drained from Chang Jinxing's face. He knew Zhang Yuwen was speaking the truth. Sometimes he saw celebrity scandals online and found them entertaining, but it would be a different story if it happened to him. Especially since he'd sent some rather explicit photos of himself to several people over the years.

Zhang Yuwen wasn't finished. "In exchange, you'll get a lot of money. You might suddenly go from rags to riches and splurge on luxury cars, branded watches, and designer brands, ultimately blowing it all. Of course, this is a once-in-a-lifetime chance at a life many people dream of. You make money with your looks, but one day, you might fade into obscurity—no. Sooner or later, you *will* fade into obscurity." Chang Jinxing made a noise of agreement, and Zhang Yuwen continued, "All sorts of 'friends' will pop up around you, each with their own motives. Perhaps they'll try to make some money off you, or worse, tempt you with drugs—maybe out of pure jealousy and spite—and drag you through the mud..."

"I get it," Chang Jinxing said.

"It's true that there are a lot of good actors. I won't deny that. But if you really want to get into acting and be a star, then you have to know a lot of things going in, including what I've said tonight."

"No. I don't wanna be a star."

"Do you really mean that?" Zhang Yuwen said. "You'd better think it through."

Chang Jinxing nodded, entirely serious, and picked up his camera bag. "I wanna be a photographer, even if I can't make money off it. You don't have to call Miss Wang. I'll talk to her myself tomorrow."

"You sure?" Before he'd heard him out, Zhang Yuwen was almost certain that Chang Jinxing wanted to get into acting. He'd seen the same excited expression on many people's faces; people who yearned for a glamorous life and hoped that, after their drama aired, there would be swarms of fans waiting for them at the airport and screaming crowds wherever they went. They dreamt not only of astronomical paychecks, but of having the entertainment industry wrapped around their finger, too...

But the reality was that most of them would remain unknown, unable to get a taste of that tempting fruit. The rest might be in the limelight for a while only to ultimately wind up as a tool for others, falling from their pedestals to become laughingstocks that people gossiped about over tea or dinner.

"Having money is great, no doubt about that," Chang Jinxing said, "but I don't wanna give up photography. I wanna stay true to myself. To me, freedom is what matters the most."

Riverbay Road
MEN'S DORMITORY

CHAPTER 33

THE HARSH WINTER had yet to pass; it was the coldest month of the year. The landscape was frigid and desolate, shrouded in a fog that seemed to envelop everything whole. The ginkgo trees by the riverside slumbered in the chilly wind. Even the flow of the river had slowed down some. In the pale daylight, pedestrians in woolen hats and thick scarves held cups of milk tea and hot coffee as they trudged wearily toward refuge.

On this particular morning, Yan Jun woke up very early. He handed Xiao-Qi her milk bottle, then went to the bathroom to brush his teeth, shave, and examine himself in the mirror. Meanwhile, Zheng Weize was still in bed, sleeping under a thick quilt. A thin layer of mist had already formed on the floor-to-ceiling window in his room. Chen Hong was in the gym doing his morning run, while Chang Jinxing was frying eggs and making coffee in the kitchen. Jarred awake by his alarm clock, Zhang Yuwen blearily put a record on and dragged himself, zombielike, to the shower. Huo Sichen, by contrast, was all dressed and ready; he drove his car out of the garage and sent a message to Zhang Yuwen, inviting him out for dinner that night.

"Last night..." Chen Hong whispered.

Chang Jinxing looked up with a smile. "Good morning."

"Morning," Zhang Yuwen said, coming down the stairs.

"Huh?" Chen Hong and Chang Jinxing were both surprised for a moment before they remembered it was Tuesday. On Tuesdays, Zhang Yuwen went to the publishing house.

"You're up early," Chen Hong noted.

"Yeah. Is there breakfast for me?"

"I'll make it now," said Chang Jinxing.

Zhang Yuwen made his own coffee while Yan Jun bade them farewell, holding Xiao-Qi in his arms. "Yuwen's early today," Yan Jun said.

As he put on his shoes in the foyer, Zhang Yuwen took Xiao-Qi from him and gave her a peck on the cheek. "Bye-bye."

Zhang Yuwen was going to be running around for almost the whole day, including his trip down to the publishing house. Right now, he was at the printer, sorting out the manuscript, when Chen Hong picked up the lease agreement he'd printed earlier.

"Have you decided on the location?" Zhang Yuwen asked him.

"Yup." Chen Hong put on his motorcycle helmet. He was ready to sign the contract with the landlord. "Are you and Jinxing okay?" They had all felt the force of Zhang Yuwen's fury the previous night.

"It's nothing," Zhang Yuwen said. "Jinxing, do your best at work today!"

"Roger!" Chang Jinxing threw him a parting shot and left too. "You too! Love ya!"

Having seen them off, Zhang Yuwen faced his empty house and realized, rather abruptly, that at some point they'd all become family to him.

As he rode his motorcycle, Chen Hong looked back, concerned. "Everything okay between you and Yuwen?" he asked.

"We're fine," Chang Jinxing reassured him. "He got me some work, but I didn't do a good job of it, so he got angry."

"Yuwen really is a great person."

Chang Jinxing said nothing. He didn't tell Chen Hong what he had inferred about Zhang Yuwen; he knew how to be discreet.

"Jinxing?" Chen Hong prompted.

"Yeah," Chang Jinxing replied, feeling a little apprehensive. "He's always so generous. He changed my life."

"I think it's safe to say he changed all of our lives," Chen Hong said.

With his printed manuscript in hand, Zhang Yuwen stood in front of the photo wall, which was now adorned with the photos from their hot spring trip. It wasn't their expressions when the fireworks went off that captivated him the most—although Chang Jinxing did capture the moment beautifully—but the handful of photos taken during their mealtimes.

In the first few shots, Chang Jinxing had taken some close-ups of Zhang Yuwen. *What was I thinking about then? Sichen?* There were also individual shots of each roommate. Everyone was happy, although their eyes each told a different story about their wishes. Yan Jun and Huo Sichen were drinking and whispering to each other, so plastered their eyes were glazed and unfocused.

The last few photos were from the second day. There was no drinking this time, and Chang Jinxing had taken a group shot of them at another meal. Someone had cracked a joke, and everyone was doubled over laughing. It was chaos. Chang Jinxing had captured that moment perfectly.

There were also photos of everyone from their late-night game of Truth or Dare. Huo Sichen was looking at his phone, and

Chen Hong had wrapped himself in his blanket. Yan Jun was glancing back at the door, where Zheng Weize was deep in thought and Zhang Yuwen was laughing...

Zhang Yuwen stood in the dining room, staring silently at the photo wall. It chronicled his life, which had practically been turned upside down in the past three months. Yan Jun said he'd changed everyone, but Zhang Yuwen really felt that he was the one who had been transformed. Compared to what his roommates had given him, his own contributions seemed negligible.

Thank you, guys, Zhang Yuwen thought. Then, he bound up his manuscript, put it in his bag, and went to knock on Zheng Weize's door.

"Weize! Get up!" A lazy, complaining sound came from within. Zhang Yuwen went to the foyer to put on his shoes, calling, "Jinxing made breakfast for you."

"Oh..." Zheng Weize opened the door and poked his head out. "Are you going out too? Oh, right, it's Tuesday."

A car was already waiting for him outside. Zhang Yuwen blew Zheng Weize a kiss and left.

As usual, they arrived at the meeting point for Chang Jinxing's job, and Chen Hong gave him a sandwich. "Break a leg today."

Chang Jinxing waved goodbye and got on the bus. The director came over and sat beside him. "Miss Wang told me that Zhang Yuwen gave her a call yesterday. Was he the one who introduced you to the company?"

"Uh... Yeah." After a brief pause, Chang Jinxing gave the director a seated bow. "I'm so sorry for the trouble I caused."

The director waved his hands and put a friendly arm around Chang Jinxing's shoulder. "We were partly to blame for not clarifying earlier."

"I was the one who didn't make things clear," said Chang Jinxing.

"No, no, none of that. So, uh, what does Yuwen-ge think? He doesn't want you to act, right?"

"Oh! He told me to decide for myself."

The director nodded and gave Chang Jinxing an inquiring look. When Chang Jinxing didn't say anything else, he prompted, "So, what do you think? Are you willing to take on the role?"

"Has a suitable actor been found yet?"

The director frowned. "That's the production crew's responsibility. We can always find someone else if you don't wish to continue."

"There are seventeen scenes, right?" Chang Jinxing asked. He didn't mind helping out, and besides, if he quit, the earlier two scenes would have to be reshot yet again, which would put a lot of strain on his colleagues. "I can stay until the end, but I really have no interest in being an actor."

"I understand." The director slapped his own thigh. "We appreciate it. We'll make sure you're fairly compensated too. Thank you for helping out."

"You're welcome..." Chang Jinxing murmured, embarrassed. He was just thankful the director didn't scold him.

The crew got into position. The coordinator had reshuffled the scenes again the previous day, hoping to complete filming for the childhood friend's scenes a little earlier. The producer was feeling a little antsy about it all too. After all, she had to make a living in this industry, and Zhang Yuwen was a big-name director. He could make her life difficult if she provoked him.

"So, are you up for it?" the producer asked Chang Jinxing.

Chang Jinxing had thought about it all night, and he'd decided that he should finish what he started. Zhang Yuwen was right, and the crew did need him. He'd do it as a one-time favor.

"Yeah," he said. "I'll do it if you need me, but I really don't want anything as big as a debut. I'm just helping out."

"Yes, yes, I understand. I'll make sure the company keeps the fan service low-key."

That was a relief. "Thanks so much."

After Chang Jinxing had his makeup done, Kong Yu came into the dressing room. He still didn't know exactly what had happened between Zhang Yuwen and Miss Wang, but he had sensed a slight shift in the producer's attitude. Seeing Chang Jinxing diligently memorizing his lines, he pulled a chair over and sat beside him, wrapping one arm around his shoulders.

"Everything okay?" Kong Yu asked. Chang Jinxing smiled, meeting his eyes, and Kong Yu patted him on the shoulder. "Looks like you got some decent sleep last night."

"Are we starting?" Chang Jinxing asked.

"Not just yet. You know, the first time I acted, I was even more nervous than you. I wanted to die when I watched it later," said Kong Yu. Chang Jinxing gave an exaggerated laugh. "I'm one of those slow learners who isn't really suited for all this, but I gradually got the hang of it. I gotta say, though, you're a natural on camera."

Chang Jinxing nodded and returned to memorizing his lines. Then, someone called for him, and he went to film. He was shooting a scene where his and Kong Yu's characters played billiards and, as usual, discussed Kong Yu's character's relationship problems. Chang Jinxing's character had to keep comforting him.

The crew had brought in a teleprompter for the day, no doubt in preparation for the newcomer, Chang Jinxing. Now that he'd read through the characters' profiles, Chang Jinxing knew he was playing a Casanova who had lots of experience in the romance department and could offer Kong Yu plenty of love advice. But that was all.

He had no romance plotline or arc of his own—he was functionally an NPC. In this kind of romance drama for young people, the supporting cast backed the main and secondary male leads, who served the female lead. The entire setup was intended just to create a sweet, romantic ambience, and that was all it needed to do.

With the previous day's experience under his belt, Chang Jinxing was able to portray his Casanova more authentically. The character's expressions and actions were second nature. But midway through filming, an unexpected visitor arrived on set.

Everyone was stunned. To think Zhang Yuwen had come in person! And he was accompanied by an industry veteran—Director Zhu, whom the producer had mentioned at the beginning!

"Oh my god!" the producer exclaimed. "Director Zhu! Yuwen-laoshi! What brings you here?!"

Director Zhu smiled. "Xiao-Zhang came to our studio today for coffee, and you guys came up during our conversation, so we decided to pay you a visit and check things out."

"Please carry on," Zhang Yuwen said, also smiling. "Don't mind us."

The entire film production crew kept sneaking peeks at them. Even the director was too startled by their visit to focus on the filming. Chang Jinxing, however, remained oblivious and continued to play his role diligently.

"That's Jinxing?" Director Zhu asked with another smile.

The production crew brought chairs over for both of them, plus an extra one that they set beside them. Zhang Yuwen waited for Director Zhu to take his seat first before sitting down to watch the filming. Behind them, the producer remained standing.

In front of the camera, Chang Jinxing pocketed the pool ball and raised an inquiring eyebrow at Kong Yu. He had a line at this part, but he felt it unnecessary.

Kong Yu, taking his cue, adopted a hesitant look. Chang Jinxing said, "You serious?"

It was interesting to watch Chang Jinxing in action. His acting was a little awkward, but it was much better than Zhang Yuwen had thought. "He's actually suitable for the role," Zhang Yuwen murmured in surprise.

"You don't say." Director Zhu grinned. "He's even adding some depth to the character."

Zhang Yuwen and Director Zhu laughed.

"Wang-jie sure has an eye for talent," Zhang Yuwen remarked.

"What's the story about?" Director Zhu asked.

"No idea. Yesterday was the first time Jinxing told me anything about this drama. Is there a script?"

The producer showed them the script. Zhang Yuwen turned to the characters' profiles, and he and Director Zhu read through them.

"Oh, he's a playboy," Director Zhu said.

"The younger generation would say fuckboy," Zhang Yuwen told him. "Honestly, Jinxing is practically playing himself. He's like this off-screen too."

Once the scene was complete, Chang Jinxing heaved a sigh of relief. He saw the director beckoning him over and grew uneasy—and then startled, when he caught sight of Zhang Yuwen. "Yuwen? Why are you here?"

Zhang Yuwen smiled at him. "This is Director Zhu. We're here to check you guys out."

"We have Jinxing to thank for standing in and saving our asses," the producer said from behind them.

"Hello, Director Zhu!" Chang Jinxing said immediately, though he didn't recognize this veteran director. Zhang Yuwen motioned for Chang Jinxing to sit beside him, and Chang Jinxing glanced around before taking his seat with some embarrassment.

"First time acting?" Director Zhu asked, amused.

"He's asking you," Zhang Yuwen told Chang Jinxing cheerfully.

"Pretty much," Chang Jinxing said respectfully. "I did two scenes yesterday."

Director Zhu made a noise of acknowledgment.

Chang Jinxing turned to Zhang Yuwen, worried he might have been offended. "Yuwen, I thought more about it after we talked. They really do need someone to play this role..."

"You don't have to explain," Zhang Yuwen said. "It's fine. A man should always finish what he started. This morning, I had another look at the photos you took, and it's obvious now that you won't give photography up. I was too harsh on you yesterday, and for that, I'm sorry."

Tears inexplicably pricked the backs of Chang Jinxing's eyes. Afraid he might tear up, he turned his head away and nodded almost numbly.

Zhang Yuwen put his hand on the back of Chang Jinxing's chair and turned to smile at Director Zhu. "His portrait work is marvelous. Every photo tells a story."

"Many successful directors start out as photographers," Director Zhu said. "Every position in the film production crew has its own strengths. The production team, the actors, even the screenwriters—they can all go on to shoot films, wouldn't you say?"

"Yeah," said Zhang Yuwen, smiling. "Actors-turned-directors have their own strengths."

"He's very handsome, and that's a fact," Director Zhu added.

"He is, among us ordinary folks. I'd give him a nine out of ten, but it's normal for the camera to detract a point or two. Some guys have wide faces or too much space between their eyes, and their photos usually get retouched."

"His looks are on par with Kong Yu's. He'll be a hit with the young girls."

Zhang Yuwen gave Chang Jinxing a playful tap on the back of his head. "He's complimenting you!"

"Thanks!" Chang Jinxing was overwhelmed by the praise. He wanted to see the scene he just filmed, but he couldn't leave. Zhang Yuwen saw through him, though, and he nudged him forward to signal that he could go.

Watching his earlier performance, Chang Jinxing realized they were right. The close-up shots exposed his flaws and made his features wider. He'd always been told that his face was flawlessly photogenic with no bad angles, but on camera, he was no match for Kong Yu's refined features.

To Director Zhu, Zhang Yuwen said, "I'm writing a novel."

"Oh? Could you show me when it's published?"

"It's so hard to make that happen these days. In fact, I'm heading to the publishing house today to receive critiques."

"It's a completely different circle," Director Zhu said. "If you're looking to do pure literature, not just writing an entertaining book for the mass market, it'll be tough."

"Yeah, man." Zhang Yuwen sighed.

Kong Yu, who had been watching them, wanted to approach. His manager kept urging him on, and finally, he mustered up his courage to go over to them.

"Hello, Director Zhu and Mr. Zhang Yuwen," Kong Yu said, having practiced his greeting earlier. This was even more nerve-wracking than acting.

"Hello!" said Zhang Yuwen. "You must be Kong Yu!"

Director Zhu gave Kong Yu a nod, and as Zhang Yuwen took the initiative to shake his icy, trembling hand, Kong Yu tried hard to smile.

"Thank you for looking out for our Jinxing," Zhang Yuwen said earnestly.

Kong Yu had been speculating earlier. Industry rumors had it that Zhang Yuwen had never been married, and with his refined demeanor, he gave off gay vibes to Kong Yu. In that case, was it possible that Chang Jinxing was his boyfriend? No...he had to be!

"He's doing a great job," Kong Yu said.

"His photography's even better," Zhang Yuwen told him. "It's full of life. I just wanted him to join the crew to learn about cinematography. I certainly never expected him to stand in as a replacement actor at the last minute."

"Kong Yu did well earlier too," Director Zhu put in. "He just gets a little distracted sometimes."

Zhang Yuwen and Director Zhu burst out laughing. Embarrassed and not catching their meaning, Kong Yu opened his mouth to humbly accept their advice, but then Zhang Yuwen added, "That's because we're here. We should stop being nuisances. Let's go eat some fish instead."

"No way!" the producer chimed in. "We're thrilled to have you both visit the set!"

Zhang Yuwen got up with a pleasant expression, and the director and producer hurried over to see him off. Kong Yu tagged along behind them.

It was then that the female lead came running out, having just finished with the makeup artist. "Director Zhu! Yuwen-laoshi! I'm so sorry! I was in the middle of getting my makeup done! I kept urging the artist—"

"It's fine," Zhang Yuwen assured her. "No worries. I'll look forward to watching your show."

Everyone, minus the absent male lead, laughed and exchanged a few more pleasantries before seeing both of them off the set. Zhang Yuwen opened his passenger seat door for Director Zhu and then took the driver's seat. He rolled down the window of his Bentley and, just before he left, said to Chang Jinxing, "Do your best with the filming!"

It was then Chang Jinxing realized that perhaps this was the entertainment industry that Zhang Yuwen had warned him about.

CHAPTER
34

ZHANG YUWEN HADN'T PLANNED on visiting the set with Director Zhu; he'd only intended to drop by Chang Jinxing's shooting location for a quick look. But first, he made a trip to the film production company to thank Director Zhu for the job referral. Director Zhu had been the mentor of Zhang Yuwen's junior—the director whom Zhang Yuwen asked for the favor—back when Zhang Yuwen's junior had first entered the industry. If Zhang Yuwen's junior had entrusted the request to his own mentor, he must have been taking it very seriously.

Director Zhu was already curious to see who this Chang Jinxing was, so when he learned Zhang Yuwen had something to do with it, he proposed that they visit the set together. Later, after they left the set, the two of them went to a country restaurant for a lunch of wild-caught fish. Then, Zhang Yuwen dropped Director Zhu off at the company and made his way to the publishing house for further education.

The deputy editor pushed up his glasses. "We've been wondering when you'd come."

"With the new year and all, I figured everyone was on vacation, so I decided not to impose," Zhang Yuwen said, smiling.

"We just had our annual editorial meeting yesterday..."

Zhang Yuwen's heart leaped into his throat. He knew the editorial meeting was the publishing house's project meeting to decide how many books would be published during the year.

"...and I proposed the subject of your book at the meeting."

Stunned and overwhelmed by emotion, Zhang Yuwen was momentarily at a loss for words. The deputy editor continued, "The outlook wasn't exactly optimistic, but it wasn't entirely pessimistic either... You know, come to think of it, why don't you give self-publishing a try?"

Hold on! Clarify first! Zhang Yuwen thought. *What do you mean by not exactly optimistic but not entirely pessimistic?!* Aloud, he said, "I still hope...to gain the editorial team's seal of approval. I really did pour my entire heart into this book."

Truly, every giant had his Achilles' heel. Zhang Yuwen, a film industry big shot just back from being worshiped on set, now found himself groveling at the publishing house. His fortune flip-flopped faster than the plot of a B-movie.

"Oh, I see." The deputy editor looked at Zhang Yuwen from behind his glasses. "Well, we all think there's still hope for you, given your linguistic proficiency and literary skills. Work harder this year, and hopefully, you'll produce a quality manuscript."

"Oh, okay." *Does that mean I still have a chance?*

The deputy editor sighed and picked up his pen. "I saw your online draft yesterday, though, and it falls short." Zhang Yuwen had to agree with him. His heart hadn't been in it since Christmas. "Are you in love? There's a lot of emotional self-expression. Skip all these Shakespearean asides." The deputy editor flipped to the corresponding section on the screen and struck out a large chunk of the text.

"All right. Got it," Zhang Yuwen said. "I'll revise it when I get back. But do you think the themes work?"

"Keep writing and see where it takes you," the deputy editor said. "Friends, family, and love are themes that have been done to death, but if the story is well-written, there'll always be a market for them."

"Okay, yeah."

Zhang Yuwen scraped together whatever bit of encouragement he could find in the critique and chewed on it. He also scrutinized the deputy editor, whose usual firepower seemed a bit lacking; he looked almost listless, and even his commanding presence seemed weaker than normal.

"The Spring Festival is around the corner," the deputy editor said. "We'll be off for two weeks. How about you?"

"I don't need to go into the office." Zhang Yuwen understood that the deputy editor was hinting that he should come back after Lunar New Year. "I'll make use of the time to revise my manuscript at home."

The deputy editor nodded and made a dismissive gesture. It was time for Zhang Yuwen to take his leave.

Trying to get a book published was *so* hard!

Zhang Yuwen heaved a long sigh as he left the publishing house. Lots of the shops around here were up for lease again now that it was the first month of the year; people liked to take the stroke of midnight on New Year's Eve as a fresh page in their lives.

He really wanted to call someone—anyone—and tell them about the day's events and all his achievements and frustrations.

Years back, when, like Chang Jinxing, he was toiling to establish his career, he'd yearned to call his partner when he was exhausted and tell him all about his day, from his accomplishments to the setbacks he faced. But his partner didn't really understand and just urged him to hurry home. This was understandable...but over time, Zhang Yuwen shared less and less, until one day, at some point after they'd broken up, he realized that, just like all the other lonely souls drifting through the big city, he had no one left to share his life with. No family to talk to about his joys and sorrows, successes and failures. Eventually, he accepted this as his fate. He got used to it and shaped himself into the man he was now.

Zhang Yuwen sat silently in his car for a moment, then connected to Bluetooth and made a call. The Fisherman's avatar flashed on the screen as Zhang Yuwen turned the steering wheel and left the garage of the publishing house.

"Hey," Zhang Yuwen said.

"Hey, what's up?" asked Huo Sichen's voice.

"What are you up to?"

"I'm in a meeting. Why?"

"Oops, sorry."

"No worries. It's almost done, and it doesn't really have anything to do with me. So, what's up? Are you calling to tell me you're going to stand me up tonight?"

"Nah." Zhang Yuwen had forgotten for a moment that he had a dinner date with Huo Sichen. Much of what he wanted to say could wait until they met.

Huo Sichen didn't probe any further. After a moment, though, he seemed to connect a few dots. "You miss me?"

There was unmistakable joy in his voice. Zhang Yuwen, on the other hand, had to pay attention to the passing traffic, the pedestrians crossing the roads, and the traffic lights on top of what Huo Sichen was saying. His processor was running on multithreading mode. "Why is your voice so hoarse?"

Huo Sichen coughed twice. "I noticed that too. My throat has felt uncomfortable ever since I woke up today. Maybe I've been talking too much lately."

"All right then, keep working hard. I'll hang up now."

"You really don't have anything else to say?"

The corners of Zhang Yuwen's lips quirked up. "Nope. See you this evening."

"See you. I love you."

Zhang Yuwen didn't say it back, a habit that stemmed from his usual circumspection. Even a simple sentence required careful consideration on his part.

He decided to get a haircut, drive home, and then wait for Huo Sichen to come and pick him up in the evening. While he was waiting at the barbershop, he pulled out his phone and found his ex's contact on the messaging app.

He couldn't help but think about the past. They were both so young back then. Zhang Yuwen may have thought he was mature, but the facts proved otherwise. He'd made a lot of mistakes, and now, he thought about apologizing to his ex for how he'd mistreated him. He'd neglected him, for example, clinging tightly to his own solitude even though he was in a relationship.

So Zhang Yuwen typed a message that expressed his sincerest apologies. He hesitated a lot, deliberating over his word choices and trying to make the message read exactly as he meant it, without giving any impression that he was trying to rekindle their relationship. Finally, he pressed send—but his message was rejected. His ex had already deleted him from his contacts.

Zhang Yuwen laughed. *What am I doing, getting all sentimental here?*

When he got home later that afternoon, Huo Sichen sent him a message: *i think im sick. cant meet tonite.*

Surprised, Zhang Yuwen called him. "Where are you?"

"In bed at home," Huo Sichen said in a hoarse voice. "It's probably the flu."

"Do you have a fever?"

"Yeah…" Huo Sichen sounded fatigued.

"How high is your temperature? Do you have medicine at home?"

"What medicine should I take? I don't usually take any. I just sleep it off."

"I'll come over and check on you."

"No." Huo Sichen was clearly exhausted, but managed to muster up the energy to talk to Zhang Yuwen. "Don't come. I think I caught the bug from my client's office. I'll call you again tomorrow when I feel better. Sorry."

"What are you apologizing for?" Zhang Yuwen asked. "I'm hanging up."

Huo Sichen mumbled an acknowledgment, and they ended the call.

It was the peak season for influenza A. Zhang Yuwen gave it some thought, then opened the medical kit at home. He sent Chen Hong a message, asking him for Huo Sichen's home address.

Chen Hong: *Bro, r u going over to catch him in the act?*

Zhang Yuwen: *Cut the crap. If u dont want ur rent raised, send me his address now.*

That was a low blow. Chen Hong obediently sent him a location. Zhang Yuwen packed up some medicine and food, got into his car, and set off.

Huo Sichen's apartment was in a high-end neighborhood. When Zhang Yuwen arrived, he only had to mention the door number and the security guard let him through. He parked in the garage and headed upstairs. The property couldn't have been cheap; Huo Sichen's mortgage payments must have been nearly twenty thousand a month.

He rang the doorbell and suddenly felt a twinge of nervousness—what if Huo Sichen was lying to him? He was showing up so impulsively... What if he saw something he shouldn't see?

"Sichen!" Zhang Yuwen yelled.

The door opened, and Huo Sichen appeared. Zhang Yuwen was a little relieved to see that he looked half dead from illness.

"Did you bring me medicine?" Huo Sichen asked. He was nearly six foot three, but he looked liable to collapse at any moment.

"Get back inside," Zhang Yuwen urged him. "Go back to bed and lie down."

Huo Sichen frowned. "You're going to catch the flu from me."

"No, I won't. I've had my flu shot." Every autumn, Zhang Yuwen got his flu vaccine, so he usually had immunity when an outbreak occurred. This was a habit that had been drilled into him growing up in a family of doctors.

"Huh? There's a vaccine for the flu?"

"There's so much more you don't know."

Zhang Yuwen got him inside and had him lie back down. Huo Sichen was wearing tight-fitting black thermal wear that accentuated his sexy, slender figure. Zhang Yuwen ogled him a few times before he remembered the guy was sick. It wasn't the time for those kinds of thoughts.

He took Huo Sichen's temperature with an ear thermometer—104 degrees Fahrenheit.

"You're in pretty good shape, young man," Zhang Yuwen said. "A hundred and four, and you can still get up to answer the door."

Huo Sichen said nothing as he shivered under the quilt. Zhang Yuwen took out a rapid test kit and swabbed his nose. Huo Sichen sneezed and started coughing again, looking absolutely miserable.

"Yup, influenza A," Zhang Yuwen announced, unperturbed. "Take the medicine to bring the fever down first. Did you eat lunch?"

Huo Sichen took the medicine without asking what it was. "Not yet. No appetite."

"You're overworked, and your immunity is down. Here, take this lozenge. Your throat will feel better."

He tidied up Huo Sichen's bed, made sure the room was suitably shaded, and tucked Huo Sichen in. Then he closed the door and made his way to the living room to boil some water.

Although Huo Sichen's home was in a pricey neighborhood and decorated in a high-end minimalist style, its amenities were basic. Or perhaps it was more accurate to say that the home felt cold and impersonal, showing few traces of the life lived inside it. It was nearly two thousand square feet and boasted three bedrooms and a living room. Huo Sichen slept in the master bedroom and, it seemed, used the smallest room as a gym.

A spacious, upholstered sofa set occupied the living room. There was a huge television there, too, but Zhang Yuwen figured it was probably only used for gaming, seeing as the remote control for the set-top box was out of battery. The kitchen came fully equipped with various utensils, but they appeared to have never been used; the dishwasher was not plugged in, the rice cooker was new, and the oven still had its protective film intact. There was a half-finished mug of tea on the dining table and, next to it, an electric kettle and an opened, expired tea bag. Huo Sichen's fishing gear was out on the balcony, and the canvas bag was slightly faded from exposure to the sun.

Everything in the house was clean, though, or at least not covered in dust. Zhang Yuwen remembered Huo Sichen telling him that he'd hired a cleaning lady through the property management company, who came every Wednesday and Saturday to clean.

Zhang Yuwen scoured the kettle clean of limescale, boiled fresh water, and added oral rehydration salts to make a saline solution. He went and set the mug on the bedside table, then opened an app and ordered takeout for himself.

In between all of this, he checked on Huo Sichen twice. He was fast asleep and had begun to sweat the fever out now that he'd taken the medicine.

Zhang Yuwen turned on the game console in the living room and started playing Huo Sichen's games. He turned out to have a lot of games that Zhang Yuwen had purchased, downloaded, and then only made it two or three percent of the way through. This was excellent material, and Zhang Yuwen couldn't help but reflect on his writing through the lens of his boyfriend's life. It was just as his university professor had said: "To write about a person's loneliness, you can't just say he's lonely. Instead, you write about the autumn wind, the spring flowers, the noisy summer rain, the romantic winter snow—and the disconnect between him and the beauty of the world. He might take a pretty photo of the view, but he has no one to share it with."

Sitting in this cold, empty house, Zhang Yuwen could almost picture Huo Sichen returning home after work late at night, taking off his coat, and hanging it up. Everything was empty, cold, and detached. The dining table was forever spotless and unused, and the curtains were never opened or closed. Whatever state his house was in when he left in the morning, that was the state to which he returned. He would shower, sit on the sofa, and turn on the game console, trying out the games one at a time but unable to get into any of them. His eyes would linger on his phone, waiting for Zhang Yuwen's messages. When the messages came, he'd chat with Zhang Yuwen for a bit, then go to his bedroom and fall asleep, preparing to face a new day that was exactly the same as the one that preceded it.

Zhang Yuwen had the thought that he was the same—but at No. 7 Riverbay Road, he realized, even if he kept all the doors to the unused rooms closed, the place would be bathed in sunlight and the plants would thrive. Maybe it felt that way because he spent most of his time at home? And now that Yan Jun, Chen Hong, and the others had moved in, his house compared to Huo Sichen's was like the tropics compared to the Arctic.

Huo Sichen's game controller felt good in his hands. He checked out some games that he was stuck on and found that the parts that tripped him up apparently posed no challenge to Huo Sichen, who had cleared most of them. *He must be smarter than me,* Zhang Yuwen thought, surprised. He'd always thought of Huo Sichen as having high emotional intelligence, but his life circumstances weren't as good as Zhang Yuwen's; he was a little short on luck...

At ten o'clock, Zhang Yuwen began to feel sleepy. He sent Chen Hong a message, telling him that he wouldn't be home that night because he was staying at Huo Sichen's to take care of him. Then, he went into the master bedroom and retook Huo Sichen's temperature—it was down to 101.3 degrees.

Huo Sichen was drinking some water, having just woken up. Zhang Yuwen did some math; six hours had passed, so he could give Huo Sichen another pill. "Time for your medicine."

Huo Sichen looked weary. Zhang Yuwen took off his clothes and got into bed.

"What?" Zhang Yuwen asked. "It's not like we haven't slept together before."

Huo Sichen laughed.

Zhang Yuwen touched his forehead. "You'll feel better in the morning."

"Let me show you something," said Huo Sichen.

Zhang Yuwen left the bedside lamp on and waited, puzzled. Huo Sichen switched on his phone to a flood of incoming messages. "You going to show me how busy you are?" Zhang Yuwen joked.

Huo Sichen irritably dismissed the notifications and pulled up a picture from his photo album.

"Oh! You found it!" Zhang Yuwen exclaimed.

It was a photo from more than twenty years ago. After being developed and printed, it had been set aside for a long time before it was digitized.

"My brother found it," said Huo Sichen. "Our whole family went to the hot spring for vacation back then, and we even went to the park to feed the deer." The photo showed a seven-year-old Huo Sichen standing and looking back in puzzlement at the deer, who were chasing a flustered child at the edge of the frame. "Is this you?"

"Yeah! Yeah, it is! That's me!" Zhang Yuwen recognized those clothes. He recalled that scene from his childhood; it had been right there, in that park. It was true, then—the family who took him out to play all those years ago had been Huo Sichen and his brother and parents!

"I asked my brother to mail the photo back," Huo Sichen said.

"Keep it here," Zhang Yuwen said. "It's too easy to lose, and that'd be a real shame."

"Then you can bring it back yourself when you come over the next time."

Huo Sichen held Zhang Yuwen in his arms as they lay together. Zhang Yuwen zoomed in on the photo again and looked at it in disbelief. "So the legend is true," he murmured.

"Hm?" Zhang Yuwen chuckled and shook his head, but Huo Sichen pressed him. "A certain legend about destined love?"

Suddenly embarrassed, Zhang Yuwen pushed Huo Sichen's face away, and they fell into a brief silence in the quiet night.

Then, Huo Sichen buried his face in Zhang Yuwen's shoulder and said, "I want to make love to you, Yuwen. We're destined to be together."

Zhang Yuwen laughed. "Careful you don't give yourself myocarditis."

Huo Sichen looked at him with a grin. "Have you ever made love with someone who has a fever?"

"No, but your fever has already gone down. Too bad. I should have grabbed my chance when you were burning up at a hundred and five degrees." Zhang Yuwen kissed Huo Sichen, thinking about how incredible fate was. It felt as if heaven had arranged for them to meet long ago. Then, he felt something, and reached down to touch Huo Sichen's erection. "Whoa, there. Look at you, misbehaving even at a time like this."

"Then, promise me we'll do it the next time we meet," said Huo Sichen.

"Sure," Zhang Yuwen agreed readily. "What made you change your mind?"

"Well, I'm still sick, after all. 'Fraid I won't be able to perform to my fullest potential."

Zhang Yuwen laughed and turned off the bedside lamp.

"Can we cuddle while we sleep?" asked Huo Sichen.

So, Zhang Yuwen turned around and hugged him. For a moment, they rubbed against each other through their pants. Huo Sichen's body was still hot, his illness transforming him into flames that devoured everything in their path.

"Hey, behave yourself," Zhang Yuwen reminded him.

Huo Sichen stopped grinding against him. In a small voice, he asked, "Did you really get vaccinated?"

"Yup. And even if I hadn't, I'd still come over and take care of you."

"I don't want you to get sick too."

"Love is like cholera; you're bound to get it sooner or later."

Huo Sichen fell silent then.

Zhang Yuwen went back to thinking about that photo. "This is so incredible," he said. When he was four, he'd gone to the hot spring park to play and ended up meeting the boy who would become his boyfriend in adulthood.

"There are two kinds of fate," said Huo Sichen. "The fate that finds you and the fate that you seek."

Zhang Yuwen cupped Huo Sichen's cheek in his palm and leaned in to kiss him. Even his lips were scalding; his blood must have been boiling. They embraced, and Zhang Yuwen didn't hesitate to initiate contact. After seeing that photo—no, after seeing firsthand how Huo Sichen lived—he understood the weight of the emotions behind Huo Sichen's nightly "Are you asleep?" messages and the loneliness that drove him to message, "Are you awake?" This photo from more than twenty years ago told Zhang Yuwen that this was all predestined, that he shouldn't hesitate anymore; Huo Sichen was the one, and there was no escaping it.

"I want to make love to you too," Zhang Yuwen said suddenly. Huo Sichen's breathing quickened. "But not tonight. Next time, when you're feeling better."

Huo Sichen didn't reply. He kept kissing Zhang Yuwen, his lips still tasting faintly of saline. Zhang Yuwen found the smell of him comforting and oddly magnetic. Although Huo Sichen lived alone, his bedroom, especially his bedding, had a pleasantly masculine scent. Perhaps their pheromone signals were similar.

"Okay, okay..." Zhang Yuwen nudged him away gently, feeling a little like he was being nuzzled by a dog. "Let's sleep now."

This time, Huo Sichen quickly fell asleep under the effects of the cold medicine.

Zhang Yuwen didn't wake him up the next morning; instead, he yawned and went to the kitchen to make breakfast. While he was at it, he heard the sound of water from the bathroom and knew that his patient had woken up.

Before long, Huo Sichen emerged and sat down at the dining table, wearing his pajamas and with his hair still damp. Zhang Yuwen took his temperature again with the electronic ear thermometer. 98.2 degrees: His fever was gone.

"What yummy food are you making?" Huo Sichen asked. "I can't believe you know how to cook."

"Of course I do," said Zhang Yuwen. "My cooking just isn't as delicious as Chang Jinxing's. I used to help my grandma cook when I was a child, so I learned by watching."

He set a cup of tea down on the table, and Huo Sichen sipped it slowly while he replied to the work messages he'd ignored while he was sick. Since their New Year's trip, Huo Sichen hadn't said another word about quitting, and Zhang Yuwen guessed that he'd weighed the pros and cons. With a mortgage to pay and a living to eke out, he probably couldn't afford to quit, so he must have just been venting.

"Your tableware is all new," Zhang Yuwen remarked offhandedly. "You've never used any of it. You didn't even tear the labels off after you bought them."

Huo Sichen looked up. "Uh...yeah. Why?"

Zhang Yuwen set the piping-hot pot of pork rib congee on the table and distributed the bowls and chopsticks. "Nothing. Let's eat."

He'd simmered the rice until it was glutinous and flavorful, and the pork ribs were so tender the meat fell off the bones. The ginger strips he'd mixed in toward the end would help fend off Huo Sichen's cold. This was one of Zhang Yuwen's grandfather's favorite dishes.

Zhang Yuwen scooped some into his own bowl and then added a spoonful of soy sauce for flavor. "Take your time," he said. "Isn't it scalding?"

Like a child, Huo Sichen stared at Zhang Yuwen without saying a word, then guiltily averted his gaze to stare at his phone.

Zhang Yuwen finished his simple breakfast, then went to grab Huo Sichen's clothes and dump them next to the washing machine. He was capable of doing housework, but most of the time, he didn't have to—and when he did it, he did it selectively. For example, even though he was taking care of his sick boyfriend, Zhang Yuwen wasn't about to wash all his clothes and hang them out to dry; instead, he would helpfully pile them up by the washing machine and make the bed.

"Are you still going to work today?" Zhang Yuwen asked a little while later, handing Huo Sichen a cup of tea. He had just cleared away the condiments and the empty porridge pot.

"I have to," said Huo Sichen. "There's a meeting at noon today, and I have a business trip tomorrow morning. You..."

Huo Sichen wanted to ask Zhang Yuwen if he would like to stay, but then he mentally compared his house to the Riverbay Road villa. The choice was obvious, so he elected not to finish his sentence.

"Where are you going?" Zhang Yuwen asked him. He was feeling uncomfortable without his morning coffee and already itching to go home for a mug.

"Singapore. I'll be going with the legal team to sign a contract in person. It'll take at least five days." Zhang Yuwen hummed in acknowledgment, and Huo Sichen asked, "What are you up to today?"

"Going home."

"How was work yesterday?"

"Uh... Okay, I guess."

"Send me a copy of your book," said Huo Sichen. "I'd like to read it on the plane."

Zhang Yuwen's anxiety kicked in again. He had completely forgotten about wanting to share his manuscript with Huo Sichen. "Maybe next time. I haven't written much..."

"You promised me, though," Huo Sichen said seriously.

Zhang Yuwen smiled. "I will, but not now."

"You also promised to mate with me," Huo Sichen deadpanned. Zhang Yuwen snorted, almost spewing his tea over Huo Sichen's choice of terminology. "I've got it all written down in my little notebook."

Zhang Yuwen managed to swallow his tea before he started laughing uncontrollably. Huo Sichen had hit the right note with Zhang Yuwen's weird sense of humor.

"In my quest for a mate," Huo Sichen continued, "I've waited for you for so long. I even built us a nest."

"Ha ha ha ha! That's enough! Stop!"

"It's been over twenty years..."

"It's your own fault for falling sick," Zhang Yuwen teased him. He found Huo Sichen's antics both funny and strangely romantic. "Okay, get dressed now. I'll drive you to work."

"No, I'll drive you home."

"It's better not to drive when you've just recovered. It's not safe when you're feeling groggy."

Huo Sichen didn't press the matter. When they entered the garage, though, his jaw dropped. "This is your car?!" he blurted out.

"Does it make you feel like you're the kept man of some CEO?" Zhang Yuwen laughed. "It belongs to the owner of No. 7 Riverbay Road."

Huo Sichen nodded in understanding and took the passenger seat. "A Bentley. This is my first time riding in one."

As Zhang Yuwen drove them away from Huo Sichen's house, he wondered when he could come clean with Huo Sichen about his actual net worth. How would he react? Shocked, then defeated? Would it change their dynamic?

If Zhang Yuwen, with his twisted sense of humor, really said what was on his mind, he would suggest that Huo Sichen quit his job, stay at home, and learn how to cook and take care of Zhang Yuwen's daily needs. He'd tell Huo Sichen that he could be a househusband by day and a bed warmer at night...because he could sense that Huo Sichen had thought the same about Zhang Yuwen. Several times, Huo Sichen had hinted at this idea—that if Zhang Yuwen didn't want to work, he could quit and move in with Huo Sichen, and they could live together and do whatever they wanted. But if Zhang Yuwen were to do unto Huo Sichen as Huo Sichen had done unto to him, he doubted that Huo Sichen would be happy about it.

That was probably why Zhang Yuwen had never fully convinced himself to commit to Huo Sichen.

When they arrived at the building where Huo Sichen worked, Huo Sichen turned around in the passenger seat and placed a hand on Zhang Yuwen's shoulder.

"There are lots of people out there," Zhang Yuwen observed. "Any of your colleagues among them?"

To his surprise, Huo Sichen leaned over and kissed him. Some people who happened to be crossing the road looked over at them; Zhang Yuwen's car was pretty conspicuous, after all.

"One of them is our marketing director," Huo Sichen said, "but it doesn't matter. They can say whatever they want. I'm leaving. See you later."

Zhang Yuwen realized then just how open and unreserved Huo Sichen was. He'd never been in a relationship with someone like that. If they'd met during their student days, he imagined, Huo Sichen might have been the type to confess his love to him in front of a crowd of people...

Huo Sichen got out of the car and walked briskly toward the building, where someone was waiting to greet him. Zhang Yuwen thought things over for a while, and then sent his novel to Huo Sichen.

Riverbay Road
MEN'S DORMITORY

CHAPTER
35

To his surprise, Yan Jun found that once he started leading a team, his workload lightened considerably. He no longer needed to run around himself; instead, he earned a commission based on his team's overall performance. Most of the time, he could stay in the office, delegating tasks to his subordinates and optimizing their proposals. Occasionally, he even read a book at work.

Whenever he had a break, he thought about going home. Even if Xiao-Qi wasn't there waiting for him, Zhang Yuwen would be at the dining table, and chatting with Zhang Yuwen always lifted his mood. Yan Jun had this sense that his life had been on an upward trajectory ever since he met Zhang Yuwen.

Some people were naturally superstitious and would draw causal lines between two unrelated events that just happened to occur one after another. For example, someone might infer that seeing an even number of black cars on the way to work would mean they'd have good luck at work that day. After he met Zhang Yuwen and moved to No. 7 Riverbay Road, Yan Jun's job had become more manageable, and he was finding more opportunities to make money. Sales negotiations went surprisingly smoothly, with the clients signing order forms like they were under a spell, and when the occasional issue did crop up, Yan Jun found that he could handle them easily.

When Yan Jun brought it up at work, his subordinates pandered to him by coming up with mystical explanations. One held that the place where Yan Jun lived was an auspicious feng shui treasure site, so powerful that even renting it could make a person filthy rich overnight. Why else would the houses on Riverbay Road be so expensive? But to Yan Jun's knowledge, Zhang Yuwen hadn't made any big bucks, which brought the credibility of this theory into question. Or had he merely shared his good fortune with the others? Yes, perhaps that was it. Yan Jun considered each of his roommates—apart from Chen Hong, all of their financial statuses did seem to have improved, so he largely accepted this explanation.

Of course, he wasn't always able to slack off and sneak away from work to go home and absorb Zhang Yuwen's good fortune, so instead, he chatted with him via instant messaging app. At first, Yan Jun wasn't sure Zhang Yuwen would even reply to him. After all, he didn't always reply to Huo Sichen; most of the time, he left the poor guy hanging and pining pitifully for his attention...

But he'd worried for nothing. Maybe it was just because they'd known each other longer, but every time Yan Jun hit send on a message, Zhang Yuwen responded promptly. It made Yan Jun's heart race like he was a love-stricken high schooler. This simple gesture told him that he held a higher position than Huo Sichen in Zhang Yuwen's heart.

At first, he was jealous that Huo Sichen had managed to start a relationship with Zhang Yuwen so easily, while Yan Jun missed his shot. Later, though, it occurred to him that they barely seemed to do anything as a couple; Huo Sichen rarely even visited. Zhang Yuwen didn't seem to need him all that much. Yan Jun comforted himself with the thought that it wouldn't be long before they broke up. And after a while, he began to feel that his existing relationship with

Zhang Yuwen was already good enough. Except for the sex, Zhang Yuwen was like his wife, waiting for him at home every day—he could live with that.

Yan Jun missed Zhang Yuwen again today. This was what love was like, especially secret, unrequited love—anxiety-inducing and shrouded in secrecy. He imagined Zhang Yuwen waking up and starting his workday. Lately, he'd been thinking of getting a car. After his pay raise, puffed up with confidence, he passed by the electric vehicle showroom downstairs and slowed down to take another look. If he had a car, he could go home at noon and have lunch with Zhang Yuwen.

The phone rang, yanking him back to reality. It was a phone he had set up with his late older brother's phone number; he'd designated a special ringtone for it. Yan Jun quickly got up and went out to the hallway to answer the call.

He lowered his voice slightly so that he sounded slightly hoarse when he said, "Ma?"

"Dai!" said his mother's voice over the phone. Yan Jun breathed a sigh of relief—thank God it wasn't someone else making the call on her behalf.

"I'm here."

"What're you busy with?" Mama Yan asked.

"Working," Yan Jun replied steadily. His brother had been even more taciturn than he was. Even with family, he didn't say a word more than necessary.

"How about Jun?"

"Working too."

"Lu Lu?"

Tears pricked the backs of Yan Jun's eyes. "At home taking care of Xiao-Qi."

Mama Yan sighed. "It's been so long since I last saw my little treasure..."

Yan Jun pinched the bridge of his nose, trying hard to hold back his tears. "I'll get Jun to send you some photos."

"My eyesight isn't good! Eh, Dai?"

"Yeah?"

"Are you at work? Is it tough? You haven't called me in a long time."

Yan Jun held the phone away slightly and did his best to compose himself. "We're talking now, aren't we?"

"Is business good at the shop?"

"Yeah. Busy, though."

"You keep sending me money. I saved some up for Jun."

"He has enough for living expenses," Yan Jun said. "Use it on yourself, Ma!"

"I bought some clothes for the little treasure too. How tall is she now?"

Yan Jun said nothing and wept in silence. Mama Yan chattered away, mostly talking to herself.

Finally, she asked, "Are you two coming back for the new year?"

Yan Jun's heart skipped a beat. "I can't close the shop for the new year," he said immediately.

"If you brothers can't come back, I'll go over to visit you. I can catch a ride with your friend."

Yan Jun's mind went momentarily blank. What was he going to do? "Let me see what I can do," he said. "Don't be in a hurry to come. It's not convenient for you to travel."

Mama Yan lived in the countryside, and she didn't care much for Christmas or New Year's. To her, the most important holiday was the Spring Festival—also known as the Lunar New Year—which she believed was a time for family reunions. Yan Jun had given it some thought before. Originally, he planned to have his mother return to her maternal home to spend the festival there, and he would tell her that he and his brother were too busy during the holidays to return home.

But so much had happened recently that he'd forgotten all about it.

What was he going to do? Yan Jun looked at the train tickets and opened his messaging app to contact a few friends in the countryside. He'd only told a handful of people about his brother and sister-in-law's passing, hoping to prevent anyone from accidentally leaking the secret to his mother. He asked his friends if his mother had asked about catching a ride to Jiangdong, and they all said no.

What could he do? Yan Jun was deeply troubled. In the end, he took the afternoon off and went home to ask Zhang Yuwen for advice. He sat with Zhang Yuwen, utterly exhausted, and sipped his coffee with a frown on his face.

"Pardon me for being blunt," Zhang Yuwen began, "but what I'm going to say might be a little..."

"You don't need to worry about my feelings," Yan Jun said.

"Okay, first, how long are you going to keep this from her?" Yan Jun didn't answer. "You know you can't hide this forever, right?"

"Yes."

"I'm going to say something a bit grim."

"Go ahead."

"There's no way you can hide this from your mother until she passes away." Yan Jun nodded, and Zhang Yuwen continued, "So, you have to start thinking about when to tell her, the potential consequences, and how to handle it in a way that keeps the potential fallout within controllable limits."

"You're right," Yan Jun said. "I've been avoiding it this whole time, and now, it's been almost a year." His brother and sister-in-law's accident happened in April of the previous year—ten months ago. In those ten months, Yan Jun had frequently played the role of two people, calling his mother every month or two. It was physically and mentally exhausting.

"Let me try to lay it out for you," Zhang Yuwen said. "She has a weak heart, cataracts, and high blood pressure, and she doesn't want surgery..."

Zhang Yuwen considered it at length. In truth, he had thought about this problem on Yan Jun's behalf already, out of occupational habit. When a director or screenwriter encountered a knotty problem in a story, they couldn't help but think, *If I were the storyteller, how would I unravel this tangled mess?*

First off, Yan Jun was right not to want to deal his mother a direct blow. Given her old age and underlying conditions, if she were to have a heart attack, the consequences could be devastating. Yan Jun's mistake, however, was failing to plan to deal with the issue in another way. Instead, he kept avoiding it.

In Zhang Yuwen's opinion, since things had already gone so far, Yan Jun might as well just go with the flow and let his mother guess the truth on her own. If he reduced the frequency of her communication with "Yan Dai," over time, she would develop her own suspicions. After that, Yan Jun should prepare by having a family doctor on standby and keeping her emergency medications ready, and when she finally asked questions he couldn't dodge, he should tell her the truth. In this way, he could mitigate the impact and then finally deal with the issue.

He explained all of this to Yan Jun, who kept silent.

"But I think she already suspects something," Zhang Yuwen said. "Wouldn't a mother have a premonition when her son passes away? Especially in a family like yours where your mother raised you two. It was the same for me when my grandparents passed."

Not long before his grandfather's passing, Zhang Yuwen had decided not to put him on a ventilator so he could bring him home. One morning, in his final moments, his grandfather suddenly asked for congee, and somehow, Zhang Yuwen knew that it was time. He made some egg congee and fed it to his grandfather, and after a few mouthfuls, his grandfather let out a dying sigh. Zhang Yuwen quickly called for his grandmother. The old man smiled and passed away peacefully with Zhang Yuwen and his grandmother by his side.

As for his grandmother, it had happened on a winter night in the same year his grandfather passed. Before he went to bed that night, Zhang Yuwen checked the temperature in her room and returned to his own room to sleep—but he woke suddenly at 3:30 a.m. with the urge to check on his grandmother. Sure enough, she had quietly passed away.

Zhang Yuwen had always believed that people could sense it when their loved ones passed away, and he was confident that Yan Jun's family was no exception. Instead of keeping the deaths such a closely guarded secret, Yan Jun should have left some room for doubt so that his mother could gradually suspect the truth, at which point he could have broken the news to her.

"I get it now." Yan Jun nodded.

"You should entrust Xiao-Qi to her care, too," Zhang Yuwen said. "People can be remarkably resilient as long as there's hope. Let me give you another grim example..."

Yan Jun motioned for Zhang Yuwen to continue, indicating that it was fine.

"Let's say that both you and your brother were gone—this is the worst-case scenario—and she had to raise Xiao-Qi alone. She would struggle, but she would also try her best to keep going. You have to believe in her."

Yan Jun nodded again. "You're right. My mother has always been a strong person. I can't let her raise Xiao-Qi, though. She's not familiar with life in the big city and wouldn't be able to adapt to Jiangdong. She's not physically up to it, either."

"That may be so, but she also needs to believe that there's still someone who relies on her." Zhang Yuwen paused for a moment, thinking, then asked, "Are you planning to go back home to visit her for the Spring Festival?"

Yan Jun had been uncertain before he spoke to Zhang Yuwen, but now, he knew he had to. "I'll take Xiao-Qi with me and tell her that my brother and sister-in-law had to stay in Jiangdong for the Spring Festival."

"That works, but you have to start preparing for when you tell her the truth."

"I will."

"I can help you find a doctor. If you decide to have the showdown here, I'll ask a cardiologist friend to be on standby for emergency assistance. I believe she can get through this."

Yan Jun considered this for a moment, grateful to Zhang Yuwen for the offer. "I'll think about it when I return after the Spring Festival."

"You might also need to record a message as your brother and play it for her during the Spring Festival."

Yan Jun came up with a detailed plan that included how to conceal the truth from his mother when he brought Xiao-Qi back home for the festival. After the Lunar New Year, he would gradually bring his mother to sense that something was amiss, then find the right time to tell her the truth.

But once she knew the details...what then? He couldn't leave his grieving mother alone in the countryside, or something terrible was bound to happen. The best strategy would be to live with her for a while and let her take care of Xiao-Qi, but where would she stay in Jiangdong? Not No. 7 Riverbay Road, that was for certain. There were no extra rooms, and besides, everyone in the house was gay. She would figure Yan Jun out for sure, and coming out to her would be another emotional blow.

Would he have to rent a house and move out? But Yan Jun had to work every day—he couldn't always be there to take care of her. In the countryside, her neighbors could watch out for her. This was another reason he wanted to buy a house; if he had his own house in Jiangdong, he'd be able to hire a caregiver, which would give Yan Jun some peace of mind about his mother being unaccustomed to life in a big city.

No. His mother would definitely ask to go back home to the countryside and take Xiao-Qi with her. Leaving aside his reluctance to separate from Xiao-Qi, he couldn't let his mother raise Xiao-Qi by herself. His mother's vision was poor, and Xiao-Qi was just starting to learn to walk, so she was at a phase where she was curious about everything. It would be dangerous to leave her alone with his mother.

"You could hire a caregiver in the countryside to take care of your mother and Xiao-Qi," Chen Hong suggested. "But no matter what, once Xiao-Qi starts kindergarten, you'll still have to return to Jiangdong."

"All of that has to wait until I come clean," Yan Jun said as he folded Xiao-Qi's clothes. The housekeepers at No. 7 Riverbay Road understood how hard it was to take care of a baby, so they always made sure to tidy up his room for him every day. Yan Jun, in turn, set aside a sum of money for them every month as a token of his appreciation.

Chen Hong empathized with Yan Jun. They both had elders and youngsters at home to worry about. Chen Hong might not have had kids of his own, but he was always worried about his younger sister. Fortunately, Chen Hong's parents were both healthy and could take care of each other.

"This is a tough time of year," Chen Hong remarked.

"And yet we have to get through it all the same every time." Yan Jun picked Xiao-Qi up and changed her into her pajamas.

"Yuwen, Yuwen," Xiao-Qi called out.

"He's not here," Chen Hong said. "Call me Hong-ge."

"How's the gym coming along?" asked Yan Jun.

"Just needs some minor renovations. It'll open for business on the fifth day of the Lunar New Year."

"I'll try my best to be back by then so I can show you my support."

"Deal." Chen Hong grinned.

Chen Hong had staked all his savings on this one gamble. It was only a hundred and twenty thousand yuan, but it was everything he had. Between the renovation costs and the rent, he was nearly broke, and now all he could do was wait for the grand opening, when he could begin to collect membership fees.

I hope things go smoothly, Chen Hong thought. *For all of us.*

CHAPTER
36

AS THE LUNAR NEW YEAR approached, it ushered in Jiangdong's coldest weather of the year, with three consecutive days of heavy snow that signaled to everyone that a year of hard work was finally coming to an end. In those last few days, nobody's mind was on work.

Everyone at No. 7 Riverbay Road was busier than they'd been at the Solar New Year. Yan Jun was finally taking a trip back to the countryside with Xiao-Qi, and Chen Hong had to visit home too. Meanwhile, the film production crew Chang Jinxing was working with had to reshoot due to the heavy snow, and since they were filming on location, he would be eating and staying with the crew. Huo Sichen left for Singapore on his business trip before the Spring Festival, but not before making plans for the Lunar New Year with Zhang Yuwen.

This left only Zheng Weize at No. 7 Riverbay Road. He had to spend the holidays alone.

"I...might go back home," Zheng Weize said. "I *should* go home."

"Oh?"

This was a bit puzzling. Zhang Yuwen had noticed that Zheng Weize seemed to have more disposable income lately and often received gifts, so he suspected Zheng Weize was dating someone, but so far he had only seen the money, not the boyfriend. Zheng Weize never said anything about it, though, so his roommates didn't pry. They just reminded him to be careful.

On the evening before everyone went their separate ways for the holidays, Zhang Yuwen ordered a ton of takeout for dinner. As they all dug in, they chatted and exchanged updates from the past month.

"Why don't you come to the film set?" Chang Jinxing asked Zheng Weize. "We're filming at a little mountain villa by the lakeside. It's surprisingly comfortable."

Chang Jinxing didn't think bringing one more person to the set with him would be a problem; he could just say that Zheng Weize was his younger brother. After more than half a month of filming, he'd gotten to know the film production crew and had even become friendly with Kong Yu. He'd run the idea by Zhang Yuwen, and Zhang Yuwen didn't see any issue with it. It was the Spring Festival, after all.

"Nah, it's fine," Zheng Weize said. "I'm still planning to head home."

"If you're coming back early, you can come over to my house," Chen Hong chimed in. "I'll give you my address."

"Or maybe you could come spend the new year at my house," Yan Jun offered. "Yuwen, are you coming?"

Yan Jun really wanted to bring someone along for backup. After all, he was taking Xiao-Qi home, and there'd be trouble if he accidentally revealed the truth. He thought it might be helpful to have a friend around to ease some of the pressure.

"Are you serious?" Zhang Yuwen asked. He was, in fact, worried about Yan Jun's trip. He had some basic first-aid knowledge from back when he helped out at his grandfather's clinic. He was often treated as half an assistant in the clinic, with the other half-assistant being the housekeeper, Liu Jingfang.

Zhang Yuwen's momentary hesitation was enough to satisfy Yan Jun. "Just kidding. You should go with Huo Sichen."

"Will you be okay there?"

"Have some faith in me."

Zhang Yuwen didn't press the matter further. They didn't drink that night because they all had things to do the next day; after a sumptuous dinner, they returned to their respective rooms and went to bed. It was a frigid night, so bitterly cold that even the heating seemed inadequate. As he nestled under the quilt, Zhang Yuwen saw Huo Sichen's message: *Miss me yet?*

Nope, Zhang Yuwen replied, although he did miss him. As he sent his reply, he thought, *When did I become such a tsundere?*

Huo Sichen sent Zhang Yuwen a selfie. He was wearing beach shorts at the hotel pool, and Zhang Yuwen had to admit that Chen Hong's lessons were well worth the price. Huo Sichen was about to turn thirty, but his body was perfectly toned, with pecs and abs that were well-defined without being bulky. This beautifully sculpted, masculine physique stoked a fire in Zhang Yuwen in much the same way that one of Chang Jinxing's gourmet dishes could whip up his appetite. Fucking this long-legged hunk, being fucked by him...it didn't matter. Both sounded appealing.

Huo Sichen sent him another message. *we gonna spend tmrw nite 2gether? I think abt u every day.*

Zhang Yuwen: *yeah.*

Huo Sichen: *nervous? ur not saying much 2day.*

Zhang Yuwen laughed and rolled over in bed. He bet Huo Sichen had no idea what was going on in his head right now.

Huo Sichen: *actually, im nervous too. yeah.*

Does he know? Zhang Yuwen thought. He sometimes wondered whether Huo Sichen knew he loved him, just not as much as Huo Sichen loved him back. He must have sensed it, but he never seemed to dwell on or split hairs over it. Maybe different people approached love differently—some excited and passionate, others restrained and rational. But love was love, and it didn't matter who loved whom more.

Zhang Yuwen figured that he should give Huo Sichen some positive feedback, lest he come off disinterested in the chat. He typed, *u haven't told me abt ur kinks yet.*

It took Huo Sichen a while to reply. The screen showed that he was typing for a long time, but when his reply finally came, it said only: *u r my kink.*

Zhang Yuwen laughed again. *I thought I'd satisfy ur desires tomorrow. U rly don't have any?*

The typing indicator appeared again, lingering as if Huo Sichen was struggling to find the right words. A whole three minutes later, he replied, *rly?*

Zhang Yuwen set his phone down and burst out laughing. Teasing this guy was so much fun.

my kink is 2 straight, Huo Sichen continued. *forget it.*

Zhang Yuwen: *so u do have one. u were just playing dumb that day.*

Huo Sichen: *I only remembered later, after u reminded me.*

Zhang Yuwen: *be honest w me. I'll make it happen.*

He knew Huo Sichen couldn't resist this kind of temptation. Huo Sichen might have had more life experience than Zhang Yuwen, but when it came to sex, Zhang Yuwen had him wrapped around his little finger.

Huo Sichen: *a soccer babe roleplay?*

Oh my god! That's so straight! Zhang Yuwen thought. *I wouldn't know where to get the outfit for that even if I wanted to!*

don't have the clothes for that, he replied. *I thought u'd ask for something like high school uniform. do u like basketball players?*

a school uniform? that'd work! Huo Sichen said. Zhang Yuwen was about to die laughing. *still got ur high school uniform?*

yeah. But Zhang Yuwen didn't feel like changing into it this time. *how bout what's underneath?*

The typing indicator appeared again, and Zhang Yuwen knew what Huo Sichen must have been thinking: *I get to choose what goes underneath?!*

Zhang Yuwen was sure he must be tormenting Huo Sichen. They chatted for a while longer, and then Huo Sichen requested a video call. Zhang Yuwen, who was playing video games, accepted the call and leaned back in his bed. He knew that he looked unruffled, and on the other side of his phone screen, Huo Sichen was lying on his side with his eyes locked on Zhang Yuwen's profile. As the night wore on, Huo Sichen fell asleep, and Zhang Yuwen followed suit not long after.

No. 7 Riverbay Road was cleared right out the next morning as the housekeepers did a thorough cleaning in advance of the Spring Festival. Zhang Yuwen woke up late, around ten, to a thermos of coffee Chang Jinxing had left on the table. Yan Jun and Chen Hong were already gone, having put the couplets and decorations up around the house before they left.

Zhang Yuwen ate his breakfast and gave red envelopes to each of the housekeepers. He'd also prepared one for Zheng Weize, who was his junior, had yet to formally enter the workforce, and was still of an age to receive money as a New Year's gift. He walked over to stick it on Zheng Weize's door and found three other red envelopes stuck there already.

He opened the door to the room that he always kept locked and had the housekeepers clean it. Then, he lit joss sticks before his grandparents' portraits and set out their favorite snacks as offerings.

At eleven thirty, just as Zhang Yuwen was changing his clothes and getting ready to head out, he heard a car parking outside. There was no doubt about it: This was the most punctual Huo Sichen had ever been. Zhang Yuwen dug out his high school uniform.

In his youth, he'd attended one of the best private high schools in Jiangdong City, and the uniform suit was fashionable even now. His ex had all sorts of kinks, from basketball players to soccer jerseys during the World Cup, and he'd often asked Zhang Yuwen to co-splay for him. In exchange, he indulged Zhang Yuwen's outdoor sex fantasies. After graduation, though, Zhang Yuwen had rarely worn the shirt, tie, and suit of his school uniform.

After getting changed, Zhang Yuwen put on his black-rimmed glasses. Huo Sichen was chatting with Zheng Weize downstairs, but the moment he laid eyes on Zhang Yuwen, he fell silent, looking awestruck. A student bag slung over his shoulder, Zhang Yuwen sat on the stair railing and slid down it as if he was a teenager again. Huo Sichen's breath quickened.

"Weize, when are you leaving?" Zhang Yuwen asked.

"Uh...um." Zheng Weize was bowled over too. Usually, Zhang Yuwen dressed in loungewear or sportswear—handsome, yes, but not *this* striking. He snapped back to his senses. "Tomorrow, I guess. Can I take a picture?"

"What's there to take a picture of?" Zhang Yuwen chuckled, but his vanity won out, and he let Zheng Weize snap a photo of him.

"Remember to turn off the lights before you go. All right, I'll leave it to you."

"O...kay."

Huo Sichen didn't say anything. He just stared intently at Zhang Yuwen, who pushed his glasses up and followed him out.

"Gege, where are we going to hang out?"

Huo Sichen was still speechless.

Zhang Yuwen even took Huo Sichen's hand, and Huo Sichen wasted no time intertwining their fingers. He adjusted his belt with his other hand, looking awkward all the while. "We'll go wherever you want to go, do whatever you want to do."

And just like that, he's hard, Zhang Yuwen thought, amused.

They got in the car. Huo Sichen seemed reluctant to even start the car; he just kept staring at Zhang Yuwen's face. Eventually, he leaned over to kiss him, and Zhang Yuwen responded by wrapping his arms around his neck and kissing back. His enthusiasm knocked Huo Sichen off his feet.

"Aren't we leaving?"

"Yes, yes, we are, right now," said Huo Sichen. "Let's grab lunch first. I've already made reservations."

"How was your business trip, Gege?"

Hearing Zhang Yuwen call him that made Huo Sichen weak in the knees. He blushed, then chuckled and shared a series of anecdotes from his business trip. Any frustration he had when he arrived at Riverbay Road was long forgotten; all he wanted to do was finish his meal quickly, take Zhang Yuwen to the hotel, and make love.

It was true: Love was the best refuge from stress. But the fact that Zhang Yuwen hadn't given in to him yet made Huo Sichen crave even more. His infatuation was unbearable.

For lunch, he had booked a private room at a Japanese restaurant for sukiyaki. They had to take off their shoes, and from that point on, there was no stopping Zhang Yuwen's teasing. He and Huo Sichen were both wearing thick black socks, and Zhang Yuwen began by rubbing his feet against Huo Sichen's insteps…only for Huo Sichen to trap them between his own legs. Then, he pressed his foot against Huo Sichen's crotch, and Huo Sichen grabbed the errant foot and started caressing it. Zhang Yuwen was hard now, too, and Huo Sichen's touch almost made him come, so he quickly retracted his foot.

Huo Sichen tried to regain some of the ground he had lost. "What else are you wearing under there?"

"Why don't you come undress me and find out for yourself?" Zhang Yuwen retorted, rendering Huo Sichen speechless.

After lunch, Huo Sichen drove Zhang Yuwen to the suburbs. This was a rare moment of alone time for them.

"Gege, drive slowly," Zhang Yuwen said teasingly.

"Okay, but I'm not even going a hundred yet."

Huo Sichen had sped up without even realizing it. Zhang Yuwen didn't dare distract him by teasing him further on the highway. But to his surprise, Huo Sichen gradually calmed down and started chatting with Zhang Yuwen about his trip to Singapore.

"Oh, and I bought you something too," Huo Sichen added suddenly. "I forgot all about it the moment I saw you."

Zhang Yuwen found himself touched by this sweet talk. He took Huo Sichen's bag from the back seat and opened it to find the gift inside: a luxury bag. "Wow! So expensive!" he exclaimed.

"I didn't know what to get you."

Zhang Yuwen grinned. "Can't go wrong with something expensive."

For a moment, Huo Sichen couldn't tell if Zhang Yuwen genuinely liked the gift or was just teasing him, so he stole a few more glances until Zhang Yuwen told him to keep his eyes on the road. The luxury bag would have run him more than ten thousand. It was clear that Huo Sichen kept to his old habits from dating girls, only this time, the gift he bought was a men's bag instead of a woman's handbag.

Satisfied, Zhang Yuwen tried out his new bag. He was playing a high school student for the day, though, so he figured he might as well go all the way: He went ahead and looked up the price of the bag on his phone.

"If you don't like it, we can exchange it," Huo Sichen said. "Just don't throw the receipt away."

"I like it," Zhang Yuwen told him, "but it's too expensive."

Huo Sichen chuckled. He didn't know what Zhang Yuwen was really thinking: *You only earn so much and have a mortgage to pay, and you give me a bag worth more than ten thousand?*

"We're finally here," Huo Sichen said as he drove into the hotel's parking lot. It was a one-stop resort nestled in the mountains, even more luxurious and modern than the hot spring hotel they'd visited, with various entertainment options. This was where they would spend the next three days of their Spring Festival holiday.

Huo Sichen checked in, and the receptionist asked, "King-sized bed, Mr. Huo?"

"Yes," Huo Sichen said without a hint of embarrassment. In fact, if he could have, he would have yelled, "This is my fucking wife!" to all the guests in the lobby.

Zhang Yuwen, dressed in his school uniform and carrying a designer bag, looked just like a high school student being kept by an elite patron. He sized up the guests around them, amused.

"Wow," he said when he opened the door to their room. It had a spacious terrace with a hot spring pool. *This is a premium suite,* he thought. *Probably not the most expensive one the hotel offers, but—*

Huo Sichen couldn't contain himself anymore. Before Zhang Yuwen could even get a good look at the room, Huo Sichen took him into his arms, bent down slightly, and kissed him.

Zhang Yuwen wrapped his arms around Huo Sichen's neck, and Huo Sichen kissed him frantically. They were both hard, and Zhang Yuwen was assailed by a familiar sensation. He was unaccustomed to being on the receiving end of a top's passionate kisses—never mind the fact that, for Huo Sichen, "passionate" looked a lot like "aggressive"—but it didn't matter. Like was like and love was love, and that didn't change just because one of them was in a different role than he was used to.

Huo Sichen held Zhang Yuwen down on the bed, and they looked at each other for a moment without speaking. Zhang Yuwen set aside his bag and unbuttoned Huo Sichen's shirt collar with one hand. Breathing heavily, Huo Sichen untucked Zhang Yuwen's shirt and leaned in to inhale the scent of his body through the fabric.

"What's under there?" Huo Sichen asked.

Zhang Yuwen grinned impishly. "That's for me to know and you to find out."

Huo Sichen unbuckled Zhang Yuwen's belt and unzipped his pants, revealing a pair of flimsy black briefs with nothing in the back but thin straps of fabric framing Zhang Yuwen's bare ass. His hard cock strained against the fabric, leaking pre-cum that proclaimed that he, too, loved Huo Sichen and was eager to fuck him.

Huo Sichen was blushing hard, but he couldn't tear his eyes away. He lowered his head and, in an obscene gesture, planted a kiss on

Zhang Yuwen's clothed crotch. Zhang Yuwen knew which buttons to hit to turn on a top, and Huo Sichen was lapping it up.

"I brought lube," Huo Sichen whispered.

He began to kiss his way down Zhang Yuwen's neck to his chest. Zhang Yuwen was enjoying himself, charmed by Huo Sichen's sincerity and earnestness during foreplay. "Let me do it," he whispered back.

He applied the lube for Huo Sichen and arranged himself in a sitting position, thinking that being in control might help him get used to being penetrated. Huo Sichen stared at Zhang Yuwen with his face beet red, and Zhang Yuwen, who was busy getting himself into position, shot him a questioning look.

"I feel like I'm dreaming," Huo Sichen said. He had no complaints about Zhang Yuwen taking the lead; he, Huo Sichen, was the inexperienced one, after all. Everything he knew about sex between men came from some last-minute cramming he'd done watching adult videos over the past few days.

Zhang Yuwen was just barely beginning to guide Huo Sichen inside him when he jolted, feeling as if he'd been struck by lightning. *Fuck! It hurts! So much!* He felt like he was being electrocuted, but he was the one who initiated this hookup, so he had to go through with it. Huo Sichen's dick was too big, even bigger than his own, and Zhang Yuwen wanted to give up even as he was forcing himself down. *What kind of torture is this?! Damn! It really hurts!*

He looked at Huo Sichen, trying his best to school his expression, but Huo Sichen was so nervous he couldn't even speak.

"Ugh..." Composing himself, Zhang Yuwen straddled Huo Sichen's waist. Huo Sichen grabbed his hands and pulled him toward him.

"You're so tight," Huo Sichen managed.

"Yeah...yeah." Zhang Yuwen frowned. It was so painful he didn't want to talk. He tried to move up and down, but suddenly, Huo Sichen sat up, wrapped his arms around Zhang Yuwen's waist, and buried his face against his body, panting heavily.

Zhang Yuwen shifted again. Still flushed red, Huo Sichen kept his head down and said nothing, and Zhang Yuwen made an inquisitive noise. Sounding utterly mortified, Huo Sichen said, "Yuwen, I came."

"Huh?" Zhang Yuwen said. "You...did?" Privately, he thanked his lucky stars. He was still in pain, and now, he could tell Huo Sichen to pull out ASAP. He started to push himself off Huo Sichen, but Huo Sichen wasn't done; he didn't want to let go. Zhang Yuwen gritted his teeth and managed to pull away.

"I...haven't shown you my full prowess." Huo Sichen's face was flushed to his ears. "You're too sexy."

Zhang Yuwen roared with laughter. If someone else hooked up with a top who finished this fast, they'd roast the guy on social media, but Zhang Yuwen had dodged a bullet; he was both amused and relieved. Huo Sichen found a towel and clumsily wiped them both down.

It was hard for a guy to control himself after such a long dry spell; Zhang Yuwen offered scientific theories to comfort Huo Sichen. "It's just because you've abstained from sex for a long time," he said.

But Huo Sichen's frustration was palpable, and none of Zhang Yuwen's cutting-edge reproductive science could dispel it. After all, he had been looking forward to this for more than a month, and for the past few days, he'd been going back and forth between flirting and trepidation. He had a lot of time to build this moment up in his head, and then he only lasted a few seconds...

Zhang Yuwen acted like it was no big deal, but deep down, he was in hysterics.

"Let's take a bath," he said, pulling Huo Sichen up by the hand. "Come on!"

Still depressed, Huo Sichen got up, and they went over to the balcony in their bathrobes. The privacy at this hotel was impressive, and the balcony had a hot tub big enough to accommodate them both. By this point, unlike the time in the hot spring, Zhang Yuwen was used to seeing Huo Sichen's body, and used to showing his own off to him.

"You must be tired lately," Zhang Yuwen said as they sat together.

"Yeah. I barely sleep more than five hours a night. But things are much better now that I'm here with you."

Huo Sichen reached out to wrap his arms around Zhang Yuwen, motioning for him to come closer.

"Sit on me," Zhang Yuwen said spontaneously. Huo Sichen hesitated, seeming to finally realize that his partner was another guy. This amused Zhang Yuwen even more. "What's wrong? You don't want to?"

Huo Sichen shifted over and sat on Zhang Yuwen's lap. It was a strange feeling, being held by another guy, whose hands were roaming all over his body and caressing him sensually. He wasn't used to it, and it felt a bit like he was being controlled by Zhang Yuwen. He couldn't help but grab at Zhang Yuwen's hands, and they both laughed.

"Don't...touch me there," Huo Sichen said, stopping Zhang Yuwen from playing with his nipples.

"Why? Are you sensitive there?" Zhang Yuwen's hands wandered further down. "What about here, then?"

Under the warm water, Huo Sichen's body flushed crimson at Zhang Yuwen's touch. "You're pretty horny yourself," he said, deadpan.

Zhang Yuwen laughed. "Name a guy who isn't."

Slowly, Huo Sichen grew used to the intimacy of sitting in Zhang Yuwen's lap. Perhaps, deep down, he yearned for someone to care for and dote on him. He wrapped his arms around Zhang Yuwen's neck and bent to kiss him. "Can I do it again later?" he asked.

Ugh, please no, Zhang Yuwen moaned inwardly. The first time was so painful...but when he saw the look on Huo Sichen's face, he couldn't bring himself to say no. He caved and said, "Oh, sure."

Now that he had a chance for his second coming, Huo Sichen's nerves came creeping back.

"Actually..." Zhang Yuwen wrapped one arm around Huo Sichen's waist, letting his other hand wander indecently over Huo Sichen's abs and thighs. "Ejaculating quickly is an evolutionary advantage. You see, most animals mate in the wild, where it's dangerous, and they risk being caught by predators at any time..."

"This is the first time I've heard someone use specialized evolutionary theory to console a guy who's come too soon."

Zhang Yuwen cracked up. "No, no," he insisted, "I'm serious. The faster you ejaculate, the better the chances of survival for you and your offspring, so this is—"

Huo Sichen got off Zhang Yuwen and picked him up in his arms.

"Wait, wait! We're all wet!" Zhang Yuwen blurted. "Second round already? Don't you need a break?"

Fully naked, Huo Sichen carried Zhang Yuwen into the room, then dried him off with a towel. After their soak in the hot tub, their skin was warm and flushed, and their firm, masculine, muscular bodies had softened.

This time, Huo Sichen took charge. *All right, then,* Zhang Yuwen thought. *Bring it on. I'll just grin and bear it; who knows, maybe it'll be over quickly again.*

Huo Sichen entered him. It hurt, but it was more bearable than the first time. Huo Sichen, finally noticing the look on Zhang Yuwen's face, asked, "Does it hurt?"

"N...no, it just...feels strange. This is my first time bottoming... Ow! Gentle!"

Huo Sichen's breathing quickened as he pushed in deeper. "Second time," he whispered.

He pressed his strong, slender body into Zhang Yuwen, pinning him down, and Zhang Yuwen's pain slowly subsided until it was replaced by a strange sensation that was both uncomfortable and stimulating all at once. Maybe this was what pain and pleasure were all about.

"Mm... Mm... Ah!" Zhang Yuwen moaned. It didn't matter how much of a top a guy was; when a particular spot inside him was stimulated, it was impossible for him to keep from moaning— perhaps even more so when he wasn't all that fixed in his role in the first place. "Slower, slower... Ah! Ah!"

The complex blend of sensations melded into pleasure, and then that pleasure only intensified. Huo Sichen paused briefly, gazing at him, entranced, and Zhang Yuwen looked back at him, panting. When their eyes met, Huo Sichen thrust in as if in appreciation for whatever he saw in Zhang Yuwen's eyes.

"Ah— Ah—" Zhang Yuwen grabbed Huo Sichen's wrists. So this was what it felt like to bottom. There was indeed a different kind of pleasure to be had, but it required the skill and cooperation of the top. While Huo Sichen lacked experience, he was gentler on the whole, and this tenderness made up for his fumbling. He always watched out for Zhang Yuwen's reactions, searching for things that made Zhang Yuwen feel good so that he could zero in on them.

"Oh, fuck..." Zhang Yuwen huffed, "you're...really big...ugh..."

Huo Sichen didn't waste his second chance. Relaxed from the hot tub and less nervous than before, he had regained his confidence and the right to call the shots in bed. Whether it was a straight man or a gay top, the person who launched the offensive in bed—the penetrating party—always had the upper hand.

I'm getting fucked. The thought hit Zhang Yuwen hard. It was a little shameful, but it was sexy too. And Huo Sichen's unit was so huge it actually kind of left Zhang Yuwen in awe. And then, amid all these complicated feelings, he experienced a new kind of climax. "Ah...ah!"

As soon as Zhang Yuwen started moaning, Huo Sichen lowered his head and kissed him deeply. Zhang Yuwen was overwhelmed by Huo Sichen's lips and tongue, his caresses, and the relentless thrusting going on below. The pleasure from all three fronts blended into one, and it held him in a vise grip that left him wanting even more.

But then Zhang Yuwen felt Huo Sichen pull out completely, thrust in shallowly a few times, then push himself all the way back in. "No, no, not like this—ah!"

"Does it not feel good?" Huo Sichen pressed his tip against Zhang Yuwen's hole, watching for his reaction.

"Oh, fuck!" Zhang Yuwen was about to lose his mind. He hadn't expected that Huo Sichen would know the technique of alternating nine shallow thrusts with one deep one; it was so hot, so overwhelming.

"You're still hard," Huo Sichen said, looking down.

Zhang Yuwen's face flushed crimson. He pressed his thumb against the base of his shaft, which was slick with cum, making it stand up against Huo Sichen's abs. "It's a compliment," he panted. "You fucked me 'til I came prostate fluid."

That turned Huo Sichen on even more. He buried himself in Zhang Yuwen, their bodies tightly entwined as he gently thrust in and out. Zhang Yuwen hugged his shoulders tightly, reveling in the sensation of skin on skin. He felt the waves of climax approaching, but each wave stopped short of crashing into him—denying him release, leaving him floating at the height of ecstasy.

"How much longer are you going to keep going?" Zhang Yuwen moaned. He was already exhausted.

"Relax." Huo Sichen kept kissing Zhang Yuwen's cheeks, forehead, and eyelids. "You're too tense."

Zhang Yuwen took a deep breath and tried to relax. It didn't hurt anymore now that he was used to Huo Sichen's enormous cock. Now, it felt custom-made for that particular spot inside him. Scalding hot and hard, it pillaged his warm, pliant body, a stark contrast to Huo Sichen's tender lips.

"I need to come," Zhang Yuwen gasped.

"Can you do it like this?"

"No. Need your hand."

"I've got you."

They separated a little, and Huo Sichen gave Zhang Yuwen a helping hand, never wavering in his thrusts. Neither of them spoke, and Zhang Yuwen gazed up at Huo Sichen, enthralled. Suddenly, he found Huo Sichen gorgeous—so handsome it took his breath away. Why hadn't he realized it before?

He knocked Huo Sichen's hand away and began to stroke himself. His eyes misted over as he raked them admiringly over Huo Sichen's form. His body was so sexy, and the knowledge that its most vital part was inside him held a powerful sway over him.

Zhang Yuwen pumped himself a few more times and practically spurted as he came. The onslaught of his second climax wiped his mind blank and set off a dazzling display of fireworks behind his eyelids.

Huo Sichen held his breath and thrust harder, and while Zhang Yuwen was still lost in the glow of his orgasm, Huo Sichen found his own release. He bent down to kiss Zhang Yuwen fiercely, whispering, "I love you. Yuwen, I love you," into his mouth.

"I love you too," Zhang Yuwen whispered back.

They embraced passionately, savoring the long-awaited release. It felt, to both of them, as if all of their past encounters, every time they'd come together and parted from one another, had been building to this very moment when they were unified.

In the afterglow, Zhang Yuwen's lust receded. He looked at Huo Sichen's face and saw a reflection of his own feelings. He wanted to kiss Huo Sichen. Even after sleeping with him, Zhang Yuwen still loved him.

But Huo Sichen beat him to it. He kissed Zhang Yuwen. "Yuwen, I love you," he said again.

Zhang Yuwen returned the kiss. "I love you too."

So it's true. Sexual intimacy really does strengthen emotional bonds, Zhang Yuwen thought. He was certain now of his feelings. *Yup. He's the one.*

CHAPTER 37

JIANGNAN CITY QUIETED DOWN on the second-to-last day before the Spring Festival as people returned to their hometowns for the New Year. Places like Jiangnan District and Xiling District, typically full of workers who'd moved there for better job prospects, cleared out overnight. Only areas with more local residents, such as Qishan Road, Jiangbei, and Riverbay, still showed signs of life.

Chang Jinxing was prepared to spend the Spring Festival on set, but to his surprise, they wrapped up early. The entire crew had been waiting for a clear winter night to shoot the final scenes—the male and female leads ice-skating, and the second male lead stargazing with the female lead—and, as if the heavens wanted them all to go home for the Spring Festival, the weather decided to cooperate. They finished shooting both scenes in a single day.

"It's a wrap?" Chang Jinxing flipped through the schedule, hardly able to believe it. There were no scenes left to shoot.

"Uh... I think so." Even the producer sounded uncertain.

The entire crew fell silent for a moment, then broke out in cheers. "WOOHOO!"

Kong Yu was freezing; it was a chilly winter night, and in his scene he wore only a sweater, sitting by the frozen lake and speaking to the female lead with chattering teeth. The female lead listened in silence. She had few lines in the scene and only needed to shed a few tears to fulfill her part of the bargain, but her trembling legs betrayed her.

"It's a wrap!" Everyone cheered again. Shaking like a leaf, Kong Yu threw his gentlemanly demeanor to the wind and ignored the female lead as he hurried over to warm himself up. Chang Jinxing immediately handed him his thermos of hot chocolate.

"It's a wrap! Yay!"

Their cheers reverberated through Changhu Park. Bundled up in thick earmuffs and scarves, a bunch of people took out the sparklers they had used during the shoot to go horse around by the lake. And just like that, Chang Jinxing's first drama concluded successfully.

"Let's have lunch to celebrate tomorrow!" the producer suggested, shivering. "Go back and get some sleep for now. It's freezing tonight."

"Wanna warm up in my room for a bit?" Chang Jinxing asked Kong Yu.

"Yeah, sure," Kong Yu said. "Thanks."

Chang Jinxing had been through thick and thin with Kong Yu over the last twenty days, and as a result, they'd become good friends. He got along well with the crew, too, and during his time on set, he'd made a lot of friends in the film industry, including production assistants, script supervisors, coordinators, lighting assistants, and so on. A bunch of ladies from the marketing and communications team even asked to exchange contact information with him on WeChat. His affable personality and handsome looks made making friends a breeze. It helped that he was well aware of his place in the pecking order as a member of the production crew, so even when he stood in temporarily as a supporting actor, he didn't harbor any delusions of overnight stardom.

CHAPTER 37

But his friendship with Kong Yu was different. In the drama, they played childhood friends with a steadfast bond that had lasted more than twenty years, and in real life, Kong Yu always guided him during filming, too. As a result, Chang Jinxing was still immersed in his role and had yet to step all the way out of it.

Once they were back in Chang Jinxing's hotel room, Kong Yu finally started to feel better. "Phew!"

Chang Jinxing was still shuttling between several different rooms, sorting out the camera equipment they'd brought back and helping his mentor with the paperwork and inventory check. The next day was set to be another busy one for him: handing the remaining footage over to post-production, checking the backups... While the actors could relax now that filming had wrapped, members of the production team were up to their necks in work. His phone was blowing up with notifications.

"How are you spending the Spring Festival?" Kong Yu asked, sipping hot water.

Chang Jinxing had been planning to spend the Spring Festival on set. Now that they'd wrapped up early, though, he realized he would have to go back home. No. 7 Riverbay Road would probably be empty, but spending the Spring Festival alone at home didn't sound too bad.

Just as Chang Jinxing was about to reply, though, Kong Yu asked, "Are you heading back to spend the Spring Festival with Zhang Yuwen-laoshi?"

Chang Jinxing figured most of the production crew were already speculating about his relationship with Zhang Yuwen. It was reasonable to assume they were a couple; they did look like one, especially with Zhang Yuwen having made arrangements for him to work as a cameraman on set. He chuckled. "We're really just friends. Believe me. And he's already gone on vacation."

"Oh," Kong Yu said thoughtfully. "You must be great friends."

"Yeah."

Kong Yu had initially hesitated to get too close to Chang Jinxing because he thought Chang Jinxing was Zhang Yuwen's lover, which put him in a bit of a pickle. On the one hand, he wanted to make influential connections, and he thought that Chang Jinxing might be able to formally introduce him to Zhang Yuwen and give his career a boost; on the other hand, he'd worried that getting too close to Chang Jinxing might draw Zhang Yuwen's ire.

"Are you going home?" Kong Yu asked. "If not, you can spend the Spring Festival at my agency. Jiang Youfeng and a couple of girls from the studio will be there too." Jiang Youfeng was Kong Yu's manager, another young man.

Chang Jinxing considered it for a moment, but then said, "Nah, I should go home." Kong Yu nodded and didn't press the issue. "When's Youfeng coming?"

"I'll text him and ask," said Kong Yu. "I should get going myself."

The door to their room was wide open while they talked, and crew members were parading past with celebratory beers in hand. Some women were wearing bathrobes and shouting excitedly. Everyone was in high spirits.

"I mean, why don't you sleep with me here tonight?" Chang Jinxing suggested. "Jiang Youfeng has been so busy today. There's no need to make him make another trip."

Kong Yu was surprised, but he realized quickly that Chang Jinxing meant he should literally sleep here. "Okay. I'll tell him not to come and pick me up."

"Sure."

Chang Jinxing was still working; he sorted out the equipment, submitted the form, and sent a message to the post-production team from his phone before finally opening a beer bottle for Kong Yu and clinking bottles with him. After three weeks of training, Chang Jinxing was adept at handling the production crew's work and capable of multitasking.

Because he was handsome and got along so well with the others, Wang Botao had tasked him with liaising with all the other departments; the girls on the crew were suckers for good-looking guys, and when Chang Jinxing asked about work, people would inevitably cooperate with him. Not even the producer or director ever turned down his requests, because they didn't want to offend Zhang Yuwen. Consequently, Chang Jinxing spent every day in multithreading mode, coordinating between the camera crew and the other various teams while still finding time to chat with Kong Yu.

"Well then, I'm gonna grab a shower," Kong Yu said.

Chang Jinxing told him to go ahead, then closed the door and went to find the director so that he could hand over a USB drive with a copy of some footage on it. When he returned, Kong Yu was blow-drying his hair.

"Look! We've got a sample clip! It's our scene!" Chang Jinxing gushed. He opened his phone and showed it to Kong Yu, and they sat on the bed together and watched. When it was done, he flopped back onto the bed in despair. "Oh my god, my acting's so awkward..."

"You did great for someone with no professional training," said Kong Yu. "What more could you ask for?"

"You're the one who rocked it," Chang Jinxing said, deflecting. "Just look at you. Your eyes are so emotive."

Kong Yu laughed. Where Chang Jinxing was embarrassed to watch himself on camera, Kong Yu found it fascinating. "That's how it is the first time you act," he said, and it was clear from his expression that he was reminiscing about his own experiences. He sighed.

It was two a.m., and Chang Jinxing needed to sleep too. After a shower, he lay down on his bed, and Kong Yu took the other one. "I'm turning off the lights," Chang Jinxing said.

"Okay," Kong Yu replied. "Are you cold?"

"I'm good. What, do you wanna come over and sleep together?" Chang Jinxing said teasingly. But when Kong Yu went silent, he backtracked. "Just kidding. Don't take it seriously."

In the darkness, Kong Yu hummed in acknowledgment.

Chang Jinxing's fuckboy instincts told him that right now, if he asked Kong Yu if he wanted to have sex, Kong Yu would agree. But he restrained himself. He turned on his phone in the darkness and watched the sample clip over and over, feeling as if, like his character, he had an old friend of many years, and that friend was sleeping in the bed next to him.

He had a sudden urge to call Kong Yu by the name of his character in the drama—Gu Youli. "Youli, what are you thinking?"

"Still in character, huh?" Kong Yu said, then adopted the tone of the second male lead. "I'm thinking, Yao Chen, that being a good actor doesn't necessarily mean you'll become famous."

Yao Chen was Chang Jinxing's character's name. "But things will improve if you persevere."

"Really?" Kong Yu said mildly. "But I get this sense that a career is like love. Working hard doesn't guarantee you'll succeed."

It sounded just like something his character—a melancholic, jaded screenwriter—would say. They'd brought their on-screen characters back to the hotel with them. Chang Jinxing sat up with his blanket wrapped around him and looked blankly at Kong Yu.

"You're breaking character, Jinxing."

Chang Jinxing grinned.

"Did they tell you a lot about me?" Kong Yu asked. He still had his back to Chang Jinxing.

"Huh? Not really." Chang Jinxing blinked, puzzled.

"Not really?" Kong Yu glanced back at him. "I see."

"Why? Who's 'they'?"

"Never mind. It's nothing." There was a beat of silence, then Kong Yu continued, "There used to be a big shot who sponsored me, but two years ago, he grew disappointed with me. Or maybe he just got tired of me. For all of last year, I couldn't get any acting gigs. Making ends meet was a struggle."

Chang Jinxing made a sympathetic sound.

"Did you overhear me and Tao Ran at the back of the ship that day?"

"Yeah, a little."

"It isn't easy to make it big. Sometimes, it's a challenge just getting by."

"Once the drama airs, things will start looking up for you," Chang Jinxing said, trying to comfort him.

"It's still up to luck. You're different, though. With Director Zhang backing you, you can play any role you want."

"You can't force it either," Chang Jinxing said wryly. "And I'm just here to learn. I'm not going to keep acting."

"So you wanna be a photographer?" Kong Yu asked, still not turning to face him. "Whatever you do, don't become an actor. Before you make it big, you'll have to sacrifice all your dignity, and it won't be much better after you become famous. Everyone is just a plaything for the rich."

"That's not true." Chang Jinxing put down his phone. "Listen to me."

"If you continue acting, you'll gradually come to realize I'm right."

"No, wait. Youli?"

Kong Yu didn't respond.

"Youli. We're just the supporting cast." Chang Jinxing went over and touched Kong Yu's shoulder. "Yu Changkong is the real protagonist."

"Right. He's the lead. We're just the supporting cast."

"But I'm really glad to have met you."

Kong Yu glanced back at Chang Jinxing, and they locked eyes.

Carried away by his emotions in the moment—bolstered by both their twenty years of on-screen bond as childhood friends and their twenty days of off-screen friendship—Chang Jinxing leaned in and kissed Kong Yu on his cheek. Kong Yu turned over, put a hand on Chang Jinxing's neck, and started kissing him.

Whoa, this is hot, Chang Jinxing thought, too surprised to do anything but kiss Kong Yu back. Chang Jinxing didn't have fucking his childhood friend on his menu of kinks, but suddenly, he thought that maybe he should have.

As they were kissing, though, Chang Jinxing's senses returned to him. "No, this isn't right." He fled back to his bed. "We'd be making a mistake if we went any further. Youli, we're best buds. We can't sleep together."

Amused, Kong Yu turned away without saying a word. Chang Jinxing's heart was pounding as he pulled up his quilt.

"I've never had a friend like this," Kong Yu said.

"Me neither."

"But after playing this role, I think I get it."

Chang Jinxing laughed. Outside, the ruckus of their drunken production crew colleagues continued unabated. It was snowing again out there. Filming had wrapped, and the show was over.

When Chang Jinxing woke the following day, Kong Yu was already gone. Most of the others were still sleeping off their night of revelry. Chang Jinxing quickly got up and went about finishing his remaining tasks. He carried the equipment back to the film production company, copied the film stills for future promotional use, and returned the form to the production department. The company was on its Spring Festival break, so the entire place was quiet and deserted.

When his work was complete, a realization struck Chang Jinxing. *That's it? It's over?*

There was, at least, a wrap party later that afternoon. The lead actor and actress came to offer a toast, and Kong Yu joined them with his manager. Chang Jinxing shared a table and some drinks with Wang Botao, who was still rather groggy, and the lighting crew. Afterward, someone suggested karaoke, but everyone else wanted to go home for their New Year's Eve dinner, so the idea was vetoed.

As they left the hotel, Kong Yu's manager ran over and handed him a gift—a brand-new mobile phone.

"Let's catch up again sometime," Jiang Youfeng said, patting Chang Jinxing on the shoulder. "And give my regards to Director Zhang." As Chang Jinxing waved goodbye to him, he saw Kong Yu getting into the car and leaving.

The project was over. With mixed feelings, Chang Jinxing turned away and walked to the subway. It had only been twenty days, but he felt as if he had experienced a completely different life.

On the subway, he received a text notifying him that his bank account had been credited with ¥135,700. He almost fainted. He checked the transaction details and found that the credit was for his wages. Then he checked his WeChat. The production crew's finance department had sent him his pay slip, and it included his salary of

¥12,000 for his work as a camera operator, ¥3,700 for travel, meals, and other miscellaneous allowances, and ¥120,000 for his role as a supporting actor.

Damn, actors make big bucks! Chang Jinxing could hardly believe his eyes. He sent a message to Zhang Yuwen, but there was no reply, and he figured Zhang Yuwen was probably enjoying his vacation. *What a windfall!*

Chang Jinxing reined in his impulse to splurge. Besides, it was the eve of the Spring Festival, and all the shops were closed for business, leaving the streets empty and desolate; even if he wanted to treat himself to a big feast, there was nowhere to go. All he could do was return to No. 7 Riverbay Road.

Strangely enough, though, when he got home, the lights were on. Chang Jinxing opened the door to find bowls of instant noodles on the dining table. The door to Zheng Weize's room was ajar, and Chang Jinxing heard a voice inside.

"Weize?" Chang Jinxing called out.

"Uh...yeah?" Zheng Weize was wearing his wig and in the middle of a video call when he heard Chang Jinxing's voice. He ended the call hastily and rushed into the bathroom to remove his makeup.

"What was that?"

"I'm taking a shower!" Zheng Weize yelled, flustered.

"Oh." Chang Jinxing had bought some alcohol and food at the shop outside the subway station, and he put it down on the table and cleared away the messy heap of instant noodle bowls and cups. "Didn't you say you'd be going home?"

Zheng Weize didn't reply; he was too tense. Fortunately, Chang Jinxing didn't come into his room. He stuffed his dress, black stockings, and all the rest into the closet.

CHAPTER 37   **161**

Unfazed, Chang Jinxing opened the refrigerator to take a look. There were still plenty of ingredients left from the last time Yan Jun went grocery shopping, including cod for Xiao-Qi, frozen shrimp, and beef. He took them out to thaw, planning to whip up a sumptuous New Year's Eve meal, and sent Yan Jun a photo with a note that he was helping himself to the food and would restock for him after the holidays. He sent him a red envelope as a New Year's gift for Xiao-Qi, too.

Yan Jun was awfully busy. He hadn't had a moment's rest since he arrived in his hometown. He'd cleaned the house, changed the bedsheets for his mother, fixed the heating pipes, cleared out the refrigerator, organized the pile of cardboard scraps and other trash that his mother had picked up from god-knew-where, cleaned the windows, and put up the Spring Festival couplets and decorations. He also had to prepare a New Year's Eve meal for three people.

Finding time out of his busy schedule to glance at his phone, he asked Chang Jinxing, *r u home? thought u'd be on set.*

Chang Jinxing explained the change in plans.

Where's Yuwen? Yan Jun asked.

dunno. prob out for the new yr. it's just me n Weize at home.

Chang Jinxing set his phone aside. Suddenly, he felt a tingle at the back of his neck, and he turned to find Zheng Weize standing at the kitchen entrance in his pajamas, looking blankly at him.

"Why are you back?" Zheng Weize asked. His eyes were red.

Chang Jinxing put down the ingredients, wiped his hands, and walked over to him. "What's wrong? Did you decide not to go home?"

Without warning, Zheng Weize stepped forward and hugged Chang Jinxing. Chang Jinxing could tell something had happened, but he didn't ask; he just hugged Zheng Weize back and patted him on the head. Then, Zheng Weize pulled away from Chang Jinxing, left the kitchen, and sat at the dining table and went back to his phone. Chang Jinxing watched him for a moment to make sure he wasn't crying. Perhaps he was just feeling low.

"Filming wrapped up earlier than expected, so I came back," Chang Jinxing explained. "I thought I'd be spending the Spring Festival alone. I'm so glad you're here."

"What are you cooking?" Zheng Weize asked.

"Steamed fish. Maybe stewed beef for you and some stir-fried shrimp. Are you hungry?"

"I just ate lunch." Zheng Weize's so-called lunch had just been instant noodles. Instant noodles were actually all he'd eaten for the past couple of days, since even the takeout delivery drivers went home for the Spring Festival. He wasn't planning on eating anything else after that bowl of instant noodles after four p.m. A true warrior could ride his hunger through the night.

Nothing had actually happened. Maybe his irregular sleep schedule and the lack of nutrition from all those instant noodles were making him feel listless. Whatever it was, the empty house only made him more emotional. It also didn't help that, during their video call earlier, he'd seen Whiskey and his whole family sharing a meal. Loneliness tended to magnify a hundredfold during the holidays, and the sight of Whiskey's family had sent Zheng Weize's loneliness through the roof. Suddenly, life felt meaningless.

Then, at his loneliest moment, Chang Jinxing had returned.

Chang Jinxing busied himself in the kitchen. "Were you chatting with your friend?" he asked, vaguely remembering that Zheng Weize was on a call when he returned.

"Uh... Yeah..." Zheng Weize had ended the video call under the pretext of an internet outage. Normally Whiskey would have found that weird, but he was busy with his family reunion dinner, so he didn't probe. "How was filming?"

Zheng Weize knew a little about his gig, but he didn't know that Zhang Yuwen was the one who recommended him for the job. Chang Jinxing grinned. "It went great. I played a small role in the show. You'll see me on TV when it airs."

"Wow!" Zheng Weize was a little jealous, but Chang Jinxing was so handsome—in fact, Zheng Weize thought he was close to perfect. From the first day they met, Zheng Weize had suspected that Chang Jinxing wouldn't be just an ordinary person forever. "Are you gonna be a star? Can I have your autograph? I can keep it as a memento when you become famous."

Chang Jinxing smiled and started serving the food. Even though this New Year's Eve dinner was just for the two of them, he'd cooked up a feast. "Nah, I won't be famous."

"That's what they all say." Zheng Weize often read celebrity gossip online, so he was familiar with the paths that stars typically took. Before their rise to stardom, they were just ordinary folks, but once they made it big overnight, temptations came knocking in the form of love interests, ex-girlfriends, childhood friends... In the best-case scenario, they never saw those people again; the worst, they'd wind up as stepping stones for opportunity-seekers trying to get further in life.

"Really." Chang Jinxing took off the oven mitts, poured some red wine for Zheng Weize, and toasted him. "Happy New Year."

"Is that the landlord's wine?" Zheng Weize asked cautiously.

"No, I bought it today."

They clinked glasses. For Zheng Weize, the night was bittersweet. He still loved Chang Jinxing and didn't want this moment to end, but his beautiful bubble of hope that his feelings might be reciprocated had long since burst.

Zheng Weize had sensed a significant shift in his crush's life after their trip to the hot springs. Chang Jinxing no longer stayed out late or pulled all-nighters, and his routine was much more regular. His face was full of hope when he left home every day with his bag. He had already embarked on another path, and he was leaving Zheng Weize behind. The thought made Zheng Weize even sadder. After tonight, Chang Jinxing was going to fly high, far beyond his reach.

Chang Jinxing was still replying to messages on his phone and taking photos to share with his friends from the production crew. "If you don't wanna be famous, then what do you want to do?" Zheng Weize asked him.

"Huh?" Chang Jinxing looked up from his phone. "Photography. I've loved photography since I was a kid. I still do."

"Are you going to keep working as a cameraman?"

"Yeah..." Chang Jinxing set his phone aside and ladled some soup for Zheng Weize. "If the production crews want me, I'll take on a few more gigs to get some more experience. But I'm considering returning to school to further my studies."

He meant it. With the payment he'd received for his work on the drama, he no longer needed to worry about his next meal or his next job pandering to others. He planned to look for a university where he could enroll in a photography program, because working with the film production crew made him realize he needed more technical knowledge. He couldn't rely on teaching himself by reading books and experimenting with his camera anymore.

"Maybe after the Spring Festival," he added.

"I really envy you guys," Zheng Weize said. "Everyone has something they want to do."

Chang Jinxing grinned. "I'm sure you have something too. What's not to like about being a streamer? Besides, you're still in school; thinking about this stuff is still premature."

Zheng Weize sighed. "You know what? I lied to all of you. I'm, uh...not actually a student."

For a moment, Chang Jinxing didn't know what to say. Maybe it was the night's atmosphere, or maybe Zheng Weize was just sick of keeping up the lie, but on this New Year's Eve, at least, he wanted to be himself and say what he truly felt.

"Oh. To be honest...I never went to university either," Chang Jinxing confessed.

They both burst into bittersweet laughter. Chang Jinxing recalled the time he first met Zhang Yuwen and moved to Riverbay Road. He told Zhang Yuwen that he'd graduated from Jiangliu University's Department of Photography. He thought Zhang Yuwen was just an ordinary sub-landlord, but now that he thought about it, how could Zhang Yuwen not have seen through him? Maybe he'd just decided not to expose Chang Jinxing to save him the embarrassment.

"You aren't a photography major?" Zheng Weize was astounded.

"Nope. I didn't have any further schooling after high school. All this time, I've just been drifting all over and muddling my way through things."

Zheng Weize nodded. "I see..."

The fact that Chang Jinxing only had a high school education seemed to close the distance between them, and knowing that Chang Jinxing, too, would lie for his own vanity made Zheng Weize feel like maybe he wasn't so far out of his league after all.

"Same for me. I came to Jiangdong to work after high school. The difference is that I ran away from home. I never told you that, did I?"

"Why'd you run away?"

Zheng Weize thought for a moment. "I have two older sisters," he said at last, "and ever since I was a kid, I've always wanted to be a girl. At the time, I didn't understand why..."

He was born into a middle-class family in Minxi County. His father was a sailor, and his mother was a housewife. His father, holding the traditional belief that girls would eventually marry out of the family, had always wanted a boy who could care for him in his old age. As the family's youngest and only son, Zheng Weize was a beloved, pampered child.

His father spent most of his time at sea, though, and Zheng Weize, growing up in a family of girls, developed traits that leaned more toward the feminine side. This made him a prime target for bullies throughout his elementary and middle school years.

Chang Jinxing listened attentively without interrupting.

"Starting in ninth grade, I took titty skittles for a while," Zheng Weize explained. "Oh, those are—"

"I know what that means." Chang Jinxing was familiar with the term: It was slang for hormone replacement therapy. Lots of transfeminine people who were unable or unwilling to have surgery took estrogen to make some of their features look more feminine.

"They found me out in high school," Zheng Weize said. "I couldn't get my hands on them anymore, and I gave up in twelfth grade. I didn't want to be a girl anymore, and being a guy wasn't so bad. Sometimes, I feel like I'm neither male nor female..."

"Don't say that." Chang Jinxing smiled at him. "You're you."

He racked his brain for words of comfort to offer Zheng Weize. If Zhang Yuwen were here, he probably could've come up with something heartwarming and impactful, but Chang Jinxing couldn't. He could only lend a sincere, listening ear.

"I suppose I realized it was easier to survive in this society as a boy," Zheng Weize continued. "But I failed the college entrance exams and got into a big fight with my family..."

"And then you came to Jiangdong," Chang Jinxing finished for him.

"Yup. I still remember the guy I liked in high school."

"He was straight, right?"

Zheng Weize blinked. "How did you know?"

"You've always been one for straight guys," Chang Jinxing said with another smile.

"He was a bad boy who liked to fool around, like you. He had several girlfriends. I really worshiped him back then, and I think he had genuine feelings for me, even though he hit me occasionally when we argued."

Chang Jinxing was offended to be compared to this guy. He would never raise a hand to anyone, no matter the circumstances. Whether the relationship was heterosexual or homosexual, it didn't matter: Violence was an absolute no-go.

"So I always believed that it was possible to turn straight guys gay," Zheng Weize added.

"But in the end, they'll leave you," Chang Jinxing reminded him. Zheng Weize said nothing. "Did you break up in the end?"

"Of course we did. Maybe he felt like I wasn't a real girl. But half a year after we broke up, I heard that he got in a tailgating accident on his motorbike. He died."

For a moment, Chang Jinxing didn't know what to say. Eventually, he asked, "So your parents and sisters don't know where you live?"

"Yeah, all they know is that I'm in Jiangdong."

Chang Jinxing glanced at his phone, his meaning clear: *You don't even contact them during the Spring Festival?* But every family had their own way of getting along, so he didn't voice those words.

"How about you?" Zheng Weize asked with a hint of anticipation.

Chang Jinxing hesitated. Zheng Weize wanted to trade secrets so that they could get to know each other better, but the thought of sharing his painful past was a little...discomfiting.

CHAPTER
38

"MY PARENTS DIVORCED WHEN I was a kid," Chang Jinxing began. "My dad was a violent guy who hit my mom a lot." That was why Chang Jinxing strongly opposed any form of violence.

"Oh, I see." Zheng Weize nodded.

"After they divorced, I lived with my father, but he left me to fend for myself once I graduated from high school. He wouldn't let me enroll in university."

"Your dad must have been very handsome," Zheng Weize remarked.

"Yup, he was a womanizer."

And so am I, Chang Jinxing thought self-deprecatingly. *Why do we grow up to become the people we hate?*

Zheng Weize looked blankly at Chang Jinxing, who continued, "There's nothing really that memorable about my childhood, actually. The things that left a deep impression were when I helped out in the kitchen of a restaurant, or times I asked my dad for money after school. Life got much easier after I started working."

"You must have had a lot of admirers."

"Yeah." When he was still at home, he used to ask his father for money. After he left home, he asked his boyfriends or girlfriends for money instead. Nothing seemed to have changed in his life.

"What happened later?" Zheng Weize prompted.

"Uh... What else? I..." For a moment, Chang Jinxing was going to say, *And then I slept around. Luckily, I didn't get HIV,* but instead he said, "Then I realized that I was...very popular. Sorry, am I being too—"

"No, no. You're really handsome."

"So, things fell into my lap, and I took them for granted. That's just how people are, right? Between the ages of eighteen and twenty-five, I never lacked for girlfriends or boyfriends." Chang Jinxing never planned to have his girlfriends spend money on him at first, but eventually, he realized that his life was much easier when he lived off of women.

"What I mean is, when did you realize you like guys?" Zheng Weize asked. He was curious.

"I had this ex-girlfriend whose boyfriend liked me too," Chang Jinxing said. "After I broke up with the girl, he started pursuing me."

"He must've been very handsome too, huh?"

"Yeah," Chang Jinxing said, though he was leaving some things out. The guy had been his junior in high school, and they'd known each other for a long time. "Actually, he was a good friend of mine. We knew each other for eight years. And when he found out that I got together with his ex-girlfriend, he reacted very strongly."

"Oh. Then you went from rivals to lovers and ended up together?"

Chang Jinxing looked a bit lost. Even after all this time, he hadn't quite sorted out the messy tangle of his feelings about the whole thing. "His girlfriend liked me first," he explained. "We... It's not like I could do anything about it, but he was angry—furious, in fact. We gradually drifted apart after high school. But we were close in junior high. Yeah, he was my best friend in junior high."

"Where is he now?"

"Abroad. His family is pretty wealthy—he ended up going to Australia. Now that I think about it..." Chang Jinxing fell silent, remembering bits and pieces from the past. Did he really like that girl? It didn't seem like it now. Perhaps, subconsciously, he'd just been trying to maintain some connection to his friend. He'd never really affirmed his own sexual orientation or gone through a whole self-discovery process the way Zhang Yuwen, Yan Jun, and the others had.

"Who topped?" Zheng Weize asked.

"We switched. Let's go set off some fireworks later. I brought home some leftover sparklers from the production crew."

"Sure, but make sure to save some for when we hang out with everyone else on the sixth day of the Lunar New Year."

They finished their dinner, and as Chang Jinxing cleaned up in the kitchen, he reminisced about his past. After he broke up with that girl, his childhood friend had invited him out so that they could chat. They sat beside a flowerbed, drinking and talking about their junior high school days. His friend was still angry, though, and when the conversation turned to the topic of Chang Jinxing kissing the girl, Chang Jinxing lost his patience and blurted out, "What's the big deal about a kiss?" He turned his head as if to say, *You wanna try it too?*

The next thing he knew, he had his arms around his buddy and was kissing him. The kiss spiraled out of control, and under the influence of alcohol, Chang Jinxing brought his friend back to his place. They had already kissed, so why not take a step further into forbidden territory, right?

His friend cried and moaned as Chang Jinxing topped him, and Chang Jinxing generously let his friend top him in return. In life and in bed, they clicked surprisingly well. They understood each other well thanks to years of friendship, and with their awareness of each other's boundaries, they were able to avoid most conflicts. Their similar experiences and living environments meant they had a lot in common and their values rarely clashed.

Before Chang Jinxing knew it, they'd been together for over half a year. The other guy even bought Chang Jinxing a camera, which Chang Jinxing used for a long time before it was stolen, just like his heart. Then his lover went abroad, and their romance, which could have lasted a lifetime, came to an abrupt end.

Chang Jinxing handed the sparklers to Zheng Weize, who happily set them off in the garden. Maybe it was past time for him to reach out, he thought. He made an overseas call.

"Hello?" The voice on the phone sounded a little tired, but, hearing it, Chang Jinxing's heart skipped a beat. They hadn't spoken in seven years. When he didn't respond, the voice became more alert. "Jinxing? Is that you? Jinxing?"

Tears pricked Chang Jinxing's eyes. Perhaps meeting Kong Yu and sharing a handful of scenes with him made him nostalgic for the past, shedding light on unspoken feelings that had long since dissipated. The sadness hidden behind subtle expressions, the true meaning of unspoken words—they all became clear to him.

"Jinxing," the voice called again.

"Yue Wen," Chang Jinxing said finally.

"It's you!" Yue Wen exclaimed. "It really is you!"

Chang Jinxing chuckled. "You didn't save my number? Why am I not surprised."

"You're the one who changed it!" said Yue Wen. "Where are you? What are you doing?"

"Happy Lunar New Year. Not doing anything much. I just wanted to say best wishes for the new year."

"Where are you?"

After a moment's thought, Chang Jinxing told him that he was in Jiangdong. Yue Wen asked how he'd been doing all these years, what kind of work he'd been doing, and if he'd been well, so Chang Jinxing stood in the garden and chatted with him.

"You must have settled down by now, right?" Yue Wen said. "Are you married or on your way there?"

Chang Jinxing looked at Zheng Weize, who was lighting up sparklers in the garden. Zheng Weize turned and smiled at him. "No, no," Chang Jinxing said, amused. "Nope. Not married."

"I would've figured you'd have a cute daughter by now."

"What? That's so not me. I'm still single. How about you?"

"I'm living with Chen Anran."

"You two..." Chang Jinxing was stunned. Chen Anran was a bosom friend of their mutual ex-girlfriend.

"No, no," Yue Wen explained, "she's just staying with me and paying me rent. She's doing her graduate studies in Melbourne."

"Oh."

"I'm still single," Yue Wen added. A moment of silence passed between them. Then, suddenly, Yue Wen laughed. "Let's do a video call. I want to see you."

Chang Jinxing switched over to the video call interface. Yue Wen was in pajamas, turning on the lights in his study and looking like he'd just woken up. He was more mature than Chang Jinxing remembered. For a moment, they just smiled at each other wordlessly. Yue Wen's eyes looked a little moist.

"You're even more handsome now," Yue Wen told him, "while I've gotten old and ugly."

Chang Jinxing burst out laughing. "Come on! You're still very handsome. Really."

"Who's that?" Zheng Weize asked, popping up in the video beside Chang Jinxing. Yue Wen said hello to him.

"He's your..."

"My good friend," Chang Jinxing filled in. He sat down in front of a lounge chair at the side of the garden.

At the words "good friend," Zheng Weize slipped back into his room, having already lit all the sparklers.

"It's cold outside," Yue Wen admonished. "Don't catch a cold."

"All right."

"You're just too picky," Yue Wen said, teasing him from thousands of miles away, on the other side of the world. "That's why you're still not married."

Chang Jinxing laughed. "You're describing yourself."

Snow began to fall around him. Each tiny flake drifted through the air to the sporadic sound of firecrackers going off in the distance. He and Yue Wen studied each other's faces, trying to recapture the feelings of yesteryear.

After a moment, Yue Wen smiled. "Do you like guys or girls now?"

"I'm open to both. You?"

"Same here." Yue Wen's face reddened, and he added self-deprecatingly, "And as a result, it works out with neither."

Another brief silence fell upon them. Chang Jinxing asked, "Are you working in Australia?"

"Yeah. I'm a product manager at a software company. How about you?" Yue Wen asked. Chang Jinxing shared some anecdotes from his time with the production crew, and Yue Wen listened, nodding. "That's great."

"I'm still far from a competent professional, so I'm thinking of going back to school. Man, this is what happens when you don't study hard."

Yue Wen paused for a moment. "It's okay. A lot of people who work in the arts aren't formally trained. If you're up for it, though, you could come to Australia for further education."

"Huh? Are there photography programs in Melbourne?"

"There are plenty! Wanna give it a try? Send me your portfolio, and I can ask around at the schools for you. You don't have to go through an agency."

"But language-wise..."

"They have preparatory courses here for learning the language. English isn't hard to learn. You'll pick it up quickly in daily life."

"How much would it cost? It must be expensive, right?"

"Not at all. If you're serious, you can even apply for scholarships."

"Let me think about it," Chang Jinxing said. "I mean, life would be pretty different there."

"Yeah, that's a major consideration." Yue Wen nodded. He didn't keep trying to persuade him. They were adults now; if Chang Jinxing decided to study aboard, he would reach out to Yue Wen.

Chang Jinxing changed the subject. "So, how's Chen Anran doing?"

"Same old, same old. You know, she used to have a crush on you."

"No way!" Chang Jinxing exclaimed, deliberately dramatic. "Awkward..."

"Half the girls in our class had a crush on you. Several of them are in Australia now, actually. We're thinking of organizing a small class reunion..."

As the night wore on, Chang Jinxing rediscovered a lot of memories from the past. He wasn't the only one taking a walk down memory lane, either.

Yan Jun held a sleeping Xiao-Qi and listened as his mother recounted stories from his and his brother's childhood.

Zheng Weize returned to his room, put on his wig, applied his makeup, and logged on to chat about old times with Whiskey, who had just finished his New Year's Eve dinner.

Chen Hong was keeping his younger sister company as she set off fireworks in the streets when he bumped into the family of his junior high classmate and began chatting about their student days.

Huo Sichen, by contrast, was sleeping like the dead. He had slept the same way the night before, when they were in bed after their dinner; at one point, Zhang Yuwen genuinely felt the need to check on him to see if he was breathing. On New Year's Eve, they ate breakfast and made love again, and then Huo Sichen went back to bed, where he slept until it was time for New Year's Eve dinner. He woke dazed and disoriented, as if his body was trying to catch up on all the sleep he'd missed in the past year.

For his part, Zhang Yuwen reminisced about celebrating the new year as a child, when his grandparents took him to the riverside to set off fireworks.

Lost in their memories and the flashes of fireworks, everyone ushered in another cycle of the four seasons. And right on schedule, spring arrived, to the tranquility of thawing river water weaving through fragments of ice.

CHAPTER

39

ON THE FIFTH DAY OF the Lunar New Year, Chen Hong's gym opened its doors with a one-month soft launch. Chen Hong's experience told him that business would likely be slow in the first month, but since the fifth day of the lunar year was auspicious, he decided to go for it and open for business anyway.

He didn't want to employ his competitors' methods of hiring part-time fitness trainers and setting them loose onto the streets like a pack of stray dogs to beg passersby for food—or, in this case, to sign up for gym memberships. Instead, he took Yan Jun's advice for his new gym and treated it like a long-term private studio: He hired only one employee, a woman, and would save as much as he could on expenses like rent.

But of course, even the most modest business needed an opening ceremony. Chen Hong invited his roommates to join him for a simple ribbon-cutting ceremony at the gym entrance, intending to follow it with coffee and a chat inside. Never in his wildest dreams could he have expected the turnout he received. The studio stood between a convenience store and a gas station, in a location that got lots of natural light, and flower baskets with signs congratulating Chen Hong on his grand opening were everywhere—they were practically spilling into the road. Each of his roommates had sent two, and Yan Jun and Huo Sichen had also sent congratulations under their companies' names.

But what really threw Chen Hong for a loop was the celebrity sighting! Kong Yu wasn't *famous*-famous, but he was still a C-lister, and when his car pulled up outside the gym and he stepped out in his suit, he oozed star power. He gave the impression that he was walking the red carpet, complete with his own entrance music. Between him, the passersby who stopped to gawk, and the old clients of Chen Hong's who came to offer their congratulations, the place was full to the brim.

"Kong...Kong Yu?" Zhang Yuwen had just arrived bearing gifts, and he was just as surprised—though for different reasons than Chen Hong.

"Is that the actor?" Huo Sichen asked.

"Seems like it," Zhang Yuwen replied. "Have you seen his dramas? He's Jinxing's friend."

"Since when does Jinxing know actors?"

"He's a cameraman for a production crew."

Zhang Yuwen motioned for Huo Sichen to go on ahead, worried that Kong Yu might blow his cover by tactlessly calling him Director Zhang. Fortunately, though, Chang Jinxing had given Kong Yu a heads-up about the situation. He was in the middle of a casual chat with Kong Yu, who looked every inch the charmer in his sunglasses, and when he saw Zhang Yuwen, he made a *don't worry* gesture. Zhang Yuwen nodded in understanding and approached them.

Chen Hong bustled around, busy with his gym. In addition to the friends who came to congratulate him, there were a lot of old clients at the opening, plus a flock of gay men from the gay dating app he'd re-downloaded to advertise his gym. Zheng Weize's live stream channel also brought traffic to his gym; he'd hyped the event up before the new year, telling his viewers, "Come for the eye candy! There'll be lots of hot guys!" Consequently, gay men thronged the studio entrance like attendees at a film festival, decked out in their cutest fits. They strolled around under the clear, sunny sky, looking like marchers at a pride parade.

Of course, Yan Jun and Zheng Weize were there too. Zheng Weize even got up early to do his makeup and style Yan Jun's hair with wax. As soon as Yan Jun arrived, someone exclaimed, "Look, a hottie!" Looking like a couple, the two of them handed over their congratulatory flowers and traded hugs with Chen Hong, who hadn't returned home the previous night because he was busy tidying up the gym. Chen Hong was surprised by Yan Jun's appearance: Between his physique and his meticulously groomed hair, his looks rivaled Chang Jinxing's.

"Jun-gege! Looking good!" Chang Jinxing snapped some photos of him. "Did Weize style your hair? And did you shape your eyebrows?"

"Keep your voice down," Yan Jun muttered, embarrassed. "Where's Yuwen?"

"Over there. They just arrived too."

Zhang Yuwen was standing outside the gym, drinking a hot beverage. When Kong Yu saw his target approaching, he took off his sunglasses and said politely, "Yuwen-xiong."

"Hi!" Zhang Yuwen grinned. "Wow! You're Kong Yu, right? I've seen your shows! Can I have your autograph?"

Kong Yu broke out in a cold sweat. Chang Jinxing had sternly instructed him not to act too subservient, and he wasn't sure what to do with himself.

Huo Sichen made an inquisitive sound, but Chang Jinxing hurriedly diverted him away: "Sichen, come look at this!"

Left alone, Zhang Yuwen and Kong Yu stood off to one side and traded pleasantries, and before long, Kong Yu's manager joined them. Zhang Yuwen knew that Chang Jinxing must have convinced Kong Yu to make an appearance by telling him Zhang Yuwen would be there. Celebrities rarely did anything that didn't benefit them, and just because they'd shot a show together didn't mean they were close friends. Their relationship would have been, at best, a mixture of friendship and mutual benefit.

They were there to support a friend's gym, so Zhang Yuwen chatted with Kong Yu for a bit longer, confident that Kong Yu didn't expect this small talk to win him any major connections or privileges. Instead, he was looking to establish himself as a familiar face to Zhang Yuwen. After about ten minutes of conversation, Kong Yu summoned the courage to ask Zhang Yuwen about exchanging contact information, and Zhang Yuwen readily agreed.

"All right, it's time!" Chen Hong announced. "Let's cut the ribbon!"

Everyone came back together for the ribbon cutting. Chen Hong looked like he wanted to drag Kong Yu up to the front for a photo op, but Zhang Yuwen stopped him.

"Listen to me," Zhang Yuwen whispered. "Don't take random promotional photos of celebrities." Kong Yu was there as a favor to a friend, so he wasn't being paid for his appearance, and Chen Hong would be hard-pressed to explain things if Kong Yu were to get caught up in a scandal or controversy down the road. Zhang Yuwen did also notice a lot of gay people among the onlookers, and if he shared a photo of Kong Yu to promote his gym, Chen Hong could risk inadvertently outing him.

Thus, once Chang Jinxing got his camera set up to take a photo of the big moment, Chen Hong cut the ribbon on his own.

After the ribbon cutting, Kong Yu politely bade Chen Hong farewell and pulled him in for a firm hug. "May your business prosper," Kong Yu said, grinning.

Chen Hong was flattered. "Thanks! Thank you so much!"

Zhang Yuwen felt a lot more relaxed with Kong Yu gone. He did, however, overhear a few of Chen Hong's clients gossiping, saying Kong Yu was his sponsor's kept man and he was clearly gay. Chang Jinxing heard it, too, and it made him furious—but this was his buddy's grand opening. He couldn't go and start shit with these people.

"You heard that?" Zhang Yuwen whispered to him. "That's what being a celebrity is like. All glamour in public, but the second you turn your back, they start gossiping."

Chang Jinxing nodded. Huo Sichen, who was wandering around the gym, asked, "How did you know that guy?"

"Our publishing house once did a book on him," Zhang Yuwen explained, "and I was the editor on the project."

"Oh." Huo Sichen accepted this slapdash explanation hook, line, and sinker.

At last, Chen Hong had some spare time to chat with his friends. Everyone signed their name on the opening ceremony's backdrop wall, and Chang Jinxing took photos of each of them. They were also able to pick stickers that read "1," "0," or "0.5" from a box and stick them on the wall where the message board was.

"Who's your primary target audience for your new gym?" Huo Sichen asked Chen Hong. This was the first time Huo Sichen had encountered so many gay guys in one place, and the box with the numbered stickers perplexed him.

"I advertised on a gay dating app," Chen Hong explained. "I'm thinking of catering to the gay community."

His employee, the female trainer, was helping him handle inquiries and signing up new clients on opening day. Between the big turnout and the promotional discount they were offering, Chen Hong expected their sales figure for the day to be decent.

"I saw the message wall," Zhang Yuwen chimed in. "You're planning to organize dating and other events too, right?"

"Yup." Chen Hong was less worried about his sexual orientation being out in the open so long as he could make money. "I'll occasionally organize murder mystery games, board games, and other stuff like that. It'll be like a small club."

Huo Sichen nodded. He was drawing plenty of glances from the people coming and going, and Zhang Yuwen had noticed Huo Sichen was popular with the gym crowd. Yan Jun, too, had his fair share of admirers.

"Everyone's so friendly," Huo Sichen commented.

"Because you seem the straightest out of all of us." *And none of those guys are even trying to hide it,* Zhang Yuwen thought.

"There's a lot of bottoms here," Chen Hong added, "but it's okay. All they'll do is ogle. You don't have to worry about them coming up and grabbing your dick or anything like that."

Huo Sichen was dumbstruck. Meanwhile, people were already hitting on Yan Jun, though Zheng Weize clung tightly to his arm, his hostility palpable: *Stay away from my gege, you hos!*

"Guys, look at the message board," Chen Hong said. "We already have eight 0s, three 1s, and twelve 0.5s..." The numbers represented whether their selector was a bottom, a top, or vers.

"Are we going to have an impromptu matchmaking later?" Huo Sichen asked. "It's like a math problem; it won't be easy to match everyone."

"This is like throwing chickens and rabbits into the same cage—a total mismatch," Zhang Yuwen grumbled, even as he grabbed a sticker for himself and pasted it to the wall.

Huo Sichen took a 1 from the box, though Zhang Yuwen had taken a 0.5. Huo Sichen then took out a 0 and raised an eyebrow at Zhang Yuwen, insinuating that he should swap to 0. Zhang Yuwen shot him a glare, and Huo Sichen burst out laughing.

Yan Jun took a 1, and Zheng Weize took a 0. Chang Jinxing went over, thought for a moment, and took a 1 too. Zhang Yuwen let out his signature "Oh?"

"Oh?" everyone else said in unison. Then they doubled over with laughter.

Chang Jinxing made an inquisitive noise. "You guys got something to say? Wanna taste of my golden cudgel?" Everyone hastily declined.

People started approaching Chang Jinxing to ask for his contact information. He gave in and added a few of them on his app, wanting to get away from them as soon as possible. Meanwhile, Chen Hong chatted with Yan Jun.

"You should be able to recoup at least 70 percent of the funds you spent on this place today," Yan Jun said, handing contracts over to Chen Hong. "I closed two deals for you."

"Thank you so much! We're short on manpower. I should have hired a few more temporary workers to help out."

Yan Jun waved off his thanks. "It'll get better after a few more days."

"You're right. I'm so glad I listened to your advice."

In a rare moment of shyness, Yan Jun smiled. "I just have more experience dealing with this sort of thing."

Chen Hong had consulted with Yan Jun before opening the business, and it was fair to say that Yan Jun deserved half of the credit for the gym. He made a lot of good suggestions: starting off small by hiring one or two employees and having them take on several people's workload in exchange for higher pay or shares in the company; saving on rent and utility costs where possible; focusing on providing excellent service to every gym member; maintaining a good relationship with regulars; and, of course, not biting off more than he could chew. Chen Hong had taken all his advice and scaled back the business, and he felt a lot more relaxed as a result.

Elsewhere, a pair of close gay friends recognized Zheng Weize. "Oh wow, are you Xiao-Tu?"

"Yeah." Zheng Weize didn't recognize them, but he smiled. "You're here too, huh?"

They both grinned. "You look just like you do on the live stream!"

Zheng Weize felt thrilled to be recognized. To think he could even meet fans offline when he had so few of them! He waited, wondering if they would ask for his autograph.

"Can we take a picture together?"

"Of course!" Zheng Weize might not have been as handsome as his roommates, but his makeup skills were excellent and he didn't shy away from taking group photos.

"All right, let's get out of here already," Zhang Yuwen said. "Our host's swamped with work."

"Where should we go?" Yan Jun asked.

"How about the flower market?" Chang Jinxing suggested. "It's still open for business, and today's the last day we can get anything."

Everyone agreed. Chen Hong's composure crumbled a little as he watched his friends prepare to leave. "I wanna go too..."

"We'll hang out tomorrow," Zhang Yuwen said. "Will you be coming home tonight?"

"We'll see. I'll try my best."

Zheng Weize took a quick photo with the fans and left. Huo Sichen was driving, so Zhang Yuwen took the passenger seat, while Chang Jinxing and Yan Jun sat in the back with Zheng Weize squeezed in the middle. Since they'd ditched Chen Hong, there was just enough room for all of them. Finally, they set off.

"Which flower market?" Huo Sichen asked.

"How about the one at Dynasty Road?" Zhang Yuwen suggested. "It's livelier there, and since it's their last day, we might even score some bargains." He glanced back at Yan Jun.

"What's wrong?" said Yan Jun. "Something on my face?"

Zhang Yuwen laughed. "To think you can actually rival Jinxing with a bit of styling."

Huo Sichen glanced at Yan Jun in the rearview mirror. "I didn't even recognize you at first."

In some respects, Huo Sichen was a typical straight guy who saw Zhang Yuwen as one of the guys. Even when his partner complimented a friend's looks, Huo Sichen showed no signs of jealousy. Maybe he trusted Zhang Yuwen implicitly after the nights they'd spent together recently, or perhaps he was just so confident in himself that he didn't see Yan Jun as a love rival... Either way, his only response was to compliment Yan Jun too.

Once again, the flattery embarrassed Yan Jun.

"Where's Xiao-Qi?" Zhang Yuwen asked.

"With my ma," replied Yan Jun.

"Can your mother take care of her on her own?" Zheng Weize asked.

"Shouldn't be a problem; my aunt is there too. I'll pick her up after the Lantern Festival."

"So you finally get a break now, huh?" Huo Sichen said light-heartedly.

"Yeah, but I'm not used to it. Sometimes, it feels like I need her more than she needs me."

Zhang Yuwen glanced at Huo Sichen and smiled. Naturally, Huo Sichen understood what Zhang Yuwen was thinking, and he murmured, "Love is all about mutual need."

Everyone fell silent. A moment later, Zhang Yuwen and Chang Jinxing spoke simultaneously:

Zhang Yuwen said, "Yan Jun?"

Chang Jinxing said, "Sichen."

Yan Jun and Huo Sichen responded in unison, but Zhang Yuwen and Chang Jinxing didn't know who should go first. After a moment, Chang Jinxing gestured for Zhang Yuwen to go ahead, so Zhang Yuwen asked, "Is Hong-ge's business viable?"

Yan Jun didn't answer. Huo Sichen was a finance expert too, but he was too busy, and Chen Hong hadn't wanted to impose on him. Even though he was the one who brought Huo Sichen and Zhang Yuwen together, there still seemed to be a barrier between them.

"Do you have a cost sheet?" Huo Sichen asked. He knew Zhang Yuwen cared about Chen Hong and wanted him to make money. "I'll know once I look at it."

"Yan Jun saw it," Zhang Yuwen said. "He was the one who gave Hong-ge advice before the grand opening."

"It's hard to say," Yan Jun replied finally, "but there's potential. It'll depend on how he manages operations down the line."

Zhang Yuwen met Yan Jun's eyes in the rearview mirror. "How about breaking even?"

"That won't be a problem, but I'm worried he'll start spending indiscriminately again once he gets there."

Zhang Yuwen nodded and said nothing more. He'd considered investing in Chen Hong's business; for him, losing a few hundred thousand or even a million yuan was no different from breaking a vase at home. If he'd become an investor, however, it would have inevitably changed their relationship. Zhang Yuwen's grandparents had always told him growing up that a person should never go into business with their buddies.

Zhang Yuwen was hoping Chen Hong could do a good job running his gym.

After a bit of thoughtful silence, Chang Jinxing said, "Yuwen."

"What's up?"

"Have you ever been abroad?"

"Are you thinking of traveling overseas?" Huo Sichen asked, butting in.

"I've been talking to a friend of mine about furthering my studies abroad," Chang Jinxing said with some uncertainty. "But the process seems pretty complicated. And the tuition is really expensive, right?"

"Tuition shouldn't be a problem," Zhang Yuwen said. "Lots of students work part-time to pay for their tuition, and schools overseas offer scholarships, too, which is like the financial aid we have here. You can apply so long as you meet the requirements... Ah, here we are, the flower market. Let's get out first."

Back at the gym, Chen Hong worked out his income. He'd signed on a good number of new members in addition to his returning clients, and even at the promotional price, he'd recouped somewhere in the range of 60 to 70 percent of his initial investment. Next, he'd have to recruit new members and sell training sessions. The opening went much better than he'd expected, and it was all thanks to his roommates' support.

Gradually, the crowd of gay men who came to gawk dispersed. Chen Hong picked up a 1 and stuck it on the message board.

Facing the wall full of 0s, 1s, and 0.5s, he was struck by a sudden pang of melancholy. It felt as if there was no refuge for his soul to seek and no direction for his body to move in. All his experiences, the people he'd loved, his family and career—they were all reduced to a simple label representing a gay sex position, pinned to the center of a board for others to gawk at and judge.

He took the 1 down, then, after a moment's thought, put it back up.

Most of the crowd was gone, and the trainer began her training session. Chen Hong picked up some forms to schedule training sessions for his new members, but just then, someone else arrived.

"Welcome, feel free to look around," Chen Hong told his new arrival. The man walked over to Chen Hong and stood in front of the coffee table. "Would you like something to drink?"

Then Chen Hong looked up and, to his surprise, saw that it was Mr. Elite.

Mr. Elite had told Chen Hong to call him Dong, and to Chen Hong's surprise, they ended up chatting a fair bit on the messaging app. Mostly, though, they just shared info about local food and entertainment; by unspoken agreement, they avoided talking about their private lives. Chen Hong did share some of Dong's messages with Yan Jun, who called him Mr. Dong.

After the first time, Mr. Dong had asked Chen Hong to hook up three more times, but Chen Hong had been busy lately, so they'd only met up once, during the day. Mr. Dong booked the room, and Chen Hong took some time off from the renovation and rode his motorcycle over the hotel to get down and dirty with him. He liked

Dong's body; his fair skin, minimal body fat, defined abs, and long legs that seemed effortlessly toned. A physique like that was all genetics, and it seemed like it ought to belong to a bottom, not a top. When Chen Hong fucked him, he asked, "Aren't you supposed to be a top? Huh? You like getting fucked? You like it when I take you like this?"

There was no doubt in his mind that their second encounter had left an unforgettable impression on Mr. Dong.

For Chen Hong, dominating someone who identified as a top was extremely sexy and gratifying. More importantly, Dong had a great body and was very cooperative. He wasn't shy and didn't hold back in bed, which made Chen Hong remember his time with his ex. After a few intimate encounters, Chen Hong considered making Mr. Dong a regular long-term hook-up partner. Maybe that would alleviate the anxiety of being single.

At his grand opening, a lot of the men who showed up couldn't take their eyes off Chen Hong, and some of them tried to proposition him. Some even tried to discreetly seduce him by asking how many credits they needed to buy for their gym membership to qualify for private lessons. Chen Hong politely declined all the offers, determined not to get involved with his gym members again. He'd had sex with his gym members the last time because he was enticed by the promise of commissions, and that led to a lifetime of regrets. He'd been young and foolish, and hadn't realized that temptation always came with a hefty price tag; he would not make the same mistake again.

In the evening, when everyone was gone, the trainer came up to him. "Boss, I'm done for the day."

"Thanks for your hard work," Chen Hong said.

"Not open for business at night?" Mr. Dong asked as he sat down at the coffee table.

"Overtime? Before the holidays are over? The staff will riot," Chen Hong said. "So...are you going to sign up for a gym membership?"

"I could sign up for one to support your business."

"What business? It's all just for fun." Chen Hong wasn't in the least bit polite with Dong, and his words were sometimes barbed. He always had the vague feeling that Dong looked down on him. Dong always had this polite demeanor that reflected his elite upbringing, but his politeness was nothing like Zhang Yuwen's—or rather, it was a bit like the attitude Zhang Yuwen had when they first met. Once they got to know each other, however, it became apparent that Zhang Yuwen saw all his roommates as his equals and treated them with empathy and respect. Dong's courtesy, on the other hand, was more obligatory; the kind that a person might show to drivers, security guards, and cleaning ladies. It was only meant to demonstrate his good upbringing: *Your manners don't matter, but I must appear polite.*

Vexed and preoccupied with scheduling his gym members for training sessions, Chen Hong ignored Dong, so Dong was watching him from his seat off to the side.

"You're being a little rude," Dong said. "I made a special point of coming here to show my support."

"You gonna sign up for a gym membership?" Chen Hong asked.

"Sure. Where's your card reader? Will it include private home training sessions?"

"Nope, I don't have time. If you sign up, you'll have to come here for your sessions."

Dong thought about it for a moment. "Fine."

Chen Hong brought over the card reader. "How many credits do you want to buy?"

"Let's do a hundred thousand."

"We don't have an option that expensive. Stop messing with me."

"Then, what's the highest tier you have? Any special perks?"

Chen Hong barked a laugh. "The Platinum VIP tier gives you priority for booking training sessions. It costs twenty thousand yuan."

"Just twenty thousand? Let's go with that, then."

Chen Hong was tempted to mock him but dropped it. A paying client was a paying client. He knew Dong must be rich, judging by his luxury car. He'd be a fool not to take money that was basically falling into his hands, so he swiped the card for twenty thousand yuan. Dong signed his name on the contract, and Chen Hong finally learned that his name was Dong You.

"When do you want to start the sessions?" Chen Hong asked.

"How about now? Shouldn't you come up with a fitness plan for me, though?"

"That'll depend on your goal. Do you want to build chest muscles? Abs? Strength? Cardio?"

"Why don't you look at my body first and see which parts I need to work on?"

"Sure. I'll take a look if you strip."

"Fully naked?"

"Fully naked."

"I'm wearing a thong today," Dong You said. "Should I take that off too?"

"You can keep it on. What color?"

"Your favorite. Want me to strip right here?"

Chen Hong closed the main door, locked it, put up the closed sign, and led Dong You to the small back room where BMI was taken. Dong You unbuttoned his shirt, revealing his fair pecs and abs. Chen Hong undressed, too, and Dong You started caressing him. Chen Hong pulled Dong You's pants down, and sure enough, he was wearing sexy underwear.

Chen Hong hadn't had sex for the whole week he went back home for the holidays, and he was so horny he could burst. He poured some massage oil onto his palm, and they had sex right there in the closed gym.

There were mirrors everywhere in the gym, but after a while, Chen Hong wasn't finding it exciting enough. He moved to fuck Dong You from behind, making him put a leg up on one of the workout machines so that he could see Chen Hong entering him. It still wasn't enough, so Chen Hong made him touch the spot where their bodies melded into one to feel it too. Dong You's face flushed red, and his moans came in a ceaseless stream as Chen Hong drove him to the brink of ecstasy.

Nearly an hour later, the two of them showered. Dong You straightened his disheveled shirt and returned to his elite self. "Wanna grab a meal?" he asked.

Chen Hong stepped out wearing a gym tank top and sports pants, and Dong You went up to him and fondled his crotch. "Why?" said Chen Hong, letting him do as he pleased. "Looking for more? Not satisfied yet?"

Dong You let go. "I know a decent restaurant nearby," he said coolly.

"Nah, I still have another thing tonight. Maybe another day."

Chen Hong knew that Dong You must have had a costly restaurant in mind. He didn't want Dong You to treat him, but if he treated Dong You instead, his wallet would weep, and asking to split the bill would make him look like a clown.

Every time, after they had sex, Dong You asked Chen Hong out for a meal. He seemed to want to get to know Chen Hong better. But Chen Hong knew that they belonged to different worlds, and he didn't want to get too involved, so he turned down every invitation that didn't involve the use of their lower bodies.

"That's what you said the last time," Dong You pointed out.

"I'm really busy." Chen Hong gestured around the gym, suggesting that Dong You could see for himself.

"Okay, but you can't turn me down next time."

Chen Hong hummed in acknowledgment. Dong You was clearly smitten with him, mostly because Chen Hong acted all cool and reticent around him, but he was pretty wild in bed—nothing like his usual, obedient-puppy persona.

Dong You hesitated for a moment, then leaned in and gave him a peck on the cheek. The gesture touched Chen Hong. In his opinion, kisses during sex meant nothing—that was only an expression that lust was running high—but kisses in the aftermath meant "I like you."

That was all it was, though: like. Chen Hong thought about it, then returned the gesture with a kiss on the lips. As Dong You was leaving, Chen Hong said, "Platinum members also get some gifts: a thermos bottle, a hair dryer..."

"It's fine, keep them for yourself," Dong You said.

All right, then. Chen Hong put down the membership gift set and watched with mixed feelings as Dong You left.

It was the last day of the Spring Festival holidays, but the flower market was still a bustling hive of activity. The guys strolled around at leisure. Zheng Weize was still clinging onto Yan Jun's arm, and Zhang Yuwen was answering Chang Jinxing's questions about life abroad, leaving Huo Sichen by himself.

This Spring Festival, the roommates' wallets were visibly bulging; a far cry from the days when they'd just moved in, when they'd had to scrimp and save every penny.

Chang Jinxing and Zhang Yuwen trailed behind the rest of them; Chang Jinxing listened to Zhang Yuwen talk, nodding now and then. The problems of language, finances, and studies could all be overcome. The biggest challenge of all, it seemed, was something that he hadn't yet considered: culture shock.

Zhang Yuwen bought a lot of flowers to decorate their home, and Zheng Weize purchased several small ornaments and picked out a small gift—a "safe travel" hanging charm for drivers. Zhang Yuwen and Yan Jun glanced at Zheng Weize when he asked the merchant to wrap it up.

The flower market's exit happened to be right in front of the food stall where Zhang Yuwen and Huo Sichen had had their first lunch date. It was noisy and bustling on the fifth day of the Spring Festival, and they all squeezed into a square table at the corner and chatted among themselves.

It was nightfall when Huo Sichen finally dropped them off at No. 7 Riverbay Road. After they made plans with him to have a barbecue at the riverside park the following day, Zhang Yuwen opened the door and entered.

Inside, the lights were on. Chen Hong was wearing an apron and arranging ingredients on bamboo skewers for the next day's barbecue. "Why are you all just getting back now?!" he howled.

"Have you had dinner yet?" Zhang Yuwen asked, realizing what had happened.

"No!" Chen Hong was crying inside. "I called you guys, but either your phones were turned off or you didn't pick up! Did you guys plan this?!"

"My phone died!" Zhang Yuwen explained quickly.

Chen Hong looked at Yan Jun. "What about you?"

"I was carrying a flowerpot the whole time, so I didn't check my phone."

"I was taking photos the whole way," Chang Jinxing added. "Sorry."

"Why didn't you call me?" Zheng Weize asked.

"I thought you guys would be back soon," Chen Hong muttered.

"I brought you takeout," Zhang Yuwen told him. "See? Fried rice and three-cup chicken in pandan leaves." Chen Hong accepted it reluctantly, and Zhang Yuwen smiled. "You can eat more tomorrow to make up for it."

Noticing Chen Hong's low spirits, Zheng Weize leaned over the dining table to peer at him. "What's wrong?"

"Huh? Oh, nothing. I'm just tired."

"How did it all turn out today?" Yan Jun asked.

"Great, thanks to you guys and Jinxing."

They all observed Chen Hong closely, trying to discern whether he was miffed about being left behind. Zhang Yuwen didn't think it warranted that much of a reaction, but Chen Hong did appear troubled. He seemed like a completely different person from the one they left behind at the gym earlier in the day.

Yan Jun made a finger heart gesture to Zhang Yuwen, who understood immediately, although Chen Hong had told him nothing about his love life recently. In truth, Yan Jun was also just speculating. He didn't see the fuck buddy Chen Hong told him about at the opening, so his guess was that Chen Hong had fallen for Mr. Dong and was sad that he didn't show up for the big day.

Everyone sat down to help Chen Hong skewer the ingredients and prepare the grill and charcoal for the barbecue. Through it all, Chen Hong was distracted, and when they were done, most of them returned to their rooms to pack for the trip. Only Zhang Yuwen and Chen Hong remained at the dining table.

"How are things between you and Sichen?" Chen Hong asked.

"As promised, you can have a one-month waiver on your rent," Zhang Yuwen said.

Chen Hong laughed. "No need for that. It's my duty to pay the rent anyway."

"I promised you, though. Or how about I give you a gift as a commission for acting as a go-between?"

Chen Hong leaned closer to Zhang Yuwen and whispered, "Can you lend me your...uh, the landlord's Bentley?"

"Oh?"

Chen Hong looked at Zhang Yuwen. Despite his pensive expression, Zhang Yuwen nodded and smiled.

Riverbay Road
MEN'S DORMITORY

CHAPTER

40

JIANGDONG WELCOMED A WARM SPRING on the sixth day of the Lunar New Year. The thin layer of ice over the Liujin River melted completely, and in the warmer weather, the temperature in the city returned to nearly 68 degrees Fahrenheit. Parks and other outdoor spaces bustled with people who were eager to take a stroll and enjoy the sun on the penultimate day of their week off.

In the men's dormitory at No. 7 Riverbay Road, the guys started getting up at around ten o'clock. Once awake, they sprang into action, and when they were all ready, they headed out to Beitan Park on the Liujin River with their backpacks to meet up with Huo Sichen; he had gone ahead to secure a spot at the riverside for their barbecue and other outdoor activities. As they got ready to go, each roommate had a strange sense that something was missing. It wasn't until they saw Yan Jun leave the house empty-handed, with only his hiking backpack, that they realized: *Oh, Xiao-Qi isn't here.*

"It's not just you. We all feel so off without Xiao-Qi around," Zhang Yuwen said.

"She's spent nearly half of her life with you guys," Yan Jun said. Xiao-Qi had been only six months old when Yan Jun started raising her, and by this point, she'd lived at No. 7 Riverbay Road for almost four months.

"Is she adjusting well to life in the countryside?" Zhang Yuwen asked. The two of them stood chatting at the side of the bus.

"To be honest, not really. But my mother wants to keep her there. When I tried to leave, Xiao-Qi kept calling for me... It was hard for me to explain, so I had to sneak away."

When Yan Jun took her home for the Spring Festival, Xiao-Qi kept calling him Papa, which struck their visiting relatives as strange. Yan Jun, scrambling, offered brotherly resemblance as an excuse.

"She never calls for Mama," Zhang Yuwen pointed out. "That'd stand out too."

Yan Jun laughed. "Yeah, she only calls for Papa and Yuwen now. My mother kept asking me who Yuwen was. She thought it was my girlfriend." Zhang Yuwen laughed. Now that they were on the subject, Yan Jun took the opportunity to ask, "How are things between you and Huo Sichen?"

"We're official now."

"Oh." Yan Jun nodded. "That's great."

It occurred to Zhang Yuwen then that interactions between Yan Jun and Huo Sichen had decreased noticeably since the night they drank together during the Solar New Year. "He said he'd like to treat everyone to a meal."

"Sure, but not today. This is supposed to be my treat."

"Yeah." Zhang Yuwen smiled.

Yan Jun didn't pry for details about Zhang Yuwen and Huo Sichen's relationship. Over the last little while, he'd come to terms with his feelings. He liked Zhang Yuwen, and those feelings had ballooned beyond a longing for his own ideal life into an uncontrollable love.

Perhaps it was because of Xiao-Qi's absence that Yan Jun's attention finally returned to himself. Or maybe it was the trip back to his hometown and his mother's insistence that he settle down that had forced him to confront his feelings again. Whatever the reason, last night he'd tossed and turned in the bed where he slept alone, his mind continually replaying Zhang Yuwen's compliment on his looks. He considered getting up to go chat with Zhang Yuwen, since it was still early in the night and he could hear Zhang Yuwen's and Chen Hong's voices downstairs, but he feared that Zhang Yuwen might figure out what was on his mind. Finally, just before eleven, he couldn't resist the urge anymore and put on his pajamas, but by the time he stepped out, Zhang Yuwen had already gone back to his room.

Now that Xiao-Qi wasn't around, he didn't have to play the role of super dad; he had time to be himself. He'd grown used to being super dad, though, and on the few occasions he was able to break away from that persona, he felt a little unmoored. To combat it, he tried hard to recall his student days and transport himself back to that time. That morning, for their outing, he carefully chose his clothes, styled his hair, and sat in the living room to wait for Zhang Yuwen. Finally, he picked up his heavy backpack and headed out with everyone else.

Surprisingly enough, the park wasn't all that crowded when they arrived. Huo Sichen was already there waiting for them, and as Yan Jun watched him set up the grill, a pang of melancholy hit him. Things had not developed in the direction he hoped for. He searched for signs that Huo Sichen and Zhang Yuwen were incompatible and told himself with conviction that they would eventually break up.

But would I have the courage to confess my love to Yuwen even if they did?

Yan Jun sighed inwardly. He had a one-year-old daughter and an elderly mother to care for. To Zhang Yuwen, he was an even less ideal suitor than Huo Sichen. That much, he knew.

"Are we cooking yet?" asked Zheng Weize, who only cared about eating. "I'm starving!"

"I'll start grilling now," Chang Jinxing said. Zhang Yuwen got the fire going, and Huo Sichen stood next to him, watching.

"Wanna try your hand at archery?" Chen Hong asked Yan Jun. There was an archery booth just next to where they'd set up. Yan Jun went with Chen Hong to shoot arrows, and Zheng Weize asked them to win him some prizes. Meanwhile, Huo Sichen, Zhang Yuwen, and Chang Jinxing prepped the food and chatted about studying abroad.

"So have you decided yet?" Zhang Yuwen asked.

"Uh... I guess I'm about 80 percent sure," said Chang Jinxing.

"You'll adapt," Huo Sichen reassured him. "You're just going for a few years. It's not like you're never coming back."

"I kind of can't bear to leave my current life," Chang Jinxing said. "It's strange. I've lived on Riverbay Road for less than half a year, but it feels like it's been much longer."

"You can go," Zhang Yuwen told him. "I'll save your room for you. I won't rent it to anyone else."

From a distance, Chen Hong called out, "Sichen! Wanna give this a try?" Huo Sichen headed over to join them at archery.

Chen Hong had lured Huo Sichen away only because he sensed that Yan Jun was feeling down. He didn't know why, but something told him that he should tear Zhang Yuwen and Huo Sichen apart and pair Zhang Yuwen up with Yan Jun. Maybe it was just that he was on better terms with Yan Jun than Huo Sichen? It would have been too obvious to send Yan Jun to Zhang Yuwen right after he'd called Huo Sichen over, though, so they shot another set of twelve arrows before Yan Jun said, "I'm going to check on things over there."

Zhang Yuwen stood at the grill with Chang Jinxing, watching him flip the sizzling food. "No. 7 Riverbay Road is mine," he said to Chang Jinxing.

"Uh-huh," Chang Jinxing said. "You're a director, right? After that whole incident, I looked you up and watched a few of your films."

"To tell the truth, at first, I was just thinking—"

"Hush." Chang Jinxing shot Zhang Yuwen an enigmatic smile, and Zhang Yuwen fell silent. "I think Hong-ge might have figured it out too."

"I'll come clean when the time is right," Zhang Yuwen said.

"That definitely hasn't even crossed Weize or Jun-ge's minds. Speaking of which...Yuwen, are you super rich? You own such an expensive house."

"Uh... Kinda, I guess?" Zhang Yuwen said sheepishly. He knew he'd acted unconscionably, and very disrespectfully, by using his roommates as material for his novel. He swore that was only at the beginning, though. Over time, he stopped thinking of them that way.

"You have tens of millions, right? Tell me so that I can get a taste of that lifestyle," said Chang Jinxing. Zhang Yuwen laughed awkwardly. "Maybe one day I'll become a famous photographer and make a lot of money too."

"Well," Zhang Yuwen said slowly, "to be honest, I don't know exactly how much I have."

"Now you're just asking for a beating!"

"I mean, I have financial advisors managing it for me."

"Figures. What's your rough estimate?"

Zhang Yuwen thought for a moment. "Maybe a few hundred million? About six hundred million including No. 7 Riverbay Road, I guess. Some of that was left to me by my grandparents, and the rest came from investments in films. My actual fee as a director isn't all that much."

Had Zhang Yuwen said thirty million, Chang Jinxing might have envied him. But six hundred million was so far beyond his comprehension that he couldn't even be jealous. Nodding dazedly, he said, "So you're way richer than Sichen."

"I...guess so?" In Zhang Yuwen's eyes, Huo Sichen's financial situation wasn't all that different from Zheng Weize's. He didn't like Huo Sichen for his wealth or success, anyway.

Zhang Yuwen trusted Chang Jinxing; he was a discreet man, and he'd kept Zhang Yuwen's secret for this long already. For all that he looked like the kind of guy who loved to shoot his mouth off, he was surprisingly sensible. Zhang Yuwen had noticed that his roommates all shared a common trait: Everyone needed money, but they never coveted what wasn't theirs.

"But I gotta warn you," Chang Jinxing said. "Remember at the hot spring, when Sichen got wasted and kept saying sorry to you?"

"Yeah. He even cried when we returned to the room. Maybe it was just work stress..."

Yan Jun arrived in time to hear the end of Zhang Yuwen's sentence. "Who's stressed at work?" he asked.

"You," Chang Jinxing and Zhang Yuwen said in unison.

"Am I? Grill more shrimp. Xiao-Qi can—oh, she's not here. Never mind."

Zhang Yuwen laughed. "Don't burn them," he said. "Watch out for dioxin." He rarely had barbecue because it was extremely unhealthy in the eyes of doctors.

"Okay." Yan Jun took over for Chang Jinxing and told him to take a break off to the side. To Zhang Yuwen, he asked, "What else?"

"Benzopyrene, sulfur oxide, and some tiny tar particles. But it's okay to have some every once in a while." Yan Jun laughed, and Zhang Yuwen called over to the archery booth, "Hey! Mr. CEO!"

Huo Sichen promptly put his bow and arrows down and came over to help. "What can I do for you, young master?"

"You're just here taking up space." His implication: *You're not contributing.*

"I can't cook for nuts," Huo Sichen explained. "I'll burn the food."

Huo Sichen had no life skills to speak of. He hadn't put any points into domestic chores in his skill tree, nor did he want to. It wasn't that he was averse to getting his clothes dirty or smelling like grease, though; to a business major like him, cooking was like conducting a chemistry experiment.

"I'll teach you," Zhang Yuwen said. "Observe carefully. Proteins denature at high temperatures, but they shouldn't come into direct contact with open flames. When a shrimp's shell visibly turns a light, pearlescent red—that is, RGB values 255, 179, 230, give or take 3— that means it's cooked."

Yan Jun stared at him, astonished.

"Next, sprinkle about 0.2 grams of salt evenly on each one and glaze them with sauce."

Huo Sichen cracked up. "This is so much easier to understand than a cooking show."

Just then, Yan Jun received a call and moved away to answer. Huo Sichen and Zhang Yuwen fiddled around with the food, and Huo Sichen was, as promised, so clumsy that he kept making Zhang Yuwen laugh. Feeling warm, Huo Sichen took off his jacket, rolled up his shirt sleeves, and got grilling. While his eyes were on the food, Zhang Yuwen's were on his face. He seemed to become more and more handsome the longer Zhang Yuwen looked at him.

After the day they finally slept together, Huo Sichen had been mostly restrained when it came to physical intimacy. Now that they were in their honeymoon phase, though, he couldn't get enough of Zhang Yuwen. Aside from the previous night, when Zhang Yuwen returned home to Riverbay Road, they'd spent every moment together from the second last day of the year to the fifth day of the new year. Huo Sichen wanted more, but he didn't want to smother Zhang Yuwen, so he restrained himself and only asked to have sex once every night. Zhang Yuwen didn't turn him down. In fact, he adapted to his new role, and what started as a painful but pleasurable experience had evolved into mutual exploration and discovery of each other's bodies.

Being with a top felt comfortable; they were both emotionally stable, a rare and valuable quality in modern men. There was no need for either of them to guess at what the other was thinking or worry about setting the other off by saying the wrong thing. This minimized the mental fatigue that they might otherwise have experienced in this stage of a relationship.

"See, you can do it," Zhang Yuwen told him.

"When are you going to move in?" Huo Sichen asked.

"Huh?" Zhang Yuwen was taken aback. He didn't understand why Huo Sichen would ask him that.

"I want to eat the meals you cook." Huo Sichen blushed and avoided Zhang Yuwen's eyes. "Will you move in and live with me?"

Zhang Yuwen gave Huo Sichen a skeptical look. Huo Sichen set the grilled meat aside and met his gaze, his eyes betraying his nervousness, and Zhang Yuwen laughed.

"I'm serious," Huo Sichen said.

"Do you know what you're asking?"

"Huh? Did I say something wrong?"

Zhang Yuwen thought for a moment. "No, you didn't."

"I want to live with you, Yuwen."

"Why?"

"You lead an interesting life. Mine is dull. I want to be close to you and live vicariously through you."

"I just don't keep office hours," Zhang Yuwen said, smiling. "Anyone who stays at home would be interesting to you."

"There are lots of uninteresting guys who stay at home out there. Don't be so modest. Move in with me instead of staying at your friend's house. I can help you move after the Spring Festival."

"You're very..." Zhang Yuwen sighed. "You haven't thought this through, have you?"

"What?" Huo Sichen was baffled. From the look on Zhang Yuwen's face, Huo Sichen could tell he was being rebuffed, but he didn't know why. His heart sank, but he didn't probe, just muttered, "Oh," and lowered his head to return his attention to the grill.

Zhang Yuwen found his reaction interesting. "Are you upset?"

"No," Huo Sichen said, his expression serious.

"What I mean is, have you really thought it through? Living together, I mean."

Suddenly, Huo Sichen saw a glimmer of hope. "Yes. I don't want to be apart from you. I want to be with you every moment of every day. It's just like Yan Jun said: Seeing you at home every day after I got off work would be a dream come true. Maybe that's all I've ever wanted in my life."

Zhang Yuwen found himself moved by Huo Sichen's words, and he decided it was time to have a serious conversation. No more beating around the bush. This wasn't the right place for it, but Huo Sichen's earnest proposal required a proper response regardless of the location.

"We really shouldn't be talking about this during a barbecue," Zhang Yuwen said, "but I love you, Sichen."

"I know. I love you, Yuwen. Does this sound like a marriage proposal? Sorry, I didn't mean to be flippant—"

"No, it's okay. But when I asked if you knew what that meant, I was really asking if you've thought about all the responsibilities we would take on. For example, who will do the household chores and cook the meals? Who will manage the finances? Will we have a joint account? Or will someone take charge of all the daily expenses? Who will have the final say if we disagree on household matters? Who will pay for the utilities and keep the house? And do we need to split up responsibilities for household maintenance? What expectations do we have of each other? What are our hopes for the future? If we fight, how will we resolve it? And..."

Huo Sichen listened to him, and what he heard in Zhang Yuwen's words was that anything was possible when they were in love and both parties went to great lengths to accommodate each other. That was what Zhang Yuwen meant: He'd compromised on his preferred sexual position, so what else was there that they couldn't accommodate? Once they started living together, however, it would no longer just be a matter of picking up the tab, exchanging gifts, or checking into a hotel for a romp beneath the sheets.

Zhang Yuwen wanted to add, *Besides, the decor in your place is too minimalist, and I ain't about to live in a high-rise,* but he restrained himself. Huo Sichen had bought that condo with his savings, and he'd shown it to Zhang Yuwen like a bird flaunting its love nest—painstakingly constructed out of dry twigs and leaves for the mate it drew in with its courtship song. Sincerity like that should be respected and never scorned, no matter what the context.

But Zhang Yuwen didn't want to move out of No. 7 Riverbay Road. He was already thinking about the best way to come clean with Huo Sichen. And now, he was caught in a trap of his own making, because he was the one who set the rule about no overnight guests. Sure, his roommates might accept a rule change, but he knew it would still feel awkward.

"You're right." Huo Sichen accepted Zhang Yuwen's words calmly. "I think we can do this."

He turned, apparently searching for something, but Zhang Yuwen said, "We should both take some time to sort out our thoughts. I need to think it over too."

Huo Sichen wanted to strike while the iron was hot and make a decision promptly, but for now, all he could do was nod.

Just then, Yan Jun returned, and Zhang Yuwen called out, "Mealtime! The food's ready, you bunch of lazy bums!"

Chang Jinxing downed the last of his coffee and came over. "Good job, you two!"

Most of them were starving, having skipped breakfast, and they began to split up the food. Yan Jun, however, surprised them all by putting on his coat and saying, "Sorry, I have to leave now."

"Overtime?" Zhang Yuwen asked.

"Someone from my hometown came to Jiangdong. My brother's friend's kid. He brought some stuff with him to visit my brother and sister-in-law."

"He doesn't know?" Chen Hong asked.

"Nope. I have to pick him up at the station."

"Want to take my car?" Huo Sichen asked.

"No need. I might not be coming home today."

"All right," said Zhang Yuwen. "Is he here to sightsee?"

"How old is he?" Zheng Weize asked.

"Nineteen. He's not here for sightseeing." Yan Jun sounded resigned. "He wants to enroll in a cram school in Jiangdong for the spring season and get into the university here. Anyway, I've got to go."

"Okay, sounds good." Everyone bade him farewell and reminded him not to rush.

As they dug into their barbecue, everyone praised Huo Sichen's cooking and told him that he had culinary talent. Their actions, however, betrayed them: They reached first for the food Chang Jinxing had made, then for Zhang Yuwen's. When all was said and done, there were still a few of Huo Sichen's masterpieces remaining, so Zhang Yuwen finished them off to spare his feelings.

This gesture may have been unnecessary, though. Huo Sichen was distracted, apparently preoccupied by the questions Zhang Yuwen had raised before their meal.

Can I bring him back 2 Riverbay Road 4 a while? Yan Jun texted Zhang Yuwen. *Idk where else 2 go, and I dont wanna sit around in the coffee shop.*

ofc. he's ur guest, it's no problem, Zhang Yuwen replied.

After a day of barbecue and outdoor fun in the park, they headed back home, chatting and laughing. When they arrived, they saw a nineteen-year-old boy sitting on the sofa. Yan Jun was making tea for him.

The boy was in sportswear, and his physique was a lot like Yan Jun's—tall and lean, but sturdy. He had the look about him of a high school basketball player.

"Hi," Zhang Yuwen said. "It's nice to meet you."

The boy, apparently a sensible young man, stood right up to greet them. "Hello."

"This is Shen Yingjie," Yan Jun said.

They exchanged greetings. Yan Jun had called him a kid earlier, so everyone was picturing a child, but when he stood up, he was as tall as Zhang Yuwen and sturdy to boot. Presumably he was of mixed highland heritage too, but his complexion was even fairer than Yan Jun's, which surprised the rest of them.

"Your name sounds like it belongs to the hero in a novel." Zheng Weize grinned, his eyes practically screaming, "Hottie! Hottie!" Zhang Yuwen shot him a warning glance, though, so Zheng Weize refrained from messing with Yan Jun's guest.

Zhang Yuwen pushed Chang Jinxing toward the kitchen. "Let's cook."

"Again?" Chang Jinxing had just returned from a day of fun, and now he had to cook again for this huge pack of young men? Usually, he filled the rice cooker to the brim, and they devoured it all. With an extra person, there wouldn't be enough rice in the pot to go around.

"Just make him some noodles," said Yan Jun. "I'll make arrangements for him again after dinner. There are some local specialties here—two freshly slaughtered free-range chickens and eggs from the countryside."

Zhang Yuwen noticed that Shen Yingjie's eyes were red, as if he'd been crying. He figured that Yan Jun must have told him the truth.

"Let's all just have noodles. I'm too lazy to stir-fry anything," said Chang Jinxing.

Of course, a chef's idea of "lazy" was different from a layperson's. He stewed chicken broth, cooked a big pot of noodles, and fried a dozen eggs with the efficiency of a cafeteria matron. In the end, the group cleaned their plates—especially Shen Yingjie, who wolfed down four bowls of noodles. Even Yan Jun was in awe. The appetite of a nineteen-year-old boy was a wondrous thing to behold.

"Look at you, and now look at him," Chang Jinxing said to Zheng Weize.

Zheng Weize couldn't stop laughing. Red-faced, Shen Yingjie looked at Yan Jun and said, "Uncle."

"Don't worry about it," Yan Jun told him. "I'll clean up."

Shen Yingjie kept thanking him, and in addition to all his thank-yous and sorrys, he addressed Yan Jun as "uncle." The roommates, finding him polite and sensible, offered Shen Yingjie New Year's gift money, and Shen Yingjie didn't dare to accept until Yan Jun told him to just take it.

"He called you uncle," Chen Hong said. "I feel old."

"His father is a good friend of my brother's, so he calls me uncle too," Yan Jun explained. He was nine years older than Shen Yingjie, so that was normal, but it made the rest of them sigh with emotion.

While uncle and nephew cleared the table and washed the dishes, everyone else returned to their respective rooms. Zhang Yuwen lay down on his bed and turned on a video game, but before he could get into it, a message from Huo Sichen popped up on his phone: *r u asleep?*

Zhang Yuwen replied to the message offhandedly and began his game, thinking about how, if they were to live together, he could watch movies or play games with Huo Sichen all night. When he got stuck in a game, he could just get Huo Sichen to help him. That didn't seem so bad.

Several more messages came in from Huo Sichen. *I thought abt it a lot. ur right. I'd like 2 talk abt our future. I've got several proposals. Wanna hear em?*

Now? Zhang Yuwen asked.

Is now ok? Or is it 2 late?

What do you think?

Huo Sichen must have decided it was late, because he replied, *Another day then. But I still wanna find time soon to talk to u abt another thing.*

I want to talk to u abt something too, Zhang Yuwen said.

Sometimes, Zhang Yuwen did not understand how Huo Sichen's mind worked. He was highly skilled in his field, and his graduate program was the most competitive one at the finance and economics university. In general, his EQ also seemed extraordinarily high, but sometimes, when they were together, it fluctuated wildly.

Perhaps men who were in love tended to speak without thinking? Zhang Yuwen himself was sometimes like that too, he realized. Especially since he and Huo Sichen made things official.

Huo Sichen had been typing for a while. Zhang Yuwen sent him another message: *Not fishing these days?*

Huo Sichen: *After I got to know u, fishing started to seem lackluster in comparison. U craving fish?*

Zhang Yuwen: *Yeah, a little.*

Huo Sichen: *Join me. I still have 1 more day off tmrw.*

Zhang Yuwen: *Yessir.*

In the game, Zhang Yuwen was about start a boss fight. He snapped a picture of the screen and sent it over so that Huo Sichen wouldn't think Zhang Yuwen was ignoring him on purpose. Tactfully, Huo Sichen said nothing more.

Midway through the fight, however, someone knocked on his door. "Yuwen?" called Yan Jun.

Zhang Yuwen had no choice but to set down the controller. "Come in, my liege. Here to play a game?"

"What are you up to?" Yan Jun entered the room and saw the game screen. "Am I interrupting you?"

"Nah. How's your nephew?"

Yan Jun sat on the edge of the bed. "I'll take him to the hotel later."

"How long is he going to stay in Jiangdong?"

"A good while. His parents are divorced. He lived with his mom, but when he failed the university entrance exams, his mom didn't know what to do. So she sent him to me."

"You highland people seem to produce a lot of fuckboys," Zhang Yuwen said. Unexpectedly, Yan Jun blushed, and Zhang Yuwen whacked him playfully with his pillow. "Did that sound like a compliment to you?! Why are you blushing?!"

In a nimble move, Yan Jun caught the pillow and made to throw it back. Zhang Yuwen tried to dodge, so Yan Jun, reluctant to actually engage in any teasing, gently set it down.

"He's planning to rent a house in Jiangdong," Yan Jun said. "Then he's going to attend cram school to prepare for the entrance exams and apply to the mechanical engineering program at Jianghan University."

"Jianghan's minimum score requirement is pretty high."

"Yeah, but he's been fascinated by machinery ever since he was a kid."

"You and he must have been pretty close."

"I watched him grow up," Yan Jun agreed. "He was already five foot nine by the age of twelve, and he's still the same height. His dad helped my brother a lot. You could say that he was like a big brother to both of us."

Zhang Yuwen smiled. He knew that men in highland indigenous communities tended to call each other "brother" and that these friendships often lasted from childhood to adulthood and even old age. They supported each other in navigating life's roadblocks and offered unwavering assistance on matters that ranged from marriage to careers.

"Just have him stay here," Zhang Yuwen said. "No need to bother with a hotel."

"No, I can't do that..."

"It's fine. Is he gay?"

"I don't know, but probably not. Why, do you think he is? He doesn't seem to have a girlfriend, now that you mention it..." Yan Jun suddenly seemed anxious, as if he weren't gay himself.

"It's really no biggie," Zhang Yuwen assured him. "Just let the others know. It makes sense for him to stay here for the time being. He came to you for help. Being alone in a hotel would be kind of lonely, wouldn't it?"

After a moment's silence, Yan Jun said, "All right. But if you guys need anything, just ask him."

Abruptly, it occurred to Zhang Yuwen that they didn't have a spare room for Shen Yingjie. Should they have him sleep on the sofa in the living room...?

"Where will he sleep?" he asked.

"He can share a bed with me," Yan Jun said. "It won't be a problem. I'll take him to look at apartments tomorrow and rent one as soon as possible. Somewhere near the cram school, nothing too fancy. Young people can endure a bit of hardship."

"Let him sleep in Xiao-Qi's crib." Zhang Yuwen laughed. Yan Jun cast him an amused look, but found himself unable to look away. "What?" said Zhang Yuwen.

Yan Jun sighed. "I hope he can get into university. Looking back, I wish I'd studied harder and gotten a bachelor's degree."

Zhang Yuwen smiled. "Hindsight is always 20/20. No use regretting what's already happened."

"But I'll make sure Xiao-Qi gets a good education and goes to university."

"Why not do it yourself? You can still go back and further your studies, can't you?"

"Eh?" The thought had never crossed Yan Jun's mind until now, but Zhang Yuwen was right. He fell silent again. Zhang Yuwen continued with his game, so Yan Jun sat in the bedroom and wordlessly watched him play.

"Yuwen?" Chang Jinxing appeared at Zhang Yuwen's wide-open door.

"What's up?" Zhang Yuwen asked.

"I missed you." Chang Jinxing flopped onto the bed and grinned. "We haven't seen each other in over a week, and I just wanted to chat."

Yan Jun shifted over a little and draped an arm around him, and a while later, Chen Hong showed up too. Zhang Yuwen knew he wanted to ask about using the car, but his first words when he saw all the others were: "Whoa! What are you guys doing? Count me in!" He squeezed himself in among them, and they all lounged on Zhang Yuwen's crowded bed, watching him play.

Before long, Zheng Weize came upstairs looking for Chang Jinxing so he could see today's photos. The room was empty, but he soon found them all in Zhang Yuwen's room.

"What are you guys doing here?" Zheng Weize got onto the bed.

"Why is everyone in my room?!" Zhang Yuwen demanded, torn between laughter and tears.

The guys started a pillow fight, and in no time, pillows were flying all over the room. It wasn't until the clock struck twelve that they returned to their own rooms to sleep.

Riverbay Road
MEN'S DORMITORY

CHAPTER

41

Zheng Weize had been on edge lately, because he was about to meet Whiskey.

According to his rough calculations, he'd received about ¥38,000 in live stream tips from Whiskey, plus gifts worth over ¥6,000. Whiskey had offered to give him a new mobile phone, too, but Zheng Weize turned it down. At first, Whiskey's timely support eased the financial pressure on Zheng Weize, but when the money kept pouring in, Zheng Weize panicked, fearing he would one day receive a court summons accusing him of fraud. And since he cooped himself up at home every day, there was nowhere for him to spend his money, so after using up a little over ten thousand yuan, he deposited the remaining money in the bank with the intention of setting up a nest egg for them.

They both agreed that Whiskey would come over on the seventh day of the Lunar New Year to meet up, chat, and have a meal with Zheng Weize. Then, he'd go back home the next day. Zheng Weize chose this date because he knew lots of shops reopened for business on the eighth day, so even if Whiskey wanted to extend his stay, he wouldn't have been able to.

"Yo, you got plans today?" Chang Jinxing asked.

Zheng Weize, who had been drinking coffee at the dining table, looked up suddenly like a thief caught in the act. With the exception of planned group activities, Zheng Weize never got up before two p.m.

"Yeah, I'm meeting friends," Zheng Weize said.

"Want me to fry an egg for you?"

"No need to trouble yourself." Zheng Weize straightened up in his seat.

"Yuwen has to eat too. He's going fishing today."

Earlier that morning, Yan Jun had taken his nephew out to rent an apartment, and Chang Jinxing went to his gym. Zhang Yuwen was already dressed, but he looked bleary as he rummaged through the refrigerator with Chang Jinxing to discuss breakfast options. Chang Jinxing's daily schedule had become a lot more disciplined after nearly a month of working on the film set. He no longer frequented nightclubs, and waking up early made his day longer, so he had a lot of free time on his hands. Recently, he'd taken to hanging around at home and using Zhang Yuwen's computer to browse information about studying abroad.

"Are you going out?" Zhang Yuwen asked Zheng Weize.

Zheng Weize hummed. He didn't want to tell them he was meeting someone from online. "Hanging out with a few friends."

"Huo Sichen is coming to pick me up later, so he can drive you. Where are you headed?"

"Railway station. Is that okay?"

"Of course."

Zheng Weize's first impulse was to decline because he hadn't put on his makeup, high heels, wig, breastforms, and other props yet. But even if he did get all dressed up at home, he would still have had to leave his room like that and risk being seen by Chang Jinxing, who clearly wasn't planning to go out today. He figured he might as well find a restroom at the station and take his time getting himself

CHAPTER 41   **221**

in order there. If Huo Sichen gave him a ride, he could get there earlier, which meant more time to get ready.

"Well, I'm off," Zhang Yuwen said.

"Have fun," Chang Jinxing told them both. "Bye-bye."

Outside, Huo Sichen honked his horn twice. Zheng Weize slapped on a light makeup base and followed Zhang Yuwen out of the house and into the car.

"Drop him off at the railway station first," Zhang Yuwen said, but as soon as he settled into the passenger seat, Huo Sichen kissed him.

When they were done, Huo Sichen glanced at Zheng Weize in the rearview mirror. Zheng Weize knew he must have looked nervous. Whiskey had been bombarding him with messages since early in the morning. There was a message when he woke up, another when he brushed his teeth, and more when he washed his face, changed his clothes, took selfies, left the house, and arrived at the station—a live broadcast every step of the way to his meeting with Zheng Weize.

Zheng Weize sent him a voice message. "I'm on my way to the railway station to pick you up."

Whiskey promptly sent one back, and Zheng Weize played it: "Okay, honey, I love you." Zhang Yuwen and Huo Sichen both heard it, but neither said a word. Zheng Weize's palms sweated profusely as he rummaged through his backpack to reassure himself that he hadn't forgotten anything.

"Did you get a good night's sleep?" Huo Sichen asked.

Zheng Weize looked up. "Huh?"

Zhang Yuwen grinned. "Knowing you were gonna take me fishing, gege, I was so nervous I couldn't sleep."

Huo Sichen chuckled. "I saw that a good friend of mine got a trophy in that game last night. Guess he must have been up real late." He and Zhang Yuwen had, of course, added each other in the game.

Zhang Yuwen started telling Huo Sichen about what he got up to gaming last night, and before long, they arrived at the railway station. Zheng Weize got out of the car, quiet and heavy-hearted, and thanked Huo Sichen.

Zhang Yuwen rolled down the window. "Want us to pick you up in the afternoon?"

"Nah, it's fine," Zheng Weize said. "You guys have fun."

"Or how about we all hang out together?" Huo Sichen suggested.

"No, thanks," Zheng Weize said hurriedly. "It's not my friend's first time in Jiangdong. We... We... Jinxing gave me some buffet vouchers earlier. We'll probably get a buffet lunch."

"All right, then. Take care of yourself," Zhang Yuwen said.

"Yup! For sure!" Zheng Weize smiled and hurried off to the high-speed railway station.

"Think he'll be okay?" Huo Sichen asked Zhang Yuwen as he watched Zheng Weize go.

"I don't know. Is he meeting an online friend?"

"Seems like it."

Zheng Weize didn't have much social experience, and he wore his heart on his sleeve. A glance was all that the more worldly Zhang Yuwen and Huo Sichen needed to discern what was up. Zhang Yuwen knew that Huo Sichen was worried for Zheng Weize's safety, since the person he was meeting was a stranger, but he figured Zheng Weize would probably be fine—he was a guy, after all.

"Should we tell Jinxing?"

"Weize is a guy, so it shouldn't too dangerous, right?" Zhang Yuwen said. He did send a message to Chang Jinxing, though, filling him in and asking if he gave Zheng Weize buffet vouchers. This surprised Chang Jinxing, who hadn't heard about the meeting.

He went to meet an online friend? I did give him vouchers, yeah. I'll call him in a bit to make sure he's ok.

Alrighty, I'll leave it to u, Zhang Yuwen replied.

The suburb of Jiangdong was even more crowded than the previous day, full of people enjoying the outdoors. Huo Sichen drove his car through the picturesque scenery to the camp entrance where they once played laser tag. Mr. You's business had finally seen a resurgence during the public holidays, and there were couples playing laser tag all over the hills and valleys.

Huo Sichen went to say hello, then effortlessly retrieved his fishing gear and slung it over his shoulders. He took Zhang Yuwen by the hand and led him to the back side of the mountain.

"You really did bring me here to fish," Zhang Yuwen said.

"Did you think I'd seize my chance and take you to a hotel?" Huo Sichen chuckled. "Honestly, though, I'd love to."

It had indeed crossed Zhang Yuwen's mind that Huo Sichen might make a sudden change of plans and take him to a hotel instead.

"Don't you have a thing for outdoor sex?" Huo Sichen added. "There's a lake back there where we can fish and make love at the same time."

Zhang Yuwen burst out laughing. Unfortunately, Huo Sichen's hopes were dashed: The place, when they got there, was teeming with people sitting and getting cozy by the lake.

"I heard there are sturgeon in this river," Huo Sichen said, "but I've never caught one."

"All year round?" Zhang Yuwen watched Huo Sichen set up his fishing rod, select a hook, bait it, and cast the line with practiced ease.

"No, only summer and winter. It's the tail end of winter now. The fish you can catch vary throughout the year, and sea fishing is different from lake or river fishing..." Huo Sichen began to explain fishing to Zhang Yuwen with complete earnestness. Zhang Yuwen rarely saw him so in his element, and though he wasn't all that keen on fishing, he listened attentively all the same. After a while, Huo Sichen seemed to notice that he'd been monopolizing the conversation, and he looked a touch embarrassed. "Sorry, am I boring you?"

"No, not at all. Keep going—I find it interesting. This is fascinating writing material."

"How's your book coming along?"

"I've been so busy with you during the holidays that I haven't written a single word." They'd been together for practically the whole holiday, up until the previous day, so Zhang Yuwen hadn't gotten any time to write.

Huo Sichen set up two fishing rods under a tree while Zhang Yuwen spread a blanket out on the ground and took out a book. Huo Sichen sat against a tree, and Zhang Yuwen reclined with his head on Huo Sichen's lap.

"Oh, is the fishing rod moving?" Zhang Yuwen asked.

"Ignore it." Huo Sichen ran his fingers lovingly through Zhang Yuwen's hair.

"Aren't you going to reel it in?"

"You need to be patient. The fish is just testing you."

Zhang Yuwen laughed. "Why do I feel like you're implying something? What are you hinting at?"

Huo Sichen laughed too. "Yuwen, do you want to live with me?"

Zhang Yuwen made a noncommittal noise. Instead of giving him a direct answer, he said, "Why do you ask?"

"When I was making plans yesterday, I really started thinking things over, about us. I took everything into account."

"I see."

"You're not that keen on becoming part of my life in that way, right?" Huo Sichen asked somberly. "You prefer maintaining your personal space while you're in a relationship."

"No, it's not that." After a moment's thought, Zhang Yuwen decided to be honest. "I mean, you're right, but that's not the main issue." He sat up, taking a moment to gather his thoughts. "I like you, but I'm reluctant to give up my current lifestyle. The thought of walking into someone else's life and having to make all those changes makes me...hesitant, I guess. But I love you, and that is a fact."

Huo Sichen looked intently into Zhang Yuwen's eyes. Zhang Yuwen had always been frank and willing to speak his mind. That was one of the reasons Huo Sichen loved him. "You're infatuated with my big cock," Huo Sichen translated, laughing, "but you don't wanna marry me."

"It's not just your cock." Zhang Yuwen didn't know whether to laugh or roll his eyes. "Damn, that's so crass. I didn't know you had it in you. I also enjoy being with you. Does it really matter so much to you if I don't want to move in with you?"

"A little."

"Be honest."

"Okay, yeah, it matters a lot," Huo Sichen admitted.

"You don't need to worry, though. I'll get over it. You win some, you lose some, right? I've gained that huge cock of yours, so I need to learn to sacrifice something."

He laughed at his own joke, and Huo Sichen's disappointment melted away.

Then, Zhang Yuwen leaned in close. "So," he breathed into Huo Sichen's ear, "when are you gonna let me give you *my* cock?"

Huo Sichen turned beet red. Zhang Yuwen loved riling him up. It was a different feeling. He knew that Huo Sichen would be willing, and he suspected the only thing holding him back was that he couldn't bring himself to say he wanted to try switching positions. Luckily, they were still in the honeymoon phase—if Zhang Yuwen struck while the iron was hot, he was confident Huo Sichen would agree.

Huo Sichen looked at him. "Do I need to do anything to prepare?"

"Nope. Just leave it to me. I promise you'll feel good."

"Okay."

He agreed? Just like that? It was almost too easy. Zhang Yuwen was beginning to realize just how much Huo Sichen loved him.

A fish bit the line then, and they both hurried over to the rod. Huo Sichen showed Zhang Yuwen how to reel in the fish, which turned out to be a crucian carp. Fish, Zhang Yuwen realized then, were stronger than he'd imagined.

"Crucian carp are real fighters, huh?" Zhang Yuwen said. He was starting to see what was compelling about fishing.

"If they don't fight, they'll end up getting eaten. Of course, they get caught in the end, anyway."

Zhang Yuwen released the fish back into the water and went back to waiting with Huo Sichen. Huo Sichen parted his legs and had Zhang Yuwen sit between them so he could wrap his arms around Zhang Yuwen from behind. They shared an intimate moment, and Huo Sichen kissed and nuzzled Zhang Yuwen's ear.

Out of nowhere, Huo Sichen said, "I'm going to resign. I'm gonna hand in my resignation letter tomorrow, as long as you're okay with that."

"Huh?" Zhang Yuwen contemplated this. "It's no problem for me, of course. So you finally made up your mind to quit, huh."

"You're really okay with it?"

"Yup! Congrats!" Zhang Yuwen pulled away from Huo Sichen and turned to face him. "You can finally take a break."

"Yeah." Huo Sichen mulled it over, avoiding Zhang Yuwen's gaze. "I'm thinking of getting a certification or enrolling in the MBA program at my alma mater. Either way, I'll take some time to recharge before I decide whether I want to find a new job or start my own business."

"Good idea. That job's been draining the life out of you. You need to de-stress." Even on New Year's Eve, he was bombarded with messages. If he were in Huo Sichen's shoes, Zhang Yuwen would've sent hitmen after his boss.

"But if I quit, I won't have an income. So, if you're willing to..." Huo Sichen paused for a moment. "I mean, well, our quality of life will drop significantly."

Zhang Yuwen understood what he wasn't saying. If they became a family, Huo Sichen would be without his biggest advantage, or rather the thing on which he most prided himself—his high salary.

"Do you have savings?" Zhang Yuwen asked.

"A little over seventy thousand."

That was puzzling, given that his annual pre-tax income exceeded a million. After tax, he should have still had more than six hundred thousand. Combine that with his stock dividends from previous years, and Zhang Yuwen didn't understand how he, a CTO who had been with the company for half a decade, could have saved only seventy thousand. What was he spending so much of his money on? Even with loans to repay, he couldn't have had so little in the bank.

But Zhang Yuwen didn't ask where his money went. Instead, he said, "That's enough. I have a salary too." Huo Sichen's eyes brimmed with hope. "You could rent out your house and offset part of the mortgage."

"You mean move in with you?" Huo Sichen asked in disbelief.

Zhang Yuwen hadn't decided on a final course of action and motioned for Huo Sichen to wait and let him think. He was in a bit of a pickle. "Perhaps you could rent a cheaper place," he said eventually.

Huo Sichen's expression calmed. "I see."

"Because, as you know, No. 7 Riverbay Road was originally..."

"Yeah, I understand."

Zhang Yuwen's hesitation stemmed from the fact that he was the one who'd set the rule against cohabitation. If he wanted to break the rule, he would have to ask his roommates first. The others would understand, of course, and they'd welcome Huo Sichen into the home, but what if, down the line, they all found themselves their own partners? Should their partners be allowed to move in too? Ten people living in their house would be far too crowded and chaotic.

After thinking it over, Zhang Yuwen only saw one solution: renting a new place with Huo Sichen. But No. 7 Riverbay Road was his house! Why should he be the one to move out?

Zhang Yuwen noticed that Huo Sichen's expression had shifted again, from delighted to despondent. "Are you angry?" he asked.

"No." Huo Sichen went to check on his fishing rod.

"I think we should be honest with each other about what we really think," Zhang Yuwen said. He felt like he'd let Huo Sichen down. Huo Sichen loved him wholeheartedly, but he was always avoiding direct conversations about key issues. "I'll start."

"No, don't force yourself. I mean it, Yuwen. You know, after what you said yesterday, I spent the whole night thinking, and I came up with a detailed plan." Huo Sichen retrieved an envelope from his bag. "These are the questions you asked me yesterday. I've added a few more, including questions about how to manage our shared life together. You can make changes to it; I don't think I'll fight you on much of it. But I know you might be disappointed in me because I decided to resign, and you might find it hard to decide whether to—"

"What?" Zhang Yuwen stared at him. "Resign? This has nothing to do with your resignation."

"Of course it does. My income is gone. I might not be able to give you what you want, and the daily necessities matter. Do you want to reconsider? I can wait for you."

"Reconsider what?" Zhang Yuwen took the envelope. "Living together?"

"Me. Reconsider whether you want to be with me," Huo Sichen replied. "For maybe the next six months, we won't be dining at expensive restaurants, and we'll have to budget our living expenses. I also won't be able to buy you gifts like I used to. We might argue over financial issues, and your love for me will gradually fade away. I don't want...I don't want to end up like that. Can you love me like this?"

"What are you talking about? Do you think I'm with you because of your money?" Zhang Yuwen asked incredulously. Huo Sichen said nothing. This was absurd. "Is that really what you think of me?"

Another fish took their bait with a loud splash. Neither of them turned to look.

"So that's how you see me," Zhang Yuwen said. "You think I'm with you for your money?"

It dawned on Huo Sichen that Zhang Yuwen was angry. In the entire time they'd been dating, he had never seen such anger in Zhang Yuwen.

"That's not what I mean," Huo Sichen said, trying to explain. "I was just trying to say that we're happy together, right? But our happiness is built on material comfort, because I've been covering expenses so you haven't needed to worry about money—"

"What gifts have I accepted from you? How many expensive restaurants have we eaten at? Mr. Huo, do you want to tally how much money we've spent dating? Let me help you calculate. Oooh, looks like a lot—tens of thousands."

"You're angry. We can't communicate like this."

"You think I love you now because of your high salary, but once you resign, I'll start to look down on you. Am I right?"

Huo Sichen couldn't hold it in any longer. "You're already starting to look down on me. I know you have higher expectations of me. You don't say it, but that's how you feel. Know how I know that? It's so hard to get a response from you, and sometimes, it's like you're an actor putting on a show for me. When I take you out for dinner or buy you gifts, or when we go on vacation, you act like you really like it, but I can tell you're not being genuine. You think I can still do better, right?"

Huo Sichen hit the nail on the head. While he was wrong about the reason for Zhang Yuwen's feelings, he was exactly right about how Zhang Yuwen behaved. The "acting" came about because he was simply too accustomed to extravagant spending and had little interest in worldly possessions. It made no difference to him whether a date involved going to the park or going to Disneyland.

The splashing intensified, sending up larger sprays of water.

"I think I need to cool down for a bit and think things through," Zhang Yuwen said. "I'd like to go home now."

Wordlessly, Huo Sichen began to pack up their things, but Zhang Yuwen stopped him.

"No, you don't need to drive me back. We'll just keep arguing in the car." He slung his bag over his shoulder, and Huo Sichen looked at him. "I'll contact you after I've cooled down. I'm leaving now. Bye."

Zhang Yuwen put the envelope in his bag, left the lake, and made his way out to catch the bus home.

Huo Sichen remained silent, regretting the impulsive things he'd said. He took out his phone to call Zhang Yuwen, but Zhang Yuwen had forgotten his own phone, and it began to vibrate nearby. Its screen flashed with the caller's name—The Fisherman ♥—which was followed by a note that said *Family*.

He hurried out with Zhang Yuwen's phone, only to find the bus departing. He ran back to pack up his fishing gear but found that he couldn't lift one of the rods. He struggled to reel it in—it began to thrash wildly, and he realized that he'd snagged a fish. Huo Sichen didn't want to waste time, so he yanked with brute force. Man and fish engaged in a furious battle, and in the end, Huo Sichen emerged victorious, hauling in a sturgeon a foot and a half long.

The fish took its revenge, however. As it left the water, it raised its tail and whacked Huo Sichen hard, leaving a distinct, vivid fishtail mark on his cheek.

The blow dazed Huo Sichen, and it took him a good while to recover. When he did, he shoved the fish into the cooler, slammed the lid shut, and hurried off to his car.

Riverbay Road
MEN'S DORMITORY

CHAPTER

42

WHEN ZHENG WEIZE ARRIVED at the railway station, he ran to the women's restroom and locked himself in one of the stalls to put on his thermal leggings, change into a loose skirt, and get his fake boobs into place. He used a high-necked shirt to cover his barely noticeable Adam's apple and spread his legs to adjust the position of his pecker in the crotch of his pants. By the time he put on his wig and stepped out of the stall, there was a queue for the restroom.

Then, he opened his makeup bag and added a few more touches to the basic makeup he'd applied in the morning. He darkened his eyeliner, applied eyeshadow, attached his fake lashes, and put on lipstick, keeping an eye on his phone for Whiskey's messages all the while. Fortunately, it wasn't summer, so he hadn't needed to shave his legs in advance. He was so focused on his makeup that he barely had time to feel nervous about meeting Whiskey.

His phone chimed with a message from Whiskey: *here. gettin off the train now.*

Zheng Weize took a deep breath, put away his makeup kit, and slipped into his high heels. *All right, here we go... It's just a meal. I'll see him off tomorrow morning, and then it'll be over. It'll be fine,* Zheng Weize reminded himself. *It'll be fine.*

He'd told Whiskey beforehand that he'd contracted influenza A so his voice would be hoarse, and they couldn't get too close to each other because Zheng Weize didn't want to infect him. He said that he didn't want to cancel the meeting altogether because he, Zheng Weize, was looking forward to it too. This moved Whiskey, who insisted on seeing "her" despite the supposed risk of infection.

Zheng Weize sent a voice message in his best falsetto, trying to make it sound hoarse from illness. "I'll be waiting for you at the exit."

"Okay," Whiskey's next message said. His voice sounded thick with anticipation. "Your voice is really hoarse. Are you all right?"

Zheng Weize put on his mask and took another deep breath to calm his nerves.

A crowd surged from the exit gate, and Zheng Weize scanned the exiting crowd with his arms crossed. A lot of people were returning to Jiangdong after their Spring Festival holidays, and there were a number of lovers waiting to pick up their other half. He witnessed a number of long-overdue embraces in the tiny old station as he himself waited for Whiskey.

Where is he? Zheng Weize wondered, standing tall and graceful. Doubt began to creep in.

Another text message came in from Whiskey: *honey, honey, i'm under the red billboard. whr r u? whr r u?*

Then, Zheng Weize saw a man wearing a mask. His heart plummeted. *No way! Are you kidding me? Fuuuck!*

At the exit stood a plain-looking straight guy in a mask. He was a five at best, and even that was generous, since the mask probably scored him additional points. He wore a brown jacket and gray suit pants, carried a laptop bag over his shoulder, and dragged a dirty suitcase along behind him.

Despite the disappointment crashing over him, Zheng Weize waved. It was indeed Whiskey. When he saw "her," he beamed, and his crinkling eyes revealed crow's feet at their corners. He quickly made his way over to Zheng Weize.

"Honey!" Whiskey shouted, oblivious to his surroundings. A bunch of people turned to look at Zheng Weize, who wanted to flee.

Sigh... Zheng Weize had forgotten that, while he sent a lot of unfiltered selfies to Whiskey to gain his trust, Whiskey himself always used beauty filters for video calls and photos. After using deceptive photos for so long himself, now Zheng Weize had been catfished into this train wreck of an online dating encounter.

As Whiskey approached, Zheng Weize forced himself to smile and give Whiskey a light hug, avoiding contact with certain important parts of himself. Whiskey grinned and asked, "Have you been waiting long?"

Are you really five foot eight? Why do you seem shorter than me?!

Zheng Weize nodded, pretending to be unwell. "Not too long. My friend drove me here." Zheng Weize's voice was very hoarse, but since he usually spoke in softer, higher-pitched tones, he sounded like a girl who'd lost her baby voice from the flu. It was awkward, but Whiskey bought it, and to sell the act further, Zheng Weize took a throat lozenge from his bag and popped it into his mouth. Whiskey didn't suspect a thing.

"Where to now?" Whiskey asked. "My hotel?"

Zheng Weize nodded and left the railway station with him, keeping his expression placid and his eyes fixed ahead. Whiskey, on the other hand, kept ogling Zheng Weize's face and chest. *Just go for a meal and get it over with,* Zheng Weize told himself repeatedly. *It'll be fine. It's gonna be fine.*

In the taxi, Whiskey removed his mask. His features looked the same as the ones in his photos, but taking them in the grander context of his face, something just seemed...off. Zheng Weize held his forehead with a hand, his mind reeling. Where he'd previously thought Whiskey was at least passable, his dreams of love were now in tatters.

That's right, Zheng Weize lamented to himself. *That's the kind of person I am. I'm ugly, but I still judge other people for being ugly.*

Whiskey gave the driver the address. Noticing Zheng Weize looking at him, he smiled, and Zheng Weize quickly averted his gaze.

"Have you had breakfast yet?" Whiskey asked.

Zheng Weize shook his head. "Just coffee."

Whiskey nodded. "Drinking coffee on an empty stomach in the morning can't be good for your digestion," he said with concern. "I'll take you to get some food later."

Whiskey assumed his wife was just shy. After all, "she'd" told him that she had depression and rarely spoke to people in real life. It took her a lot of courage to come out and see him.

Whiskey rambled for a bit, then placed his hand on Zheng Weize's thigh. Zheng Weize removed it, and Whiskey, unperturbed, draped his arm around his shoulders and touched his waist. Zheng Weize shot him a few annoyed looks, trying to hint that he should stop, and Whiskey chuckled and dropped it.

When they arrived at the hotel, Whiskey went to check in, and predictably, he wanted Zheng Weize to go up to his room with him. Zheng Weize turned him down, of course.

"No," Zheng Weize said, upset. "We agreed on this."

Whiskey could tell from "her" expression that "she" wasn't happy, so he didn't push it. "All right. I'll be right down after I change my clothes."

Zheng Weize waited in the hotel lobby's café, wondering if he should ask a friend to help him slip away. But he didn't really have any friends other than his roommates, and he didn't want them to know about his cross-dressing.

While he was thinking it over, Chang Jinxing called. Zheng Weize picked up immediately.

"Where are you?" Chang Jinxing asked. "What are you doing?"

Zheng Weize eyed the elevator. "I...I'm meeting my elementary school classmate. What's up?"

"Wanna grab a meal together?"

"He's leaving soon. He'll only be in Jiangdong for a few hours."

"Oh," said Chang Jinxing, unconvinced. "Is everything okay?"

"Yup. I'll be back for dinner. I'll go grocery shopping later."

Chang Jinxing couldn't dig further; asking too many questions might have exposed that Zhang Yuwen was worried about Zheng Weize. "All right," he said eventually. "Call me if you need me."

Zheng Weize hung up. He really wanted to leave. The contrast between the Whiskey he knew online and the guy he just met was too jarring! But he'd spent so much of Whiskey's money...

Oh. Money. Zheng Weize realized that was the crux of the issue and started to panic. If he rejected Whiskey, what then? Would he have to return the money and gifts? But he'd already spent a lot, and the platform had a no-refund policy for the tips and gifts a user gave to a streamer—there was no reason for refunds if they were paying for a live streaming service.

Sigh. How did things turn out like this? Zheng Weize had so many regrets. He never should have agreed to meet Whiskey. Wouldn't it have been better to keep this fantasy online? What in the world had gotten into him?

Whiskey came back down to the lobby before long, having only changed his jacket. "I got you this gift," he said, pulling a music box shaped like a red crystal heart out of his bag. In their ten minutes apart, he seemed to have adjusted his expectations and realized he couldn't rush things with a girl. "I assembled it myself at the factory. You told me not to get you anything expensive because it's the thought that counts—well, this is okay, right?"

Zheng Weize opened the music box. Touchingly, it tinkled with the melody of *Eternal Love*. He retrieved a wrapped gift from his own bag—the safe travel charm he bought from the flower market—and handed it to Whiskey with both hands.

"This is for you," Zheng Weize said. "I prayed for it at the temple."

Whiskey glanced at it and put it into his pocket without opening it. His mind was consumed with thoughts of getting "her" into bed. Rubbing his hands together like a fly, he looked at Zheng Weize and grinned. "Are you hungry yet? Let's grab some food. I didn't eat breakfast either, and I'm starving."

Zheng Weize nodded with a smile and led him out of the hotel to a buffet restaurant he booked. He handed over the meal vouchers Chang Jinxing had given him and sat down to dine with Whiskey. Finally, he took off his mask, allowing Whiskey to get a clear look at the lower half of his face. Whiskey seemed mesmerized.

Zheng Weize didn't have noticeable facial hair, so as long as his voice didn't give him away, he wouldn't be exposed. He did his best to act like a girl, and Whiskey seemed satisfied with "her" appearance and figure, falling all over himself to get food for her from the buffet.

"You're pretty tall," Whiskey said, smiling.

"I had a growth spurt after I hit sixteen."

"Any old photos of yourself? Can I see?"

Zheng Weize had prepared some photos in advance, and he sent them to Whiskey from his phone. To cement the idea he was a girl in Whiskey's mind, Zheng Weize showed Whiskey old photos of him from when he was little, when his gender wasn't as apparent. There were also cheeky snapshots of him in a dress from the time back in elementary school when his sisters dolled him up like a girl for fun. Whiskey glanced at the photos happily, then went back to staring at Zheng Weize, apparently unable to tear his eyes away. He was clearly head over heels.

Zheng Weize, for his part, nibbled slowly at his food. He was starving, but he had to restrain himself and eat like a girl instead of giving Whiskey a fright by gobbling his food down. Gradually, he realized that he was getting used to Whiskey, who no longer seemed as ugly to him as he did at first. And there was still the emotional bond they had built up over time talking online day after day. Zheng Weize couldn't bear to just ditch him after lunch.

"I still don't know your name," Whiskey said. He'd just been calling Zheng Weize "honey" this whole time.

"My name is Zheng Jintu," Zheng Weize replied, making up a random name. "What about you?"

"I'm Yang Xie. Where do you live?"

Zheng Weize answered, but it wasn't long before he realized that he had nothing to talk about with Whiskey. Whether the details about their lives were real or fabricated, they already talked about it all online. They both racked their brains for topics to discuss, and Zheng Weize grew even more uncomfortable; he still had to be mindful of his hoarse voice and not talk too much, lest he rouse Whiskey's suspicion.

"What do you wanna do after this?" Whiskey asked. "Are you full? You only ate a bit."

Zheng Weize nodded and raised his eyebrows. "Hm, where do you have in mind?"

"Wherever you want to go. I've been to Jiangdong a few times before. I don't mind just spending time doing nothing if that's what you want."

Zheng Weize fell silent. He knew he must look to Whiskey like he was thinking hard about places to take him, but in truth, he was wondering when exactly he could make his escape. Whiskey had come here to see him, though, and it didn't seem right to ditch him. Zheng Weize was in a tough spot.

"How about going to the mall?" Whiskey suggested. "Do you want anything? I can take you shopping and buy you some clothes. Do you like bags? I can buy you one. Or maybe jewelry?"

Zheng Weize hurriedly waved his hands to say no, but he felt a little touched. Whiskey was slowly but surely winning back points, which just made Zheng Weize's decision more difficult. "Why don't we go to the park and get some sun?"

"Sure."

As it happened, it was a sunny day. Zheng Weize took Whiskey for an afternoon stroll along the river. He rarely wore high heels, though, so the walk was excruciating—his feet ached, and he was getting blisters on his heels. He hadn't bought any band-aids, either. After a short, painful distance, he decided to find a nearby spot where they could take a break.

Evidently, there were a lot of differences between a cross-dresser and a real girl who wore heels regularly.

Riverbay Road lay on the boundary between Jiangnan and Jiangbei. There was a large square by the river, and next to it was a municipal park where the sun was shining brightly. They could see a handful of kids flying kites there. Zheng Weize chose a spot in the garden to sit and take off his high heels.

The park was packed with couples on romantic strolls. Whiskey asked Zheng Weize to rest his head on his lap, and Zheng Weize didn't want to but had no choice but to lie on his side and obey. Whiskey reached out and stroked his hair. From the outside, it was a heartwarming scene, but Zheng Weize was on tenterhooks, worried that Whiskey might pull off his wig.

"Is your business going well?" Zheng Weize asked.

"Not too bad, I guess. It won't make big bucks, but it's enough to support you."

Zheng Weize imagined that they were a real heterosexual couple who had been in a relationship for a while. Work had kept them apart, but now they were enjoying a rare moment together.

"When are you coming to my house? My mom wants to meet you," Whiskey said. Zheng Weize didn't reply. "I know it's a hard proposition."

"And yet you're still asking me?" Zheng Weize said reproachfully.

"It's just that lately, I keep thinking about it," Whiskey continued. "I can't help it. I want to marry you, honey. I want to live with you as husband and wife. You can move into my house after we marry, or if you prefer to stay in Jiangdong, that's fine too. My mom said she'll buy me a house in Jiangdong when I get married. When the time comes, I'll expand my business out here. You don't need to work or live stream anymore. Not that I'm jealous or anything..."

Whiskey had stumbled into the usual pitfall of straight men, lost in his own fantasy and going off on a monologue, drawing up a blueprint of their future together—not unlike Huo Sichen. Zheng Weize listened without interrupting, feeling touched by his words.

"My heart aches to see you always staying up late," Whiskey went on, "and your health isn't good either. See, you catch the flu as soon as the flu season comes around. You need to take care of yourself so you can bear me a few kids..."

As Whiskey spoke, he stroked Zheng Weize's back, and he slid his hand around Zheng Weize's waist several times to try to touch his chest. Each time, Zheng Weize fended him off, so Whiskey changed tack and played with the clasp of Zheng Weize's bra. Zheng Weize tensed up, anxious despite how moved he was by Whiskey's words, and swatted his hand away.

"Can you not?!" Zheng Weize snapped. "Can't we just have a normal conversation?"

"Were you listening to me?" said Whiskey, momentarily stunned. Zheng Weize's outburst had sounded a little masculine, but Whiskey quickly dismissed that as his own imagination.

"I am." Zheng Weize lay down again.

"Do you want to?"

Zheng Weize remained silent, and he reached behind his back to secure the loosened bra strap. Whiskey offered to help, but Zheng Weize wouldn't let him. He was on edge; his breastforms had slipped to his abdomen while he was lying on his side.

"What's wrong?" Whiskey asked.

"N-nothing." He reached into his clothes to adjust them. "Don't look!"

"Okay, fine." Whiskey grinned and closed his eyes.

He thought Zheng Weize would kiss him, but Zheng Weize didn't. Instead, he hastily readjusted his fake boobs, relief setting over him once they were back in place.

"You won't need to lift a finger," Whiskey added. "I'll hire someone to do the housework. You just need to take care of the kids.

I want a boy and a girl. We'll raise them well. I hope they take after you, since you're good-looking and tall..."

For some reason, Zheng Weize thought of his parents. Was this what it was like for them when they were dating? On the day he moved into Riverbay Road, he'd dreamed of a life like this, and now, Whiskey was offering him everything he ever wanted. A beautiful future was beckoning to him.

It was four in the afternoon, and Zheng Weize knew he had to leave. If Whiskey kept talking, he was going to cry.

"Are you leaving?" Whiskey asked.

"Yeah, I don't feel well. My throat still hurts, and I think I have a bit of a fever."

"I'll go with you and take care of you. I can't leave you alone with no one to care for you when you're sick."

As they left the municipal park, Zheng Weize did his best to dissuade Whiskey. He assured him that he could take care of himself and suggested that he return to the hotel, promising to meet him again tomorrow. As for tomorrow—who knew? He'd cook up another excuse then. New day, new excuse. Where there's a will, there's an excuse.

But Whiskey wanted Zheng Weize to have dinner with him before he went back to the hotel. Then he flip-flopped and insisted on buying a bento meal. Zheng Weize's thoughts were all over the place, and his emotions were rocketing up and down like a roller coaster. The sweet nothings and touching expressions of concern made Zheng Weize feel like Whiskey really was his ideal partner, but his slipping breastforms were a constant reminder that it was impossible between them... He walked for a while, eventually taking off his high heels because his feet were killing him, and continued along the road in his thick black tights—a fatal temptation to a straight guy like Whiskey. Whiskey kept following Zheng Weize, who just wanted to get away from him as soon as possible.

They stopped and stood at the side of the road. Zheng Weize wanted to call a taxi for Whiskey so that he could return to the hotel, at which point Zheng Weize could walk back home alone along Riverbay Road. But Whiskey called out, "Jintu, my wife."

Under the afternoon sunlight, Zheng Weize whipped his head around, and Whiskey grabbed his hands and moved in for a kiss. Caught unaware, Zheng Weize shoved him away.

"You're not interested in me, are you?" Whiskey's eyes were filled with disappointment.

"No, it's just... I'm a little scared," Zheng Weize said. "You're too... direct..."

"Do you like me, then? Give it to me straight."

Zheng Weize looked into his eyes, and for a moment, he forgot everything else. It had been so long since he last felt loved, and now, standing in front of a straight guy on this warm spring night, he'd finally rediscovered what that was like.

Whiskey took his pause a sign that he still stood a chance. He wrapped an arm around Zheng Weize's waist and kissed him. This time, Zheng Weize didn't push him away; he wrapped his arms around Whiskey's neck, lost in his role.

This was the first serious kiss Zheng Weize had ever had with someone he was dating—never before in his life had he been in a relationship where both parties were in mutual love. At twenty years old, no one he'd fallen for had ever truly loved him back. His unrequited loves always ended in disappointment, and his sex life was limited to casual hookups. When one of those hookups did kiss him, it was Chang Jinxing-style fuckboy encouragement: noncommittal, just part of the act. Once it was over, they both went their respective ways.

Whiskey's kiss was the first one that truly told him, *I love you.* Zheng Weize could feel it. Tears welled up in his eyes. Whiskey was far from his ideal type, but he felt his heart stir.

But a moment later, Whiskey paused, looking bewildered. "What's that?"

He'd been embracing Zheng Weize, and their bodies had pressed together as they kissed. It didn't take long for the kiss to make Whiskey hard, but just as he was about to reach out and fondle Zheng Weize's chest, he felt something pressing against him.

Zheng Weize was hard too.

"Fuck." Whiskey reached out to touch it, and in the blink of an eye, his expression transformed from bewilderment to realization and, finally, shock.

Zheng Weize had completely forgotten. He jumped away from Whiskey, who instantly understood that he'd been deceived. Even worse, he'd just been kissing a man, or a woman with a dick!

Whiskey's eyes went wide. "Fuck! You're a guy?! What the fuck!"

Zheng Weize looked at him in a daze, and Whiskey reached out to grab him in an apparent attempt to confirm what he'd felt. Zheng Weize dodged his grasp and broke into tears.

"Motherfucker!" Whiskey bellowed. He looked like he was having a mental breakdown. "Fuck you! *Fuck* you! Why did you lie to me?!"

"No...it's not like that," Zheng Weize tried to explain. "I didn't mean to lie to you..."

Whiskey lunged and made a grab for him. Zheng Weize turned and tried to flee, but Whiskey grabbed his bag and yanked, sending its contents spilling all over the ground. Zheng Weize turned back and bent down to pick them up.

"Don't do this!" he cried. "We're in public! Let's go somewhere else, and I'll explain—"

"*Fuck you!*" Rage consumed Whiskey, and he started punching and kicking at Zheng Weize. One of his kicks landed, and Zheng Weize stood up to run—only to receive a punch that made his head spin.

Just then, a voice rang out that sounded familiar to Zheng Weize: "Hey, you! Stop!"

They were at the back gate of the park, a place where cars rarely passed by. Riverbay Road was just a turn away. A Mercedes-Benz pulled over at the curb, and a man in outdoor gear leapt out from the driver's side.

"What are you doing?!" the man's voice boomed. It was Huo Sichen. He charged over, shoved Whiskey aside, and helped Zheng Weize up. "Are you all right?"

He didn't recognize Zheng Weize, whose eyes were bloodshot from the beating, his nose still bleeding. Huo Sichen was just passing by the park on his way to Riverbay Road to return the phone to Zhang Yuwen when he saw, to his shock, a man beating up a woman. No matter what their relationship was, Huo Sichen couldn't tolerate violence, so he got out of the car.

"Fuck!" Whiskey roared. "Mind your fucking business! What is this, a badger game?!"

Whiskey lunged to grab Zheng Weize, who was hiding behind Huo Sichen, but Huo Sichen assumed a fighting stance. In one swift motion, he charged forward and tackled Whiskey, grabbing him by the waist and slamming him to the ground. The maneuver was so powerful it knocked Whiskey's shoes off his feet. Zheng Weize was stunned.

Suitably intimidated, Whiskey clambered to his feet, limped over to his shoes, and put them on. With a terrified glance back at Huo Sichen, he turned and fled without so much as another word.

Huo Sichen's fury subsided some. He'd been feeling agitated, almost to the point of looking for a fight, and it was Whiskey's bad luck to run into him. Still, he did hold himself back from punching Whiskey in the head.

The contents of Zheng Weize's bag were strewn across the ground: eyebrow pencil, lipstick, foundation… Off to one side lay a shattered music box playing the tinkling notes of *Eternal Love*, now a broken melody.

"Do you need me to get you to the hospital?" Huo Sichen asked. Zheng Weize shook his head, and Huo Sichen finally got a clear look at his face.

"Weize?" he said in disbelief.

CHAPTER
43

ZHANG YUWEN HADN'T BEEN on the bus for long when he realized that he'd forgotten his phone. That was fine, though. He knew Huo Sichen would bring it to him. And what if Huo Sichen forgot or didn't notice it? Well, then it was Huo Sichen's fault, and he could damn well buy Zhang Yuwen a new one.

During his phoneless ride, he thought things over and reflected on himself in a calm, rational manner. He'd always been aware of his own shortcomings. A person's flaws and strengths were often two sides of the same coin. Say, for example, his strong points were his rationality and emotional stability; the flip side was his indifference to others, which tended to make him come across as sexually apathetic. Not even Zhang Yuwen would have dated someone like himself. If he encountered such a person in the wild, he would think, "The hell is up with that holier-than-thou attitude?"

And speaking of emotional stability... Well, his emotions weren't actually that stable. He didn't get angry very often, but every so often, a landmine would inexplicably trigger him and make him blow up in rage. The recent incident with Chang Jinxing's producer was a classic example. His reaction to Huo Sichen's words today was another.

Moreover, he was selfish in love. He didn't want to change his lifestyle and would prefer for his partner to compromise. This was evident in his last relationship, and old habits died hard. Now, he was acting the same way with Huo Sichen, treating him like a kept boy who was at his beck and call. What was more, this kept boy tirelessly lavished him with money and love.

When all was said and done, this boiled down to the bad habits of the upper class—or, more bluntly, the arrogance of the rich. It was natural for others to compromise and accommodate Zhang Yuwen, but God forbid he made even the tiniest concession himself. If he was late for a date, well, things happen. If the other party was late, though... He might not voice them aloud, but he'd certainly entertain some thoughts about their sloppy time management.

Zhang Yuwen had too many shortcomings to list. He knew the seed of arrogance had been planted in his heart a long time ago and watered and nurtured over the years by money and flattery. Now, it was a towering tree, and all his other flaws were the tree's lush leaves. By the time he realized this tree was a problem, it was too late to take an axe to its robust trunk, so he let it be. What else could he do? It was what it was.

On top of all that, he was super lazy. He was doing well as a director, but he lacked ambition, and after producing only two films, he wanted to rest on his laurels and enjoy his life. When he wasn't creating literary trash, he was just playing games at home... Was it possible that he was jealous? Zhang Yuwen didn't think he was the type to get jealous. Still...suppose Huo Sichen became stronger and more successful than him. Would Zhang Yuwen be able to take it, or would he just flat-out reject him? He examined his own criteria for selecting a partner and realized that he may have had an underlying criterion he wasn't aware of: a partner who wasn't as good as him.

People were easier to control that way.

No doubt, a large part of Zhang Yuwen's overconfidence stemmed from the fact that he was richer than Huo Sichen and lived a freer, more leisurely life. It was the same with his roommates. He greedily absorbed their trust and friendship, and he demanded Huo Sichen's love. However much they offered him, he took it all, but he never told them the truth.

At first, Zhang Yuwen had hidden behind a façade as a precaution, but even after the deception became routine, he reveled in it. On some level, seeing them down on their luck gave him a perverse sense of satisfaction. He magnanimously treated them to meals and hypocritically doled out small acts of kindness because it gave him a sense of superiority. He was just like those wealthy elites who engaged in philanthropy because they wanted to see how the masses struggled so that they could compare it against their own blessed lives.

And who am I to judge him? Zhang Yuwen thought as he opened his front door. *Didn't I assume the others were after my money? Why else would I keep hiding it from him?*

These thoughts depressed Zhang Yuwen even more. He practically checked all the boxes for the seven deadly sins. He had the advantage when it came to material wealth, but in spirit, he wasn't worthy of Huo Sichen. Huo Sichen was sincere, had a sense of responsibility, and was willing to invest in their relationship, while Zhang Yuwen was a hypocrite who contributed nothing. Other than their positions in bed, he had made no concessions to Huo Sichen.

But bedroom positions are important too! Zhang Yuwen's inner voice argued. *And besides, it's not like Huo Sichen doesn't have his own shortcomings.* The flip side of having a sense of responsibility was chauvinism and a need for control.

Let me see what he wrote in his letter...

Back at home, Zhang Yuwen changed his shoes with a somber expression on his face. He brewed some coffee, then sat at the dining table and opened the envelope Huo Sichen handed him, which contained his hopes for their future. It was a detailed spreadsheet that came attached with two bank cards and a credit card. It only took a glance at it for Zhang Yuwen to want to give Huo Sichen a call. His anger had subsided, and he wanted to apologize for losing his temper.

The rows on the spreadsheet were labeled with various aspects of their future lives together, and there were two columns: one for Huo Sichen and one for Zhang Yuwen. Huo Sichen had checked certain items under his own name and marked some for Zhang Yuwen, with white stickers attached at the side so that Zhang Yuwen could cover them up and make amendments as he saw fit.

The first row was *Management of Household Finances and Expenses*. The tick was under Zhang Yuwen's name, meaning he would be the one managing it. A comment stated that Huo Sichen would hand over all his income and use a supplementary credit card, while Zhang Yuwen would pay the bills monthly. Essentially, this meant that he would give Huo Sichen an allowance to spend.

Next up was *Work, Relocation, Changing of Cities & Other Related Matters*. Huo Sichen had ticked both of their names, suggesting that any significant life changes would be joint decisions. Zhang Yuwen thought for a moment, then tore off a sticker and pasted it over the tick under his name. Huo Sichen could make the decisions himself.

The third row was for *Home Renovations, Décor & Other Matters Not Affecting the Place of Residence*. Huo Sichen had only ticked under Zhang Yuwen's name.

And so it went. The spreadsheet covered topics like pets, gatherings with friends, holiday celebrations, vacations... Zhang Yuwen reviewed each line, making some additions to the spreadsheet as he went.

When he flipped to the second page, he came across a section on *Properties*. Under the last item, *Real Estate*, both of their names were ticked, with a reminder in the comment field to "add Zhang Yuwen's name to the deed of the current apartment."

Zhang Yuwen was moved by this gesture. Yes, it meant that they would be jointly responsible for paying off the mortgage for Huo Sichen's apartment, but Huo Sichen had already paid down more than a million. Adding Zhang Yuwen's name was a sign of trust and a gesture of sincere commitment: Essentially, he was offering Zhang Yuwen at least half a million yuan with open hands.

Touched, Zhang Yuwen decided to withdraw a paltry ¥1.2 million from his ¥600 million fund and pay off Huo Sichen's mortgage in advance. But this still didn't involve making any actual compromises. If Huo Sichen was willing to add Zhang Yuwen's name to his apartment, then the principle of reciprocity dictated that Zhang Yuwen add Huo Sichen's name to No. 7 Riverbay Road.

Uh, here's the thing... No. 7 Riverbay Road is valued at 120 million! That's a hundred times more than your 1.2 million! Unable to decide, he eventually opted to set a deadline.

If we can stay together for four years, I'll add his name to the deed.

Chang Jinxing yawned as he came down the stairs, having just woken from a nap. "When did you get back?"

"Just now." Zhang Yuwen put the bank cards away and folded the spreadsheet back into the envelope, wondering why Huo Sichen hadn't shown up yet.

"Where's the fish?" Chang Jinxing asked.

They looked at each other. Zhang Yuwen had forgotten all about the fish. "Huo Sichen will bring it over later."

Then again, Huo Sichen probably hadn't been in the mood to fish after he left. Maybe Zhang Yuwen should just take everyone out for dinner.

At that moment, Huo Sichen stood at the entrance of the villa complex on Riverbay Road, still unaware that he'd be entitled to at least sixty million of Zhang Yuwen's assets four years down the line. One side of his handsome face was still stinging, bearing the imprint of the slap from the sturgeon.

"Don't tell them," Zheng Weize pleaded. He didn't want his roommates to know about his humiliating encounter.

"How can we not tell them?" Huo Sichen said. "Look at the state of you. Weize, what happened? You need to tell us so we can all help you figure something out. What if he comes looking for you again when we aren't around? Do you realize how much danger you were in today?"

Huo Sichen had his rough estimations of what happened: Zheng Weize received a beating after he met up with his online friend. But when Zheng Weize went to the railway station earlier, he wasn't dressed as a woman, so Huo Sichen was struggling to connect all the dots. He assumed it was some kind of role-play.

Of course, Huo Sichen knew that Zheng Weize was Zhang Yuwen's roommate, but in his mind, Zheng Weize was a passive bottom, just like a girl—mindful of the imagined gender difference, he didn't drag Zheng Weize into the house. "You have to tell them," he said, though, somberly. "They're going to ask you anyway."

Zheng Weize wiped at his bloody nose. He couldn't stop crying. Eventually, he nodded, and Huo Sichen led him into the house.

Zhang Yuwen and Chang Jinxing were talking when they saw Huo Sichen and Zheng Weize enter—Huo Sichen with half of his face bruised, and Zheng Weize with a badly battered face. They both froze in shock.

"What the hell? What happened?" Chang Jinxing demanded. When Zheng Weize saw Chang Jinxing, he burst into tears again.

Huo Sichen shot Zhang Yuwen a vexed look. "Your phone."

"What happened to your face?"

"A fish slapped me with its tail."

Zhang Yuwen gestured to Zheng Weize. "And Weize?" Huo Sichen shrugged, indicating that he didn't know. Zhang Yuwen was speechless. They looked at each other, then Zhang Yuwen went to get the medical kit. Huo Sichen turned to leave, and Zhang Yuwen asked, "Where are you going?"

"To get the fish!"

He carried a cooler box in and set it down in the kitchen. Zhang Yuwen applied medicated ointments for Zheng Weize, but Zheng Weize wouldn't stop crying, so Zhang Yuwen passed the responsibility for comforting him on to Chang Jinxing. He then had Huo Sichen sit at the dining table and applied an ointment to his bruised cheek. When Huo Sichen looked up at Zhang Yuwen, his gaze lingered on Zhang Yuwen's lips.

"Does it hurt?" Zhang Yuwen asked.

"A lot," Huo Sichen confirmed.

"Sorry," Zhang Yuwen said in a small voice.

"About what?"

"I shouldn't have lost my temper at you like that."

"It was my fault," Huo Sichen said in a similarly small voice. "If you're not angry anymore, can I kiss you?"

In full view of Zheng Weize and Chang Jinxing, Zhang Yuwen leaned in and kissed Huo Sichen, keeping it chaste.

Zheng Weize cried even louder and buried his face in Chang Jinxing's chest. "What happened?" Chang Jinxing asked as he patted Zheng Weize on the back. "Who did you get into a fight with?" But Zheng Weize clearly didn't want to talk about it—he just wanted to get his feelings out.

Suddenly, Zhang Yuwen put two and two together. "Weize, was it that online friend of yours?"

With tears still streaming down his face, Zheng Weize nodded. "Yeah..."

For the second time that day, Zhang Yuwen blew his lid. He felt like he might need some fast-acting heart medication. "Why?!" he bellowed. "Where is he?!"

"It's all my fault," Zheng Weize insisted, fearing that his roommates might escalate the situation. If Whiskey called the police, things would get even worse. "I shouldn't have deceived him by pretending to be a girl..."

Understanding dawned on Chang Jinxing. "Fuck! Where is he?"

The clock struck five, and Yan Jun and Chen Hong returned together. When they caught sight of Zheng Weize, they both stared at him, floored.

Finally, after nearly forty minutes of crying, Zheng Weize recounted what had transpired. Everyone was enraged.

"Which hotel is he staying at?" Yan Jun asked. "Don't worry, Weize. I won't hit him. I just want to have a word with him."

"Please don't. I shouldn't have been greedy for his money. Just leave it. He's gone now. We won't be in contact anymore."

"How can we just leave it?" Chen Hong demanded. "This has to be dealt with!"

"How much of his money did you spend?" Chang Jinxing asked.

Everyone was sitting around Zheng Weize, which made him even more nervous. "I...I don't know. Tens of thousands, probably. I met him on the live stream channel, and he gave me gifts..."

Zhang Yuwen looked at Huo Sichen. "Did you beat that guy up?"

"I didn't use that much force," Huo Sichen said. "I just tackled him to make him back off. I didn't recognize Weize at first. If I had known, I'd have beaten him to a pulp."

Zhang Yuwen was impressed. It was hard to hold back in a fight; it required an absolute advantage in strength and skill over the other person. His attention now diverted, Zhang Yuwen wondered who would win if he and Huo Sichen were to fight. "Where did you learn to do that?"

"I was on the rugby team in high school. But don't worry: I swear I won't ever lay a hand on you if we fight. I'm afraid of divine retribution. See, I already got my comeuppance after you left today, and we were just arguing."

The mention of divine retribution amused Zhang Yuwen, but alas, Zheng Weize was still upset. The feelings welling up inside Zhang Yuwen were really too complicated for him, anyway.

Although Zhang Yuwen had been the first to fly into a rage, his fury dissipated quickly. After hearing the whole story, he felt that Zheng Weize himself bore half of the blame. He had, it seemed, fallen for a straight guy and spent his money.

"But no matter what, we have to get even," Zhang Yuwen said.

"Yeah," Yan Jun agreed.

"Let's do it tomorrow," Zhang Yuwen said. "We'll go and look for him together."

"No, please don't," Zheng Weize said in a small voice. He tugged Yan Jun by the hand. "It's okay. Please. I don't wanna see him again."

Zhang Yuwen got up, saying nothing, and went to the kitchen. He opened Huo Sichen's cooler to find a sturgeon so enormous it resembled a prehistoric monster. It had been on ice for hours, but it was still alive and kicking, and Zhang Yuwen barely managed to dodge in time to avoid its tail.

"Careful there," Huo Sichen said, entering the kitchen to help and almost getting himself slapped a second time.

"Forget it. We'll order takeout tonight," Zhang Yuwen decided, shoving the whole sturgeon into the freezer for Chang Jinxing to deal with later.

"Or we could eat out?"

"How are we going to eat out with all of that happening?"

Huo Sichen took out his own phone to order takeout, but Zhang Yuwen stopped him from paying. "Have you looked at the spreadsheet?" Huo Sichen asked.

"Yup. It's on the table. I made a few revisions," Zhang Yuwen told him. Huo Sichen hummed in acknowledgment. "I was thinking we could rent a house and live together. My monthly salary will cover the rent. We can cook at home and eat simply..."

Huo Sichen broke into a grin immediately. This was the biggest surprise he'd ever received, and he fixed his eyes on Zhang Yuwen in uncontainable delight. "For real?"

"Yeah." Zhang Yuwen had been thinking about it. Once upon a time, he'd considered returning to live in Jiangnan. Jiangbei was a good neighborhood, but it lacked local character. He'd lived in Jiangnan for a while as a child, in the apartment above his maternal grandfather's clinic. There was a bustling food market downstairs, and at night, the street was crowded with all sorts of vendors.

Renting a small house in a residential area and living there with Huo Sichen, experiencing the hustle and bustle of everyday life... It didn't sound like such a bad idea after all.

Riverbay Road
MEN'S DORMITORY

CHAPTER
44

THE NEXT DAY, EVERYONE BUT Zheng Weize showed up in black suits. They wore different styles, but they still looked like a mob gathering for action, especially in contrast to Zheng Weize's casual outfit. Huo Sichen, Zhang Yuwen, Chen Hong, Yan Jun, and Chang Jinxing all entered the hotel lobby and sat in the coffee bar area. After a long silence, Zheng Weize finally dialed Whiskey's number.

Zhang Yuwen had insisted that this matter had to be resolved, and everyone unanimously concurred. They were more worldly than Zheng Weize and had faced more challenges in their lives, so they knew that, without closure, this matter would remain an insurmountable hurdle in Zheng Weize's heart for years.

But they didn't explain this to Zheng Weize. Instead, they adopted stern expressions and forced him to take them to the hotel to meet Whiskey. Zheng Weize had pleaded with them not to get involved, but they remained unmoved.

The elevator dinged, announcing Whiskey's arrival, but when he emerged and spotted all the tall guys in suits, he panicked and made to leave. Too late: Everyone had seen him, and he'd seen Zheng Weize.

Chang Jinxing was sitting in the middle of the sofa, and Zheng Weize sat next to him, looking pitiful. "That's him?" Chang Jinxing asked. Zheng Weize nodded, so Chang Jinxing beckoned to Whiskey. "Hello."

Whiskey was left with no choice. He braced himself and walked over, keeping a wary eye on the others all the while. They were in the hotel's coffee bar; surely these people wouldn't assault him in broad daylight. But the menacing aura the group was giving off still made him nervous.

Chang Jinxing politely took off his sunglasses and stood up. "Hello," he said again, and shook Whiskey's hand. Whiskey shot an apprehensive glance around at everyone before his gaze rested on Chang Jinxing.

He couldn't stop himself from stealing a few more glances at Zheng Weize, though. Zheng Weize didn't look back at him. His face was bruised from the beating Whiskey gave him.

Before they arrived, they agreed that Chang Jinxing would do the talking. The others would play the role of Chang Jinxing's underlings, sitting nearby silently and exerting invisible pressure with no communication whatsoever. Huo Sichen was wearing a black face mask, but Whiskey had already recognized him as the tall, strapping guy who'd intervened yesterday, and he knew that things weren't going to go smoothly for him today.

"Hello." Cautiously, Whiskey sat down, taking note of the position of the sofa in case things turned violent and he needed to make a run for the doors.

"Weize is my younger brother," Chang Jinxing began, his tone unusually calm. "He has some...unusual hobbies, but most of the time, they're harmless. I rarely concern myself with who he makes friends with, but I heard there was some unpleasantness between the two of you yesterday, so I brought him here to clear the air rather than let it fester."

Tears sprang into Zheng Weize's eyes. The others looked at Chang Jinxing as if waiting for his command.

"I...I was at fault," Whiskey said uneasily. "It was me. Yeah...it was all me. Sorry. Sorry!"

Whiskey was an adaptable person. He knew how to change his behavior as circumstances required, and he also knew that he was in another city. Even if he called someone for backup now, it would take them four hours on the highway to get there. There was no point fighting while he was outnumbered.

Zheng Weize turned his face away, avoiding Whiskey's eyes. The others sized Whiskey up from behind their sunglasses. Huo Sichen even cracked his knuckles a few times, clearly still fuming about what happened the previous day. He hadn't gotten his fill of kicking Whiskey's ass, and now, he was feeling the itch.

"Don't you have anything to say?" Chang Jinxing asked Zheng Weize. "He's apologized to you."

Whiskey glanced around. Then, holding onto the coffee table for support, he knelt before Zheng Weize. This cross-dresser who liked to deceive straight men could very well have been a mafia scion! If he'd known, he would never have laid a hand on him. But he wasn't usually a violent person, he assured himself; he'd reacted on impulse yesterday because of the shock of the situation.

Zheng Weize finally looked at him. "Forget it."

Still on his knees, Whiskey hurriedly explained, "I was too impulsive last night. I shouldn't have acted like that. You can hit me back, or I can compensate you—"

"Who wants your money?" Zhang Yuwen scoffed. "You think he's after your money?"

This was a subtle jab at Huo Sichen, but Huo Sichen wasn't exactly free to talk back to his partner. He started to get up to intimidate

Whiskey instead, but Zhang Yuwen tugged at his sleeve and made him sit back down.

Whiskey slapped himself hard on the cheeks to demonstrate his sincerity. Two crisp smacks rang out, and his face began to swell. The coffee bar's servers and customers all looked over, but no one dared to approach them. Whiskey couldn't have cared less about his dignity. No one in Jiangdong knew him, anyway.

"I said, forget it." Zheng Weize finally looked him in the eyes. The sorrow weighing down on him nearly spiraled out of control again, and it took everything he had not to burst into tears. *I must have a screw loose. How in the world did I ever fall for him?*

"I hear you've given my brother quite a lot of money?" Chang Jinxing asked.

"No! Not at all!" Whiskey just wanted to escape this predicament. Screw the money! "Those were just ordinary gifts."

"Uh-huh." Chang Jinxing thought for a moment. "As I understand, he also received physical gifts from you?"

"He can have them as mementos. Just keep—"

"Who cares about mementos?" Yan Jun said suddenly. "What's he supposed to remember? You beating him up?"

Whiskey trembled in fear. Zheng Weize felt put on the spot, too.

"Get up," Chang Jinxing said. "So, tell me, how much did you spend on his channel in total? I'll transfer it all back to you, including the amount you spent on the gifts."

Whiskey was sweating profusely. "No need, no need."

"How much in total?" Chang Jinxing repeated.

"Really, there's no need. I'm always glad to make friends..."

"How much in total?" Chang Jinxing asked a third time. The others stood up, and Chen Hong came over and sat down on the sofa next to Whiskey.

"Over thirty thousand!" Whiskey blurted. "I-I don't know the exact amount..."

"Calculate it now," Chang Jinxing said. "Try to be as accurate as possible."

Whiskey was on the verge of tears. He looked around. "I really can't remember. Let's...just say it was thirty thousand."

"Fine. Do you have a QR code for me to make the transfer?" Whiskey unlocked his phone, and Chang Jinxing added, "After all, you've known each other for so long. I can't let you come all the way here in vain."

Then, he transferred the money to Whiskey as if it were no big deal. Zheng Weize turned to Chang Jinxing, in shock, looking like he wanted to say something, but Chang Jinxing's gaze turned severe. His meaning was obvious: *Stay quiet.*

"O-okay, got it." Whiskey had received the money, but from his understanding of the mob, he was pretty sure the next step was a group beating. He didn't think his offense warranted too heavy a punishment, and with so many people watching, he wasn't about to be beaten to death and dumped in the river...but a beating was inevitable.

"So, are we even now?" Chang Jinxing turned to Zheng Weize. "Anything else you want to say?"

"Nope, but I'd like to return this to him." Zheng Weize took out a broken music box and set it on the coffee table. It was the gift Whiskey had made for him.

"You two will have nothing more to do with each other going forward, correct?" Chang Jinxing said.

"Y-yeah," Whiskey said, trembling uncontrollably on his knees. His T-shirt and jacket were drenched in sweat. He looked like he'd been fished out of the river.

Chang Jinxing paused for a long moment. Finally, he said, "Then let's go."

As one, the group got to their feet and left the hotel. Chang Jinxing took Zheng Weize by the hand and led him to the Bentley. Yan Jun opened the car door for them and took the passenger seat while Chen Hong acted as the driver.

Meanwhile, Zhang Yuwen got into Huo Sichen's Mercedes-Benz. Huo Sichen drove, following the Bentley out of the hotel parking lot.

Whiskey couldn't believe he'd gotten off so lightly. He craned his neck and watched them drive away in their luxury cars. Then, at last, his knees gave out, and he slumped to the ground.

In the car, everyone burst into laughter in the car. Zheng Weize felt both touched and embarrassed. As soon as they were out of the parking lot, he asked Chang Jinxing, "Why did you give him back the money?"

Chang Jinxing just patted the back of Zheng Weize's head and laughed.

"I'll pay you back!" Zheng Weize said. "I didn't spend it all. There's still a little more than twenty thousand left."

Chang Jinxing glanced at Zheng Weize. Zheng Weize insisted again that he accept the money, so he agreed. "Fine, but leave some for yourself for living expenses and food."

"Damn," exclaimed Chen Hong, "you played the role of a mafioso's son so well!" Chang Jinxing cracked up again.

"I almost believed it for a moment," Yan Jun chimed in. "Can't believe I was thinking of asking Yuwen to play the role instead."

"Yuwen has the strongest presence," Chen Hong agreed offhandedly. "I didn't expect Jinxing to pull it off so well, either."

Yan Jun turned around and saw the Mercedes-Benz following them. Slowly, they returned to Riverbay Road. Once they were back in the house, they all broke into laughter again.

"Your acting skills really improved on set!" Zhang Yuwen told Chang Jinxing, grinning. "Sichen couldn't stop talking about it in the car."

"Thank you, thank you," Chang Jinxing said. "I've always wanted to play a mafia brat. Thank you, gentlemen, for giving me this opportunity. Ha ha ha ha!"

The guys sprawled out on the sofa, some making coffee first and others opening cans of cola. Liu Jingfang, the housekeeper, had finally returned to work that day, freeing Chang Jinxing from his duty of cooking three meals daily for a huge pack of guys.

"What is this?!" Liu Jingfang demanded. She was startled by the prehistoric monster in the refrigerator.

"That's a fish Sichen caught," Zhang Yuwen explained. "Can you help us prep it? Jinxing will cook it three ways for dinner tonight."

Liu Jingfang got to work on the fish and had it cleaned up in no time. It was a bright, sunny day today, so everyone brought their quilts outside to air them out under the sun. The housekeepers weren't responsible for cleaning any of the bedrooms other than Yan Jun's, so without prompting, everyone began their spring cleaning. Zhang Yuwen put on some music, and the roommates went wild, jumping all over the place as they cleaned.

"I'm gonna get a job," Zheng Weize told Chang Jinxing as he tidied up his closet. "I'll pay you back the rest of the money over time."

"Sure," Chang Jinxing said with a smile. He was going around snapping photos. "No rush."

Zheng Weize carefully looked through his stuff and packed up his wig, skirts, and fake boobs.

"You know, you look pretty as a girl," Chang Jinxing said. Zheng Weize gave him a sad smile, and Chang Jinxing sat on the edge of the table. "Have you joined any groups for that kind of thing? The kind where everyone really understands each other."

"I don't actually know if I'm a cross-dresser or transgender," Zheng Weize said. "Maybe I'll figure it out later."

"There are lots of guys who are into that kind of thing. Just be yourself."

Zheng Weize knew that Chang Jinxing was encouraging him. He meant that it didn't matter whether Zheng Weize was trans or a cross-dresser; as long as he was serious about dating, he'd find true love. Zheng Weize wanted to thank him—thank all of them—but the words "thank you" felt inadequate. He'd been thinking about it the entire journey home. He didn't know how to repay them; they probably didn't even expect him to.

Sunlight shone in his room once more.

Chang Jinxing noticed the contents of the cardboard box and made an inquisitive sound. "Can I try them?"

"Go ahead," Zheng Weize said, his mood brightening. So, Chang Jinxing put on the wig, took a couple of selfies, and went out into the hall to show his roommates.

Hysterical peals of laughter broke out, and Yan Jun came in. "Do you have more? Let me try one!"

Zheng Weize dug out another wig and put it on Yan Jun for him. This produced more hysterics, and this time, Zhang Yuwen popped into his room. "Quick, dress Sichen up too." And on it went.

"Oh, my god!" Chang Jinxing exclaimed when he saw Chen Hong with a wig. He even had the fake boobs on. His sturdy, muscular physique was totally at odds with the feminine outfit. Huo Sichen, with his unshaven beard and bruised cheek, looked even more ludicrous. Surprisingly, though, Yan Jun made it work—he looked like an aloof classical beauty.

"Jinxing is the prettiest!" Zheng Weize declared. "Yuwen's not bad either!"

Zhang Yuwen was discovering that a fair complexion really hid flaws. He and Chang Jinxing were the fairest of them all, so they looked more natural dressed as girls. Height aside, either of them could pass for a girl, more or less. Yan Jun, on the other hand, had a slightly darker complexion, so he came off as more androgynous.

"Come on, guys, let's take a group photo!" Chang Jinxing said.

Thus, all the residents of No. 7 Riverbay Road changed into women's clothing and gathered for a group shot. Zheng Weize stood in the middle, making a peace sign.

At the sound of the camera shutter, a door clicked open. With concerted effort, the roommates finally pushed open the door that had been sealed shut in Zheng Weize's heart for a long, long time.

CHAPTER

45

THE SPRING FESTIVAL HOLIDAYS came to an end, and Zhang Yuwen threw himself back into his manuscript. *New year, new beginning,* he told himself, hoping to get his manuscript approved this time. Zhang Yuwen—having finally developed psychological trauma from being repeatedly put down by a certain deputy editor—procrastinated for the first few days after the Spring Festival so as to avoid dealing with that editor. A day delayed was a day survived without being humiliated. But just as an ugly bride must eventually meet her in-laws and garbage must ultimately be incinerated, he reached a point where he could no longer put it off, because it was another holiday tomorrow.

During this period, Huo Sichen went to his office sporting a bruised face and resigned. Though he downplayed it with a few casual remarks, Zhang Yuwen knew that Huo Sichen's business partner must have been shocked. He even finally showed some concern about Huo Sichen's life: According to the report Huo Sichen relayed of his conversation with his partner, he mentioned feeling "liberated," and his partner asked delicately, "Are you in a relationship?"

Huo Sichen didn't tell him much about Zhang Yuwen, though. He also wasn't free of his job just yet: He still had to tie up loose ends and hand over his work, which would take about a week. After all, Huo Sichen had been the company's second-in-command. The handover process involved calling on his clients with a colleague, his successor, in tow so that he could introduce her to the clients and give them her contact information. His successor was a capable career woman in her thirties. Zhang Yuwen had seen her photo and thought she had decent looks.

The process also involved drinking with clients, and twice, Huo Sichen got himself drunk. Zhang Yuwen went to pick him up and drive him home on both occasions. It hadn't, he reflected, been easy for Huo Sichen to earn his salary. Meanwhile, Zhang Yuwen had been out of touch with society for so long that he didn't even bat an eye at a gross annual income of one million yuan.

Zhang Yuwen wanted to spend this time editing his manuscript, so he didn't bother Huo Sichen. He knew Huo Sichen would be free before the Lantern Festival, in any case. When Tuesday rolled around again, Zhang Yuwen printed out his manuscript to take to the publishing house, having already sent the digital copy by email the previous day. As it was printing, Chen Hong emerged from his room with his motorcycle helmet in hand and sat at the dining table, whistling.

Zhang Yuwen didn't even have to look back to hear the smugness in that whistle. "He agreed?"

Chen Hong chuckled and snapped his fingers. "Gimme a cup of coffee first, baby. What are you doing? Going to work today?"

"Yeah. What did Mr. Dong say?"

Chen Hong looked at his phone. "He finally stepped up today and asked me out. I said I was busy, so he suggested dinner together the day after tomorrow."

"Did you forget that the day after tomorrow is the Lantern Festival?"

"Yeah!" Chen Hong grinned. "He probably thought I'd turn him down as usual, but I surprised him and said yes. Ha ha ha!"

Zhang Yuwen listened with great interest, saying nothing. What did a date during the Lantern Festival signify? *When the moon rises over the willow trees, lovers unite in twilight...* The Lantern Festival was considered the Valentine's Day of the East, and asking someone out for a Lantern Festival date implied commitment—it meant that the asker hadn't asked anyone else out for the Festival. Perhaps that sounded like an obvious statement, but it was important, because it demonstrated how highly the person receiving the invitation ranked in their partner's heart. Those who could put aside other matters to meet their date for this special night were more likely to end up together in the long run. It was just one night, yes, but it was time together.

Even before the Spring Festival, Huo Sichen had booked a table at the Sky Promenade restaurant for the Lantern Festival. He would be busy until that afternoon but free to meet Zhang Yuwen in the evening. That was when they planned to discuss living together.

"No," Zhang Yuwen told Chen Hong, "what I mean is that the day after tomorrow is the Lantern Festival. So, uh, you might find it hard to get dinner reservations."

Chen Hong's grin froze on his face. It hadn't even occurred to him. When Mr. Dong came knocking, all Chen Hong thought about was their impending hookup. Dressing up, eating, transportation, booking a room—these things were all in service of the end goal. He hadn't even considered the problem of dinner. "Oh, right," he muttered to himself. "What am I gonna do?"

"Maybe you can just have dinner at home?" Zhang Yuwen suggested. "Get Jinxing to be the chef, Weize to play the waiter, and Yan Jun to act as the butler? Give them some money, and they'll be happy to do it. But that isn't going to impress Mr. Dong very much... Or, well, I guess that depends on what kind of guy he is. It could actually make it way more impactful. Who knows, right?"

Chen Hong didn't respond. He never explicitly admitted to having feelings for his masochist-leaning Mr. Elite. Mostly, when he spoke of him to Zhang Yuwen, it was about how the very sight of Dong You pissed him off. But Zhang Yuwen knew that Chen Hong had a plan to knock Mr. Elite off his high horse: He was going to package himself as a wealthy young heir to a family conglomerate, with the gym as a side project he established as a hobby.

If anyone else brought this plan to him, Zhang Yuwen would have dismissed it as absurd and naive, but Chen Hong's plan also carried a hint of mischief, and his roommates found the idea of joining in irresistible. That was why Zhang Yuwen and Yan Jun had teamed up to advise Chen Hong on the entire romantic endeavor; while Yan Jun analyzed Mr. Dong's psychology, Zhang Yuwen gave Chen Hong a makeover in the hopes of fooling a genuinely rich guy and making him fall for Chen Hong's act.

Zhang Yuwen agreed to let Chen Hong borrow the luxury car, and Huo Sichen lent him a tailored designer suit. Yan Jun researched all sorts of topics, like "the daily life of the rich," to help Chen Hong familiarize himself in advance. Everyone had a blast. The plan involved a lot of details that even Zhang Yuwen found overblown, but that was fine. They gave Chen Hong a complete makeover and prepared him for the prank.

"Let's see if I can get you a table." Zhang Yuwen grabbed his phone and made a call. "Hello, I'm Zhang Yuwen. I'd like to make a reservation for dinner on the evening of the Lantern Festival. Is it still possible to book a table?"

Chen Hong was restless, and part of him wanted to message Mr. Dong with an excuse and a request to reschedule. Zhang Yuwen waved him off, still talking on the phone.

"Yup, yup. It's for my friend. Yeah, I've already made a reservation for myself. Do you have any tables left? Okay, thank you, thank you so much... Oh? Really? That's marvelous! Yes, we'll be there on time tomorrow night." Zhang Yuwen hung up and said to Chen Hong, "I got you a reservation. It's at a restaurant owned by an old acquaintance—Sky Promenade."

"Isn't that place really expensive?!" Chen Hong exclaimed.

"Uh..." Zhang Yuwen hadn't even considered the price.

"It's fine!" Chen Hong insisted quickly. "Yeah! This is perfect!"

"All right," said Zhang Yuwen. "They still had a few tables, so I reserved another one for Jinxing and the others."

"Oh?"

"Wear a Bluetooth earpiece and keep the call connected. Yan Jun will prompt you through it."

Chen Hong burst into laughter. "Awesome!"

Zhang Yuwen went upstairs and returned a moment later with a watch. "Here, wear this. It belonged to my grandfather. The good thing about it is that it's durable, not at all delicate, and also very understated."

According to Zhang Yuwen and Yan Jun's plan, on the day of the operation, Chen Hong would knock Mr. Dong's socks off by picking him up in the Bentley and driving him to a high-end restaurant for dinner. Their only regret was that they wouldn't be there to witness it firsthand. But Mr. Dong had chosen to go on a Lantern Festival date, and Zhang Yuwen had managed to book them all a table— now, everything was perfect. They could pretend to be customers at another table and eavesdrop on Chen Hong's date with Mr. Dong. It would be better than watching a drama!

None of them, however, had thought yet about how to wrap up Operation: Tall, Handsome, and Rich.

"He's gonna be furious, isn't he?" said Zhang Yuwen. "That is, if he finds out."

"I'll come clean. I just want him to understand. Like, 'See? If I had the same status and wealth as you, you'd treat me differently, but I'm still me and always have been. What's the difference?'"

Zhang Yuwen nodded. "Since I know the owner of the restaurant, I can ask the head chef to come out and greet you to make it seem like you're a regular. How does that sound?"

"No, no. That's too much. I won't be able to pull it off. Let's leave it at what we've already planned. I need to go now." Chen Hong snapped out of his fantasy, put on his helmet, and returned to the harsh reality of cleaning gym equipment. For his part, Zhang Yuwen packed up his manuscript and headed out to the subway so that he could go to the publishing house. Chen Hong's plan was very amusing; perhaps he could add it to his book.

While Zhang Yuwen was en route, Huo Sichen found time in his busy schedule to message him, so Zhang Yuwen sent him a snapshot of the subway. Huo Sichen had left that morning on a business trip to another city so that he could complete the handover. He was going to return to Jiangdong the next afternoon, at which point he would finally be free. Zhang Yuwen told him a bit about what Chen Hong was up to. Intrigued, Huo Sichen promised to be at the Sky Promenade early the next evening to grab a seat for the show.

The publishing house was half empty when Zhang Yuwen arrived with his manuscript and walked into the deputy editor's office.

"Aha, you're here," the deputy editor said. "I was wondering when you'd come. Here, have a cup of coffee."

Zhang Yuwen perched anxiously at the edge of his chair. "Th-thanks." He had noticed his printed-out manuscript on the deputy editor's desk. This time, it bore no red-ink annotations.

What does that mean? Was it approved? Or maybe only the first page is clean and the rest are littered with comments...

They always made small talk before they started discussing the manuscript. "How did your Spring Festival go?" the deputy editor asked as he made instant coffee at the water dispenser.

"Pretty good." Zhang Yuwen smiled. "Did the other staff leave early for the Lantern Festival?"

The deputy editor came back with two mugs of coffee and handed one to Zhang Yuwen. Instead of bringing up the manuscript, he said, "As I recall, you were introduced to us by an author we have a long-standing partnership with."

"That's right." Zhang Yuwen smiled. The author was a screenwriter Zhang Yuwen once collaborated with, one who'd published a few books. Zhang Yuwen sometimes wondered how it was that some people could publish book after book, while for him, getting even one published was an uphill battle.

"Okay, so, your book," the deputy editor said in a meaningful tone. "Personally, I think it's decent. You're not professionally trained, but you lack the typical shortcomings of those who are. You have a better grasp of storytelling than a lot of other authors do, and your characters are quite distinctive..."

"Really?" This was by far the highest praise Zhang Yuwen had received from the deputy editor, and for a moment, he didn't know how to react.

"But," said the deputy editor, and Zhang Yuwen's heart sank. "Your book doesn't fit with the times. It's outdated, but somehow it also feels ahead of its time. Outdated because the core ideas are still stuck in your vision of a bygone era. And ahead of its time because you aren't satisfied with that past—you're trying to look at it through a different lens, deconstruct it, and build something new upon its ruins. But that era is long gone. Other people have built a world completely different from the one you've envisioned here, and that makes your blueprint confusing."

Zhang Yuwen listened attentively, mildly confused himself.

"No one writes like you anymore, you know? No one." The deputy editor's expression turned solemn. "All right, let's put aside your original intention for this work and talk about the story itself. Look at all the books on the market right now. Which category do you think yours fits in? Can't think of one, can you? Book categories are like a person's personal labels. You don't understand genre writing. Readers have tastes. Some like it salty, some spicy; others like it sweet or sour. They look around for restaurants that suit their palates, just like they look for partners based on labels. A person can be tall and handsome, but not handsome and ugly. You can be either a man or a woman, but not both, and certainly not neither."

More puzzled than ever, Zhang Yuwen looked at the deputy editor. Something seemed off about him today, but Zhang Yuwen couldn't quite put his finger on what.

"Yes, you must be thinking, 'That's the only kind of book I can write,'" the deputy editor continued, sounding both sympathetic and resigned. "To be honest, writers in the past were like this too. Just look at *Waiting for Godot* or *The Legend of Guatemala*—can you categorize them? Of course, I'm not saying your book is in the same league as those classics. I just want you to understand that the world changed a long time ago, because failing to grasp that is your biggest problem. Do you find it frustrating that your manuscript keeps failing to make the grade?"

"Uh, not really..."

"There will be no end to revising your manuscript, because in the end, you don't want to satisfy readers or make money. You just want to create what's in your heart, which means writing stories that are significant for you but don't mean shit to anyone else. You're hoping for someone to resonate with you and reach into the depths of your innermost self, but you don't realize that you might as well just go beg on the streets! It's the same thing. The audience comes and goes, and they'll ignore you or scorn you, at best. More often than not, they'll mock you. They don't care what you're thinking. They just see what they want to see. Take this publishing house, for example: The authors are scrambling to understand the readers' preferences and jumping around like clowns to put on a show for them. If the audience wants to see acrobatics, the authors will jump through hoops of fire for them. If they want tragedies, the authors will kneel on stage and wail. The readers have no qualms about making assumptions, either. Write about an abandoned woman, and they'll say, 'The author must have been abandoned too.' Write about a criminal, and they'll say, 'The author must have a twisted mind.' Isn't writing just another way of selling yourself, after all? The writer bravely bares all, and the brazen readers peek and click their tongues and offer comments on the shape, color, and characteristics of your genitals..."

Zhang Yuwen stared at him.

"We signed an author who was a full-time housewife. She couldn't write anything noteworthy no matter how she tried, but then her husband cheated on her and divorced her, and suddenly, she was a single mother struggling to get by while raising a four-year-old daughter.

When she finally found the time again, she wrote a new book. The protagonist is her alter ego, and the book is a collection of her tirades against life and fate. And the readers went wild and feasted on her like a shoal of piranhas. They gathered around her and said all sorts of things: 'The author must be just like this! How tragic! She brought it all upon herself!' She begged them for money and fame, and in exchange, she bared her scars so that they could rip her apart and dig into her festering flesh! And guess what? She became famous overnight! But when she was still a housewife, she was just a talented woman who wanted to write some literature.

"What is literature?" The deputy editor pushed up his glasses. "Tell me. What is literature?"

"Well, to be honest," Zhang Yuwen said, "I didn't think that much about it. I just felt like I had a story I wanted to tell—"

The deputy editor went on as if he didn't hear Zhang Yuwen. "Literature? When I read her manuscript, I asked myself, 'Where *is* the literature?' Where can you find literature now? Literature is long dead! Literature was dragged off its pedestal and robbed and violated! Author or reader, everyone has a hand in this, and I think literature itself even enjoys it! And so, over time, this violation morphs into consensual adultery and spawns a horde of grotesque monsters with three heads and six arms each. These monsters dolled themselves up and prowled the world in search of prey, and people patronize their businesses seeking novelty.

"These, these...and these... Look at the bookshelves. The monsters are the books we publish! They're devouring the souls of humankind! Everyone sells their souls to the monsters in exchange for gratification and pleasure. That's right! Reading for pleasure! What was originally a joke has become a universal truth. Can you imagine? Making a deal with the devil, letting them shit in your mind, all for a fleeting moment of satisfaction! And worst of all is if you actually take a liking to one of these books. Just imagine the devil taking up permanent residence in your soul, piloting your entire life!

"Meanwhile, books that document lives, tell human stories, and explore deeper meanings either go unnoticed or are subjected to moral censorship by those who cannibalize literature. They're shoved right back into the womb and barred from ever being born."

Zhang Yuwen was beyond words.

"Look at these books," the editor went on. "Do you know how many manuscripts we reject every year because of moral censorship? If you're in the minority, you're not allowed to exist. 'Don't like this,' 'that feels offensive'—so let them all just disappear from the world! But of course, anything that's popular with the public is acceptable! Even pedophilia is allowed if it's packaged as a brother-sister relationship. And are underage lolitas not a problem? The author smiles knowingly, and the readers go along with it—it's abhorrent! Sexual fetishes are everywhere! Watch out! They stress that not all fetishes are created equal, that fetishes can be noble or vulgar, but it's really no different from how members of the LGBT community discriminate against each other despite already being marginalized by the general public. These people wear their fetishes like badges, showing them off proudly, categorizing them, ranking them—'mesmerizing voices' and 'broad shoulders' are restrained, choice kinks, but being urinated on is the basest kink of all; to say 'I like black stockings' at a gathering is harmless, but the moment someone says that they like being pissed on—"

Zhang Yuwen couldn't take it anymore. He leaped up, opened the door, and called, "Is anyone there? Your deputy editor's lost his mind!"

At the same time, he tried to think of a way to calm this guy down. Normal people were all alike, but every lunatic was crazy in their own way. He didn't know what in the world had triggered the deputy editor—he was starting to wonder if he should recommend a psychiatrist.

"You can stop shouting," the deputy editor said gravely. "You think I'm crazy, right? I'm telling you, Mr. Zhang, nobody out there will listen to you. Our publishing house has gone out of business! After tomorrow, we'll shut down and declare bankruptcy! Your manuscript is pretty good, and I'm willing to see it to the end, but that's only because I, personally, want to do so."

Zhang Yuwen froze, stupefied.

"So that's it, I guess," the deputy editor said. "Go write some novels that can actually sell. Join the bandwagon! This is my parting wisdom for you. Stop talking to yourself. We're all talking to ourselves. You think I'm crazy, but are you any different? It's just that my madness is in the words I'm saying, while yours is in the book you're writing."

Zhang Yuwen peered out the door and saw editors and proofreaders packing up their stuff and leaving with cardboard boxes in their arms. "How...how can that be? You're closing down? Just like that?"

"Yes." The deputy editor seemed to have returned to his normal self. "Poor management, a broken capital chain, and outstanding accounts receivables. No one's investing in us anymore. What's more natural than a publisher going under?"

"But...you've been in operation for forty years! My grandfather used to take me to your bookstore when I was a child..."

"That bookstore closed a long time ago. How many people read novels these days? Forty years... So what? Dynasties have lasted hundreds of years, but they still died when their time was up. And why would you, a storyteller, care about such trivial matters? Right. So you see, that's why your work didn't make the cut."

Zhang Yuwen had been knocked completely off-balance. After a while, he asked, "Is the financial situation really that bad?"

"The company owes a whopping twelve million yuan. With this meager salary of mine, it'd take me eighty-three years without eating or drinking to pay it off. This has dragged on long enough. From two years ago to last year, and finally this year... We can't go on anymore. Our staff haven't been paid in three months. Didn't you notice that there were fewer employees every time you came?

"You should go now, Mr. Zhang. It's been nice knowing you. Here's your manuscript. You must have spent a lot on the paper and ink. Take it back and give it to your kids so that they can make paper airplanes."

Zhang Yuwen left the publishing house, still shaken, with his manuscript in hand. That evening, he sat by the riverbank that evening and watched some kids playing in the park after school hours. He was overwhelmed by complex emotions, and he didn't call his friend to ask for recommendations for a new publishing house. What he needed was to calm down and reflect on his life, just as Huo Sichen did before he decided to resign. Maybe he really wasn't cut out for writing.

The deputy editor's feverish raving had shocked him more than anything. He knew that a lot of people in the world—maybe as many as 10 percent?—had a few screws loose. Far more than most people thought, though certainly fewer than other lunatics imagined. The only thing that separated the madmen who walked among ordinary folks from those in institutions was an ability to hide in plain sight; the ones who had that skill seemed no different from other people until they either lost it in real life or went cray cray online. Interestingly, these two kinds of madmen tended to operate in different circles, and Zhang Yuwen had just had the fortune of catching one in action.

The really frightening part, however, was that his words actually made sense to Zhang Yuwen.

Maybe it meant he was a lunatic too.

Not wanting to dwell on that thought, he removed a sheet from his manuscript, folded it into a paper plane, and tossed it at the kids. They giggled and came over to ask for paper. Zhang Yuwen took his manuscript apart and folded a ton of paper planes for them. They threw the plans, and he watched them soar through the sky.

In the end, a park attendant spotted him and barked, "Hey! No littering in the park!"

"Sorry! Sorry!" Zhang Yuwen jumped up to gather the pieces of his masterpiece. He spent a full twenty minutes collecting them and then, finally, shoved it all into the bin and left the park.

CHAPTER

46

"You okay there?" Chen Hong asked. He'd noticed that Zhang Yuwen seemed a bit restless over the past couple days. "Huh?" Zhang Yuwen snapped back to his senses. Since he returned from the publishing house, he seemed to have lost his drive. He'd been reflecting on his life and his goals. What exactly was he seeking? To be successful and famous and leave his mark on history? Or to breeze through a smooth, uneventful life? Was there even a meaningful difference between those things? "It's nothing. Come on, get changed."

It was the day of the Lantern Festival, and Chen Hong was buzzing with anticipation. He was getting ready to meet Mr. Dong, his regular hookup, in order to vent his spleen and get his revenge for all the times Mr. Dong had humiliated him.

"When you drive," Yan Jun reminded him, "remember to keep only one hand on the steering wheel. Don't just stare straight ahead with both hands on the wheel. That'll make you look uptight, like a luxury car chauffeur."

"Got it," Chen Hong said. "Just like how Zhang Yuwen drives, casual and relaxed." Everyone nodded and agreed.

"You have to have the kind of confidence that says, 'Who cares if I crash into a utility pole?'" Yan Jun added. "'I'll just leave it by the curb and buy a new one.'"

"Not like you need to worry, anyway," Zhang Yuwen chimed in. "The car owner has great insurance. Ooh, yeah! That's it, perfect!"

Chen Hong was wearing one of Huo Sichen's casual suit jackets, which fit him surprisingly well and made him look extremely classy. He paired the jacket with a better-fitting pair of pants from Zhang Yuwen's closet. Who could have predicted that the love between Zhang Yuwen and Huo Sichen would manifest itself on a fitness trainer? Zheng Weize had also styled Chen Hong's hair, done his eyebrows, and applied the kind of light, barely noticeable makeup favored by men. With that, Chen Hong transformed from a beefy gym bro into a polite, handsome, wealthy young man.

"So handsome!" Zheng Weize gushed, hamming it up.

Everyone else echoed him: "So handsome!"

"People with broad shoulders always look good in anything," said Zhang Yuwen. "Go on. Mr. Dong is going to fall head over heels in love with you."

Chen Hong chuckled, grabbed the car keys, and glanced down at his phone as he made for the door. Then, he put on his earpiece and called, "See you at Sky Promenade!"

The roommates—all but Yan Jun—blew kisses at him and returned to their rooms to change clothes. Yan Jun followed Chen Hong out and got in the passenger seat. Chen Hong had agreed to drop him off at his workplace to take care of some business.

"That restaurant is super expensive," said Zheng Weize.

Zhang Yuwen laughed. "Yeah. Don't worry, though. Sichen has promised to treat us all." He'd announced as much earlier that day. Sky Promenade was pricey, it was true, but they had reasons to celebrate: Zhang Yuwen and Huo Sichen were officially dating, and Huo Sichen had quit his job.

Chang Jinxing whistled as he went to change his clothes. He was planning to take Zheng Weize out to lift his spirits; the incident with the straight guy seemed to have left Zheng Weize with some serious trauma. He hadn't talked to them about it, but his lifestyle had undergone some tremendous changes. Instead of staying up late every night to live stream, he kept more regular hours, and he also went out for a while every morning.

Zhang Yuwen changed his clothes and walked with the rest of them to the subway station. The entirety of Riverbay Road was decked out for the Lantern Festival, with colorful lanterns on the trees and in front of the greenbelt. When night fell, the lanterns would all illuminate together, creating a dazzling array of lights.

Huo Sichen, meanwhile, was on his way back to Jiangdong. He messaged Zhang Yuwen, *bit of a traffic jam. u guys go on ahead.*

Zhang Yuwen knew this was a special day for Huo Sichen, who was about to start a new chapter in his life. He walked ahead of the others and messaged Huo Sichen back. Chang Jinxing and Zheng Weize trailed behind him, making conversation.

The subway, when they reached it, was empty; everyone had gotten off work early to celebrate the Lantern Festival. The three of them stood together in a corner of the subway car and chatted. Suddenly, Zheng Weize asked Chang Jinxing, "When are you going abroad?"

His question caught Chang Jinxing off guard. He thought for a moment. "Next month, I guess? I can leave as soon as the visa is approved."

"That soon?" Zhang Yuwen asked, surprised.

"I asked Yue Wen to enroll me in a one-year prep course. After that, I'll pursue a two-year undergraduate degree in photography."

"Where will you be staying?" Zheng Weize asked. "Have you found a place?"

Chang Jinxing smiled. "Yue Wen's house. I'll clean and cook for him for a while in exchange for a room. Once I've settled down, I'll find a new place or move into the dorm at university."

His roommates had a rough idea of who Yue Wen was, due to being introduced to him over video calls before, but Chang Jinxing never told Zheng Weize about his past relationship with Yue Wen, only that they were buddies in high school.

Zhang Yuwen was going to miss Chang Jinxing, but he was happy for him. At least Chang Jinxing had found his direction in life. "That's good," Zhang Yuwen said. "You'll do well. I'm sure of it."

"Thank you," Chang Jinxing said earnestly. Zhang Yuwen also heard what he didn't say: that if Zhang Yuwen hadn't introduced him to the production crew, he might have taken a lot longer to make this kind of life-changing decision.

"I'll miss you so much," Zheng Weize said. He was melancholy about it all, but his feelings for Chang Jinxing had settled down a lot. In the aftermath of the incident with Whiskey, he'd come to see Chang Jinxing as a very good friend and nothing more.

Chang Jinxing grinned and pinched his cheek. "I'll be back. It's only three years."

"Uh-huh," Zheng Weize said. "Actually, Yuwen, I might move out too."

"Huh? Why?" Zhang Yuwen asked, startled. "I can waive your rent— Uh, I mean, you can pay me when you're financially stable."

Zheng Weize's eyes went wide. "Really?!"

"Uh... Sure," Zhang Yuwen said hesitantly. Not because he cared about the money, but because it didn't seem right to put it like that.

"Thank you... That's really sweet of you. I've been looking around for a job lately, and I've been to a few companies, and there's one I might be able to handle. They'll provide the food and accommodation, but I have to do free training first, and then I'd be working in Jiangnan, so...commuting all the way from Riverbay Road might be a problem."

"Oh? What kind of job is it?"

Zheng Weize showed them on his phone. His morning outings, it turned out, had all been for job interviews. The best option by far was a sales position with a cosmetics company. The salary was based on sales, with an overall monthly income of around eight thousand yuan. The company also offered employee dormitories.

"Is this the kind of work you want to do?" Chang Jinxing asked.

"It's okay, I guess," Zheng Weize said. "With this job, I could save up some money, whether it's to go to school or upgrade my skills..."

"How about other options? You could keep looking, you know," Zhang Yuwen suggested.

"Yuwen already said he can waive your rent," Chang Jinxing added. "You don't have to rush it."

Zheng Weize sighed. "There's another one here. See? But the pay's too low." He showed them another job—an apprenticeship at a fashion design studio.

"Oh, I know this one," Zhang Yuwen said. "It's run by a gay couple. There's a clothing store with a design studio at the back."

The job only paid a little over five thousand. It did also come with free meals and accommodations, but the shifts were longer—nearly ten hours—and the job would require him to help with sales in the shop.

"Honestly, I'd rather go to the fashion design studio," Zheng Weize said. "I've liked design since I was a child. But the salary is too low." Zhang Yuwen and Chang Jinxing didn't respond, instead just looking at the pictures on Zheng Weize's phone. "I'll think about it some more."

"Take as much time as you need," Zhang Yuwen told him. "Ah, we're here!"

The whole of Jiangdong was adorned with Lantern Festival decorations. The city was ready to offer all the romantic ambiance it could muster for its residents who were in love, and to slap all its singles in the face. As for Sky Promenade, it was packed, with every table booked up for the evening.

Huo Sichen, who was waiting for them outside the shop, took Zhang Yuwen's hand. "Chen Hong isn't here yet," he said.

"That's fine." Zhang Yuwen smiled, and they walked into the restaurant hand in hand. They were seated at the same table for two as last time, situated right by the floor-to-ceiling window. Chang Jinxing and Zheng Weize sat at a small table for four and saved a spot for Yan Jun, who would arrive later. Zhang Yuwen grinned. "Many thanks to Mr. Huo for the treat."

"You're welcome," said Huo Sichen, ever the gentleman. "But my goal here is to thank the matchmaker. You're just my plus-one. It's the matchmaker who deserves my gratitude."

Chen Hong might have left No. 7 Riverbay Road brimming with confidence, but he started trembling as soon as they were on the road. Yan Jun's encouragement did help him regain some confidence, but the moment Yan Jun got out of the car, his nerves surged back. Just a tiny scratch on this car, and the repair bill would cost as much as two of Chen Hong's gym...

He couldn't fend thoughts like that off entirely, but as he drove to pick Dong You up, he found that driving the Bentley wasn't all that bad. All the other cars on the road kept their distance from him, and no one tried to cut him off. Chen Hong reminded himself of Yan Jun's advice: *Don't just stare straight ahead.*

He drove the car to the designated spot and sent Dong You a message: *I'm here.*

5 min, Dong You replied. *Wait for me downstairs. Did you drive here? This meeting will be over soon.*

Chen Hong didn't reply. He parked the Bentley by the curb, and a security guard from the office building came over. "Sir, you can park inside," the guard said respectfully. Then, he removed the barrier in front of the building and guided Chen Hong to a reserved parking spot.

In that moment, Chen Hong felt the difference between his life and the lives of the elite. If he arrived at a place like this on his e-scooter like normal, the security guards would have told him to get lost and get out of the rich people's way. He sighed, adjusted the watch on his wrist, and put his phone in the designer bag on the passenger seat—another loaner from Zhang Yuwen.

It wasn't long before Dong You emerged. He was chatting with his colleagues, and once they left, Dong You slung his bag over his shoulder and turned toward the parking lot. Chen Hong honked the Bentley's horn, startling him, and a complicated expression came over Dong You's face.

Here we go! It was the moment Chen Hong had been waiting for! *Click*—he took a snapshot, his phone at the ready. Then, he rolled down the window and said to Dong You, "Who are you looking for?"

Dong You was speechless. It was the first time Chen Hong had seen him lose his composure.

The disbelief on Dong You's face gave way to a chuckle. He looked at Chen Hong as if seeing him for the first time, then strolled over and peered curiously at the passenger seat—confirming that no one else was there, and Chen Hong really was there to pick him up.

"What are you looking at? Get in," Chen Hong said impatiently. He was acting the same as he always did, but deep down, he was delighted.

Maintaining his silence, Dong You opened the door to the passenger seat and got in. Chen Hong steered the car one-handed out of the parking lot and merged into the traffic on the street.

Dong You, who still hadn't fully recovered from his surprise, kept glancing at Chen Hong. "Having fun?" he asked.

"What?" said Chen Hong, confused. "Having fun with what?"

"Are you messing with me?"

"Messing with you? Why would I?" Chen Hong asked. Inwardly, though, he was howling with laughter. It took all his willpower to keep his face straight, and his lips betrayed him by turning up slightly at the corners.

"What does your family do?" Dong You asked.

"Gyms. You've seen mine, haven't you?" Chen Hong was gratified to see Dong You a little flustered. For the first time since they met, Mr. Elite's arrogance was nowhere to be found.

"Right. The gym is just something you do for fun," Dong You filled in.

"I told you that, didn't I?" Chen Hong gloated. "I told you right from the start it was just for fun."

"So where do you live? You can tell me now, right?"

"Why? You gonna visit my parents?"

Dong You didn't answer. What Chen Hong failed to realize was that by presenting himself in this way, he was sending Dong You unintentional hints about his expectations for their relationship. To Dong You, Chen Hong revealing his true identity as the scion of a wealthy family perhaps suggested that Chen Hong intended to pursue him. To Chen Hong, however, it was just a prank.

"I live on Riverbay Road," Chen Hong said finally.

"Oh," said Dong You. Then, a moment later, "I see."

They were waiting at a red light, and Chen Hong glanced at Dong You, wondering if he was prepared to go to a hotel with him after dinner. He also wondered what Dong You was wearing under that suit...

Dong You met his eyes. "So you've been lying to me all this time."

Chen Hong chuckled. "What did I lie about?" He hadn't really lied about anything, but he'd been going around in circles with Dong You. He knew what these trust fund babies were like. With Chen Hong calling the shots like this, Dong You had no way to make his move.

Dong You chuckled again, accepting this response. He even seemed to find it amusing. He reached out and caressed Chen Hong's thigh. "Let me feel it. How many days has it been?"

"About a week, I suppose." Nearly a week without sex. The moment Dong You touched him, Chen Hong got hard. "Hey, don't."

"There's a traffic jam."

"You'll ruin my pants if you make me come," Chen Hong said impatiently. Dong You unzipped Chen Hong's pants and leaned in, but Chen Hong grabbed him by the wrist, stepped on the gas, and continued driving. "I'll let you have your fill tonight. Now, how about calling me daddy?"

Dong You said nothing. He only called Chen Hong "daddy" when they were having sex; once sated, he reverted to his usual, aloof self. Chen Hong wanted to see if he could get Dong You to say it when they weren't mid-coitus. For the first time, Dong You didn't immediately tell him to fuck off.

While they were waiting at the next red light, Chen Hong reached over and pinched Dong You's nipple through his thin white shirt. Dong You snatched his hand away. "Let's not do this now, daddy!"

Chen Hong was on cloud nine. He really had to thank Zhang Yuwen for letting him experience a day in the life of the rich.

"Where are we eating tonight?" Dong You asked.

"Oh, some restaurant I picked randomly. I made my reservation too late, and all the other restaurants were full." Chen Hong had rehearsed this line. So far, it seemed, Dong You didn't suspect a thing. He'd bought right into Chen Hong's persona as a rich kid being trained for entrepreneurship.

"Does this car belong to you or your dad?" Dong You asked.

This question wasn't in his script, but Chen Hong knew how to answer it. "A friend gave it to me as collateral for a loan. I hardly ever drive it."

"Oh? Why?"

"Makes me look like a chauffeur, don't you think?" Chen Hong said. Dong You laughed knowingly. "That Porsche of yours is gorgeous, though."

"That's my brother-in-law's."

Chen Hong said nothing. He knew that he had Dong You at his mercy now, because Dong You's usual air of superiority came only from thinking that he was richer than Chen Hong. Chen Hong already had the authority of a top, so without his disadvantages, Dong You was powerless against him.

"How's business at the gym?" Dong You asked.

Chatty today, aren't you? Chen Hong thought. *You rarely ask about stuff like this.* Aloud, he replied coolly, "Fine, I guess." Usually, he put on a disaffected air because he didn't want to be dominated; now he needed it to maintain his persona.

He drove the car into Sky Promenade's underground parking lot, and the moment he cut the engine, Dong You embraced him with both arms. Chen Hong kissed him, and before long, they were making out in their seats. Chen Hong caressed every inch of him, not holding back.

"Let's go to the back seats," Dong You gasped. "You wanna see what I'm wearing today?"

Chen Hong snapped back to his senses. Given his close relationship with Zhang Yuwen, he could probably get away with it, but it wasn't really the best idea to have sex in a friend's car. "Let's eat first. I didn't have lunch, and I'm starving now."

Dong You nodded obediently and followed Chen Hong out of the car. Chen Hong couldn't believe it. *He's so docile today!* Normally, Dong You would have said, "So what? I'm starving too," and whipped his pants off without regard for what Chen Hong wanted.

Chen Hong led the way, and Dong You followed him across the parking lot. They searched around for the elevator but only managed to find the emergency exit. "Forget it," Chen Hong said. "Let's take the stairs and switch to an elevator when we find one."

Dong You tugged at Chen Hong's hand a few times as they walked, and when they entered the stairwell, he cupped Chen Hong through his pants again. Unable to resist any longer, Chen Hong turned around, pushed him up against the wall, and kissed him. Dong You was clearly pleased; this was exactly what he'd wanted. For his part, Chen Hong said nothing more about being hungry.

Dong You unzipped Chen Hong's pants and sucked him off right there in the stairwell. Chen Hong pulled him up again a few minutes later, yanked Dong You's pants down far enough to expose his ass, took out his lube, and fucked him. The thong Dong You was wearing was incredibly sexy, and his shirt partially covered him as he rested one foot on the stairs, giving Chen Hong easy access in and out. The stairwell echoed with Dong You's suppressed moans and Chen Hong's heavy breathing. Even while they went to town, they remained alert for sounds from above, and they occasionally heard footsteps or the doors from the lobby on the ground floor opening and closing. The risk of being caught only heightened the thrill factor, and Chen Hong lasted only twenty minutes before he came.

"That was quick," Dong You gasped.

"Any longer, and you won't be able to close up." Chen Hong took the opportunity to cop a feel.

"Will there be more later?"

"Of course." Chen Hong continued with his groping. "We'll circle back once you're ready for me again." This was just the appetizer, but it was enough for them to savor for a while.

They straightened their clothes. Dong You even buttoned Chen Hong's shirt for him before giving him a long, lingering kiss. They made their way up to the ground floor and entered the elevator. Chen Hong pressed the button for the top floor.

"The Sky Promenade?"

"Yeah, why?" At Dong You's surprised look, Chen Hong added, "We can go somewhere else if you don't like it."

"It's fine. Let's just stick with this. Every restaurant is the same."

Given Dong You's usual style, Chen Hong guessed his objection wasn't to the price. "You only have an appetite for huge cocks," Chen Hong mocked him mercilessly.

Dong You had no comeback for that. When someone else joined them on the elevator, though, he asked Chen Hong, "What did you say?"

With a mischievous grin, Chen Hong slung an arm around Dong You's shoulder, leaned in, and whispered in his ear, "You just wanna eat your daddy's huge cock."

Dong You managed to keep a straight face, and they arrived at the restaurant. Chen Hong led him in, and they took their seats. Behind them, not far away, sat Zhang Yuwen and Huo Sichen; seated at another table off to the side were Chang Jinxing and Zheng Weize. When they saw Chen Hong arrive, the roommates all took a sip of water to covertly glance at Dong You.

"Let me see what's on the menu today," Zhang Yuwen said, grinning. "Mr. Huo's gonna get quite a bill." Huo Sichen was paying for two tables, while Chen Hong would pay for his own.

"It's fine," said Huo Sichen. "I'm going to have to depend on you after today, anyway."

A waiter approached. "Sirs, we're offering a set menu today."

Zhang Yuwen didn't know whether to laugh or cry. It turned out the restaurant had made the decision for them—at 888 yuan per person.

"How did it go with your manuscript?" Huo Sichen hadn't heard any complaints from Zhang Yuwen about his visit to the publishing house, so he assumed the manuscript was approved.

"The deputy editor's gone crazy."

"Huh?"

"Yeah, the publishing house went bankrupt."

While Huo Sichen tried to wrap his head around that, Zhang Yuwen kept one eye and half of his attention on Chen Hong's table.

Meanwhile, Chang Jinxing and Zheng Weize were waiting for their dishes to be served.

"It's so expensive here. This meal's gonna cost over a thousand. I bet you'll have a lot of Western food when you're abroad," Zheng Weize said, and Chang Jinxing nodded. "You're going to lead such a great life; I know it. I could tell the first time I saw you."

"Thank you," Chang Jinxing said with a sad smile.

"Sorry, I'm always getting ahead of myself. I've caused you so much trouble lately..."

"It's really nothing. We're friends, aren't we?" Zheng Weize laughed, and Chang Jinxing explained, "I think of you as a younger brother, you know. Everyone likes you. You're a kindhearted kid."

"If only I'd met you earlier," Zheng Weize lamented. "Maybe things would be different now."

Chang Jinxing felt his eyes threaten to tear up, and he gestured for Zheng Weize to stop talking. Zheng Weize was always apologizing, but in his heart, Chang Jinxing knew that he was the one who'd let Zheng Weize down by teasing him and leading him on.

After a bit of thought, Chang Jinxing said, "I think the fashion design studio is the better fit for you. The salary isn't great, but you'll be able to learn a lot about things you're actually interested in."

"That's what I'm thinking too. But I'm worried that I won't be up to the job and they'll reject me. That studio is so exclusive, and there are only two bosses..."

"That won't happen. You have to believe in yourself." Zheng Weize hadn't had any contact with society for almost half a year, and his social anxiety was a genuine problem for him. His previous job was something he had to do to earn a living, not something he loved. With a grin, Chang Jinxing added, "And besides, what if a handsome guy comes to buy clothes and falls for you?"

"Even if that happened, I wouldn't entertain the idea of depending on him," Zheng Weize said solemnly. "I want to rely on myself."

"That's great. I mean it; I used to be the same way. I know you'll succeed."

Standing on their own feet was a step everyone had to take, and Chang Jinxing understood this better than anyone. Slowly, over time, he'd become his own person. And it seemed this journey was the most typical of life's many challenges.

Chen Hong leaned back airily in his chair and waited for their food.

"I'm going to the washroom," Dong You said.

"Want me to go with you?"

"No, it's fine." With an oddly evasive look on his face, Dong You hurried off.

Chen Hong took the opportunity to greet his roommates. He made a gesture, and everyone responded with an "okay" sign. Zhang Yuwen shot him an inquiring look—did Chen Hong need to use the phone?—but Chen Hong waved his hand; he had it all under control.

Dong You returned then, and the waiter brought over their soup and bread rolls and set them in front of Chen Hong.

"Only my portion?" Chen Hong said.

"Aren't you starving?" Dong You asked. "You can dig in first." He'd transformed into a considerate gentleman, completely upending Chen Hong's perception of him.

"What kind of work do you do?" Chen Hong asked offhandedly. Despite his tone, he really was curious.

"I'm helping out with the family business. It's in the entertainment industry. My sister and brother-in-law are the ones who call the shots in the company."

Chen Hong nodded. "Oh, I see."

"How about you?"

"Gym."

Dong You smiled at him. "Can't you be a little more honest?"

Chen Hong snorted. *Honest? You're asking me to be honest?*

"This is the first time we've had a conversation like this, right?" he asked, restraining himself from saying *a conversation on equal footing.*

"I've always wanted to get to know you," Dong You said, "but you wouldn't give me a chance. You're always running off the second you get your pants back on."

Was Dong You really interested in him? Impossible. Chen Hong doubted they'd even be talking about this if he weren't putting on this act. "I really do run a gym," he said. "I borrowed the car and watch from my friend just to have a meal with you and make you happy."

Dong You laughed again. He'd laughed more times today than in their entire acquaintanceship up to this point. "Are you an only child?"

"I've a younger sister. She lives with our parents." Dong You nodded and sighed, and Chen Hong asked, "Are your parents pressuring you to get married?"

"No," Dong You said, snapping back to his senses. "They hardly pay me any attention at all. It's mostly my sister who looks out for me."

Thinking about it, Chen Hong thought he could guess why Dong You had sighed. "It must be tiring working for a family business."

"It is, but you get used to it."

"You haven't come for a training session at my gym yet."

Dong You grinned cheekily. "I haven't bought my gym clothes yet. I don't know what to wear."

"Whatever you want. You can choose not to wear anything at all, if you like."

"What will you be wearing, then?"

"I can buy you a set of workout clothes," Chen Hong said with a raise of his eyebrow. It only took one look at Dong You's expression to know what he was thinking.

Dong You had lowered his voice, so Zhang Yuwen and Huo Sichen couldn't hear what they were saying, but they could tell from the atmosphere that Chen Hong and Dong You were probably flirting.

"Chen Hong's in love, too," Huo Sichen observed.

"Is that so surprising?" asked Zhang Yuwen. "Everyone has the right to love and be loved."

Huo Sichen chuckled. "I'm just worried they...um..."

"Won't last?" Zhang Yuwen had actually had the same thought. Chen Hong was unique. His relationship had started with sex, but was sex enough to overcome all the inevitable conflicts of everyday life?

"Then again, other people might see us that way too," Huo Sichen said matter-of-factly. "Are you coming over to stay the night?"

Zhang Yuwen thought about it. "Sure."

"I really, really, really miss you. I nearly couldn't control myself this morning and almost got myself off thinking of you. But since I knew I might get to spend the night with you, it was my duty to endure that trial."

Zhang Yuwen couldn't stop laughing. Huo Sichen was always saying outrageous things in a serious tone to amuse him, and his words were always so vivid and evocative.

"We can go and look at some houses tomorrow," Zhang Yuwen said.

"So, we're going to rent a place?" asked Huo Sichen. "You've made up your mind?"

"Yeah." Zhang Yuwen wanted to try moving out of No. 7 Riverbay Road. "There are a few places I really like." In fact, it wasn't so much that he liked the places as that he wanted to relive memories from his childhood—those little moments of life with his grandparents in Jiangnan.

Just then, a long-haired woman in a black dress and high heels materialized from nowhere and approached their table, interrupting their conversation. "Huo Sichen?"

Zhang Yuwen glanced at her, then at Huo Sichen, whose expression had transformed in an instant. "What are you doing here?" Huo Sichen asked.

"I should be asking you that, Huo Sichen. You have the money to eat at a fancy restaurant, but not to pay your debts?"

"You... Don't create a scene here, Shiyu. Get out!" Huo Sichen shot to his feet. Zhang Yuwen's mind went momentarily blank at what he was hearing.

"Huo Sichen! When are you going to pay alimony? I've been waiting for almost two months, and you're worried about me causing a scene?!"

"You— You're crazy! Get out now!"

Huo Sichen reached for her, but she shook him off. She clearly knew he couldn't use force here at this restaurant. "Are you scared of people hearing, you scumbag?! If you have the guts to do it, why are you afraid that people will find out?! Instead of paying your debt, you come here and splurge? If you had just answered the phone *once* when I called—"

"Shiyu! Calm down!"

She was extremely agitated. Zhang Yuwen, by contrast, was stunned silent. It was a scene straight out of a melodramatic soap opera where someone caught their cheating spouse. He never imagined it would happen to him.

Shiyu's shrill voice drew the attention of everyone else in the restaurant. All around them, heads turned to her in astonishment. Huo Sichen was in a serious predicament; he couldn't stay and let her do this, but neither could he chase her off, and his frustration showed on his face.

"Don't you dare touch me!" Shiyu spat. "Don't think I won't report you for rape!"

There was a clattering sound as every diner in the restaurant put down their cutlery in tandem. Chen Hong stared at the woman in disbelief.

"Who is this woman?" Zhang Yuwen finally asked Huo Sichen.

"I'm his wife!" she interjected. "Can you tell him to pay me already? Stop avoiding my calls—"

"Enough already!" Huo Sichen said. "Come with me. We'll talk outside."

"So you do have some shame! That's a surprise, given how thick your skin is." She turned to Zhang Yuwen. "Did you know that he's a homosexual who tricked me into marrying him? You'd better stay away from him in case he infects you with AIDS. He cheated me of my dowry, too! He's a complete fraud! Rotten to the core! Really—"

Huo Sichen took a deep breath and grabbed her by the wrist.

Chang Jinxing and Zheng Weize hesitated. The woman's fury was directed at Huo Sichen, and everyone who knew him was stunned. Chen Hong, too, started out just observing, but when Zhang Yuwen asked who the woman was, he couldn't sit still anymore. He got up so that he could go over and intervene. After all, he was the one who'd introduced Zhang Yuwen and Huo Sichen.

"What's wrong?" Dong You asked. He could tell what Chen Hong intended to do. "Is that your friend?"

"Yeah." Chen Hong paused briefly, trying to think of a way to persuade her to leave. Huo Sichen was already trying to pull her away by the wrist, but her tirade was still going strong, right in front of Zhang Yuwen.

Dong You glanced over again. "Which one?"

Chen Hong started to say "both" but changed his mind. "The tall one."

"Let me handle it." Dong You put down his napkin and got to his feet. Chen Hong followed him over.

"He scammed me out of my dowry, and now he won't answer my calls or reply to my messages," the woman was telling Zhang Yuwen when Dong You and Chen Hong came up to them.

"Oh, wow! Shiyu!" Dong You exclaimed. "It's you! What are you doing here?"

Everyone was bewildered again, even Shiyu herself. She looked at Dong You. "Who are you? What are you doing? Don't you touch me—"

In one swift motion, Dong You grabbed her arm and dragged her aside. The restaurant staff instantly understood his intention, and several servers rushed over to assist.

"You're a mischievous one, aren't you?" Dong You was saying. "Come with me! Stop messing around!"

Huo Sichen finally breathed a sigh of relief. Sweat dripping down his forehead, he turned to look at Zhang Yuwen.

"Aren't you going to check on her?" Zhang Yuwen asked. His face had gone dark.

Shiyu was being dragged screaming toward the back of the restaurant. Worried that things might escalate, Huo Sichen followed them.

Dong You was faster, though. The moment they left the dining area and entered the kitchen, he grabbed the woman by the throat with one hand and pinned her against the wall.

"Listen here, beautiful lady," Dong You said calmly and deliberately, "I don't care who you are. I'll let it slide today, but never make a scene at my family's restaurant again, or I'll send someone to do. You. In. If I had the inclination, there are plenty of means at my disposal to make your life a living hell."

Shiyu stared at him, terrified. His grip on her throat was so tight that she couldn't even make a sound.

"Now," Dong You continued, "please take the service elevator down to the ground floor and get lost. If I ever see you here again, I'll slice off that pretty face of yours with a knife. I mean what I say. If you don't believe me, you can go and ask people who I am."

All the staff stood in an orderly semicircle behind Dong You with their hands by their sides. The moment Dong You released Shiyu, she fell to her knees on the ground, coughing violently and looking at him in fear. The service elevator dinged, announcing its arrival, so Dong You hauled her up again and shoved her in. A restaurant security guard took his cue and followed her.

Huo Sichen caught up just in time to see her being taken into the service elevator at the staff exit. Dong You gestured at him to go back, and Huo Sichen looked back at the dining area and thanked him. Dong You nodded. Chen Hong traded a glance with Huo Sichen, his meaning clear: Now, Huo Sichen had to explain things to Zhang Yuwen.

"So sorry, everyone," Dong You said to the diners as he returned to the dining area. "She's a friend of mine, and she hasn't been herself lately. She misses her ex-husband terribly and often shows up here to choose some lucky guy to create a scene. We're sorry you all had to see that. To make it up to everyone, dessert is on the house. Sorry again."

The diners no longer looked curious. By this point, the scene was just a minor interlude in their dinner. Other people's joys and sorrows were personal matters and not always worth paying attention to. At worst, outbursts like Shiyu's were annoying.

But what about Huo Sichen? He returned to the table to find that Zhang Yuwen had already left. Huo Sichen grabbed his coat and car keys and hurried out to catch the elevator.

There was a ding, and two elevators arrived simultaneously. Just as Huo Sichen stepped onto one that was headed for the ground floor, Yan Jun stepped off the other.

"Huo Sichen?" Yan Jun called when he saw Huo Sichen's back.

But Huo Sichen was too weary to even muster up the strength to greet him. That dinner had spelled Huo Sichen's end.

CHAPTER
47

NO. 7 RIVERBAY ROAD.

Zhang Yuwen lay on his side on his bed, his face illuminated by the white glow of his phone screen. He was scrolling through the messages he and Huo Sichen had sent to each other since they first met and reminiscing about the little moments they'd shared.

It had only been half a year. Six months. A hundred and eighty days. Long enough for two hearts to go from strangers to acquaintances to mutual understanding to flying sparks...before finally fading back into silence. Sometimes, time stretched for so long that you could know a person for a lifetime without ever really knowing them at all. At other times, it was so short that all of your beautiful memories were like five fleeting minutes of light on the river when its water caught the evening sun at just the right angle.

Zhang Yuwen put down his phone and sighed. When he left the restaurant, his only thought was: *Fucking hell, how did I come so far and still get screwed over by life?!*

He could have a new boyfriend every week, topping or bottoming as he pleased. No need to compromise on positions or learn about the other guy's preferences. If he ever wanted a stable familial relationship with someone, they would jump at the opportunity. *But would they like the real me?*

Zhang Yuwen had always wondered if love, for him, was just a re-packaged fiction. It wasn't like he could just go outside and trip into love, but finding it didn't require much effort when all was said and done. He couldn't be sure of authentic feelings in easy relationships like those, though. He didn't want to force anyone or be deceived, and so he preferred to steer clear of love altogether.

There were only two times he had ever been certain it was true love. The first was his relationship with his ex-boyfriend. Neither of them had any money back then, so Zhang Yuwen's ex couldn't have loved him for his money. Perhaps the saying "you should not abandon the wife who has been through hard times with you" was based on this principle.

The second was his relationship with Huo Sichen, who didn't know anything and even thought, naively, that Zhang Yuwen would be displeased to have to experience hardships by his side.

Zhang Yuwen didn't know what to do. The accusations he'd heard from Huo Sichen's ex-wife didn't make his love for Huo Sichen disappear. On the contrary, her words made him even more aware of his feelings. Yes, he loved Huo Sichen; if he didn't, he wouldn't be so depressed right now. He'd been wrong to think that he only loved Huo Sichen a little. In the restaurant tonight, he realized that his love for Huo Sichen ran much deeper than he'd thought. Why else would he be so angry?

He wondered for a moment whether Huo Sichen knew the truth of Zhang Yuwen's circumstances all this time and just played along with him. When he thought back on their time together, however, Zhang Yuwen dismissed this possibility. Huo Sichen's atti-tude had always been consistent, and his confidence and demeanor when they were together proved that he didn't know who Zhang Yuwen was.

What exactly did she say, again? Zhang Yuwen was foggy on the latter half of their conversation. His mind was blank. All he remembered were key concepts, like ex-wife, scam, and debt.

But he didn't think Huo Sichen would resort to fraud. Huo Sichen had a proper job. Zhang Yuwen had read the chat history of his company's group chat, and he'd even visited the building where Huo Sichen worked. He had undeniably been the vice director of his company. Huo Sichen had no vices, and his lifestyle was simple. He didn't covet material comforts, either. How could he have been in debt?

Zhang Yuwen wasn't concerned about the marriage part of it. A person couldn't be stripped of his right to love and to be loved simply because he'd been married before. In his heart, Zhang Yuwen began to defend Huo Sichen. People leaned toward the explanations they wanted to believe; Zhang Yuwen, rational though he was, was no exception. In this respect, he wasn't all that different from Zheng Weize with his unrequited love for straight guys.

But were Huo Sichen's marriage and divorce the key issue? No. The deception was the main thing—Huo Sichen had not told him the truth.

But haven't I been deceiving him, too?

Round and round in circles he went, and now, he was back at the root of the problem. They'd both been hiding secrets from each other. In fact, they'd admitted as much to each other before. Zhang Yuwen had permitted secrecy as long as it wasn't a matter of principle, like cheating. Anything else, and he wasn't really bothered. This was his philosophy about love: Both people in the relationship were allowed to hold back.

Now, Zhang Yuwen was in even more agony than someone in the throes of a complete relationship breakdown. It would have been a lot easier if he could be sure he no longer loved Huo Sichen; a few days of gaming and drinking, and he would have been able to forget and move on. That was what had happened with his ex. When they broke up and Zhang Yuwen watched him leave, his love suddenly vanished, and once that halo was gone, his ex was a stranger. Alas, he still loved Huo Sichen, which made things harder, and the only solution was to forgive Huo Sichen and give him a chance to explain.

Maybe, one day, Zhang Yuwen would suddenly stop loving him. When that happened, he could settle scores both old and new and give him a kick out the door. Until that happened, though, Zhang Yuwen couldn't let go.

That night, all of Jiangdong was ablaze with lanterns. Lights twinkled on the Liujin riverbanks from Jiangnan to Jiangdong. Their sparkling reflections on the water called to mind a fairytale palace.

Huo Sichen arrived, parked his car outside No. 7 Riverbay Road, and walked up to the door, where he hesitated like a child sent to stand in the corner as punishment.

Meanwhile, Zhang Yuwen's roommates were in Yan Jun's room, talking in hushed, tense tones. Life was often painful, and while Zhang Yuwen suffered on his bed and Huo Sichen stewed outside the front door, Yan Jun and the others fretted on the ground floor.

"Is he asleep?" Yan Jun asked anxiously.

"Nope," Chang Jinxing said. "I checked his door. It's slightly ajar."

Chen Hong nudged Yan Jun. "Go and talk to him."

Yan Jun had gotten a general idea of what happened from his roommates, but he just couldn't muster up the courage to go comfort Zhang Yuwen. "He probably wants to be alone now," he said anxiously.

"Just go!" Chang Jinxing insisted. "Now's your best chance. Go for it!"

But Zheng Weize was less confident. "I don't think it's a good idea," he said uncertainly.

With the experienced Chang Jinxing egging him on, Yan Jun was on the verge of going upstairs to keep Zhang Yuwen company, but Zheng Weize's words stopped him in his tracks. His morals kicked back in, and he hesitated again.

Chen Hong thought for a moment. "Just knock on the door and ask?"

Of Zhang Yuwen's roommates, Chang Jinxing was the most firmly on Team Yan Jun. He witnessed the scene that night at the hot spring when Huo Sichen hugged Zhang Yuwen and cried. His intuition as a honey-tongued fuckboy told him that Huo Sichen was lying to Zhang Yuwen about something, and today's events had proved him right. He was also less close to Huo Sichen than the rest of them and tight with Yan Jun, so he stood firmly on his buddy's side and believed that Yan Jun and Zhang Yuwen were a good match.

Zheng Weize, on the other hand, was Team Huo Sichen. Without Huo Sichen's intervention, he would have been beaten to a pulp by that straight guy. At least for the moment, Zheng Weize still felt grateful to him. He didn't want to see Huo Sichen sent to the guillotine or his relationship with Zhang Yuwen broken off before he ever had a chance to explain himself.

And Chen Hong? He was the most indecisive. Previously, he'd supported Yan Jun, and at one point, he even thought that Yan Jun should try to steal Zhang Yuwen away. He thought Yan Jun was a better match for Zhang Yuwen and that he and Huo Sichen wouldn't last. After the events in the restaurant, though, he found

Huo Sichen even more pitiable than Yan Jun, and he had some sympathy for his bro. Maybe he was just too much of a bleeding heart—he couldn't help rooting for the underdog, whoever that happened to be.

He weighed his friendships with Yan Jun and Huo Sichen again. Huo Sichen had signed up for a gym membership, lent him a suit jacket for the date, and treated him to a meal twice... However, signing up for a membership was, in essence, just a way to purchase training sessions with Chen Hong, which was a fair exchange and shouldn't have added points to the friendship meter. Yan Jun, on the other hand, had given him advice on love, come up with an operation model for his gym, and treated him to meals, coffee, and barbecue; they'd even shared the same bed...

Ding-dong! The doorbell chimed. Everyone fell silent.

"Yuwen," Huo Sichen called from the other side of the door. "Give me a chance to explain. I'll leave after I'm done."

"Don't open the door yet," said Chang Jinxing. Yan Jun looked conflicted.

"How can you do that? Jinxing!" Zheng Weize shot Chang Jinxing a reproachful look. Out of consideration for Yan Jun, however, he didn't say anything else. Chen Hong stayed silent too, still facing a dilemma.

Yan Jun sighed. The incident at the restaurant, as his roommates had described it, was absurd and outrageous. It was the kind of cli-chéd plotline you'd only see on the most melodramatic TV drama series.

The doorbell rang again. Zhang Yuwen still didn't come downstairs to open it.

"Let Yuwen decide for himself," Chang Jinxing said.

The scale in Chen Hong's heart tipped slowly in Yan Jun's favor. "If Yuwen is willing to hear him out, he'll go and open the door himself," he said. "Right?"

They all fell silent again. The doorbell rang several more times before it finally went quiet.

"He's gone," Chang Jinxing said. "Go now, Yan Jun. You don't need to say a word. Just sit with him."

"No, he hasn't left." Yan Jun walked to the window near the garden and glanced out. "His car is still there. He's waiting outside."

Zheng Weize couldn't take it any longer: He left the room and opened the front door. Huo Sichen was sitting on the steps outside No. 7 Riverbay Road with a document folder in his hand. Hearing the door open, he jumped up, and when he saw it was Zheng Weize, he nodded. "Thanks. I'm sorry you guys had to see that today."

"There's no need for you to apologize to me," Zheng Weize said. "It has nothing to do with me. But you really should apologize to Yuwen."

Huo Sichen took off his shoes and dashed up the stairs.

"That poor thing," Zheng Weize said when he returned to Yan Jun's room. "He was supposed to treat us to dinner today, but here he is, apologizing to me."

"More like Yuwen would have treated us," Chang Jinxing retorted. "If he'd already maxed out his credit card, then wouldn't Yuwen have to pay for him? And Yan Jun was the one who actually footed the bill today!"

Zheng Weize, with his limited social experience, didn't always see the dark side of human nature, and Chang Jinxing's words enlightened him. It made sense now—Huo Sichen had promised to treat them, but he'd left early, forcing Yan Jun to foot the bill of

¥6,000, including the service charge. He even paid for Chen Hong. Yan Jun didn't get to eat anything himself, having just arrived at the restaurant when Huo Sichen was leaving, and here he was, ¥6,000 poorer.

Now he was starving even as he thought about pursuing Zhang Yuwen, the man he'd long harbored unrequited feelings for. And here Zheng Weize was, sabotaging him by letting his rival in! Zheng Weize felt guilty.

"Sorry." Zheng Weize was on the verge of tears. He felt like everything he did was wrong.

"It's okay," said Yan Jun. "You did the right thing. I didn't want it to turn out like this either."

Chang Jinxing opened the door a crack, trying to hear what they were saying upstairs, but he was too far away to hear anything.

Zhang Yuwen was lying on his side when Huo Sichen came in and sat down on the swivel chair next to the bed. He'd only turned on a desk lamp, so most of the room was dark. Outside the floor-to-ceiling window, though, the colorful lanterns on Riverbay Road shone bright.

After a long silence, Huo Sichen sighed. "I'm sorry, and I'd like to explain. I sincerely hope you'll give me a chance to."

Zhang Yuwen kept his back to Huo Sichen and said nothing. Realizing that Zhang Yuwen wasn't going to respond, Huo Sichen opened his document folder with slightly trembling hands, took out a stack of documents, and offered them to Zhang Yuwen.

"These are my divorce papers," Huo Sichen said. "They detail the circumstances of my previous marriage, with an official court seal, a breakdown of my debts, and the reasons for the divorce. You can find the court's judgment online if you want to verify that it's real.

They're all public records. I should have come earlier, but I had to go home to get these, and then I got stuck in traffic."

Zhang Yuwen glanced back at Huo Sichen, then went back to his phone.

Huo Sichen remained composed. "I'll be frank with you about my circumstances. I swear, from now on, everything I say is the truth. I won't lie to you again."

"Go on," Zhang Yuwen said. "I believe you now."

Huo Sichen hummed in acknowledgment. "I'm not sure if you've ever experienced this, but growing up, I wasn't my parents' favorite kid."

"Nope. I'm an only child, and I wasn't raised by my parents," Zhang Yuwen said. *Can't play the victim card now, can you?*

"In families with two sons, the parents often play favorites, even without meaning to," said Huo Sichen. "In my family, the favorite was my older brother. He's smarter and all around better than me. All the affection went to him. As it says in the Gospel of Matthew: 'For whoever has, to him more will be given, and he will have abundance; but whoever does not have, even what he has will be taken away from him.'

"I'm not saying this to get your sympathy. I just want to explain why I made the choices I did. It's just like you told me: When you're writing a novel, the character's past, background, and experiences all influence their decisions during significant events. My brother's name is Huo Siting. He got into Pennsylvania State University, and I did my undergraduate studies in California. My parents wanted me to work on Wall Street, but I couldn't. I wasn't as exceptional as my brother, so I decided to come back and develop my career here. I did my graduate studies in Jiangdong, and during a class reunion in my second year of grad school, I decided to partner with

Wu Peifeng, my classmate from elementary school, to start a foreign trade company using his family's resources."

Huo Sichen paused, and Zhang Yuwen said, "I'm listening."

"I hold some shares in the company. At first, I wanted to do all I could to take the company public and achieve financial freedom. People think I'm tall, rich, and handsome, but I knew deep down that I was just a bookworm. I don't have many life goals, and I don't know where my future will end up. Jiangdong was an environment I was familiar with, at least, and I felt more at ease living here. I don't have any opinions about love or family. In junior high and high school, the girls I liked were all Chinese, tomboyish, lively, and open-minded. It never occurred to me that I might one day like another guy. Those relationships were also very short-lived...

"Since I was entering a new phase of my life, I took on a new identity. I worked at other companies for a while, but eventually, at Wu Peifeng's insistence, I joined the foreign trade company as the vice director to help him manage the business. Our relationship wasn't smooth, but we managed to stumble forward. He thought we could be on even closer terms, so he introduced me to a girlfriend— Jia Shiyu, who you met earlier."

"I see," Zhang Yuwen said.

"When she first came into my life, she did bring me lots of tenderness and happiness. She has a close friend who dated Wu Peifeng around the same time Jia Shiyu and I went official. Peifeng and his girlfriend broke up before long, though, and I kept dating Jia Shiyu. You always say I'm very straight, and you're right. I never thought of messing around. It takes a lot of time and thought for me to decide if someone is right for me, but once I've decided, I'm committed to spending a lifetime together. Maybe it's because of my career; as you know, you always have to make prudent choices in trade. There's no backpedaling once you've made a decision.

"We dated for almost eight months. We argued a lot, but I was always able to smooth things over with gifts and sweet talk... I'm sorry. This is my fault. I didn't consider your feelings, and I brought old habits from that relationship into our life together."

"Go on. What happened next?" Zhang Yuwen asked.

"I married her," Huo Sichen said. "She moved into my house, but once we were married, I discovered that she was very materialistic and high-maintenance. She wanted to dine at high-end restaurants and take vacations in the Maldives... To top it off, she was buying things all the time. With my salary, I struggled to keep up. I tried to talk to her about it, hoping to get her to change her lifestyle, and that led to a major crisis."

"She thought you were wealthy when she married you," Zhang Yuwen interjected, "only to realize you weren't as rich as she thought."

"That's right," Huo Sichen admitted readily. "I wasn't her ideal partner."

"Uh-huh."

"Eventually, I cut back on the household expenses. I still needed to pay the mortgage and save for the future."

"Did she work?"

"She had a cushy job at a friend's company. Four thousand a month." After a moment of silence, Huo Sichen went on, "She started borrowing money to fund her extravagant lifestyle, thinking I'd help her pay the loans off because we were married. I think it was out of spite; she wanted to get back at me. 'You're a stingy one, aren't you? Let's see if you can get out of paying now.' She didn't just buy luxury goods for herself; she also kept treating her girlfriends to afternoon tea, creating this wealthy lady persona. If that was all she did, it would've been manageable, but she was naive too. One time, when she was on vacation in Macau with her girlfriends, she was introduced to a junket operator and got addicted to gambling..."

"Uh-huh."

"There's information on her debts here." Huo Sichen offered the legal documents to Zhang Yuwen again, who finally sat up so that he could flip through them. There were, indeed, IOUs for loan companies, signed by Jia Shiyu herself. And the details of the court's judgment were just as Huo Sichen described.

"At first, she won a fair bit, like gamblers often do. In her naivete, she thought she could make a lot of money this way and get me off her case. Then, her bets got larger as she tried to recoup her losses. Over time, the interest piled up, and the debt snowballed."

Zhang Yuwen was still looking through the documents. "And that's when you finally decided to divorce her."

"I had no idea how astronomical her debts were. It was like a bolt from the blue when I found out. I still had the mortgage to pay. She incurred the debt during our marriage, and I couldn't prove that I was unaware of it, so it became a joint debt."

"You only need to pay back half of it," Zhang Yuwen said dispassionately. "So you're not at the end of your rope yet."

"Yup," Huo Sichen said. "I thought about shirking responsibility. 'Why should I pay her debts? What does any of that have to do with me?' I've been under immense pressure, having to pay off a debt that isn't mine. And on top of that, I have to pay her three thousand a month in alimony until she finds a job. It really feels like a raw deal."

"But complaints aside, you still started paying it off."

"Yeah. If the company had gone public without a hitch, I would have had a chance to turn things around. But when the economy started to decline, the company's business deteriorated. One time, when Wu Peifeng and I were chatting over drinks, he got drunk and accidentally blurted out the truth: When he introduced Jia Shiyu to me, he knew that we wouldn't last, because she and her friend were hedonists who went around searching for rich men to sponge off of. Plenty of men in the elite circle had been their victims before.

"I asked Wu Peifeng why he didn't tell me earlier, and he looked remorseful. He said he didn't expect Jia Shiyu to borrow from loan sharks; he assumed she just wanted creature comforts and that, with my salary, I could afford it. He thought that he could keep me bound to the company by playing matchmaker. Because of this, a rift formed between us that eventually grew into a chasm. We ended up arguing every day, and I gave up on the company..."

A thought occurred to Zhang Yuwen. "That day at Elephant Gorge, you received a call. At first, I thought it was your girlfriend. Who was it?"

"Who?" Huo Sichen didn't remember this. He made a give-me-a-second gesture and thought it over, scrolling back through his call log.

"The other person wanted to go to your house, and you said no one was home," Zhang Yuwen added.

"Oh, that was Wu Peifeng. I used to go fishing every week and meet him for drinks afterward," Huo Sichen explained. That made sense to Zhang Yuwen. "Anyway, Jia Shiyu shifted the blame for her own mistakes onto me. She argued that she bought a lot of things for me, too, when we were dating. That's why she kicked up a huge ruckus today and accused me of cheating her out of her dowry. During the divorce, I sold off whatever I could to pay down the debt and started setting aside twenty thousand a month to pay off the rest. That left eight thousand for my own living expenses. Factoring in the interest, I'd need at least twenty years to pay it all off."

"You'd have been nearly sixty years old by the time you paid it off," Zhang Yuwen said. Huo Sichen fell silent. "But you resigned. It won't be easy to find another job with an annual net income over five hundred thousand..."

"Even if I hadn't resigned, I'd still have needed to take a voluntary 50 percent pay cut due to all the problems the company is facing."

"That would double the repayment period." It was basic algebra. "At that rate, it would take fifty years, and you'd be eighty before you were debt free."

The pressure on Huo Sichen was immense.

"So, how much exactly do you owe? In total?" Zhang Yuwen felt overwhelmed just looking at the long breakdown of debts. Some were even from loan shark companies with extortionate interest rates.

"As per the court ruling, for my half of the debt, I'm responsible for part of the interest and the full principal amount. Once the judgment takes effect, the interest will stop accruing. Jia Shiyu is responsible for her own portion—"

"The total," Zhang Yuwen repeated.

"The joint debt is 11.2 million. I need to pay 5.6 million, plus the mortgage of 1.2 million. The total is 6.8 million."

"Okay." Zhang Yuwen was still looking down at the court judgment. It even included Jia Shiyu's assertion that Huo Sichen was impotent, which she likely used as leverage to get more compensation in the divorce. He could almost see Huo Sichen's embarrassment during the divorce proceedings. It was awful to be attacked like that.

After a moment's silence, Huo Sichen said, "I know—"

"No, you don't." Zhang Yuwen put the documents aside, picked up the game controller, turned on the TV, and started up his game. "You don't know anything. You think our problem is that you deceived me and that this has always been a landmine between us, ready to blow you to pieces at any moment. Am I right?"

"You're right," Huo Sichen said. "I admit, I acted with bad intentions in our relationship. What I did was abhorrent. I wanted to secure our relationship first and wait until we were in love and living together for a while before I told you the truth, or let you find out on your own. I hoped that, that way, our bond would make it harder for you to think of breaking up, or...or..."

"Or maybe, by then, you'd have no more regrets," Zhang Yuwen finished for him. "Better to have loved and lost..."

"Nurturing love between us and then using it to blackmail you... That was despicable of me. To me, Jia Shiyu is a nightmare, but she saved you from me and gave me a hard slap in the face—a reminder of just how worthless I am."

"You see," Zhang Yuwen said, "that's what you don't understand. Of course, it's true that it's not easy to admit to your own despicable behavior."

Huo Sichen gave him a puzzled look.

"You think I'm going to dump you because of all of this, right?" Zhang Yuwen glanced at the court judgment on the table. "But I'm not. Remember when you thought I was after your money? Now, you think I'm going to dump you because you're a pauper with a debt of...how much again?"

"Six point eight million."

"Right. Whatever the figure is, I don't care." Zhang Yuwen didn't look at Huo Sichen as he resumed his game from where he previously got stuck. "You keep spiraling over this same issue."

"No, I don't." Huo Sichen was a little angry but knew he had no right to argue with Zhang Yuwen, so he explained, "I lied to you. The issue is the deception."

"Then why do you think I would care about this deception?" Zhang Yuwen retorted. "Pulling out a bank card with six million on it to spend as I wish would be a surprise, while giving me an IOU of six million is a shock. But what makes one thing a white lie and the other malicious deception?"

Huo Sichen looked baffled.

"Maybe you'll say that a lie that results in loss and harm is deception, and a lie that brings the other person joy and happiness is a nice surprise. But lies are lies. What's the difference? I guess I have to remind you, Huo Sichen, that this isn't what our conflicts are really about. The question is, how exactly do you see our relationship?"

The loading screen appeared, and Zhang Yuwen glanced at Huo Sichen, looking him up and down. *He's still gorgeous,* Zhang Yuwen thought. If Huo Sichen were to strip naked now and ask for breakup sex, Zhang Yuwen felt like he might actually agree to it.

Huo Sichen fumbled for a response, clumsy in his sincerity. "I want to be with you, hear your opinions—"

"No, no." The game loaded, and Zhang Yuwen's attention returned to the screen. "All this time we've been together, you've always seen me as some kind of male woman."

Huo Sichen shut his mouth.

"That's right, a woman," Zhang Yuwen went on. "That's how you see your other half in a marriage. When I say 'woman,' I'm not talking about gender, but social and functional roles in life. You see yourself as the 'man' and your other half as the 'woman.' I'm a male woman, and you see Jia Shiyu as a female woman. Leaving aside all the shitty things she's done, one of the reasons you chose her is that she's very feminine—she fits your idea of what your other half should be. I can tell that your family must be very traditional. Your family might promote a rigid worldview, yes, but your upbringing is no excuse. You've read so many books, but your values haven't budged an inch."

It was rare that Zhang Yuwen had an opportunity to deliver such a critical hit, and he was fighting the boss in his game and verbally destroying Huo Sichen at the same time. Huo Sichen looked at Zhang Yuwen's profile. For a moment, his thoughts couldn't keep up. When he should have been focusing on what Zhang Yuwen's words meant, he only had one thought: *Humanity created the Tower of Babel only for God to destroy it, and for that, the masses no longer shared a common language.*

"'One is not born, but rather becomes, a woman,'" Zhang Yuwen said, quoting Simone de Beauvoir. "I said 'female woman' and 'male woman' because the mere fact of being biologically female doesn't mean Jia Shiyu has to play the role you expect her to play. Your views are deeply ingrained, and you've carried them over to our relationship."

"That's not fair. It's a division of labor," Huo Sichen protested.

"Right. Ignore a person's professional value and self-worth, and free up the family member with the highest earning potential to focus on making money and providing for the family—this all sounds reasonable. But let me ask you: If you had already resigned and had zero income when we first met, and I earned more and had more savings than you, would that have meant that I could fuck you as I pleased?"

"You can fuck me as you please. I want to be fucked by you. Does that satisfy you?"

"Are you telling the truth? Or are you just saying what you think I want to hear?" Zhang Yuwen asked. Huo Sichen had, after all, promised to tell the truth about what he truly thought.

"Honestly speaking? No, I don't want it," Huo Sichen admitted. "But I'm willing to try whatever makes you happy."

"See? You're still stuck in the same mindset. You'll get fucked to make your wife happy; it's how you show that you dote on your wife."

It seemed like Huo Sichen was starting to understand, but he still wasn't entirely there.

"That's the mentality of a prideful top. Your value is high and mine is low, so you're the man and I'm the woman, regardless of my actual gender. You could do the housework, cook, and take care of the family, but always as the man. Even if you have no income, it's only temporary, like Ang Lee and Jane Lin. But by your own logic, you should now voluntarily and willingly become the 'woman' in our relationship. That's it. That's all I have to say."

Huo Sichen sat in silence as Zhang Yuwen fought a fierce battle against the boss in the game. After a while, Huo Sichen looked at the screen. "Need help?"

"Thanks, but I'm good."

"You can't adjust the difficulty in this game. All you can do is hone your skills by challenging it again and again. I had to reload my save a lot of times before I was able to get past it." Zhang Yuwen didn't reply, and Huo Sichen continued, "Sometimes I think it would be awesome if life had save files too. But it doesn't. I can't go back and avoid all the bad choices I made. One small mistake can have a domino effect that leads to total ruin."

"I don't like save scumming," said Zhang Yuwen. "When I play PC games, I always use cheats, like money hacks and stats mods, and hack and slash my way through. But there's no way to use cheats on console games."

"You can't use cheats in life, either."

They both fell silent.

"I don't have any expectations here," Huo Sichen said at last. "I know you're utterly disappointed in me. Thank you for giving me the chance to explain."

Zhang Yuwen still didn't respond.

"I'll leave the document folder here," Huo Sichen said earnestly, and Zhang Yuwen didn't look at him. "Please leave my bank card in the folder. Maybe you still want to look through it, or maybe you're not interested anymore, but in any case, when you're done, you can leave it on the table. I'll come pick it up in a few days. I'll give you a heads-up first."

Huo Sichen seemed certain that Zhang Yuwen didn't want to see him ever again and that giving Huo Sichen this opportunity to explain himself had been an act of great mercy. He waited for a while, but Zhang Yuwen was still locked in a fierce battle with the boss and didn't reply to him.

"Well, then." Huo Sichen stood up. "Thanks again, Yuwen. I wish you happiness always."

"Don't block the TV!" Zhang Yuwen snapped impatiently.

Huo Sichen fell silent for another few seconds, then turned and left Zhang Yuwen's bedroom. He went down the stairs, put on his shoes, opened the door, and left.

As the door swung shut behind him, the roommates finally reached a consensus.

"Go!"

"Go for it!"

"They broke up," Chang Jinxing said. "They definitely did! Otherwise he wouldn't have left."

"It's weird to confess right after they broke up!" Yan Jun protested.

"Go, even if you're not confessing!" Chen Hong pushed Yan Jun, eager to get him to stop hesitating.

Yan Jun took a deep breath and anxiously tried to fix his hair in the mirror. Zheng Weize said, "Stop combing your hair already!"

Zhang Yuwen flopped down on the bed. After a tough struggle, he was mercilessly KOed by the boss. In the past, he would have angrily activated a cheat engine to boost the protagonist's combat power to 9,999,999 and OHKO the boss right back to let it have a taste of his despair. Unfortunately, he couldn't do that on console games.

"You can't use cheats in real life," Huo Sichen had said. But Zhang Yuwen could.

"Huo Sichen!" Zhang Yuwen hollered, in a terribly bad mood, but Huo Sichen was already gone. Zhang Yuwen rolled off the bed, stung that Huo Sichen didn't even linger in the living room for a bit. Furious, he bellowed, "Huo Sichen! Get your ass back here and beat this boss for me before you leave!"

Barefoot, he rushed down the stairs and out of No. 7 Riverbay Road, just in time to see Huo Sichen's car driving away. Huo Sichen stared ahead in silence, not once looking in the rearview mirror.

Everyone kept urging Yan Jun on. "Go, man!" Finally, Yan Jun steeled himself, opened the door, and followed Zhang Yuwen out of the garden.

Zhang Yuwen stood under the dazzling lights of the Lantern Festival. The lights in Jiangnan were like a mirage, forming a kaleidoscope of colors, making the long, endless night look like a dreamscape. Huo Sichen was gone, leaving him to face this grand but elusive dream alone.

"Yuwen?" Yan Jun called out in a small voice.

"Yeah?"

"It'll be fine."

Zhang Yuwen glanced back at Yan Jun. "I know."

Yan Jun's hand was trembling. He wanted to hug Zhang Yuwen, but he didn't have the courage.

"There are still...plenty of fish in the sea." It was all Yan Jun could think to say. "You'll meet someone better. You have a long future ahead of you, and there will be no lack of opportunities for you to meet someone new."

"It's all right." Zhang Yuwen sighed and walked past him to return to No. 7 Riverbay Road.

Riverbay Road
MEN'S DORMITORY

CHAPTER

48

HUO SICHEN DROVE DOWN the brightly lit Riverside Road. The night lights from both banks shone upon his soul, making everything all seem like a long dream.

Not wanting to return to his cold, cheerless home, he stopped outside Riverbay Park and walked toward the public square along the river. Wearily, he sat on a bench, rubbed the middle of his forehead with his fingers, and looked around. Couples were out in full force, celebrating the festival and admiring the lanterns. They strolled around in pairs and bathed in the glow of the lanterns, gazing up at the crisscrossing arrays of lights with stars in their eyes, as if the lanterns promised a dreamy future.

A full moon hung in the night sky, casting a silvery glow over the earth. He'd seen the same moon countless times, but tonight, it seemed unreal. Just like everything that had happened to him.

How did I end up like this? Huo Sichen gazed over the waters of the Liujin River. He regretted so many of his choices. From the moment he returned to China, every decision he'd made was wrong. It started that night in grad school when he picked up Wu Peifeng's call, and he had been veering down a path of no return ever since.

He remembered the time when several of his elementary school classmates, slogging their way through life in Jiangdong, had found out he was back in town. They invited him along to a gathering they'd planned. Huo Sichen couldn't even remember their names, and during the gathering, he had an absurd thought: *Are these really my elementary school classmates? What if they aren't?* He had to just go along with it and assume they were. Anyway, they had a great time catching up that night, and that was when Huo Sichen realized he was a lonely person. Abroad, he'd avoided parties and other get-togethers; he considered them a boring waste of time. Now that he was back in Jiangdong, though, he discovered that he liked these kinds of gatherings. They seemed a lot more interesting than he had given them credit for.

Afterward, he kept frequent contact with Wu Peifeng, who was in the process of setting up a foreign trade company and needed Huo Sichen's professional advice. They grew close, rekindling the friendship that they had forgotten for nearly twenty years. Huo Sichen graduated and found an easy, well-paying job at his professor's recommendation, which allowed him to save for the down payments on his first apartment and car. But some people get restless when life goes too smoothly, and Huo Sichen felt a certain itch: He needed more challenges and possibilities in his life. The next time Wu Peifeng invited him to join his company, Huo Sichen accepted.

At the time, they were both brilliant talents whose futures held infinite promise. The company was a custom-made stage for Huo Sichen to showcase his talents. When tiny seeds of conflict began to sprout in his interactions with Wu Peifeng, Huo Sichen chose to turn a blind eye. His parents were intellectuals, not businesspeople, so they'd never instilled in him that it was unwise to go into business with friends. Their company was like a tree that Wu Peifeng had planted and Huo Sichen watered. They had high hopes for it, and they believed that, if they worked hard enough, it would one day go public and grant them the glory they deserved in the secondary market.

Then, things began to spiral out of Huo Sichen's control. Trivial matters started weighing him down, and he was exhausted from constantly scrambling to clean up other people's messes. Meanwhile, Wu Peifeng blew hot and cold; sometimes he was a hands-off boss, but when his anxiety kicked in, he wanted to strangle every employee in the company.

Fortunately, Huo Sichen was tenacious, and getting through grad school had given him a thick skin. At least in theory, nothing could scare him off. He developed the company single-handedly, training key personnel, drawing up development plans, and taking charge of both external and internal affairs—all of which kept him awfully busy. Wu Peifeng gradually came to realize that Huo Sichen was an invaluable asset and compensating him for his contributions with shares, IPO, and empty promises wasn't going to be enough. Up to that point, Huo Sichen had been working away without complaint, but Wu Peifeng knew there would come a day when Huo Sichen realized he deserved better.

When Wu Peifeng introduced Huo Sichen to Jia Shiyu, he expected their relationship to remain a casual one, like a senior management perk. He didn't realize that, despite years of exposure to a foreign culture, Huo Sichen was more conservative at heart than most people. After Huo Sichen and Jia Shiyu had been dating for a while, Huo Sichen began thinking about marriage.

Huo Sichen had virtually zero experience with dating, and his understanding of marriage came from his family. His parents were intellectuals who knew their places at home and didn't engage in any passionate displays of affection. Instead, they stressed self-discipline and propriety; this was how most of the Chinese diaspora lived.

Huo Sichen's older brother married an Asian woman he met in college, and all Huo Sichen's classmates thought he was a nerd. They saw him as a tedious bookworm who didn't smoke weed or go to parties. Heck, he'd never even gotten properly drunk. If he had any hobbies, they were nerdy ones. He liked the world depicted in *Walden* and wished he could just fish peacefully there.

He had sexual fantasies about women, but they were just that—fantasies. Tall, fit, and handsome, he could probably have snagged a white girlfriend if he put some effort into dressing up. Lots of people would have been willing to date him, if only to add "Asian guy" to their dating resume, but that was just dating. Marriage required more careful consideration.

Huo Sichen knew everyone around him looked down on him, though, so eventually he returned to his native country. It wasn't for the sake of seeking an easier playing field; he just felt that there was no place for him in Los Angeles, and he preferred to live in an environment that was more linguistically and culturally familiar.

When he started graduate school, several of his classmates pursued him. Everyone saw Huo Sichen as a hidden gem. They speculated with each other about him, slapping on several buffs and tagging him with attributes and personas he didn't have. Huo Sichen found it both amusing and exasperating, though he said nothing about his past setbacks. He was tall, rich, and excelled academically in school; however, none of the girls at his university caught his eye. By instinct, he rebelled against his older brother's example. Dating and marrying a classmate was tantamount to imitating Huo Siting, whose shadow had hung over Huo Sichen's entire life. Just the thought of it was suffocating.

But one good thing came out of it, and that was the boost to his confidence. He kept up with his previous lifestyle, focusing on fitness, reading, and, occasionally, gaming. From enrollment to graduation to work, everyone who knew him lauded him for being mellow, gentlemanly, polite, and humorous. Even in video games, he was idolized in the ones he excelled at, with other gamers praising him for his intelligence. Through all these affirmations, Huo Sichen received a shining halo. The things that were once his shortcomings became his strengths, and he became a new and improved version of himself.

When he met Jia Shiyu, his confidence was at its peak. Later, he learned that Jia Shiyu and her friends shared a lifelong goal of snagging a rich husband—they squatted at the entrance of Nora Helmer's house, waiting for her to leave before they swooped in and took what was hers. But at the time, Huo Sichen was smitten with Jia Shiyu.

She packaged herself up meticulously, playing the role of a pretty young lady from a once-wealthy family who had fallen on hard times. She pandered to Huo Sichen's preferences like a job seeker attending an interview with a fake resume. She bought him a fair number of expensive gifts, played musical instruments that she had painstakingly learned for his sake, went fishing with him, and even read Kafka's *The Castle* to him while he fished.

She was an independent woman with refined taste, and despite her father's bankruptcy, she seemed to be doing her best to maintain her own lifestyle and stand on her own feet. She sometimes engaged him in debates, pretended to lose, and then praised him to high heaven. How could Huo Sichen not adore a person like that? He was happy to splurge on her; he had nowhere else to spend that money, anyway.

Jia Shiyu's friend, who had already been used and discarded by Wu Peifeng, was jealous of Jia Shiyu for successfully landing the rich, naive Huo Sichen. She tried several times to drop hints to this golden goose about what was really going on, but Huo Sichen didn't pick up on it. He was completely oblivious to the darker side of society. He might have been immaculately dressed and successful, yet he was still an inexperienced bookworm at heart.

His relationship with Jia Shiyu became intimate, and Huo Sichen experienced the pleasures and wonders of sex for the first time in his twenty-some years of singlehood. Jia Shiyu used this as leverage to pressure Huo Sichen to make an honest woman of her, and Huo Sichen readily agreed. Jia Shiyu couldn't believe it; she didn't even have to resort to her backup plan of trapping him into marriage with pregnancy.

Wu Peifeng was just as surprised. He tried his best to dissuade Huo Sichen from marrying Jia Shiyu, though he didn't dare reveal what his actual intentions in introducing the two of them had been. Unfortunately, Huo Sichen had already decided Jia Shiyu was the one. She made him happy. When it came to family, his parents had only ever given him one piece of advice: *Marriage is like drinking water; only the person drinking it can say whether the water is hot or cold enough. All that matters is that you're happy.*

Huo Sichen didn't realize that "happiness" had an expiration date—that it was easy to find fleeting happy moments, but sustained, long-term happiness was a different story. So, he married Jia Shiyu.

It wasn't long before his life took a 180-degree turn. Most things in the world tended to balance themselves without the need for divine intervention; they'd find equilibrium on their own. However happy Huo Sichen had felt during courtship, his misery in married life matched it. Jia Shiyu didn't do the housework or take care of him. She just couldn't be bothered. Her demeanor changed drastically; the flattery and adoration she'd showered on him vanished the moment they tied the knot. She was like an actor who, at the play's climax, abruptly left the stage without so much as a word or a bow, leaving a mortified Huo Sichen standing in her wake in awkward silence.

He tried to communicate with her. It was okay if she didn't want to do the chores—he could hire someone to do that—but what kind of life did she want? He did his best to schedule his time so that he could tag along with her whenever she went out dining, drinking, and having fun. Gradually, however, he realized that her problem wasn't with his attitude. Her problem was that Huo Sichen wasn't as rich as he'd appeared to be when they were dating, and she felt deceived. His generosity when he was courting her gave her the impression that his net worth was significantly higher than it truly was. And to maintain the façade that she wasn't materialistic, she'd never inquired about his financial status. In fact, she'd even bought him gifts in turn.

At first, Huo Sichen found her spending habits charming. He paid off the credit card debts she'd racked up before marriage and reminded her to save a little. He also gave her a supplementary card with a monthly allowance of twenty thousand yuan and budgeted four or five thousand for himself for social expenses. Not only that, but he even arranged a cushy job for her at a client's company so that she could save some money for their future children. When she received the card, she was thunderstruck by Huo Sichen's poverty. His annual income was a mere five to six hundred thousand yuan. She'd completely misjudged him!

Of course, she realized how unseemly it would be to make a scene, and she didn't want to risk losing her monthly twenty thousand, so she resigned herself to riding this diligent donkey of a husband while she returned to her hunt for a rich, handsome stallion.

Unfortunately, she was a married woman, and her girlfriends always announced that fact to remove her from the competition. Divorcing and remarrying at this point would also result in a steep decline in the quality of potential rich husband candidates. Marriage was like the life count in a video game, where resurrection came with a brief period of vulnerability. During this cooldown period, Jia Shiyu had no choice but to endure married life with Huo Sichen, despite her disdain for him.

She refused to take this lying down, though, and her attitude toward Huo Sichen quickly grew cruel. She nitpicked and found fault with everything he did. Gaming at home after changing out of his suit? He was being unambitious. If he had the time to read a book, he might as well work overtime... She refused to have sex with him, too, claiming that he hurt her—even that he'd traumatized her. Huo Sichen went from treading on eggshells around her to going flaccid the moment she frowned.

Jia Shiyu was relieved when Huo Sichen developed erectile dysfunction because it gave her a new excuse to scorn him. It was also the perfect excuse to file for divorce so she could find a new husband while she was still young and pretty. But before the divorce, she wanted to squeeze as much out of Huo Sichen as she could. With her friends egging her on, she decided to borrow money and have Huo Sichen repay the debt. Eventually, she got hooked on gambling, and things spiraled out of control. Huo Sichen couldn't believe his ears when he found out.

The day he received the bill, for tens of millions, he'd sat alone by the Liujin River just like he was doing now, reflecting on his life and where it all went so wrong. He believed now that Zhang Yuwen was right: All the problems in his life stemmed from his immaturity and ignorance. He didn't understand love or marriage at all.

Huo Sichen gazed at the lanterns. The sightseers around him had dispersed, and everything had gone quiet, leaving him with a hollow emptiness. The moon hung high in the sky, illuminating the countless lonely souls who wandered on the earth below.

He believed, foolishly, that love and marriage were just facts of life, eternal and unchanging since time immemorial just like the moon above. At most, he thought, they waxed and waned within a finite, predictable range. When two people fell in love, the natural next step was to start a family. The wife would stay home to dutifully support her husband by raising their children, which freed the husband up to build himself a successful career. Together, they would teach their children to repeat the same path...

Huo Sichen didn't know what he was living for. He stood up, trudged over to the railing, and gazed down at the river.

Yup, it was all meaningless.

Come to think of it, he'd spent most of his relatively short life so far feeling lost—over his studies in the U.S., his career after he returned to China, and his marriage after he tied the knot. He'd always wondered what the point of life was, but countless philosophers before him had pondered the same question with no success. Huo Sichen certainly wasn't qualified to find an answer.

Life was meaningless to begin with. That was true for everyone, but some people, like Huo Sichen, seemed to have even less of a reason to exist than others. Tens of millions of yuan in the hole, and to repay even half of that debt, he would have to work until he was fifty or sixty. He didn't bother appealing the outcome of the divorce proceedings; the lawyer told him there was no point. He'd been sitting by the riverside when he received the written court judgment, too, and when he saw what it said, he wondered if he should just die.

The Liujin River had taken countless people seeking release into her gentle embrace. At least eighty every year, if not a hundred. And the year was young: The Lantern Festival had only just ended. There were still plenty of places to be filled. Couldn't one of them go to him?

But, Huo Sichen thought, the water would be cold if he jumped in now. When it filled his lungs, it would be excruciating. Clearly, he wasn't seeking death, precisely; he was seeking the beautiful, grand escape it offered. With one jump, he could end his suffering and solve all his problems. Wasn't a sure bet like that worth any cost, including the momentary agony of suffocation? A few minutes of pain in exchange for eternal release... In the eyes of someone who truly longed for death, this small price was no price at all.

Rejecting that price proved to Huo Sichen that he still had some attachment to life.

As he thought back on the fleeting moments of happiness he'd experienced, he realized something: The only time he'd found any meaning in his life was when Zhang Yuwen was in it. Zhang Yuwen had a powerful, reassuring presence that soothed his roommates just as it soothed Huo Sichen. He was surrounded by an invisible shield, and anyone he allowed behind that shield was safe from existential crisis.

While Zhang Yuwen's shield protected him, time had seemed to stand still. Huo Sichen hadn't needed to think about death, poverty, or any of the things that caused him anxiety. Zhang Yuwen kept him far away from troubles like these. In his presence, Huo Sichen was able to escape reality and step into a beautiful utopia. From the moment Huo Sichen first saw him, he knew that Zhang Yuwen was special. That there was no one else in the world like him.

Huo Sichen knew gay people, and he didn't discriminate against them. But before he met Zhang Yuwen, he had never imagined his own sexual orientation could change. While he was traditional and conservative in some ways, he was exceptionally open-minded in others. Maybe it was a result of the bombardment of Western media he experienced during his formative years; perhaps the ardent advocacy for LGBT rights in the West had convinced him that it was okay for men to experiment. His failed marriage and the trauma he carried from it had certainly left him alienated from women.

Sometimes, he attributed his marriage's failure to a mutual inability to understand each other. Other times, he blamed it on gender differences—though, of course, most gender issues also arose from a lack of understanding, and it rarely occurred to him that he might need to put himself in another person's shoes. In any case, he'd turned to men. Men understood his struggles. They understood his role in society, and, to varying degrees, most had experienced the same confusion as him.

That day, when he first looked across the lake and saw Zhang Yuwen, he felt an inexplicable urge to approach him, strike up a conversation, and get to know him. Looking back now, that could have been because Huo Sichen and Zhang Yuwen met as children—the memories buried in his subconscious might have compelled him to approach Zhang Yuwen. But Zhang Yuwen protected him during the laser tag game, and Huo Sichen—rifle in hand, heart pounding, and hiding behind cover—turned to see Zhang Yuwen hoisting his sniper rifle. When Zhang Yuwen scanned the area from his vantage point, his focused expression captivated Huo Sichen utterly.

In that moment, Huo Sichen felt like a child who needed someone to protect him. Sometimes he thought that all he needed was a few minutes of protection in the long grind of his life, a reprieve to allow his depleted health bar to fill back up. Then he could reemerge and face the challenges life threw his way that had left him battered and bruised.

He had a hunch that Chen Hong and his friends were gay, so he figured that Zhang Yuwen probably was too. But this wasn't Huo Sichen's primary motive in getting close to him. Whether Zhang Yuwen was gay or not, Huo Sichen wanted to be friends with him, to spend more time with him, even to live closer to him. He needed a companion, and the question of whether they might eventually progress to lovers didn't seem so pressing then. He did still have erectile dysfunction, after all.

After that day, he couldn't resist reaching out to Zhang Yuwen, and Zhang Yuwen responded to all of his messages. This was the tenderness of a man: gentle, steadfast, and reliable. It was different from a woman's tenderness, which was like a spark from within igniting hope anew, telling you that everything had meaning. A man's tenderness was like brilliant sunshine, and it thawed Huo Sichen's frozen body until he came to life again, his vitality renewed.

Gradually, they came to understand each other. Zhang Yuwen didn't flatter him, but Huo Sichen could see from the curiosity in Zhang Yuwen's eyes that he wanted to get to know Huo Sichen better. They didn't just share the same way of thinking; they were similarly cautious, like two snails on a branch tentatively probing each other with their antennae. Huo Sichen partially hoped to build a friendship with Zhang Yuwen and confide in him about his loneliness, but he wanted to go a step beyond that, too. The more he came to understand Zhang Yuwen, the more Huo Sichen wanted to be with him. Huo Sichen was certain he could feel at peace with Zhang Yuwen, even if they weren't doing anything. Yes, Zhang Yuwen was often blasé about things, but he always gave Huo Sichen just the right response, and that made Huo Sichen feel like the effort he put in was never in vain.

It wasn't until their hike in Elephant Gorge, when Huo Sichen saw Zhang Yuwen's abs, that he felt a certain other kind of desire awaken in him. Before that, he had treated Zhang Yuwen as a friend and, he hoped, an eventual confidant: someone with whom he could share a bed, travel, or lounge around on the sofa on weekends, gaming. The idea that he could bare not only his heart to his friend but also his body—that he could make passionate love to him—ignited a forbidden flame in Huo Sichen. The blaze intensified, even without anyone stoking it, until it burned so hot it disoriented him. And that night, he discovered that his erectile dysfunction had been cured!

At first, he panicked, not knowing how to approach his developing relationship with Zhang Yuwen. He even started to avoid Zhang Yuwen, but before long, he came to his senses. Composed and cautious, he reflected again on his life, and this time, he realized that there was no reason he couldn't date a gay man. His family had never been able to stop him from doing what he wanted. His parents would have a lot to say about his choice, but they would come to terms with it once all was said and done. And Huo Sichen could even take Zhang Yuwen abroad and marry him.

Standing by the river, Huo Sichen realized that Zhang Yuwen was right. He had been acting like a blind chauvinist. No, scratch that—he *was* a blind chauvinist. When he fell for someone, he started to plan out their lives together before he even stopped to consider whether the other person would want to marry him. He was a fool in love, an idiot who wasn't sure of anything other than that his "love" came from the heart. He was drawn to Zhang Yuwen, and he understood that he was fond of him.

For the first time in many years, Huo Sichen truly understood: He had fallen in love. He wasn't a machine fueled by hormones and fleeting lust, programmed by his mortal flesh to pursue well-meaning missions. He had fallen in love with another person as a free soul.

When he realized he had feelings for Zhang Yuwen, Huo Sichen had Chen Hong help him play a joke so that he could break down the barrier between himself and Zhang Yuwen and make his feelings known. He pursued Zhang Yuwen, but his failed marriage still had a hold on him, and, without meaning to, he avoided coming clean to Zhang Yuwen about his life.

Huo Sichen clung to two unrealistic fantasies. First, he hoped that if their relationship was strong enough, it could withstand the truth coming out—that even if he was angry at first, Zhang Yuwen would get over it because he couldn't bear to leave Huo Sichen. (This thought was so despicable that Huo Sichen refused to let himself dwell on it.) In his second fantasy, he dreamed of working harder and miraculously taking the company public. If that happened, he could free himself of his financial shackles entirely.

He repackaged these two thoughts repeatedly, tossing them around from one mental box to another. Sometimes, he put them together and stuffed them somewhere they wouldn't be found, then tossed the whole thing under the bed while he progressed toward a new, alluring life.

Zhang Yuwen had changed him. His life was so rich that it forced Huo Sichen realize there was more to life than working and earning money. There were so many things to look forward to that had nothing to do with money. Even if all they were doing was having a meal together, they could banter and laugh. Zhang Yuwen seemed to have no worries at all; a monthly salary of only six thousand, but he knew how to be content with that. Insulated from all anxieties, he believed everything would work out in the end. If all working people lived like Sisyphus, then he was a Sisyphus who took it easy, letting go of the boulder midway up the mountain to find a spot to bask in the sun.

He had a fatal pull over Huo Sichen. He listened to everyone's opinions, and when he disagreed with Huo Sichen on something, a sly look appeared in his eyes. He understood Huo Sichen's bad jokes, and—even better—twisted them around to deliver punchlines that took Huo Sichen by surprise. They grew closer and closer, developing their rapport and deepening their bond. When Huo Sichen said, "You don't love me as much as I love you," he was touched by Zhang Yuwen's response, and his spirits soared when they finally made love at the hotel. The long-overdue orgasm made up for all those years he spent without true love, and he was so dizzy with unexpected joy, his mind went blank.

All he wanted was to give Zhang Yuwen everything he had, to please him and make him happy however he could. In bed, he worked hard to find Zhang Yuwen's sensitive spots, and Zhang Yuwen's responses thrilled him. He got hooked on the pleasure of sex, and his capacity for rational thought flew out of the window; all he could think about was making love to Zhang Yuwen. During those times, he didn't want to leave Zhang Yuwen's side for even a second. He wanted to tell Zhang Yuwen over and over just how much he loved him. Why had it taken Zhang Yuwen so long to find him again as an adult after the promise they made when they were kids? Did he know how much Huo Sichen had endured while he was waiting for him?

Theirs was a slow-burn romance, even though Huo Sichen fell in love with Zhang Yuwen at first sight, and Huo Sichen enjoyed the burn. This, he realized, was what love was. Unfortunately, his dating skills were lacking, and his whirlwind marriage had left him with nothing but debt. To make up for it, he studied the male leads in movies and dramas, and even downloaded romance novel audiobooks to his phone so that he could listen while he was driving and learn how dating worked. This was the life of a bookworm; even romance called for learning materials.

Old habits, however, died hard. Over time, driven by muscle memory and his choice of learning materials, he reverted to his old modus operandi. Without even realizing it, he'd slipped back into his well-worn "husband" role, where he saw Zhang Yuwen as his precious, beloved wife. The only difference was that his new wife had a middle leg. At some point, it dawned on Huo Sichen that this wasn't appropriate, so he started to remind himself to treat Zhang Yuwen as both a buddy and a lover, but this sometimes made him feel like he was on shaky ground.

After today's thorough castigation at Zhang Yuwen's hands, Huo Sichen thought he was finally starting to understand. What bothered Zhang Yuwen had nothing to do with the deceit or debt; it was their relationship dynamic. That fit with what Huo Sichen knew about Zhang Yuwen too. He just wasn't a person who cared much about material possessions. Did that mean there was still hope for them?

This thought made Huo Sichen want to go back to Riverbay Road, but it was already 5:30 a.m. His tedious self-reflection had taken so long that the moon had sunk past the end of the river, and the first rays of morning light were breaking through the horizon. Mornings belonged to the elderly—early risers who seemed far removed from the previous night's festivities. Old ladies dragged their shopping trolleys along the riverside, on their way to buy groceries at the market, and old men strolled around the park with their dogs.

Huo Sichen sat on the bench, having gone the whole night without sleep and, as a result, looking like he fit right in with these older people. He often wondered about his own life in old age; it probably wouldn't amount to much. For a time, the thought of growing old alone scared him, but ever since his divorce, he thought it might be for the best. At least by then, he would have repaid his debt.

Suddenly, he spotted a paper airplane in the bushes beside the bench. He picked it up and found that the paper had some text printed on it:

...Yuan Mu abandoned everything he once had—lover, family, wealth—and came to this place alone, hoping to recapture long-lost feelings and gain possession of himself once more. But what awaited him was an endless sea of wolves that pounced from the horizon and devoured the night's last glimmer of starlight.

In the wilderness, surrounded by wolves, he set the grass beneath him ablaze. The flame would consume him, and by the time the sun rose, he would be nothing but ash. If he were unlucky, he wouldn't even get to see the dawn of a new day.

It was all worth it, though. In that moment, he finally found himself again. He was no longer the man who merely resigned himself to his fate.
—The End—

I'm also a man who just accepts whatever life throws at me, Huo Sichen thought. Watching the sun rise and spread its light across the Liujin River, he sighed. Then, he got up, went to his car, and drove it to the designated chop shop for handover and inspection. The proceeds would be enough to offset a year's worth of loan repayments, and the creditor had promised not to bother him again for a year after the sale. Before last night, Huo Sichen had planned to trade his car for a year of breathing room, which he intended to use for wholeheartedly loving both Zhang Yuwen and himself before he started afresh. That plan had gone up in smoke, but he had already quit his job—he still had to pawn his car.

From this moment on, he'd have to walk life's many paths on his own. He wandered around aimlessly, like an empty shell devoid of its soul, and somehow, he ended up back on Riverbay Road.

CHAPTER

49

ZHANG YUWEN WAS still asleep. First, he dreamed he was fighting with Huo Sichen, and money was scattering all over the ground; then, he dreamed that Jia Shiyu was crying at him about Huo Sichen, that heartless cad... The crying lingered in his ears, and Zhang Yuwen kept saying, "Stop crying," but she just wouldn't listen. Meanwhile, Huo Sichen was off to the side, anxiously calling, "Yuwen! Yuwen!" Irritated, Zhang Yuwen sat up with a shout.

"Yuwen!" Chang Jinxing was in his bedroom, still dressed in his pajamas. "Can you get up? What time did you get to bed last night?"

The crying was still there—it was coming from the living room— but the voice sounded older than Jia Shiyu's, and it was breaking up with hysterical sobs. Zhang Yuwen startled fully awake. "What's wrong?"

"Yan Jun's mom is here! I don't know how she found this place. There's someone else with her..."

The gravity of the situation was immediately clear to Zhang Yuwen. This was Yan Jun's worst fear. He jumped out of bed, threw on some clothes, and ran to the living room. Chen Hong and Zheng Weize were already awake, too, and everyone was in the living room, comforting an old woman with gray hair. Mama Yan was wailing her heart out on the sofa, seemingly oblivious to the others. Zheng

Weize picked Xiao-Qi up and walked around the hall with her, but Xiao-Qi, who was probably frightened by the crying, burst into tears too.

In addition to grandmother and granddaughter, Yan Jun's nephew—the sporty guy named Shen Yingjie—was there, and sitting next to him was another crying woman. This woman was in her forties, and from the resemblance between them, Zhang Yuwen assumed she was Shen Yingjie's mother.

Zhang Yuwen immediately understood what must have happened. He went in search of some medicine without stopping to comfort Mama Yan. "Where's Yan Jun?"

"I've already called him," Chang Jinxing said. "He said he'll be back in five minutes."

"Where's Auntie Jing?!" Zhang Yuwen yelled. "Where are the heart pills and the red sage root tablets?"

Liu Jingfang hurried out of the kitchen and opened the highest drawer to get them for him, and just as Zhang Yuwen was twisting the bottle cap open, Yan Jun entered through the front door and saw what was going on. Without a word, he stormed over to Shen Yingjie and slapped him hard, causing chaos to erupt.

"Oh, my son!" Mama Yan cried.

"Oh no! Quick! Where's the medicine, Yuwen?" Chen Hong shouted when he heard her breathless cries. He knew from past experiences with older people that Mama Yan's heart must not be able to take the shock, and he hurried to rub her back.

Zhang Yuwen motioned Yan Jun over. Yan Jun took the heart pills from him while Liu Jingfang went to pour a glass of water. "Make sure she takes this first," Zhang Yuwen said, then grabbed the tablets.

"Ma!" Yan Jun began to cry too. That made four crying people in one living room.

"How long has your brother been dead? Why didn't you say anything?!" Mama Yan wailed. "Oh heavens, how could this happen?! My son! Oh, my Dai! How can you abandon me like this? How heartless... All these years I spent raising you..."

Chen Hong, Zheng Weize, and Chang Jinxing silently retreated to their rooms. Yan Jun knelt in front of his mother, laid his head on her lap, and cried again. Seeing this, Xiao-Qi cried even louder and reached out to Yan Jun for a hug, but Yan Jun was in no state to look after her. Zhang Yuwen scooped her up in his arms, and Xiao-Qi sobbed, "Yuwen, Yuwen!"

Zhang Yuwen had no children, so he couldn't comprehend the agony of losing one. Even so, his eyes reddened. Shen Yingjie's mother was crying, too, seemingly reminded of her own sorrows. The atmosphere in the hall was so thick with the grief of Yan Jun's sobs, Mama Yan's broken cries, Madam Shen's wails, and Xiao-Qi's whimpers that Zhang Yuwen found himself tearing up too.

The doorbell rang. Remembering that he had plans to meet his childhood friend, Liang Zheng, Zhang Yuwen went to open the door with Xiao-Qi in his arms. Instructions for Liang Zheng to wait outside were on the tip of his tongue when he realized it was actually Huo Sichen, exhausted after a sleepless night.

"Where's your car?" Zhang Yuwen asked. He hadn't heard a car pulling up, and Huo Sichen usually parked right outside.

"I pawned it to pay off part of the debt," Huo Sichen said uneasily. "I'm here to get my bank card back. I'll leave right as soon as I have it."

Zhang Yuwen beckoned him in. Huo Sichen had hoped to get another look at Zhang Yuwen and was prepared for a rebuff, but he'd thought Zhang Yuwen would still be sleeping; he was a little dazed to instead see Zhang Yuwen in this state. Everyone was still crying in the living room, too, which startled Huo Sichen. He didn't know what was going on.

"Upstairs," Zhang Yuwen told him. Huo Sichen quietly walked past Yan Jun and headed up the stairs, his face full of questions. Zhang Yuwen followed him, still holding Xiao-Qi in his arms, and pointed to his bed. "Wait here. I have some stuff to deal with. We'll talk later."

Huo Sichen nodded numbly and sat on the edge of the bed.

Downstairs, a second round of crying began and gave Zhang Yuwen a splitting headache. Xiao-Qi, who was having trouble sleeping, burst into tears again. Zhang Yuwen felt as if his heart was about to explode. He soothed Xiao-Qi again, and as he set her down in the crib in Yan Jun's room, he heard Mama Yan crying, "Oh, my son, Mama's coming to see you... Where are you?"

"Get your ass to school now!" Yan Jun was fuming at his nephew when Zhang Yuwen emerged. He grabbed Shen Yingjie and manhandled him to the foyer, where he kicked at him so that he'd leave.

"Hush!" Zhang Yuwen said, motioning for Yan Jun to tone it down. Xiao-Qi had finally fallen asleep. Yan Jun regained his composure and stepped into his room, his eyes red as he nodded his thanks to Zhang Yuwen.

Zhang Yuwen glanced at the living room. Mama Yan had survived the first wave of shock and was now sitting dazedly on the sofa, still weeping, while Shen Yingjie's mother comforted her.

"I told her I'd come and pick Xiao-Qi up after the Lantern Festival," Yan Jun said. "She probably sensed something was amiss and decided to come here by train with Xiao-Qi. The other lady is Yingjie's mother. They took the overnight service and showed up at Yingjie's place..."

"I get it now," Zhang Yuwen whispered. "So your nephew brought them here. You can't blame him. He had no choice."

Shen Yingjie was neither a skilled liar nor an experienced one. He'd inadvertently let slip the truth to his mother after just a few words. Really, it had been inevitable ever since he first came to Jiangdong to seek refuge with Yan Jun.

"I'll find somewhere to put my mother up and figure something out," Yan Jun said.

"Let her stay here. The others can watch her for you. Don't make her move around again; her body can't take it. And I'll call the hospital later. You should take her in for a checkup tomorrow."

Yan Jun breathed a long sigh, and then he started crying again. Zhang Yuwen gave him a hug and patted his back, then gestured for him to look at Xiao-Qi and cast a meaningful glance at the door: It was time for Yan Jun to step up and shoulder the responsibility for what he'd done. Yan Jun nodded his understanding.

"With Xiao-Qi here," Zhang Yuwen added, "your mother will pull through."

The doorbell rang again, and Zhang Yuwen opened the door.

"Hellooo," said Liang Zheng, playing with his car key.

"Don't come in," Zhang Yuwen told him. "Wait for me out here for a while."

Liang Zheng peered curiously into No. 7 Riverbay Road, and Zhang Yuwen shut the door in his face, leaving him bewildered.

Zhang Yuwen returned to the living room to finally greet Mama Yan and Madam Shen. He went over, sank to one knee at the sofa just as Yan Jun had done, and listened to Mama Yan's heartbeat. Not knowing what he was doing, Mama Yan patted him on the head and touched his ears and nose.

"Who are you?" Mama Yan asked.

"I'm Zhang Yuwen. I'm Yan Jun's friend. Auntie, please stay seated. I'll get someone to pour you something to drink."

"Oh, so you're Zhang Yuwen," Madam Shen said. "I've been hearing Xiao-Qi call out for someone named Yuwen."

Zhang Yuwen nodded and gestured to Yan Jun not to worry; his mother would be fine for now. Leaving Yan Jun with his mother, Zhang Yuwen stepped into the kitchen. Liu Jingfang and the other housekeeper were sitting there, because it didn't feel right for them to go out in the hall.

"Auntie Jing, please arrange for a doctor to make a house call this afternoon," he said. "We have to ensure there are no major issues with Mrs. Yan."

"Sure," said Liu Jingfang. "What are you looking for?"

"Ginseng tea."

"I've got it." Liu Jingfang made ginseng tea and brought it to Mama Yan.

"Set aside everything else for the day today," Zhang Yuwen told Liu Jingfang, "and make sure to keep an eye on her. If something crops up, call an ambulance immediately and administer first aid."

Liu Jingfang was aware that something must have happened, so she nodded. Zhang Yuwen dug a few more heart pills out of the bottle and swallowed them.

"Give me some too," Yan Jun said. He'd been tossing and turning all night, unable to sleep, and now, his heart felt like it was about to give out.

"Take them all. There are more in the top drawer. I have an appointment today, so I'm heading out for a while. If it all goes well, I'll be back by noon."

Yan Jun nodded. "Okay, do what you need to do."

Zhang Yuwen hurried up the stairs, pushed the door to his room open...and found Huo Sichen fast asleep in his bed. The sight rendered him speechless. Rather than waking him, however, Zhang Yuwen covered him with a blanket, then changed his own clothes and headed out to meet Liang Zheng.

"What's going on in your house?" Liang Zheng asked, looking bewildered.

"It's a long story." Zhang Yuwen felt overwhelmed. Everything was happening all at once. "Where's the lawyer?"

"We're going to pick him up now." Liang Zheng drove out of Riverbay Road. "Have you thought this through?"

"Yeah." Zhang Yuwen unlocked his phone. He was planning to activate a life cheat today, and a move like this was all or nothing. If he was going to do it, he might as well go all out.

Liang Zheng picked up the lawyer and her assistant, who had been waiting for them for a long time. He briefly explained the situation as he drove, and finally, he parked at the building where the publishing house was.

Zhang Yuwen entered the publishing house and shook hands with the editor-in-chief and the boss. He'd scheduled this meeting with several senior executives and the general manager at two o'clock that morning. Now, sitting in the conference room, he still felt a little sleepy.

"First things first," Zhang Yuwen began. "I have a lot on my plate today, so please pardon me if I appear to be a little out of it."

The deputy editor looked strangely at Zhang Yuwen, and the chief editor and general manager listened attentively. No one said a word.

Zhang Yuwen thought for a moment, then continued. "I'll keep it simple. I don't claim to be a highly cultured person, but I hope to make whatever small contribution I can to the development of human civilization."

The chief editor said, "As I recall, you're—"

"Director Zhang!" the general manager cut in. "You're really too modest!"

The chief editor's mouth snapped shut.

"So," Zhang Yuwen continued, "I intend to invest in your company and make sure this publishing house's forty-year history doesn't end here. I previously spoke to the deputy editor, who gave me a ballpark of the current financial deficit. I have a studio in my name, and we can inject some capital by buying shares. I think I can bring your company back out of the red."

The deputy editor gaped at him. It seemed to be taking him a while to wrap his head around this.

"I won't interfere in any of your operations. I'm only investing. Everything will remain as it is. I think things like... I mean, I know that a book's worth cannot be measured solely by its commercial value. For me, books create more than just economic returns, so this investment is worthwhile." Everyone opened their mouths to speak, so Zhang Yuwen quickly concluded his opening statement. "This is Liang Zheng, a good friend of mine. He will make some decisions on my behalf. And this is Attorney Lin and her team, whom I've granted authority to handle the full investment process."

Liang Zheng went over to shake hands with them, and the lawyer did the same.

"All right, I have to go now," Zhang Yuwen said. "For some reason, I'm particularly busy today. Please excuse me."

"Please have a cup of coffee, at least!" The general manager immediately went to make the coffee himself. He knew that Zhang Yuwen, like other wealthy individuals, was a behind-the-scenes boss and rarely showed up in person to make a deal. He and his team had discussed it last night when they received the meeting request—why was this Director Zhang suddenly asking to meet with the publishing house's senior management? This stroke of good fortune had come knocking so suddenly that they still couldn't believe it; they needed more time to digest the news.

"The schedule and memos are in your hands now," Liang Zheng told the lawyer.

"No problem," Attorney Lin said. "I'll proceed and send the finalized draft to you and Mr. Zhang."

Zhang Yuwen accepted the instant coffee, gulped it down, and shook hands with everyone to bid them farewell. And so it was done: He used a cheat code to change everyone's lives, straight up acquiring the publishing house that had rejected his manuscript countless times.

"What on earth has gotten into you?" Liang Zheng asked as they got into his car. "Why the sudden decision to buy it out? Are you planning to pivot to publishing?"

"Nope," Zhang Yuwen said. "I still want to write and get my books published. This publishing house was going out of business because of mismanagement."

"So? Can't you just submit your manuscripts to another publisher? Oh, but I guess you can publish whatever you want now that you own the company."

"I want to be a writer, not just publish books. What's the point of forcing them to publish my book, Mr. Rich Guy?"

"What's the point of acquiring the publisher, then? It can't really just be that you feel bad for them because they've been around for forty years."

"It's a bit of everything, I guess." When Zhang Yuwen was a kid, a lot of the books in his grandparents' house were translated and published by this publishing house. That included both his grandfather's professional books and Zhang Yuwen's personal favorite, *The Three Musketeers*.

"How's it going with your hubby?" Liang Zheng asked.

"You mean my wifey? The same, I guess. He's got a lot of pride, so it's going to take some work."

Liang Zheng burst out laughing. "All men have pride. Maybe you're just too domineering."

"Me? Domineering?" Zhang Yuwen scoffed. "Please. I go along with everything he says, short of dressing up in women's clothes!"

"That's how straight guys are. You're just asking for it at this point."

"I don't have a thing for straight guys. I just happen to have a thing for this one. What can I do? All right, we're here. Let's go."

"Why are we at a Mercedes-Benz dealership?"

Without answering him, Zhang Yuwen walked into the store and made a beeline for the year's latest model. "Do you have this model in stock right now? I'm not too particular about the specs," he said to the salesperson, who was stunned into silence.

"This is your first time buying a car, Mr. Rich Guy, so you aren't familiar with the process," Liang Zheng quipped. "Allow me to explain—"

"I'm aware of that. I can pay extra."

Liang Zheng laughed. "That's so nouveau riche. I love it."

"Please give me a moment," said the salesperson. "This is going to be tough, but I'll ask for you."

"Do you really *have* to drive a car back today? It's a 2.2-million-yuan car. Don't put the salesperson on the spot."

"I just want it today," Zhang Yuwen said.

"Waiting a few more days won't kill you, you know?"

"Then what's my wifey gonna drive?"

"Your Bentley."

"He doesn't like Bentleys. He only likes Mercedes."

The salesperson finished his call. "There's one in stock, sir, but even if we expedite the process, it'll take a week. Give me a minute. I'll get the spec sheet for you—"

"Just place the order for me." Zhang Yuwen took the spec sheet and glanced through it. "I don't understand any of this anyway, but I'm sure your dealership won't scam me."

He fished out his card and gestured for the salesperson to go ahead and swipe it. The salesperson had been around in the world and, having listened in on their conversation while he was making his call, he'd switched to "Dubai Mode" for Zhang Yuwen. He knew that what mattered most to these people was 1) stock availability and 2) minimal fuss. Buying a car was like buying groceries to these clients, who were busy people and would leave as soon as they made their purchase. So the salesperson quickly brought the contract over. Zhang Yuwen gave him Huo Sichen's personal details to fill in the paperwork with, completed the payment with his card, grabbed two bottles of water, and left with Liang Zheng. In their wake, a group of salespeople remained at the entrance of the dealership, ready to celebrate with fireworks.

"How much have you spent today?" Liang Zheng asked.

"Uh... A little over ten million?" The publishing house acquisition was around ten million, and the car was another two.

Next, Liang Zheng drove him to the bank, where he'd scheduled an appointment with the vice president. He handed the man Huo Sichen's bank card, cross-checked the debt records, and instructed him to transfer the funds ASAP. The vice president handled it himself, and escorted Zhang Yuwen out once he was done.

Huo Sichen was still sleeping. Off to the side, bank notifications for twelve consecutive transfers popped up on his phone, each valued at one million.

Zhang Yuwen returned to No. 7 Riverbay Road at noon and bade Liang Zheng a cheerful farewell. When he went inside, only Madam Shen was still sitting on the sofa. *Where are the others?* Zhang Yuwen thought, puzzled.

"Auntie Bai is resting inside," Madam Shen whispered. "She should be asleep by now. Xiao-Qi is asleep too. She didn't sleep well on the train last night." Zhang Yuwen nodded. "Yan Jun's inside too," she added. "Weize and Chang Jinxing are both in their rooms. Chen Hong said he was going to his gym, but he wants you to wait for him so you can have lunch together."

Madam Shen had been at No. 7 Riverbay Road for less than four hours, and she had already cracked the names of his roommates and was on to trying to learn their marriage and family statuses.

"Okay, sure thing." Zhang Yuwen wiped the sweat from his brow, sat at the dining table, then got up again to make coffee. He glanced upward, guessing that Huo Sichen was still asleep. He probably hadn't slept last night.

"How many people should I cook for?" Liu Jingfang whispered.

Zhang Yuwen had too many thoughts running through his head. "Don't worry about it. I'll order delivery."

"I'll cook some rice, then. The elderly woman's fine. Dr. Wang was here earlier to check on her—her blood pressure and heart rate are stable, though her cataracts are severe. She'll need surgery for those as soon as possible."

"Yan Jun said his mother is reluctant to go for surgery. Cataract surgery comes with some risks. It's not my place to persuade her."

Liu Jingfang opened the rice cooker and rinsed the rice. "Your grandfather had a student who's an ophthalmologist now. He's going to retire next year, but he's an excellent surgeon. There shouldn't be any problems if he performs the operation."

"Oh, Dr. Li." Zhang Yuwen remembered him. Were his grandfather's students that old now? Just then, Yan Jun stepped out of the room, having heard Zhang Yuwen's and Liu Jingfang's conversation. Zhang Yuwen looked back at him. "Yan Jun?"

Yan Jun watched Zhang Yuwen with an indescribable expression in his eyes.

"Did you hear that?" Zhang Yuwen was still waiting in front of the coffee machine.

"I did," Yan Jun said.

"I'll give you Dr. Li's number," said Zhang Yuwen.

"Okay. I was thinking the same thing anyway. In a few days, once my ma's mood has stabilized, I'll take her for a checkup, then arrange for her to have the surgery in Jiangdong."

"You'd need to apply for some time off to stay by her side at the hospital."

"Yeah," Yan Jun said in a small voice. "I plan to move to Jiangnan first. It'll be more convenient to take care of them all there—it's a three-bedroom place. Xiao-Qi and I will share a room, my ma will have a room to herself, and Yingjie can sleep in the living room. His mother likely won't be leaving anytime soon either."

The food delivery arrived, and Zhang Yuwen went to call everyone down for lunch. Liu Jingfang set the table and filled bowls with rice for them all. Meanwhile, Zhang Yuwen hauled a bleary-eyed Huo Sichen out of his bed and announced, "Lunch time."

Xiao-Qi woke up just as Yan Jun was taking his seat, so he returned to his room to soothe her. Being apart from Yan Jun for almost two weeks seemed to have made her aggrieved, and she clung to him and refused to let go. Madam Shen sat down at the table too, and everyone dug into the food.

Chen Hong hurried back, only to find that his roommates had started eating without him. "Damn it, didn't I say to wait for me?"

"It's not too late for you to join us," Zhang Yuwen said. "What's up? Something important?"

Chen Hong wanted to talk to him about Huo Sichen and Dong You, but it wasn't like he could do that with all these other people present, especially when the other people included a woman he didn't know and Huo Sichen himself. He said, "Nothing important," and took the seat across from Huo Sichen.

Between the presence of the extra guest and Zhang Yuwen and Huo Sichen eating as if nothing had happened the night before, it was an awkward meal. Nobody knew quite what to say, so they all just kept quiet.

"Have some fish," Zhang Yuwen said, picking some for Zheng Weize.

"Thanks," said Zheng Weize. "That's my favorite."

"The fish last night was good too," Chang Jinxing added. "Too bad I didn't get to savor it."

"I ate all of mine, but Yuwen probably didn't even get to have a bite," said Chen Hong.

Zhang Yuwen shot a stern look at Huo Sichen, finally remembering. "Did you leave? Then who paid the bill?"

"Yan Jun," Chen Hong answered for him. "Except he didn't count his share because he didn't eat anything."

Oh, okay, Zhang Yuwen thought. "I'll transfer the money to him," said Huo Sichen.

"Forget it," everyone else said in unison.

"Actually, Dong You's family runs that restaurant," Zhang Yuwen explained to Chen Hong. "Lucky us—otherwise things would have been even more embarrassing for us."

Chen Hong raised an eyebrow at him, indicating he knew about it already. Zhang Yuwen responded with a mischievous grin.

"Mr. Dong's that rich?" asked Chang Jinxing.

"His older sister owns a media company," Zhang Yuwen explained. "Kong Yu's character, Gu Youli, is based on Dong You."

Chang Jinxing lifted his head and stared at him.

Having listened to their conversation thus far, Madam Shen butted in. "Uh, Yuwen?"

Zhang Yuwen wasn't accustomed to eating with strangers, but since she was a family friend of Yan Jun, he responded politely and warmly. "Yes?"

Huo Sichen, meanwhile, ate in silence, occasionally sipping his water.

"You're from a family of doctors, right?" Madam Shen asked. "I see lots of medical books here."

"My grandfather was a doctor, and my grandmother was a pharmacist."

"Oh, very impressive. So, what do you do for work?"

"I work in publishing." For once, Zhang Yuwen was perfectly within his rights to claim publishing as his main profession— because he had just bought a publishing house.

"Oh! A family of intellectuals!" Madam Shen exclaimed. Everyone, including Huo Sichen, thought her next question would be, *Are you married?* But no! Instead, Madam Shen hit them with a question out of left field. "Then you must know some psychiatrists, right? Can you ask them something for me? How do I cure homosexuality?"

It took a moment for everyone else at the table to register her question—they were too shocked. Complicated expressions crossed each of their faces as they all fought the urge to turn and gape at her.

Zhang Yuwen, too, was thrown off by the abrupt change in topic. "Wh-what?"

"Yeah." Madam Shen sighed, looking troubled. "No shame in telling you. Some time ago—last year, actually—Yingjie got involved with his desk mate. I was so shocked when his homeroom teacher told me about it!"

Everyone was speechless.

"I said that was impossible," Madam Shen continued. "How can a guy be 'involved' with another guy? The teacher said he's gay, and I said my son couldn't possibly be gay. Good grief. Apparently, they were on the rooftop..."

The table of gays all wore different expressions. Huo Sichen, who had just taken a sip of water, nearly spit it out.

"Oh, so he's gay." Zhang Yuwen nodded. "To be honest...nobody has found a special cure just yet, I think...?"

"How about electroshock therapy?" Zheng Weize suggested, stunning everyone else into silence again. "My dad tried it on... I mean, someone told him that it was a treatment option."

Zhang Yuwen put his head in his hands.

"You know gay, right?" Madam Shen said.

"Yeah, I do..." Unable to bear it any longer, Zhang Yuwen decided to let Yan Jun handle this himself. "Yan Jun! Come out and eat already!"

Yan Jun finally emerged, and Madam Shen turned to him. "One of the reasons I came here is to cure Yingjie of his condition."

"What?" Yan Jun looked like a deer caught in the headlights. "What condition?"

"He's gay!" Madam Shen repeated. "I need to find a doctor to correct it as soon as possible."

Yan Jun didn't know what to say to that.

Everyone kept their heads down and quickly finished their meals, and they each heaved a palpable sigh of relief as they made their escape. Huo Sichen started clearing the bowls and chopsticks, but Yan Jun stepped in. "Let me do it."

"I've got this," said Huo Sichen. "Go and take care of your mother."

"You're not working today?"

"I quit."

"Congrats."

Liu Jingfang cooked porridge for Yan Jun's mother, and Yan Jun brought it to his mother before leaving. Zhang Yuwen helped to clear away the plates and cups, taking them to the sink.

"Let me do it," Liu Jingfang said.

"It's okay, I can handle it," Huo Sichen replied.

Liu Jingfang insisted, but Huo Sichen rinsed the dishes and loaded them into the dishwasher.

"Let him do it," Zhang Yuwen said. "That way, he'll get to stay a little longer."

Liu Jingfang started giggling, and Huo Sichen set down the bowls and chopsticks. "All right, I'll go back now."

"Nu-uh-uh. You do it." Liu Jingfang smiled. "You're all good kids."

Still, Huo Sichen excused himself politely and left the kitchen. Zhang Yuwen followed him up the stairs, curious to see his reaction. He obviously still hadn't noticed the additional twelve million in his account, since he'd left his phone behind on the bedside table when Zhang Yuwen woke him up.

"You're leaving already?" Zhang Yuwen asked. Huo Sichen looked back at him in disbelief, and Zhang Yuwen held his phone out to him. "Don't you want your phone?"

Snapping back to his senses, Huo Sichen pocketed it and put on his jacket. "Can you give me back my bank card and the written court judgment?"

"Sure. You want them now?" Zhang Yuwen gave him the document folder.

"Thanks." He went down the stairs, and Zhang Yuwen followed him. Huo Sichen turned back. "You don't have to see me off."

"I'm not. I'm heading out too."

Huo Sichen nodded, pushed the door open, and left. He walked along Riverbay Road, bathed in the spring wind, and Zhang Yuwen trailed behind him. No matter what, he had to see Huo Sichen's reaction with his own eyes when he discovered the twelve million in his account.

But Huo Sichen was a stubborn one. He hadn't even thought about checking his phone yet today, nor did he have any desire to. As always, when they were together, his attention was focused entirely on Zhang Yuwen.

Zhang Yuwen walked with him for a whole ten minutes, and at no point did Huo Sichen do what he'd been anticipating. Finally, Zhang Yuwen blurted out, "Are you angry?"

"No, I'm not." Huo Sichen stopped in his tracks, turned around, and looked at Zhang Yuwen. Zhang Yuwen paused too. "Actually, you're right. I am angry—with myself. I feel horrible now, and it's killing me."

Zhang Yuwen looked at Huo Sichen and smiled.

"I don't know why I'm like this." Huo Sichen's voice grew heavy, and his eyes reddened. Then, the emotions he had bottled up for so long erupted right in front of Zhang Yuwen. His words quivered with his sobs, and his voice was choked; tears distorted his handsome face. Even the most beautiful child could look comical when they cried from genuine sorrow. "I thought about it all night," he wept. "I've let you down. I love you, Yuwen. I don't know what I'm supposed to do without you... It took me so long to find you, and then I messed it up...with my mistakes and stupidity... I don't know who I can talk to. I...I don't want to give up, but I... Please, just don't ignore me. I can accept just being friends with you, as long as you don't drive me away..."

Zhang Yuwen slowly walked over and hugged him. Huo Sichen buried his face in Zhang Yuwen's shoulder and broke down in the gentle spring breeze.

"Let's go for a cup of coffee," Zhang Yuwen suggested, his conscience pricking at him. Here Huo Sichen was, humbling himself and putting himself through such agony just to exchange a few more words with him, all while Zhang Yuwen was gleefully trailing him to see the outcome of his prank, as if Huo Sichen's suffering had nothing to do with him. Huo Sichen nodded, and Zhang Yuwen added, "There's something else I want to say to you."

So Zhang Yuwen led Huo Sichen back along Riverbay Road, but this time to No. 6. As they walked, Huo Sichen gradually calmed down. With Zhang Yuwen by his side, that protective shield could envelop him again and dispel his pain.

Zhang Yuwen sat down at the sunlit terrace of Sunny Day Cat Café while Huo Sichen went to buy the drinks. Still curious, Zhang Yuwen watched his back. Huo Sichen ordered the drinks at the counter and fished out his phone to pay the bill.

When he saw the notifications on it, he froze. He scrolled down in disbelief, then looked all around him, apparently in a daze. He must have thought he was dreaming.

"Sir? The total is 79 yuan," the cashier said.

Huo Sichen didn't reply. He looked back at Zhang Yuwen.

He noticed it! He noticed it! Zhang Yuwen doubled over the table with the effort of containing his laughter, like a kid who'd successfully pulled a prank.

"Yuwen? Look at this. What's going on? I don't know if it's a system error or...?"

Zhang Yuwen couldn't hold it in any longer. He erupted in hysterics. "Ha ha ha ha!"

Huo Sichen looked baffled. In a voice laced with anxiety, he asked, "How did this happen? Why are you laughing? Ten million appeared in my account out of the blue, and I have no idea how it got there..."

Zhang Yuwen composed himself. "I activated a life cheat this morning and transferred it to you," he said seriously. Then, he broke into laughter again, leaning back on the sunlit sofa.

"Huh?" Huo Sichen didn't understand.

"Sorry!" Zhang Yuwen said to the cashier. "I'll pay the bill."

"Oh! It's you, Director Zhang!" The cashier smiled, recognizing him. "It's been a while! You can pay later. Let me make the coffee for you."

"Thanks! I haven't been coming as much because I have a tenant who makes great coffee," Zhang Yuwen said. Then, he turned to Huo Sichen and grinned.

Huo Sichen looked at his phone, then at Zhang Yuwen.

Zhang Yuwen moved to sit beside him. "You can pay off your debts now. I'm sorry, Huo Sichen; I've been lying to you too. I sincerely apologize, but I know you'll forgive me, just like I forgave you."

Riverbay Road
MEN'S DORMITORY

CHAPTER

50

HUO SICHEN'S PERCEPTION of the world suffered an enormous blow that morning. There had been signs all along—the house at No. 7 Riverbay Road itself was proof—but love had halved his intelligence and made his capacity for more competent thought walk out on him. He'd never even questioned it.

"I'm really not worried you were after my money," Zhang Yuwen clarified earnestly. He realized, though, that at times like this, it didn't matter what words he used to explain himself or how sincere those words were—everything made it sound like he was asking for a beating. "And it's not like I'm addicted to playing a pauper or I'm a compulsive liar or anything. It's just that...I like you, and that's it. Nothing else factors into the equation."

"Yes...of course." Huo Sichen was holding his phone, at an utter loss for what to do with the twelve million yuan weighing down on him. This development had far exceeded the bounds of his understanding of the world around him and the materialistic society they lived in. For a moment, he even had the fleeting thought that Zhang Yuwen was some kind of backend programmer for the universe.

"You should know that feeling," Zhang Yuwen said.

"Yes." It was all Huo Sichen could say. He looked at Zhang Yuwen, who explained his initial reason for renting out No. 7 Riverbay Road, as well as the origins of his fortune. Huo Sichen nodded. "That makes sense."

"I think you probably need some time to digest this. Why don't I go home first? You can come over any time. Oh, I bought a car for you, too, but it won't be here today. If you don't want to drive mine, we can walk."

"No, I'm okay." Huo Sichen grabbed Zhang Yuwen's hand. Some part of him feared that if Zhang Yuwen left now, he'd lose him forever. With his other hand, he finally set down his phone. "You've really forgiven me?"

"Of course I forgive you," said Zhang Yuwen. "I kept things from you too. I was planning to bring you up to speed on it gradually once we were together, just like how you planned to slowly break the news about your marriage to me. I needed the right opportunity, and I didn't know if you'd be angry or find it hard to accept."

"It's not the same," Huo Sichen said, though he was still preoccupied by the fact that Zhang Yuwen wasn't angry anymore. They could be together. The money issue seemed insignificant now, or at least, it no longer dominated Huo Sichen's thoughts. Everything else in his mind had to give way.

He kissed Zhang Yuwen, cutting off his words. Zhang Yuwen kissed him back and wrapped his arms around Huo Sichen's neck. They sat like that on the sunlit sofa, kissing, oblivious to the world.

When they separated, Huo Sichen felt like he'd returned to reality. With his hand that wasn't holding Zhang Yuwen's, he picked up his phone and glanced at it, then looked at Zhang Yuwen. "You're seriously giving me this much money?"

"Yeah. Why? You're the one who handed me your bank card, aren't you?" Zhang Yuwen asked, and after a brief pause, Huo Sichen nodded. "You're free to transfer the money to the debt collectors and settle the debt."

Huo Sichen put down his phone and looked at Zhang Yuwen again, this time with mixed feelings. He finally understood the real meaning behind Zhang Yuwen's words.

"But if you do, you'll owe me," said Zhang Yuwen.

"I'd like to spend my whole life paying you back," Huo Sichen said, "if you're willing to let me."

Zhang Yuwen wanted to joke that Huo Sichen was getting the better deal, but he corrected his thinking and adjusted his attitude. He loved Huo Sichen too. When they were together, it always seemed like Huo Sichen needed Zhang Yuwen more than the other way around, but Zhang Yuwen knew deep down that he needed Huo Sichen just as much.

"All righty," Zhang Yuwen decided. "You can still fuck me with that big cock, as long as you occasionally let me fuck you too."

Huo Sichen didn't really know how to respond to that. His breathing quickened. If sex with Zhang Yuwen was on the table, he was fine with topping or bottoming—but alas, he couldn't act on his desires in broad daylight. He was finally listening to his instincts, but Zhang Yuwen only had to look at his expression to know what he was thinking.

"We can go to your place," Zhang Yuwen suggested.

Huo Sichen bolted to his feet and left, pulling Zhang Yuwen along by the hand behind him.

Chen Hong was at his gym, drawing up schedules and plans for his members. He thought about going home for lunch and asking Zhang Yuwen for his thoughts, but things really hadn't gone as he'd expected, so he'd just grabbed lunch and gone back to work. His student base was gradually stabilizing, and everyone had signed up for a membership, which meant that he could keep the gym going for a while, at least. Still, he couldn't afford to get complacent.

Three o'clock in the afternoon was the gym's quietest period. People would start trickling in again around seven to sweat it out in the gym until ten. But to Chen Hong's surprise, someone walked in; Chen Hong glanced up to see it was Dong You.

"You didn't make an appointment," Chen Hong said, "so no training today."

"I'm not here for training."

"Your daddy's very busy today."

"I'm not here for a hookup either. Wanna grab some coffee?"

That didn't sound like a bad idea. Chen Hong gathered up his plans, and they went to a nearby café.

Dong You ordered coffee and watched Chen Hong work. Occasionally he asked a few questions, mostly about cardio, diet, and training. Chen Hong answered all of them. When he was done with his paperwork, he took a photo of the forms and sent it to the group chat.

"You know Zhang Yuwen," Dong You stated.

"Yeah," said Chen Hong. "I'm renting his place. I'm actually very poor—just an ordinary fitness trainer who happened to rent a room in his house." Dong You laughed. "I told you that last night."

"My family owns the Sky Promenade restaurant," said Dong You.

"I know. Yuwen told me."

Dong You seemed intrigued by the legendary young director. "I can't believe he actually rented out the house he's living in. It's not like he's short on money." He'd heard that Zhang Yuwen was a young director when they parted ways last night.

"Yeah." Chen Hong didn't want to gossip about Zhang Yuwen, who was, after all, his good friend. "I don't know the specifics. You'll have to ask him yourself."

Dong You didn't probe. "I guess it sounds like something he'd do," he said. "They say he's free-spirited. Kind of a romantic, even."

"Unlike boring old me."

"I wouldn't say that."

"I doubt there's anything about me you'd find interesting, apart from my dick."

"No, not at all. Not true. And to tell you the truth, my family isn't all that wealthy. We look well-off, but we owe more money than we make."

"That, I'd believe. So, what's up? Here on a mission to ask Zhang Yuwen to shoot a film for you?"

"Nah. I don't interfere in my family's affairs."

"Then why are you here? You've been rambling on and on for a while."

"No particular reason." Dong You looked baffled by the question. "Can't I just come see you because I missed you?"

"Yeah, right," Chen Hong scoffed. "What? You're not seriously telling me you wanna be in a relationship with me, are you?"

"No more hookups. I mean it. I want to date you."

"Sure. A celibacy contest? Fine with me. Let's see who can hold out and who throws in the towel."

"You're out of your mind."

"Yeah. I absolutely am."

"Why are you so domineering? You always have to come out on top."

"That's the way I am. If you wanna tame me and make me your dog, you'll have to see if you have what it takes." Dong You looked

Chen Hong over, and Chen Hong grinned. "No way, you fell for me? Awkward. Falling in love with a hookup? What are we going to do now? Man, what a mess."

"You're right," Dong You said in all seriousness. Chen Hong looked at him. Had he misheard? "Yeah, I've fallen for you. But you're probably not interested. You just want to fuck me." After a pause, Dong You took out a small paper bag. "This is for you."

"Huh?"

Dong You got up and left.

"Hey!" Chen Hong shouted after him. "It's not true that I only want to...fuck you. What's this?"

Chen Hong opened the paper bag. Inside were two clumsily handmade rings. He ran to catch up to Dong You.

"What are these?" he asked again in a small voice.

"I made these for you when I took my nephew to a crafts workshop a few days ago. Your initials are engraved on the inside."

Chen Hong tried to take Dong You's hand. Dong You automatically pulled away, but then he realized what he was doing, and he grasped Chen Hong's hand.

"All right...let's give it a try," Chen Hong said.

Dong You took a deep breath. His expression said, *Damn it, why am I confessing first? Don't you have any shame?* But Chen Hong's smile made it hard for him to stay mad.

"What do you mean, give it a try?" Dong You asked, raising an eyebrow and moving closer to him—so close that he physically felt Chen Hong's reaction. Dong You narrowed his eyes. "You think we won't last, don't you?"

That thought had indeed crossed Chen Hong's mind. He still thought it was worth trying for happiness, though, even if that happiness was fleeting.

Dong You licked his lips. "What do you like? I'm willing to *try* it all." All Chen Hong wanted in that moment was to kiss him. "Well, if you won't tell me, then never mind."

"I'll tell you later," Chen Hong said. "I have to get back to the gym. I've got a class to run."

Embarrassed, he turned to leave—he was relieved to see that no one was outside the café but them. He adjusted his pants and started walking, but Dong You caught up to him. "Tell me, what other things do you have in mind?"

As he thought about his own kinks, Chen Hong's face went red, but Dong You was relentless. He followed him all the way back and only stopped probing him for answers when Chen Hong escaped into the gym, and even then only because Chen Hong's students had already arrived. Instead of leaving, he sat at the reception desk, opened the laptop, and started clicking around.

Chen Hong started his class, but his attention was all on Dong You. "What are you doing?"

"I'm looking at your financial statements," Dong You said, "and your fixed monthly expenses."

Chen Hong couldn't be bothered to stop him. In Dong You's eyes, the numbers were probably miniscule—they might not even come close to Dong You's own typical spending.

He finished his class in the evening. To his surprise, Dong You was still there typing away on the keyboard, making spreadsheets. "Now what are you doing?"

"Making a budget for you. Did you get advice from an expert at some point? Your financial situation is pretty good. I'm thinking of investing in your gym."

Chen Hong stared at Dong You without saying a word.

"Would you be okay with that?"

"I'd need to think about it." Chen Hong sized up Dong You, wondering if it was practical to partner with a fuck buddy. But after their conversation at the café, were they really fuck buddies anymore? Or were they now...lovers?

"What are your plans for tonight?" Dong You asked.

"Dinner, then a training session at a member's house."

"Let's go together."

"Did you drive here?"

"Nope." Dong You's voice betrayed a hint of impatience. "I told you, that was my brother-in-law's car."

"You don't have your own?"

"I'm saving up for one."

Why didn't you say that earlier? Chen Hong thought as he handed a helmet to Dong You. He drove Dong You to dinner on his motorcycle, then headed to the member's house for their private training session while Dong You killed time watching a movie at a nearby cinema. When the lesson was done, Chen Hong took Dong You back to the gym.

"Are we doing it today or not?" Chen Hong asked him.

"I thought you said—"

Chen Hong didn't give Dong You time to finish his sentence. He picked him up and carried him into the gym's storage room. "I admit defeat, okay?!"

Chen Hong had put a bed in the tiny storage room, and as they made love inside, a strange feeling came over him. Entering Dong You from behind—their favorite position—he leaned over Dong You and whispered into his ear, "I was born to fuck you."

This was his confession of love, a marker of their official beginning as a couple.

Spring came to Jiangdong. The night brought with it a spring breeze that sighed past thousands of trees, gracing the entire city with blossoms. This was a rare, balmy spring, one that seemed to have been foretold during the harshest depths of winter.

Life at No. 7 Riverbay Road continued as usual. Both the front and back gardens were in full bloom. The warm, pleasant weather roused hibernating creatures, including the roommates, who became unusually busy.

Zhang Yuwen didn't move out of No. 7 Riverbay Road as planned. His roommates, on the other hand, were all headed for other pastures, and Huo Sichen would be moving in soon after they left. It was a long farewell, but one that was destined to happen. Zhang Yuwen had lived through all sorts of partings—with family, with hastily assembled film crews, friends, and even with other versions of himself. Separation was a fact of life, and reunions were short-lived, but did that mean fleeting relationships were destined to be mourned and only the ones that lasted were worth cherishing?

Of course not. Zhang Yuwen had long since adopted a philosophical attitude to partings, and he hoped their farewells signified better futures for them all.

Chang Jinxing had been accepted to study overseas, and he'd already bought his plane tickets. He planned to leave at the end of the month for Australia, where a person he once loved awaited him anxiously. Maybe they would rekindle their romance; maybe they wouldn't. Chang Jinxing was nervous about the uncertainty of it all.

Zheng Weize had found a new job and joined a fashion studio as an apprentice. His two bosses looked good together, and their chemistry reminded him of Zhang Yuwen and Huo Sichen. More importantly, they treated Zheng Weize well. The studio would cover his food and lodging, and in turn he would take on responsibilities for their sales. To save money and focus on learning fashion design, he gave up his room at No. 7 Riverbay Road. He still live streamed, and he tried on the studio's clothing—men's and women's—with surprisingly good results, helping to drive more traffic to the store.

Chen Hong eventually agreed to let Dong You invest in his gym and to wear the ring Dong You made for him. The ring for him was a little bigger than the one for Dong You, but somehow, it fit Chen Hong's ring finger perfectly. It made Chen Hong suspicious that Dong You had somehow taken his measurement in secret, but Dong You insisted that he'd just gone with his gut. Maybe they really were meant to be. Under Dong You's relentless questioning, Chen Hong finally, albeit hesitantly, confessed his kinks. It was strange how he wasn't the least bit shy about talking to his roommates about it, but found himself hemming and hawing in front of the person he liked. When Dong You finally learned what turned Chen Hong on, his eyes lit up. He'd clearly spotted an opportunity to take the upper hand with Chen Hong, but he managed to restrain himself.

Like Chang Jinxing and Zheng Weize, Chen Hong canceled his lease at No. 7 Riverbay Road. He decided to rent a studio apartment above his gym so that he wouldn't have to commute on his motorcycle. In his new apartment, he could be with Dong You whenever he wanted.

Yan Jun, meanwhile, made an appointment at the hospital for his mother to undergo surgery. He was able to get a slot quickly thanks to Zhang Yuwen's connections. The surgery was a great success, and when Mama Yan came out safe and sound, everyone breathed a sigh of relief. Yan Jun arranged for his mother to live in Jiangnan District in a spacious rental apartment that had plenty of room for four adults and one baby. He could afford it now, at his current salary. His mother had no choice but to stay in Jiangdong now that she'd learned the truth about Yan Jun's brother, and Shen Yingjie's own mother, a divorcée, also hoped to live with her only son, who was gay. Two mothers, two sons, and one baby thus came together to form an unconventional family unit, where Madam Shen took care of Mama Yan and Xiao-Qi at home, and Yan Jun encouraged his nephew to study hard to get into university.

Unsurprisingly, then, Yan Jun canceled his lease at No. 7 Riverbay Road as well. His mother needed him, and he had to step up to take care of her. He couldn't let her return to living alone in the countryside.

One day, during a thorough cleanup of the apartment in Jiangnan, he sorted through the old belongings sent from his hometown and found a photo of himself and his family from a vacation at a hot spring hotel. His brother had still been alive then, and his father was there too. In the photo, Yan Jun himself was only seven years old, and his mother was young and beautiful. Now, her hair had gone gray.

Shen Yingjie noticed the photo in his hand. "Who's that?"

Yan Jun didn't respond. He put away the photo.

As the final movement of this farewell symphony began, the roommates suggested another gathering. This time, it was to celebrate Zhang Yuwen's birthday. He was a Pisces, the last of the twelve zodiac signs, which embodied all the strengths and weaknesses of the twelve constellations—not that Zhang Yuwen would have admitted it.

"How's the company coming along?" Zhang Yuwen asked.

Huo Sichen, who was driving the new Mercedes-Benz his wife had given him, focused on the road ahead. He'd paid off all his debt and become history's greatest kept man. "All good."

The thing that had worried Zhang Yuwen the most about coming clean was the possibility of hurting Huo Sichen's pride. He thought Huo Sichen's attitude toward him might change subtly once he learned how much money Zhang Yuwen had, so he'd prepared various contingency plans to "correct" the perceptions they both had, much in the same way that Madam Shen tried to "correct" her son's homosexuality. Of course, the main objective was to correct *Huo Sichen's* perception. But things didn't play out the way he expected. Huo Sichen adapted at an astonishing speed, and he embraced this new knowledge without bringing any emotional baggage into play. He even made a conscious effort to switch his role in their relationship from hubby to knight.

One day, after they made love in bed, he told Zhang Yuwen, "You're my prince, Yuwen. I will always protect you." It took a second, but Zhang Yuwen remembered that Huo Sichen had once mentioned a fantasy of his: to be a guardian knight in an inverted power dynamic. It was such an anime-style fetish that it had completely slipped Zhang Yuwen's mind!

Sometimes, Huo Sichen also said things like: "I adore you, my dear wife. You're not only a skilled professional but also a very lucky one." Every time this happened, Zhang Yuwen was over the moon to hear it. It was one thing for a bottom to express his adoration of his partner, but hearing it from a top was something else entirely.

Still, Huo Sichen also believed that life wasn't a roleplaying game; there was no need to pretend to be someone you weren't or to stick to a specific role. What could be worse, after all, than losing Zhang Yuwen and being stuck paying off a debt until he was sixty?

"Preparations for the new company are going smoothly," Huo Sichen said as he pressed the elevator button. "I've already taken over most of Wu Peifeng's clients."

Zhang Yuwen had wanted to buy out the shares of another shareholder in Huo Sichen's old company, which would have given Huo Sichen majority ownership. While that alone wouldn't have been enough to force Wu Peifeng out, it was sure to make things unpleasant for him—maybe even unpleasant enough for him to rage-quit. But Huo Sichen didn't think that was necessary. His time was precious, and he decided he'd rather register for a new company. In a few months, he was going to sell his condo, pay off the mortgage, and use the remaining proceeds as start-up capital to establish a new company from scratch. With the issue of capital and shares out of the way, he would have nothing more to worry about. For the first time, he actually felt confident about the future.

He kissed Zhang Yuwen and said, "Happy birthday, my little prince. Text me when you're done." Zhang Yuwen returned the kiss and entered the restaurant.

They were meeting at a very famous hotpot restaurant. Whenever a customer celebrated a birthday, the staff swarmed in with LED signs, belting out the restaurant's signature birthday song and forcing their tired bodies to dance along. It was a ritual guaranteed to mortify its unfortunate victim. When Zhang Yuwen heard that they would be dining at this restaurant, he braced himself for the mockery that was sure to come his way.

His roommates had already arrived, and when they saw him coming, they all greeted him with a "Yoo-hoo!" As Chang Jinxing was ordering the food, Chen Hong said, "You didn't come home again last night! Spill it! Where did you go?! Fess up!"

"How's that glass house you're living in? You didn't come back either!" Zhang Yuwen shot back mercilessly. "Actually, wait, how did you know? Did you go back to Riverbay Road last night?"

He hadn't, and nor had Yan Jun or Zheng Weize. Chang Jinxing raised his hand with a grin.

"Where's Sichen?" asked Yan Jun.

"He's having his meal downstairs," replied Zhang Yuwen. "He said he's not coming."

Yan Jun nodded. "He probably wants to celebrate your birthday with just the two of you."

"Who knows?" Zhang Yuwen laughed.

No one had ever asked about the fight between Zhang Yuwen and Huo Sichen, but they knew Zhang Yuwen forgave Huo Sichen. After the fight, Yan Jun came to understand that Zhang Yuwen and Huo Sichen weren't, in fact, just casually dating; they were truly in love. He was relieved that he hadn't listened to the others that day when they insisted that he confess his feelings.

"Have you finished moving your stuff?" Zhang Yuwen asked Zheng Weize.

"Yeah. Jinxing is going back later to get his suitcase. I'll be going with him."

"I'm going to return to my hometown for a bit," said Chang Jinxing. "I'm leaving tonight on the overnight bus, then catching a flight from Changhai. Don't come to see me off."

"No one's planning to," Yan Jun said, laughing. "Don't flatter yourself."

Everyone else started laughing too. Chang Jinxing had ordered a lot of food; five grown men could eat a lot. Chen Hong ordered alcohol, too, and they clinked glasses noisily, bantering all the while. No one brought up their impending goodbyes.

Zhang Yuwen had a lot to say, but whenever he tried to broach certain topics, the others forcibly steered the conversation away.

"I'm keeping all the rooms at No. 7 Riverbay Road for—"

"You know, I'm kinda curious," Yan Jun said before he could finish. "What's in that room that's always locked?"

Zheng Weize's face went pale. "Don't tell me it's some horror story shit!"

"No! Not even close!" Zhang Yuwen insisted. He was, by this point, a little tipsy. "Listen to me, guys! There are photos of my deceased grandparents in that room. No. 7 Riverbay Road is the inheritance they left me—"

"I knew it!" Chen Hong exclaimed. "Let's drink! Cheers!"

"Let me finish, or I'm going to get mad! It's my birthday today. What ever happened to listening to the birthday boy?" Everyone fell silent. Zhang Yuwen took a deep breath. "Actually...I need to apologize to you all. I've been lying to everyone for a long time. The house is mine! I'm sorry! Really sorry!"

They all laughed. "It's all good!"

"I should be thanking you," Zheng Weize said. "If not for you, I'd have ended up sleeping under a bridge."

Chang Jinxing smiled. "Let's just drink already!"

"Let me finish!" Zhang Yuwen said loudly, still feeling bad. The table fell silent again. "At first, I did a stupid thing. I can't write novels, so I decided to find a few people to rent the other rooms in my house so I could observe them and use them as writing material. I never told you guys about this. That was despicable of me."

"What are you talking about?" Yan Jun laughed wryly. "Do you even hear yourself?" Everyone else cracked up.

"Isn't researching source material a necessary part of creation?" Chang Jinxing said. "If you didn't observe us, you'd have to observe someone else. So what's the problem?"

Zheng Weize, on the other hand, was concerned about something else. "Are you going to write me into your book? Wow! Oh my god, am I going to be a character in the story? Is it gonna be made into a drama?"

Zhang Yuwen really didn't know what to do with them. "I...I'm still trying my best at writing. I hope to write some quality literature one day."

"You can do it!" said Chen Hong.

"He's right," Yan Jun chimed in. "You definitely can do it, Yuwen. You're the best."

"If you use any embarrassing deets, remember to give me a pseudonym or redact my name, okay?" added Zheng Weize.

"I won't write it like that," Zhang Yuwen said. "Uh... What was I going to say? Look! You guys keep interrupting, and now I've forgotten everything!"

"Send us each a copy when it's published," said Chen Hong. "It has to be autographed."

Zhang Yuwen gave up. "Okay, okay. Sure. And you guys can come back anytime and stay whenever you want. You can bring whoever you want to spend the night, too. No. 7 Riverbay Road will always be your—no, will always be *our* home."

The table quieted down again as soon as the words left his mouth. No one said a word. Chang Jinxing's hand trembled as he poured another glass for Chen Hong, who coughed twice and rubbed his eyes hard. Zheng Weize held his glass against his forehead wordlessly, and Yan Jun looked at Zhang Yuwen, his eyes going suspiciously shiny. A moment later, Yan Jun got up and left the private room.

Chen Hong was the first to recover. "Here's the last bottle!"

Zhang Yuwen was about to say okay when Yan Jun reentered with a towel in his hand—he must have gone to wipe his face. He sat down, then immediately sprang back up and turned off the light. In the darkness, the staff entered bearing a birthday cake with lit candles.

"Oh my god!" Zhang Yuwen exclaimed. "This is so awkward! Help me!"

The light signs were in position, and the rhythmic birthday song started up. The staff wasted no time putting a party hat on Zhang Yuwen and counting down with their fingers. It was Zhang Yuwen's first time celebrating his birthday there, and the others fished out their phones, intent on recording this embarrassing moment.

"Today! Today is your birthday! All good wishes come your way!

What a special day this is! There's a smile like sunshine rays!

Let's sing a birthday song for the one we hold so dear!

Health and peace are on their way in the coming year!"

Then came the chorus: "To all woes, say bye-bye! To all joy, say hi-hi!"

Zhang Yuwen was speechless.

As if that wasn't enough, his roommates chimed in and sang along. "My love! My love! Happy birthday! Every day is a wonderful day!"

"There's more?! Do we have to finish the whole song?!" Zhang Yuwen implored. "How long is this thing?!"

Finally, the interminable birthday song ended. Zhang Yuwen breathed a sigh of relief and made his wish for the year. He wished

that everyone at the table, plus the absent Huo Sichen, would one day gather again at No. 7 Riverbay Road and that, when that day came, they'd all bring their own stories to share.

Zhang Yuwen blew out the candles, and Yan Jun turned the lights back on. The sudden brightness made them all squint, traces of tears still visible on their faces.

Huo Sichen parked his car outside the mall and waited. He had come to pick up Zhang Yuwen and say hello to the others. He knew they would all be drunk, and sure enough, they soon stumbled out the doors.

Zhang Yuwen gave each of them a final hug. It wasn't their last night in Jiangdong, but they wouldn't be seeing each other every day anymore, and Chang Jinxing would be going overseas. Zhang Yuwen hugged him the longest. When they finally let go of each other, Zhang Yuwen whispered, "Take care of yourself out there. Give me a call if you run out of money."

"Of course!" Chang Jinxing said, and everyone laughed.

"How are you guys getting back?" Zhang Yuwen asked.

"We're taking the subway," said Zheng Weize, standing with Chang Jinxing.

"I'll call for a taxi," said Yan Jun.

"I'll ride my bike." Chen Hong put on his helmet. "Yuwen, Sichen, you guys get going."

And so, Zhang Yuwen turned his back to them and walked toward Huo Sichen. One step. Two steps. A few steps more, and he opened the passenger door to the Mercedes and got in.

"We're leaving," Huo Sichen told the rest of them. "All good things must come to an end. Take care, everyone."

"You're not going back to Riverbay Road tonight?" Chen Hong asked.

Huo Sichen shook his head. "Nah, I'm taking him to my place. The move is tomorrow, and he said he'd feel too emotional if he went home. It'd be too much."

Everyone took turns patting Huo Sichen on the shoulder and saying goodbye to him. Then, Huo Sichen got into the car and fastened his seatbelt. Zhang Yuwen remained silent next to him in the passenger seat.

Huo Sichen glanced back to see Chen Hong, Yan Jun, Zheng Weize, and Chang Jinxing still standing by the road, watching them leave. He rolled down the car window, letting the night breeze in, and drove the car away slowly. Meanwhile, the others nudged Yan Jun and told him not to wait any longer.

Finally, Yan Jun ran forward, stopped, and shouted, "Zhang Yuwen!"

Zhang Yuwen couldn't help but look back, and when he did, he could no longer contain the sadness in his heart. Like floodwaters bursting through a dam, he started to cry.

"Be happy!" Yan Jun shouted. "May you be happy always, Zhang Yuwen!"

Chen Hong rode up on his motorcycle. "Thank you, Zhang Yuwen! I wish you happiness!"

"Yuwen! Be happy!" Zheng Weize shouted through tears.

"Thank you, Yuwen!" Chang Jinxing called to him. "I wish you happiness and joy! I'm sure you'll be happy!"

Zhang Yuwen pressed his fist against the bridge of his nose and broke down. He'd directed many crying scenes, but none had captured sorrow as real as this. Tightly knit brows, trembling lips—

he was far beyond visual cues like those. When genuine sorrow hit, he turned into a blubbering mess.

Huo Sichen stopped the car. "Do you want to get out?"

"No, no. Don't stop," Zhang Yuwen choked between sobs. "Let's get going." He kept glancing back, looking quite wretched from all the crying. Huo Sichen reached over and placed his hand over Zhang Yuwen's, and gradually, Zhang Yuwen calmed down.

Parting was a fact of life, but it wasn't all-powerful. From the moment they had come together to form a new family, they were shielded from separation. As long as they didn't forsake each other, that shield would protect them until the very end. Not even death could tear them apart.

As Huo Sichen turned onto Riverbay Road, their faces were illuminated by a kaleidoscope of lights. Dreams, like shimmering lights, soared over the Liujin River, carrying the fantasies and hopes of countless people in the city as they spread their wings and flew to the other side of the stars.

THE END

Riverbay Road

MEN'S DORMITORY

APPENDIX

CHARACTER & NAME GUIDE

CHARACTERS

Zhang Yuwen 张宇文

The owner of No. 7 Riverbay Road. A film director who dreams of being a writer, he decides to rent out his spare rooms so that he can spend time around people in real life to make his writing more realistic.

Yan Jun 严峻

The first of Zhang Yuwen's tenants. An office worker who takes care of his niece since his brother and sister-in-law passed away.

Yan Yuqi 严玉棋

Yan Jun's baby niece, usually called Xiao-Qi. Calls everyone "Papa."

Zheng Weize 郑维泽

An unsuccessful live streamer, the youngest of the tenants at twenty-two, and the only one who considers himself a bottom.

Chen Hong 陈宏

The third of Zhang Yuwen's tenants, a twenty-nine-year-old fitness trainer struggling to find clients after having to close his gym.

Chang Jinxing 常锦星

The fourth tenant, a self-proclaimed photographer. A bit of a playboy who's used to using his looks to get ahead.

Huo Sichen 霍斯臣

A rich, handsome friend of Chen Hong's who starts spending time with the group after he strikes up a friendship with Zhang Yuwen.

NAME GUIDE

Diminutives, nicknames, and name tags:

A-: Friendly diminutive. Always a prefix. Usually for monosyllabic names, or one syllable out of a two-syllable name.

DOUBLING: Doubling a syllable of a person's name can be a nickname, e.g., "Mangmang"; it has childish or cutesy connotations.

DA-: A prefix meaning big/older.

XIAO-: A diminutive meaning "little." Always a prefix.

-ER: An affectionate diminutive added to names, literally "son" or "child." Always a suffix. Can sometimes be a fixed part of a person's name, rather than just an affectionate suffix.

Family:

DI/DIDI: Younger brother or a younger male friend.

GE/GEGE/DAGE: Older brother or an older male friend.

JIE/JIEJIE: Older sister or an older female friend.